GUN STREET GIRL

ALSO BY ADRIAN McKINTY

The Cold Cold Ground

I Hear the Sirens in the Street

In the Morning I'll Be Gone

The Sun Is God

A Detective Sean Duffy Novel

GUN STREET GIRL

Adrian McKinty

**BLACK
STONE**
PUBLISHING

Printed in the United States of America

978-1-09-408101-4
Fiction / Mystery & Detective / General

3 5 7 9 10 8 6 4 2

CIP data for this book is available
from the Library of Congress

Blackstone Publishing
31 Mistletoe Rd.
Ashland, OR 97520

www.BlackstonePublishing.com

I do not yet know what your gift is to me, but mine to you is an awesome one: you may keep your days and nights.
Jorge Luis Borges, "Blue Tigers," 1983

CONTENTS

1: A SCANNER DARKLY

*S*sssssssssssssssssssssssssssssss . . .

Silence.

Sssssssssssssssssssss . . .

Silence.

"I can't get it, sir."

"Keep trying."

"Yes, sir."

Midnight.

Midnight and all the agents are asleep, and on the beach there are only disaffected, cold policemen silently sharing smokes and gazing through binoculars at the black Atlantic, hoping to catch the first glimpse of the running lights on what has become known to the ironists in Special Branch as the *Ship of Death*.

Sssssssssssssssssssss . . .

Drizzle.

Static.

Oscillating waves of sound. A fragment of Dutch. A DJ from RFI informing the world with breathless excitement that "*EuroDisney sera construit à Paris.*"

We're on a beach near Derry on the wild north coast of Ireland. It's November 1985. Reagan's the President, Thatcher's the PM, Gorbachev has recently taken the reins of the USSR. The number-one album in the country is Sade's *Promise*, and Jennifer Rush's torch song "The Power of Love" is still at the top of the charts where it has remained for a dispiritingly long time . . .

Sssssssss and then finally the young constable in charge of the short-wave scanner finds the radio frequency of the *Our Lady of Knock*.

"I've got them! They're coming in, sir!" he says.

Yes, this is what we were waiting for. The weather is perfect, the moon is up, and the tide is on the ebb. "Aye, we have the bastards now!" one of the Special Branch men matters.

I say nothing. I have been brought in purely as a courtesy because one of my sources contributed a tip to this complicated international operation. It is not my place to speak or offer advice. Instead I pat my revolver and flip back through my notebook to the place where I have taped a postcard of Guido Reni's *Michael Tramples Satan*. I discreetly make the sign of the cross and, in a whisper, ask for the continuing protection of St Michael, the Archangel, the patron saint of policemen. I am not sure I believe in the existence of St Michael the Archangel, the patron saint of peelers, but I am a member of the RUC, which is the police force with the highest mortality rate in the Western world, so every little bit of talismanic assistance helps. I close the notebook and light a cigarette for some evil-eyed goon who says he's from Interpol but who looks like a spook from 140 Gower Street, come to keep an eye on the Paddies and make sure they don't make a hash of the whole thing.

He mutters a thank-you and passes over a flask which turns out to contain high-quality gin.

"Cheers," I say, take a swig, and pass it back.

"Chin, chin," he says. Yeah . . . MI5.

A breeze moves the clouds from the face of the moon. Somewhere in the car park a dog barks.

The policemen wait. The spooks wait. The men on the boat wait. All of us tumbling into the future together.

We watch the waves and the chilly, black infinity where sky and sea merge somewhere off Malin Head. Finally at 12:30 someone shouts, "There! I see her!" and we are ordered off the beach. Most of us retreat behind the dunes and a few of the wiser officers slink all the way back to the Land Rovers to warm up over spirit stoves and hot whiskies. I find myself behind a sandbar with two women in raincoats who appear to be Special Branch Intel.

"This is so exciting, isn't it?" the brunette says.

"It is."

"Who are you?" her friend asks me in a funny Cork accent that sounds like a donkey falling down a well.

I tell her, but as soon as the word "Inspector" has passed my lips I can see that she has lost interest. There are assistant chief constables and chief superintendents floating about tonight and I'm way down the food chain.

"About time!" someone says and we watch the *Our Lady of Knock* navigate its way into the channel and toward the surf. It's an odd-looking vessel. A small converted cargo boat, perhaps, or a trawler with the pulleys and chains removed. It doesn't really look seaworthy, but somehow it's made it all the way across three thousand miles of Atlantic Ocean.

About two hundred meters from the shore it drops anchor, and, after some unprofessional dithering, a Zodiac is lowered into the water. Five men climb aboard the speedboat and it zooms eagerly toward the beach. As soon as they touch dry land the case will come under the jurisdiction of the RUC, even though all five gunrunners are American citizens and the ship has come from Boston.

Skip, skip, skip goes the little Zodiac, oblivious of rocks or hidden reefs of which there are many along this stretch of coast. It miraculously avoids them all and zips up the surf onto the beach. The men get out and start looking around them for errant dog walkers or lovers or other witnesses. Spotting no one, they shout, "Yes!" and "Booyah!" One man gets on his knees and, emulating the Holy Father, kisses the sand. He has dedication, this lad—the tarmac at Dublin Airport is one thing, but this gravelly, greasy beach downwind from one of Derry's main sewage plants is quite another matter.

They open a bottle and begin passing it around. One of them is wearing a John Lennon sweatshirt. These young American men who have come across the sea to bring us death in the form of mortars and machine guns.

"Yanks, eh? They think they can do what they like, don't they?" one of the Special Branch officers says.

I resist the temptation to pile on. Although these Irish American gunrunners are undoubtedly naive and ignorant, I understand where they're coming from. Patriotism is a hard disease to eradicate, and ennui stamps us all . . .

The men on the beach begin to look at their watches and wonder what to do next. They are expecting a lorry driver called Nick McCready and his son Joe, both of whom are already in custody.

One of them lights a flare and begins waving it above his head.

"What are they going to do next? Set off fireworks?" someone grumbles behind me.

"What are *we* going to do next?" I say back, loud enough for the Assistant Chief Constable to hear. I mean, how much longer are we going to have to wait here? If there are guns on the boat we have them, and if there are no guns on the boat we don't have them, but either way the time to arrest them is now.

"Quiet in the ranks!" someone says.

If I was in charge I'd announce our presence with a loudspeaker and spotlights and patiently explain the situation: *You are surrounded, your vessel cannot escape the lough, please put your hands up and come quietly* . . .

But I'm not in charge and that is not what happens. This being an RUC-Gardai-FBI-MI5-Interpol operation we are headed for debacle . . . A high-ranking, uniformed policeman begins marching toward the men on the beach like Alec Guinness at the beginning of *Bridge on the River Kwai*.

"What the hell is he doing?" I say to myself.

The gunrunners don't see him yet and the one with a flare is making it do figures of eight in the air to the delight of the others.

The uniformed officer reaches the top of a dune. "All right, chaps, the game's up!" he announces in a loud *Dixon of Dock Green* voice.

All right, chaps, the game's up?

The Americans immediately draw their weapons and run for the Zodiac. One of them takes a potshot at the uniformed peeler, making him hit the deck. *I say, chaps, that's a little unsporting*, he's probably thinking.

"Put your hands up!" another copper belatedly yells through a megaphone.

The Americans fire blindly into the darkness with an impressive arsenal that includes shotguns and assault rifles. Some of the policemen begin to shoot back. The night is lit up by white flares and red muzzle bursts and arcs of orange tracer.

Yes, now we have well and truly crossed the border into the realm of international screw-up.

"Lay down your arms!" the copper with the megaphone shouts with an air of desperation.

A police marksman brings down one of the Yanks with a bullet in the shoulder, but the gunrunners still don't give up. They're confused, seasick, exhausted. They have no idea who is shooting at them or why. Two of them begin pushing the Zodiac back toward the surf. They don't realize that they're outnumbered ten to one, and that if by some miracle they do make it back to the *Our Lady of Knock*, they're just going to get boarded by the Special Boat Service.

The surf tosses the Zodiac upside down.

"This is the police, you are surrounded, cease firing at once!" the men are ordered through the megaphone. But blood has been spilled and they respond with a fusillade of machine-gun fire. I light another ciggie, touch St Michael, and make my way to the car park.

I walk past the rows of Land Rovers and get in my car. I turn the key in the ignition and the engine growls into life. Radio 3 is playing Berlioz. I flip to Radio 1 and it's a Feargal Sharkey ballad—Feargal Sharkey's successful solo career telling you everything you needed to know about the contemporary music scene. I kill the radio and turn on the lights.

A box of ammo explodes with a deafening blast and an enormous fireball that I can see from here. I lean my head against the steering wheel and take a deep breath.

A very young constable in charge of car park security taps on the driver's-side window. "Oi, where do you think you're going?"

I wind the window down. "Home," I tell him.

"Who said you could go?"

"No one said I had to stay, so I'm leaving."

"You can't just leave!"

"Watch me."

"But . . . but . . ."

"Move out of the way, son."

"But don't you want to see how everything turns out?" he asks breathlessly.

"Farce isn't my cup of tea," I tell him, wind the window up, and pull out of the car park. The me in the rear-view mirror shakes his head. That was a silly remark. For out here, on the edge of the dying British Empire, farce is the only mode of narrative discourse that makes any sense at all.

2: A PROBLEM WITH MR. DWYER

Fireworks behind. Darkness ahead. And if that's not a metaphor for the Irish Question I don't know what is.

Once I was off the slip road I drove insanely fast on the A6 until the carriageway ran out at Glengormley. From Glengormley it was just a short hop up the A2 to Carrickfergus. It was a cold, wet, foggy night which discouraged both terrorists and the British Army's random roadblocks, so the run was relatively easy; and fortunately, I didn't kill myself doing 110 mph on the stretches of motorway.

I got back to Coronation Road in Carrick's Victoria Estate at just after 1:20.

In the middle class streets after midnight all was quiet, but out here in the estates there could be *craic* at any hour. The *craic* now was two doors down, where a bunch of lads were drinking Harp lager, eating fish and chips, and playing what sounded like Dinah Washington from a portable record player on a long lead outside Bobby Cameron's house. Bobby had clearly hijacked the owner/operator of a mobile chip van and forced him to provide food for him and his mates. Bobby was the local paramilitary commander who also ran a two-bit protection racket and dealt unexcised cigarettes and drugs. His stock had been low for years around here but lately had risen because, with the assistance of the Glasgow Orange Order, he had kidnapped back and deprogrammed a Carrickfergus girl from a branch of the Unification Church in Scotland. The Moonie temple had been burned to the ground in the incident and half a dozen Moonie guards had been shot in the kneecaps. "Stay out of Scotland and Northern Ireland!" was the message the crippled security personnel had carried all the way back to Korea. It was a big win for Bobby and now you sometimes heard people muttering that if "you want something done, don't go to the police, go see Bobby Cameron," which was exactly the sort of thing that the paramilitaries loved to hear.

Our eyes met. Bobby looked a bit like Brian Clough, but Brian Clough after a three-nil home defeat to Notts County.

"You're a wanted man, Duffy," Bobby said.

"Oh yeah?"

"Didn't you have your police radio on?"

"No."

"We've been listening to the scanner. They've been looking for you, Duffy. Miss Marple's not available so why not the intrepid Inspector Duffy, eh?"

"Thanks for the tip," I said and locked the car.

"You want a fish supper?" Bobby asked. "I'm paying."

I walked over to the chip van and looked at the driver, an older man with an abstract sadness about him. "I'm a police officer. Are you being held against your will or coerced to be here tonight?"

"Oh no, not at all," he said quickly. "I'm just doing Bobby a favor."

I didn't know whether I believed him, but he didn't look afraid for his life, which was something. "In that case I'll take a sausage supper."

The other diners moved aside to let me get to the chip van window. It was quite the collection of crooks and ne'er-do-wells, and when my life becomes a BBC drama the casting director will love this little scene as an opportunity for showcasing his ugliest and weirdest extras.

The hijacked chip man gave me a sausage supper wrapped in newspaper and I thanked him and offered him a quid.

"On the house," he said, and gestured toward Bobby.

I ate a chip or two. "How was Scotland?" I asked Bobby.

"You heard about that?"

"Interesting fact. The Reverend Moon was raised as a Presbyterian. The Moonies are basically radical Korean Presbyterians."

Bobby shook his head. "I won't debate theology with you at two in the morning, Duffy, not when you've got a busy night ahead of you, but I will say that the problem with you Catholics is that you don't understand the Protestant religion."

"No?"

"Unlike your Church, which is a top-down faith—Pope, cardinal, bishop, priest, congregant—ours is a democracy. Our ministers, our moderator, our elders, and our congregants are all equal. That's why the *Reverend* Moon, as you call him, could never be considered a Presbyterian, cos he sets himself above his flock."

The Jesuits had beaten the Counter-Reformation dialectic into me to such an extent that even at this unholy hour I could have martialed half a dozen arguments against Luther, Calvin, and the other heretics, but I was just too weary for any of that now. "Maybe you're right. See ya," I said, and went inside my house.

I turned on my pager and carried the phone into the living room. If they really were looking for me they'd keep trying until they got me.

I got some ice and poured myself a pint glass of vodka gimlet and put on the best album of 1985 so far: the much-delayed release of Sam Cooke's *Live At The Harlem Square Club*.

I drank half the pint and cranked the volume on "Bring It On Home," which built to the vibe of an old church revival. When I was sufficiently solaced I dialed the station. "Duffy," I told Linda at the incident desk.

"Thank God, Inspector! Chief Inspector McArthur has been looking for you."

"I'm not supposed to be on tonight. Sergeant McCrabban is duty detective."

"Chief Inspector McArthur specifically asked for you. He's been very insistent. Where have you been?"

"I was up in Derry. I just got in. I'm shattered. I really need to go to bed, Linda, love."

"I'm sorry, Sean, but the Chief Inspector has been pulling his hair out. He's got a real situation on his hands. He's asked for you specifically."

"Where is he?"

"Uhm, the, uh, the Eagle's Nest Inn on the Knockagh Road . . ." she said with more than a trace of embarrassment.

"McArthur is there right now?"

"That's what I've been led to believe."

"And he's got himself into some kind of trouble?"

"I'm not, er, privy to the details, Sean."

"All right, if he calls again tell him I'm on my way."

"Do you know where it is?"

"Uh, yes, I've been there before . . . in a professional capacity."

"Of course."

I scarfed another couple of chips, pulled a leather jacket over my jeans and sweater, and went back outside. Bobby and his cronies were playing petanque with scrunched-up beer cans, and Mickey Burke was walking his aged toothless lioness on a leash at the other end of the street, something he promised me he would stop doing.

"Ah, they found you, Duffy!" Bobby said triumphantly.

I held up a finger to tell Bobby I'd deal with him in a minute.

"Mickey, what have I told you!"

"Just getting her some air, Inspector Duffy," Mickey said apologetically.

"Get her back inside! We've discussed this!"

"She's got no teeth, she's harmless and—"

"Get her inside!"

Mickey hustled the full-grown lioness back indoors.

"There should be a law against keeping lions in a council house," Bobby said, his face now like Brian Clough after he'd found a dead bluebottle in his Monster Munch.

"There should be," I agreed, and looked under the BMW for mercury tilt bombs.

"There's no point doing that, Duffy. We've been standing here the whole time. No one put a bomb under your car."

"How do I know you didn't put a bomb under my car?" I replied, and kept checking under the chassis.

"You're my pet copper, Duffy. I wouldn't kill you."

I ignored him, finished the search, and opened the car door.

"And besides, if I wanted to kill you you'd already be dead, mate," Bobby added.

"Shortly followed by you, pal. I've seen to that," I told him with a wink.

I drove out of Victoria Estate and along the Greenisland Road to the Eagle's Nest Inn, which was halfway up Knockagh Mountain.

The B road became a private road that wound its way through light woodland and then a broad piece of manicured parkland before it arrived at a seventeenth-century Scottish baronial house overlooking Belfast Lough. The house was converted in the seventies into first a hotel, then a spa, and was now a high-class brothel. It was all completely illegal, of course, but the owners paid off at a level so elevated that you'd need a Sherpa to get close to them. A criminal investigation out here would suck you into some really heavy shit: Internal Affairs, Special Branch, the local MP, government inquiries . . .

I parked the Beemer next to two Mercedes Benzes and a Roller.

I was met at the entrance by a bright young man in a three-piece suit with a name tag that said Patrick on it, which was a likely story.

"Are you Inspector Duffy, by any chance?" he asked in an English butler accent which also sounded bogus.

"Yes."

"If you'll come with me, please," he said.

He led me through the building in a manner that can only be described as a kind of fastidious, subdued panic.

I followed him up a wide oak staircase to the second floor. There were pictures of horses on the wall, hunting scenes and the like, all originals or pastiches of Stubbs and John Frederick Herring. Chandeliers illuminated the corridor and light classical music was playing from discreet speakers. It was a chilly, unerotic environment, but they probably thought that was what the well-heeled punters wanted. Hell, maybe it *is* what they wanted. Maybe the madam had handed out questionnaires.

There were several male bouncer types waiting for us at the top of the stairs. They pointed at an open door and we went inside Room 202, to quite the little diorama.

A half-naked young man was sitting on the floor with blood oozing from a wound on his scalp. He was crying and being attended to by a bald man in a bathrobe and another much younger man in jeans and a sweatshirt. A girl wearing a basque and black stockings was sitting in a chair by a writing desk. An older woman in a harsh red wig was sitting next to her. A glum-looking Chief Inspector McArthur was sitting on the edge of the bed. Behind them all there was an open French window that led to a balcony, an elaborate fountain, and a manicured lawn.

Peter McArthur was my new boss, new being the operative word here as he'd been the station commander at Carrickfergus RUC only for about six weeks. On paper he was very much the high flyer: Cambridge University, Hendon Police College, a Chief Inspector at the age of only thirty-one, but in person he was less impressive. Long nosed, weak chinned, and a dreamy, soft vagueness to his girlish, brown eyes. He was Scottish but the fey New Town Edinburgh type rather than Glasgow roughneck.

"Thank heavens, Duffy, where in the name of God were you?"

"Derry. Special Branch op."

"I can't have you gallivanting off to Derry. Can't you see we're in big trouble here?"

"There are plenty of constables at the station."

"Uh, loose lips sink ships. This is, uh, a rather delicate matter, don't you think?"

"I can't tell what the matter *is* yet, sir."

The man in the sweatshirt got up and looked at me. "And who is this?" he asked in a pleasing American accent.

"Inspector Sean Duffy. He's the head of our CID unit. You can trust him."

The man looked dubious.

I raised my eyebrows at the Chief Inspector. *What the hell is going on here, Chief?*

McArthur lowered his voice as a stab at some kind of intimacy. "Look, Duffy, you've been around longer than I have, what are we going to do? I don't want to pass it up the chain. Not yet. It doesn't have to become a big issue, does it?"

He was sweating and looking anxious in his sharp brown suit and crimson tie. McArthur was only about three calendar years younger than me, but he avoided the smokes, the sun, and the booze, so he looked about twenty. And if he was already out of his depth here I'd hate to see the eejit in a real emergency.

I sat down on the edge of the bed. "Perhaps you could apprise me of the situation, sir?"

"Ach, I'll tell ya, so I will," the girl said in a chainsaw West Belfast argot.

"All right. What happened, love?" I asked her.

"The gentleman and I were about to get down to business. And he said I should have some . . . *rocket fuel*, he called it. I said no. He said come on and try it; it would make us go all night. I said no. He gets all eggy and starts screaming and yelling and I says, right, I'm calling security. He goes bonkers and tries to bloody choke me and I pick up the lampshade and clock him with it."

"Good for you," I replied.

"And I immediately called Carrickfergus RUC. I'll have no nonsense like this in my establishment," the woman in the red wig said. Obviously the lady of the house. A Mrs. Dunwoody if I recalled correctly.

"Where is this rocket fuel?" I asked.

Chief Inspector McArthur handed me a large bag of white powder. Enough to power an army. I tasted it. High-quality coke cut with nothing. Probably pharma cocaine manufactured in Germany, worth a bloody fortune. I sealed up the bag and put it in my jacket pocket.

"Have you weighed the cocaine?" I asked the Chief Inspector.

"No."

Excellent. "I'll do it at the station and enter it into evidence."

"Is it cocaine?"

"Oh yes. Very high-quality gear too. And there's a lot of it. We could get him on intent to deal if we wanted. Not that we'll need to. Possession alone of this much is at least six months."

Chief Inspector McArthur shook his head. "I'm not sure you're seeing the big picture, here, Duffy . . . Do you recognize who this is?"

"No."

"He's an actor. Famous. American."

I looked at the half-naked guy. He seemed vaguely familiar. Strong jawed, bright eyed. I might have seen him in something. Now his tears took on another dimension. Fake. The Chief Inspector gave me the do-you-catch-my-drift nod. *Aye, I do.* Celebrity was the coin of the realm even in far-flung places like Northern Ireland. We wouldn't be prosecuting this character. We won't be bringing the wrath of the higher-ups and the long beaks of the media into our little parish. But on the other hand, Mrs. Dunwoody, or her employer, was clearly protected, and she wanted justice . . .

"Actor? Were you in *The Swarm*?" Mrs. Dunwoody asked.

"No," he said.

"Are you sure? You look awful familiar."

"I wasn't in *The Swarm*!"

"What is your name?" I asked the actor.

"David Dwyer," he said. And yeah, I recognized it. He'd been in the tabs for assaulting a photographer and beating up an ex-wife, but in Tinsel Town that counted for nothing next to his million-dollar acting chops.

"What are you doing in Ireland, Mr. Dwyer?"

"I was researching a movie," he said, slurring his words slightly. But I could see that he wasn't *that* drunk. I wondered for a moment whether he ever stopped performing. When he was alone in his room, perhaps, with no audience but himself.

"Well, Mr. Dwyer, I suppose you realize that you're going to be charged with possession of cocaine and with common assault."

"I never saw those drugs in my life!"

"Now, now, Mr. Dwyer, we know that's not true, don't we?" I told him, the policeman's *we* throwing me fully into *my* character.

"And what about that bitch? She attacked me first!" he squealed, looking at me and then the Chief Inspector in a relentless shot/counter-shot scheme.

"She attacked you and someone planted that cocaine, is that your tragic tale, sir? It's a good job my sergeant isn't here; he's a weeper. That one would have him bawling his eyes out."

"It's true!" he insisted.

"The young lady was acting in self-defense, sir, and take it from me, any Irish jury you care to find is going to see it that way."

The bald man in the bathrobe got to his feet and addressed the Chief Inspector. "I'm done here, OK? No internals, the bleeding's stopped and he'll need a couple of stitches. Be right as rain in the morning."

"Thank you, Doctor . . .?" McArthur asked.

"I'd rather my name didn't come into this, if you don't mind."

"You probably should get back to your friend, Doctor. They charge by the hour," I said.

"No! This one's on the house; be sure and tell Samantha," the madam insisted.

The doctor smiled meekly and exited the scene . . .

"I don't know what kind of an operation you guys are running here, but you do not want to piss me off, believe me. I could buy and sell you people ten times over!" Dwyer snarled, getting to his feet. He was quite short but there was a tremendous physicality to him. I didn't know whether he'd ever done stage work, but if he had he must have commanded the room. He poked a finger into my jacket. "When Ireland is finally free you fuckers will be first up against the wall. You know that, don't you?"

I took the finger and bent it backward. He winced and his knees buckled. I forced him back down onto the ground more aggressively than I needed to just to make transparent the true power dynamic in the room.

The Chief Inspector looked at me with alarm. I shook my head so that he didn't open that gob of his. "You're quite the dangerous hombre, Mr. Dwyer, but me and the Chief Inspector are your only friends here. We're the only obstacles between you and several years in a Northern Irish jail," I explained before letting his finger go. He gasped and fell into the fetal position.

The man in the sweatshirt helped Dwyer to a more comfortable sitting posture and then stood and smiled apologetically.

"I'm Thomas, Mr. Dwyer's assistant, and I can assure you we didn't mean to cause any offense. Please tell us what we should do to facilitate this inquiry and help resolve this situation as quickly and as amicably as possible," he said.

I looked at the Chief Inspector, who shrugged. The ball was in my court.

I lit a Marlboro.

"The young lady has received quite a shock and will no doubt want to take a vacation to get over her distress. I would say that a personal check to her for, say, two thousand—"

"Five thousand!" she interrupted.

"Five thousand pounds will cover her expenses. And the lady of the house will have to replace the damaged—"

"Antique," she said.

"Antique lamp and I expect that two thousand pounds would cover the cost of that?"

Mrs. Dunwoody nodded. Two grand would be quite sufficient.

"We will expect you to leave the jurisdiction immediately and we must stress that it is in your best interests that you do not return."

Thomas was smiling deferentially, pleased that his boss had got off so lightly. "Thank you very much, Officers, Mr. Dwyer is very appreciative of all your trouble," he said.

"I want *him* to thank us for our trouble. And I want him to apologize to the young lady for scaring her."

"Like hell I will!" Dwyer muttered.

I pulled the little shit to his feet by the scruff of the neck.

"You'll do it, sunshine! The last wee bastard that gave me your attitude pisses blood through a catheter to this very day. Do you get me?"

"I get you. I get you. Relax, buddy. I get you."

Dwyer apologized.

Thomas wrote checks.

The lady of the house and the girl thanked me.

The Chief Inspector walked me back to the lobby and wondered whether perhaps I went a bit overboard with the celeb. I ignored him. He asked me if the thing with the catheter was true. I said it wasn't. He seemed relieved so I didn't tell him that in fact the last guy who gave me attitude like that I ended up shooting and leaving for dead in a village north of Brighton, just before I got blown up with half the Tory Cabinet in the bombing of the Grand Hotel . . .

"Any time you're feeling lonely and you want a friend, you know where to come. It'll be on the house. We've got girls to suit every taste," Mrs. Dunwoody said.

"That's OK, I—"

"Or maybe in your case, Inspector, you'd prefer boys, young men I mean, attractive young men."

I looked her in the eye. How did she know about that weird, out-of-character, one-time experience all those years ago? How did madams always know your innermost secrets?

"Uh, no thanks," I said.

She put her arm in mine and walked me outside.

"All sorts in here," she mused.

"I'll bet."

"Had one gentleman last week wanted Veronica to throw darts at his bare arse."

"Really?"

"But I wouldn't let her. She's left handed. They'd go all over the place, wouldn't they? Into me nice pictures."

I opened the BMW's door and got inside.

"Have you heard this one, Inspector? A man goes to a taxi driver in North Belfast and he says, 'Ladas Drive,' and the taxi driver says, 'No way! You'll have to sit in the back like everybody else.'"

I'd heard it before but I laughed dutifully.

Mrs. Dunwoody smiled. "Come back if you're lonely; even if you just want to chat, we've got some very good listeners," she insisted.

I nodded, closed the door, and drove home along the water into Carrickfergus.

The big Norman castle spoke of English power as it had been doing very effectively for the last eight hundred years. I angled the Beemer into the castle car park. No prying eyes. A coal boat from Latvia at one pier and the pilot boat tied up on the other. I took out an evidence bag, removed the bag of pharma coke from my pocket and poured out about half of it, sealed it, and put it in the glove compartment.

I drove the half-mile from the castle to the police station.

Empty but for Sergeant Dalglish, huddled by the electric fire and reading a book.

"Who's there?" he asked.

"Well it's not the Ghost of Christmas Future if that's what you're worried about."

"Ah, Duffy. The Chief Inspector was looking for you."

"He found me."

"Wee bit lonely here, Duffy, do you want to stay and chat? I'm working my way through Paul's second letter to the Corinthians; it's fascinating stuff. Pull up a chair."

"Uh, no thanks, pal. I think I'd rather fucking shoot myself. I'm away. And do please remember that DS McCrabban is duty detective tonight, not me, OK?"

"OK."

"After I type this report up, I don't expect to be bothered again until tomorrow."

"Relax, Duffy, no one'll bother you. Go on home and get your beauty sleep; looks like you need it."

I typed up a quick incident report for the Chief Inspector to sign. Under "Officer Action" I wrote that Mr. Dwyer had been let off with a caution. I went to the evidence room, weighed the coke, marked 3.1 ounces on the bag, and put it in the night locker.

Back outside. Beemer. Ninety mph on the two-minute journey to Coronation Road. Parked the car, grabbed my half of the coke, got out. Timex said 3:55 a.m. Light drizzle. No cars. No pedestrians.

Inside 113 Coronation Road. I grabbed a torch, went out to the shed, and hid the coke in a nail box next to a slab of engine grease so ancient and rancid that even the best sniffer dogs wouldn't go near it.

Inside again. I undressed quickly in the hall and walked naked up the stairs.

I lit the paraffin heater. Lights off.

I tossed and turned for an hour and finally gave up.

Downstairs again. Vodka gimlet. Sam Cooke on the stereo. Sam The Man Cooke whose raw masculine power was so intense that he seemed to bring to a climax half the audience during the medley of "It's All Right/For Sentimental Reasons."

When the record was done I let the silence wash over me. I put the chilled pint glass against my forehead. I lay there on the sofa in the pallid starlight, in that *light of other days* . . .

And the house was quiet.

And the street was quiet.

And my eyelids were heavy.

And the rain was falling.

And the phone was ringing.

3: MURDER WAS THE CASE THAT THEY GAVE ME

I picked up the phone. "This better be good."

"Sean, is that you?" Detective Sergeant McCrabban asked.

"Anyone else would have told you to fuck off by now. Course it's me. Do you know what time it is, Crabbie?"

"Uhm, about six o'clock?"

"Aye, six o'clock, and I haven't even been to bed yet."

"I'm really sorry, Sean, but we've got a situation."

"What sort of situation?"

"It's a double murder in Whitehead."

"*Ecoutez*, my esteemed colleague. Isn't that why they promoted you from humble flatfoot to detective sergeant? So that you could handle double murders in Whitehead without involving me on my so-called night off."

"The murder isn't the problem, Sean."

"OK, I'll play along, what *is* the problem?"

"It's a jurisdictional dispute."

"That's a new one. Go on."

"Larne RUC are saying that this is their case because the road the house is on is technically in their patch. But the house itself is over the line in Carrick RUC's turf. It's our case, Sean."

"Jesus, Crabbie, if they want it so badly let them have it!"

"Husband and wife shot in the head. The husband is a bloke called Ray Kelly; he's got a lot of money."

I sighed. "So you don't want Larne to have it because it's a dead rich guy?"

"Well, Sean, first of all, it is *our* case. Larne have no right to be here at all. Secondly, it's an interesting one: a dead millionaire and his wife in a whopping big mansion in Whitehead, you know?"

"And what has all this got to do with me?"

"I need you, Sean. I'm a detective sergeant; you're an inspector. I can't hold Larne RUC off by myself. I'll owe you one, mate."

I groaned into the receiver. "All right, Crabbie, I'll come down. I wasn't sleeping anyway."

"You might want to wear something respectable. There's a full-of-himself Chief Inspector Kennedy from Larne RUC here."

"What's the address?"

"64 New Island Road, Whitehead, just beyond the lighthouse. Do you want me to send a constable for you?"

"I'll find it."

"May I ask how your trip to Derry went last night?"

"The gunrunners?"

"Aye."

"As fine an example of RUC-Gardai-Interpol cooperation as I've ever seen."

"Oh dear. That bad?"

"That bad. See you in fifteen, Crabbie. Hold the fort, don't let those Larne culchies tramp their dirty boots all over our crime scene."

"I won't."

Crabbie hung up and I put the kettle on and pushed the preselect on the stereo for Radio 1. I rummaged in the cupboard above the sink for the RUC map of East Antrim, found it, and unfolded it on the kitchen table. The kettle clicked off and I made myself a cup of tea. I grabbed a couple of McVities chocolate digestives and examined the map.

I noticed that the boundary line between Carrick RUC and Larne RUC districts skirted through Whitehead town itself, but 64 New Island Road, on the Blackhead cliff, was just over the line in our manor. I might have to do some yelling and screaming but Crabbie was right; for better or worse, if we wanted it, this was *our* case.

Radio 1 began playing "Ever Fallen in Love with Someone?" by the Buzzcocks. I poured a dash of Lagavulin into the tea and lit a Marlboro.

Tea, ciggies, McVities chocolate digestives, Lagavulin: the breakfast of bloody champions.

"All right, Duffy, time to get serious," a croaky voice that sounded a bit like mine said aloud. I found a sweater and a pair of jeans that didn't look too minging. I laced up my Doc Martens, grabbed my revolver and a black raincoat, and went out onto Coronation Road.

I looked under the BMW for bombs and got inside.

I turned on Radio 1 and The Cure's "Close To Me" began its jaunty but cunningly irritating melody. I drove up Coronation Road, turned right on Victoria Road, and drove to the bottom of the hill where the Antrim Plateau met the sea. There was no traffic at this hour and I paused at the junction; to my right Carrickfergus Castle was lit up by spotlights, and behind the castle Belfast was a wet film of light and shade under the Black Mountain.

I turned left, and, as there were no other cars on the road, I let the Beemer's big M30 straight-six engine stretch itself.

The speedometer was registering a ton and change as I zoomed past the abandoned factories in Kilroot, and before Robert Smith had even got to "Wish I'd stayed asleep today," we were deep in the Irish countryside.

I made it to Whitehead in less than four minutes, coming suddenly on that great cliff bend in the A2 known as the Bla Hole, where for a dazzling second you could see all of the North Channel and a good chunk of Western Scotland.

The road curved to the left and on the passenger's side there were fields filled with sheep, and on my side a hint of sun now in the eastern horizon . . .

Pink sky.

Blue sky.

"Close To Me" ended, and because no one was listening at this hour anyway, the DJ put on the twelve-inch of "Blue Monday," which would comfortably take me all the way to my destination.

I turned right on Cable Road.

Whitehead, County Antrim.

Imagine Vernazza in the Cinque Terre on the Italian Riviera. No, wait, don't imagine that. It's nothing like that; this is Northern Ireland we're talking about here. OK, but maybe imagine it a little. A town under the cliff, a town with brightly painted houses on the seashore.

I took out the map and found New Island Road.

The crime scene was not difficult to locate.

Sergeant McCrabban had brought down two Land Rovers from Carrick RUC. Larne RUC had shown up with a couple of Land Rovers of their own, and there were two Land Rovers from the forensic unit in Belfast. Add to that a couple of cars from local media, a dozen lookie-loos from surrounding streets, and the outside broadcast van from BBC Radio Ulster.

The house itself was a kind of folly, a scaled-down copy of Dunluce Castle, which famously had fallen into the sea a few miles up the coast. There was a central "keep" in thick grey stone with turrets and flying buttresses, high arched windows, and a flat walled roof. There were several outbuildings and a guest cottage and all around the property a thick nine-foot-high stone wall.

The hundred-foot cliff protected the property to the east, south, and north, so if an intruder was going to get in he'd have to come over the wall to the west or through massive iron front gates.

I parked the BMW behind the BBC radio car and walked up to those huge wrought-iron gates where Crabbie was waiting for me.

"Morning, Sergeant McCrabban," I said cheerfully.

"Morning, Sean."

"Jesus, this is some pile," I said. "These people must indeed be loaded."

"You can see why Larne RUC want it, can't you? It's the sort of case that newspapers like, the sort of case that builds careers."

"Or sinks them," I said with a significant drop in cadence.

"Aye, but most of us don't have your luck, Sean," Crabbie pointed out.

"What did you say this guy did? He was a bookie?"

"He runs a chain of bookies."

"Who reported the killing?"

"Mrs. McCawly, the housekeeper."

"How did she get in?"

"She has a code for the front gate."

"When did she get here?"

"Five on the dot."

"Bit early for a cleaner, no?"

"She worked from five until eight every day. Mrs. Kelly liked to have the place spick and span first thing in the morning."

"Doesn't the Hoover wake them up?"

"Well, not today it doesn't."

"So Mrs. McCawly gets here at five and finds Mr. and Mrs. Kelly shot dead?"

"Yes."

"Were these gates open when she got here?"

"No."

"How did the killer get in? You'd need a siege tower to get over that wall."

"Or a ladder."

"Yeah, true, but what self-respecting hit man drives around with a ten-foot ladder?"

"A well-prepared one?" Crabbie said with Jeevesian sangfroid.

"So you're thinking an outside job?"

"No, quite the opposite in fact."

Crabbie was getting on my nerves. "Let's see this crime scene, eh?"

He led me through the gates, along a gravel drive, into a wood-paneled entrance hall, and finally into a large, open-plan, living room that overlooked the North Channel. The place was full of coppers and other hangers-on, some of whom turned to look at me the moment I stepped into the room. I ignored them.

The sun was up now and Scotland was so close that you could see chimney smoke from the villages on the other side of the sea. The living room itself was hung with tasteful, presumably original, artwork. Furniture: big stylish sofas, comfy chairs, a nice mahogany dining-room table on to which a whole bunch of police forensic equipment had been placed. Floor: hardwood with massive, expensive-looking Persian rugs on top. The TV was on, but at this time of the day the only thing showing was the BBC test card: the little girl and the creepy clown playing noughts and crosses forever in a nursery hell.

Of course the focal point of the *mise-en-crime* were the two bodies sitting facing one another on two armchairs either side of the TV set.

The man was wearing tracksuit bottoms and a Ralph Lauren lime-green polo shirt. He was in his fifties. Chubby. Grey curly hair, a goatee, a signet ring, and a wedding ring. The bullet had made a tiny impression on his left temple and a presumably larger exit wound on his right temple. His mouth was half open. He was facing the television, not the assassin. The killer had shot him first.

His wife had been shot next. Twice. Once in the heart. Once in the forehead. She was a deeply tanned, dark-haired, trim woman in a white bathrobe over blue pajamas. She was about forty-five years old. You wouldn't say attractive but perhaps once she had been. She had attempted to get out of the chair after her husband had been shot, but the killer had immediately plugged her in the chest to gentle her condition; and before she could get going with the screaming, he had crossed the room, gotten real close, and single-tapped her in the forehead, blowing the top fifth of her head off. He'd been so efficient that there wasn't even a defensive wound on either one of her hands. (Normally when you know your number's up, instinct brings your hands up to cover your head, but this guy had been quick.)

"What's your take, Crabbie?"

"The killer shot him first and her a few moments later."

"Did you notice that she has no defensive wounds?"

"Yes."

"Which means?"

"Either there were two shooters or the guy was fast."

"I'd bet one shooter but forensics will tell us for sure."

"Aye."

I examined the bodies. Nasty exit wounds. Death would have been instantaneous. The undertaker would have a real job with both of them if the family wanted to go open casket.

"Kids, relatives?" I asked McCrabban.

"One son, Michael, who is missing."

"Missing, how?"

"His car's gone from the garage," McCrabban said significantly.

"It's normally in the garage?"

"Yes it is."

"How old is this kid?"

"Twenty-two."

"Quite the difficult age for a young man."

"Aye."

"And he was living here with his mum and dad?"

"Yup."

"He was living here and now he's vanished in his car?"

"His Mercedes Benz."

"Everything quiet and peaceful chez the Kellys?"

"Mrs. McCawly didn't think so."

"Did she not?"

"No she didn't. There were arguments. Especially arguments between father and son."

"Ah, now you're talking."

"Heated arguments, she says."

"Pushing and shoving?"

"No, but yelling matches."

"About?"

"The boy's future. The boy's friends. Late nights, the usual thing."

"What does this kid do for a living?"

"He's unemployed."

I nodded. "OK, so that's one track. But leaving that to one side for the moment, what about signs of forced entry?"

"On an initial inspection, none."

"Firearms in the house?"

"Shotgun for rabbits, nine-millimeter handgun for personal protection."

"Whose personal protection?"

"On the license Mr. Kelly said that he feared that he would be subject to kidnap because of his wealth."

"Where is this nine-millimeter now?"

"It's not in the drawer where Mrs. McCawly says he kept it."

"Do you think these victims were shot by a nine-millimeter?"

"Again forensics will tell us for sure, but if you ask me the wounds are consistent with a pistol of that caliber."

"Yeah. Almost certainly."

"But you're not happy?" he said, reading my expression accurately.

I shook my head. "I don't know, Crabbie, I can see where you're pointing me, but this thing has a professional killing vibe about it, don't you think?"

"It's certainly very clean and those head shots are impressive."

"But you still like the son for it, do you?"

"I'm not jumping to any conclusions just yet, Sean."

"You have alerted our stout comrades in Traffic Branch about this kid and his car?"

"Of course. Would you like to talk to Mrs. McCawly?"

Before I could answer that a big vacant-eyed arsehole with a black 'tache got in my face. "Are you Duffy?" he asked, looking at me with slow-boiling fury.

"That's what they call me. Sometimes The Space Cowboy or the Pompatus of Love," I said, winking and offering him my hand. He let the hand dangle.

"I'm CI Kennedy, Larne RUC. Listen to me, Duffy, your fucking sergeant won't let my men get started because he says this is *your* case. This isn't your case. The cleaner, Mrs. McCawly, called Larne RUC. *We* were the first responders, and if you look at the map you'll see that this is . . ."

I let him drift out. His 'tache, his big red face, his trousers too short for his ankles, and his ankles swollen by too-tight shoes are the early signs of congestive heart failure. Chief Inspector Kennedy was that most common and dangerous thing, the old man in a hurry. Passed over for promotion and keen to retire with a rank and commensurate pension that would allow him to pay his golf club dues and get his missus her winter bronzing holidays in Tenerife.

The Cure's "Close to Me" started replaying in my head. It would really be a much better song if they cut the saxophone. Most pop songs would be better without the saxophone. Bruce Springsteen's works the prima facie case for this, and perhaps *Live At The Harlem Square Club* a rare counter-example.

"Duffy?"

Kennedy had ceased his initial rant.

He was staring at me in a way that could get a civilian sectioned under the Mental Health Act. In fact the whole room had fixed their peepers on me. Half a dozen bleary-eyed coppers. A photographer. Men in boiler suits from the new forensic unit in Belfast waiting to get started. Classic zugzwang situation. As long as I stood here nobody would do anything and everything would be fine, but any move I made was going to piss someone off. If I let Kennedy have the case, Crabbie would resent me for months, and Kennedy looked like he'd throw an atomic eggy if I tried to poach this juicy murder from under him.

"Wait one second, please," I said to Kennedy.

I took McCrabban out onto the living-room balcony which overlooked the Gobbins cliffs and the bottle-green Irish Sea beyond.

I clapped him on the shoulder, partly just to see the uptight eejit shudder at the touch of a fellow human.

"Let's let them have it, eh, mate? That Larne copper's clearly demented. If we insist on the strict letter of the law he'll likely pop a blood vessel in his brain and add to the carnage in there," I said.

Crabbie thought about this and then shook his head. "No, Sean. It's not fair. It's not their case. They've got no right to be here. It's a question of justice."

"You know there's no such thing as justice."

"Says you."

I shrugged and looked the big Calvinist ganch in the eye. He was unflinching.

"You feel strongly about this?" I asked.

"I do. And besides, they've been very high handed to our men. They want taking down a peg or two."

I sighed and the sigh became a yawn. I was exhausted. Not just from the long night, but from ten years of this shit.

Ten years with no end in sight.

"You'll have to be lead, OK? You're the duty detective."

McCrabban grinned at me. I was saying all the right things today.

"I can pick your brain on it, though?" he asked.

"Of course. But not now and I'm not interviewing this Mrs. McCawly woman or anyone else for that matter. If you want the case, fine, but I'm going home to my bed."

McCrabban nodded. "Fair enough," he said.

We walked back to Chief Inspector Kennedy.

"Well?" he said. "Can we finally get fucking going?"

"If by going, you mean get going back to that ruinous cesspit of incompetence and inadequacy known as Larne RUC, then yes, you can get going, Kennedy, and if you want I'll come down and give you boys a seminar on how to read a fucking map, because clearly you fucking morons didn't twig that this property is a good two hundred yards on our side of the jurisdiction line."

Kennedy's blimpish purple face began to swell up like Violet Beauregarde's.

"I've got something to say to you, Inspector . . ." he sputtered.

"Well, go ahead and say it, then, you big dozy cunt," I told him.

He's going to explode, everyone in the room was thinking . . .

And yes, he did explode, but I'll spare you the details because the scene itself was not exactly Oscar Wilde and George Bernard Shaw swapping barbs at the Albemarle Club—unless Oscar was a lot more sweary than history has led us to believe. Kennedy started yelling. One of his underlings started yelling. And when they had exhausted their rather limited capacity for invective, Kennedy started in with the threats: "I play golf with the Assistant Chief Constable!" "I can get you posted to the border," etc.

Me and the Crabman said little, which only infuriated them more, and rather than observe the veins throbbing in Kennedy's forehead, I watched the big red and white car ferry chug out from Larne Harbor in the direction of Stranraer across the Irish Sea. Kennedy and his sidekick burned themselves out, like a failing double act at the Glasgow Empire, like colonels spluttering over their toast at the latest outrage in the *Daily Mail* . . .

When the rant was done they stormed out.

It was a bad example for the younger officers.

"That's a bad example for the younger officers," I said to Crabbie.

"Yes," he agreed.

We set the photographer to work and turned the Belfast forensics officers loose on the crime scene.

"And while we're on the subject, where is the new blood?" I asked McCrabban.

"Oh, they'd just get in the way, wouldn't they? I'll brief them later."

"You wake me up and I'm not even on duty but you let the new detectives lie in bed?"

"They're kids, Sean, they need their sleep."

"*I* need my sleep. If I had any feelings left they would likely be resentful ones. And that resentment would be directed at you and them. But fortunately with age I have acquired wisdom and patience."

We had two new officers, one of them a slip of a girl, the other a likely lad, but neither of them an adequate replacement for our late lamented colleague Matty McBride, who'd been killed last year in a small, random mortar attack on our police station. There would never be closure over Matty's death because his killer had never been caught and, in fact, never would be caught.

"Wisdom and patience," I reiterated. "Like the prophet Elijah. He's the one that made the bears eat the kids who were laughing at him, right?"

"I believe that was the prophet Elisha, Sean."

"You gotta give me points for only missing it by a letter."

"Bloody Larne RUC. They couldn't organize a bum rape in a barracks," one of the forensics officers muttered as he got to work.

"That's not what I heard," McCrabban said in a very rare moment of levity.

I gave him the once-over. There wasn't even a smirk at the edge of his long, dour, ashy, Presbyterian face.

"You're in fine fettle today, aren't you?" I said.

He nodded, took me to one side, lowered his voice even lower than the normal Ballymena burr. "Just between us, Sean, and I don't want to tempt fate or anything, but, God willing, it looks like the clan McCrabban might be increasing. Only two months along. You're supposed to wait until three, but, well, I know I could tell you."

"Well done, mate!"

"Thanks, Sean."

Crabbie put a finger in his shirt collar and looked at his Marks and Spencer shoes. He had something more to say, the big eejit. "Sean, I've talked it over with Helen and you wouldn't . . . you wouldn't . . ." he muttered and couldn't finish the sentence

"What?"

"You wouldn't be interested in becoming the bairn's godfather at all, would you?"

I was touched. I was positively moved. A fierce, Free Presbyterian farm boy like McCrabban asking me, a Fenian left-footer, to be the godfather of his baby? Tears. No joke. Tears welling up.

"I'm thrilled, mate. Really. Of course I'll do it. It would be an honor."

There was no chance of a hug, but we shook hands and I patted him on the back.

"What do the twins think?"

"John's enthusiastic. Thomas is furious."

"He'll come round."

We chewed the fat some more, but Crabbie could see that I was fading.

"I'll walk you back to your car," he said.

I nodded, coughed, yawned again.

"So what do you want me to do regarding the case?" he asked when we made it to the Beemer.

"It's your case, mate."

"What would you do if you were me?"

"You know what to do. Get the dirt from Mrs. McCawly on family arguments, disharmony, that kind of thing. The boy's twenty-two and he's still living at home? Why? Full forensics on the victims, look for signs of intruders, canvass the neighbors, financial specs on Mr. Kelly's company, any recent threats, did he have any enemies, etc. All the standard stuff."

Crabbie nodded.

"I'd also alert border security and make sure the kid doesn't leave the country. Find who his friends are and what he does with himself. Tracking him down has to be priority one."

"Already took care of that. Airport watch and watch at the ferry terminals in Larne and Belfast."

I yawned. "Good. Good. You know the ropes, mate. And don't forget a preliminary report to our new boss, Chief Inspector McArthur. Typed. In a binder. Let's dazzle him with the efficiency of our department, eh?"

Crabbie nodded.

A final handshake and I got in the Beemer, then reversed it out of its spot and tried hard not to kill a reporter who was standing in the middle of the road attempting to intimidate me into an interview.

"BBC Radio . . . what can you tell us about the incident?" he asked.

"No comment," I told him. "I am not the investigating officer. If you want a quote for the press you'll have to wait for Sergeant McCrabban."

"Is it worth staying for? Can you at least tell me that?"

"I imagine that you and your comrades in the fourth estate are going to be spilling some ink over this one, yes," I said, and drove home along the Raw Brae Road.

It was time for the Radio 1 *Breakfast Show* now. Mike Read read Mystic Meg's astrology predictions from the *Sun* and introduced a new Duran Duran single with his own prophetic avowal that "it would be a sure-fire hit from the Beatles of the 80s." I turned it off after the tenth bar.

When I got back to Coronation Road I was barely thinking about the Kelly murders. It was McCrabban's case, not mine, and with the locked house gates and no sign of forced entry and the nine-millimeter wounds and the troubled kid fleeing the scene it seemed straightforward. I didn't foresee problems and maybe even Mystic Meg couldn't have predicted the epic shitstorm that was heading our way across the cold grey waters of the Irish Sea.

4: THE NEW BLOOD

I slept for a solid six on the living-room sofa and woke to the sound of knocking. Mrs. Campbell from next door was standing on the porch with a Black Forest gateau she'd made, presumably, as a thank-you for getting her off a speeding ticket.

I opened the door and said hello. She was wearing a little black PVC miniskirt and a white blouse with the top two buttons undone. Her red hair had been cut short and spiked in a style that was reminiscent of mid-period Sheena Easton. Despite that she looked fantastic. She was talking about the cake, about how no one in her house liked cherries, but she knew that I had "more adventurous tastes."

You don't know the half of it, sister.

I thanked her and gave her a little kiss on the cheek which she would pass off as some Catholic thing rather than a perv move.

I made a cup of tea and had a slice of the Black Forest. I remembered about the pharma coke, went outside, and nailed a line so pure it was like getting yelled at by God. Yorkshire tea, Mrs. Campbell's Black Forest, Bayer cocaine—*the lunch of champions.*

The BBC *Afternoon News*: a story that I tuned out at the time but in retrospect should maybe have paid more attention to:

"...A spokesman for Shorts could not confirm whether the missile systems had been lost as part of a shipment overseas or whether they had been stolen from the factory itself pre-shipment: 'At this stage we just don't know how many missiles, if any, have gone missing. We are conducting an internal inquiry the results of which will be made known to the police and the DPP.' And that concludes the news. Now Sam with the weather..."

I went outside, looked under the Beemer for bombs, and drove along Coronation Road, navigating the ragamuffin children playing 123 Kick-A-Tin and football. I turned right on Victoria Road, right on the Marine Highway, and drove down to the station. There were columns of black smoke coming from several locations in Belfast that could mean anything. I parked the car in the spot marked "DI Duffy" and went inside the barracks.

The talk was of last night's fiasco with the gunrunners. Apparently it had made the front page of all the local papers. One of the Americans was dead, the rest were wounded, and no less than eight policemen had contrived to get themselves injured. The RUC were presenting it as a triumph. The Northern Ireland Secretary had been flown to the scene and posed for photographs against the beached ship.

"And Prince Potemkin smiles in his far-off grave," I muttered to myself.

"I heard *you* were there, Inspector?" Constable Iain Sinclair asked me.

"Me, there? Nah, I was supposed to go, but I couldn't be bothered in the end. I'm sure you all know more about it than I do," I told him, to kill that and any other potentially tedious Q&As about the debacle.

CID had recently been moved back to the window offices overlooking the lough and that's where I found Sergeant McCrabban setting up an incident room and schooling our two new DCs in proper protocol.

I hadn't really paid close attention to the new officers yet. Both of them were young and I'd been somewhat neglectful of my responsibilities by having Crabbie break them into the ways of the station. The female officer, Helen Fletcher, was, perhaps, the slightly more interesting of the two. This was only her second posting after an obligatory tour on the border. She was a brunette, reasonably pretty, with green eyes and very pale skin. Her personnel file said she was twenty-two, but she looked younger. She hadn't gone to college but had done OK in her A-levels before joining the cops. She didn't smoke or drink, but McCrabban told me that this was for "health reasons" rather than some kind of religious thing—which, of course, was much weirder: if you were that worried about your health, why would you join the RUC?

On her first day at the office I witnessed her get completely stumped by the coffee machine, which didn't herald brilliance, but on the other hand WPC Strange told me that Fletcher's hair was always done up in a fiendishly complicated plait that she said implied hidden skills on the part of the plaitee. The male detective constable was a handsome, blond-haired kid, with an easy charm, good humor, and obvious intelligence. Four As in his A-levels: Maths, History, French, and Further Maths (whatever that was). His name was Alexander Lawson and he really was a kid, with pimples and everything. Everyone else in the station seemed to like him already, but I couldn't help feel a little bit irritated by his slickness, and I could see that Crabbie felt the same. Lawson had gone to some posh Belfast school and joined the cops straight after. He hadn't said three sentences to me since he had arrived on the same day as our new chief inspector, but we could sense that we were not destined to become fast friends. Both new arrivals were Protestants, of course, and with the transfer of Constable O'Reilly to Ballycastle RUC, I was again the only Catholic police officer in the building. I didn't mind. Everyone knew better than to fuck with me. I was the second-highest-ranking copper in the place, and my boss, Chief Inspector McArthur, now owed me a favor.

I sat down at the conference table and lit a smoke while Crabbie went on with his spiel: ". . . the victims, Mr. and Mrs. Kelly, were shot at close range with a nine-millimeter semi-automatic pistol. Both from the same gun. The cleaning lady, Mrs. McCawly, had observed a nine-millimeter semi-automatic in the desk drawer next to Mr. Kelly's bed. This gun is now missing. Also missing is Michael Kelly, Mr. and Mrs. Kelly's son. The boy is twenty-two years old and has been living at home now for the last year after dropping out of Oxford University. Mrs. McCawly had been witness to several arguments between father and son. The nature of these arguments seems to be over Michael's failures to take responsibility for his future, as well as more general complaints from Mr. Kelly about Michael's demeanor, friends, and attitude. On several occasions these arguments had, quote, 'almost come to blows,' unquote, with Mrs. Kelly intervening between the two of them."

Constable Lawson was writing furiously in his notebook and, copying his example, Fletcher was doing the same thing, but with less obvious enthusiasm.

"There were no signs of a forced entry at the Kelly home and Michael Kelly has been missing from the house since the incident. We have, of course, alerted traffic, customs, border patrol, and the army," Crabbie continued.

He passed around photocopies of what turned out to be Michael Kelly's RUC file. "Teenage convictions for joyriding and embezzlement," Crabbie said.

The joyriding wasn't terribly interesting, but the embezzlement was a sophisticated little scheme to steal money from his school ski trip fund, only rumbled because Michael Kelly's co-conspirator had blabbed. Charges dropped, of course, after Mr. Kelly had contributed money for the school's new gym . . .

Constable Lawson, adorably, put his hand up in the air.

"Yes?" Crabbie asked him.

"How many bullets did the killer or killers fire?"

"According to a preliminary forensic report three nine-millimeter rounds. All now recovered and entered into evidence. We can't, of course, tell if it was Mr. Kelly's gun because we haven't yet recovered the weapon. On an initial examination we think that the father was shot first, followed seconds later by the mother."

"Why do you think that?" Lawson asked.

Crabbie passed over the crime scene photographs. "Take a look, he's still watching the TV. Hasn't moved a muscle. She has partially turned to look at the shooter."

Now Constable Fletcher put her hand in the air.

"Yes?" Crabbie asked.

"So, it looks like Michael Kelly did it?" she asked uncertainly.

"We can't make that assumption at this stage."

"But if there's no forced entry, it's his father's gun, and he's gone missing . . ." Constable Fletcher continued.

"Yes, Michael Kelly would seem to be the obvious suspect. We'll need to find out if he has a girlfriend or other close friends that he may be hiding with. Guest houses and hotels have also been alerted."

"How long a head start would he have *if* he did the killing?" Lawson asked.

"Patho estimates time of death at just before midnight, so he could have five hours on us before the alerts went out."

"Plenty of time to get a ferry over to Scotland," I said.

"Why not just go to the airport?" Fletcher asked.

"For a flight you need ID, to cross the border into the Irish Republic you need ID," Crabbie explained. "But to get the ferry to Scotland you just pay your money and hop on."

Fletcher still didn't quite grasp it. "But he still could have flown somewhere. No one knew to stop him until this morning."

"They keep records on computer. We've told them his name. If he'd crossed the border or taken a flight we would know about it by now," Lawson explained.

"I get it. So he either took the ferry or he's still in Northern Ireland," she said.

"Exactly. There were four ferries he could have taken last night before the alarm went out. A one a.m. to Stranraer, a two-thirty a.m. to Cairnryan, a four a.m. to Stranraer, and a five-thirty a.m. to Cairnryan."

"So he could be anywhere in the middle of Scotland by now," Fletcher said.

"He could be anywhere in the middle of Britain," Crabbie said. "But the alert's gone out for him and his car. So maybe we'll get lucky."

"Lawson, you look troubled," I said.

"I don't know . . . it, er, doesn't feel quite right," Lawson said.

"What doesn't feel right?" I asked.

Lawson's cheeks reddened. "Well, if you're going to shoot your dad after months of provocation you're going to have it out with him first, aren't you? You're going to yell at the bastard and tell him what you think of him and then shoot him."

"So?" I said.

"So the mother isn't just going to be sitting in the chair watching

TV during all this, is she? She's going to be between the two of them, or, you know, at least out of her chair."

"Hmmm. Inspector Duffy, perhaps you should share with our new officers the concerns you had this morning, too," Crabbie said.

I lit another ciggie and offered the pack around. Neither of the newbies wanted one. Non-smoking was the fashion. It wouldn't last too long after their first gun battle or riot duty.

"Concerns? Well, minor concerns. I'd say the chances are that the boy did it."

"Didn't you have an issue with the wounds on the victims?" Crabbie insisted.

I took a puff of my Marlboro Red and cleared my throat. "Well, in a similar vein to Constable Lawson, my observation of the scene was that it didn't look much like a 'rage killing' to me. Nice clean shots to the temple and the heart. An angry man doesn't shoot that accurately. Professional killers do, but college dropout layabout sons who crack up because of constant nagging from the old man don't."

Lawson nodded vigorously. "Don't rage killers tend to 'overkill' too? Multiple stab wounds, multiple gunshots. He'd probably fire the whole clip at the old man, wouldn't he?" he said.

"Yes," I agreed.

"And maybe he'd spare the mother. I mean, it's the father who's giving him grief and it's the mum who's sticking up for him, right?" Fletcher said.

Crabbie skimmed the statement from Mrs. McCawly and slid it over the desk toward me. "It *was* the dad who was hassling him," he said.

"Once he's shot the father, it's in for a penny, in for a pound, isn't it?" I said.

"What's your alternative theory, Constable Lawson?" McCrabban asked.

"If Mr. Kelly had a firearm for personal protection he must have had enemies?" Lawson suggested.

"That's one of the things we are certainly going to find out," Crabbie insisted.

"Any forensic info from the shell casings?" I asked.

"There were no shell casings," Crabbie said. "He took them with him."

"Oh, I assumed when I got there that they'd already been tagged and bagged by the forensic officers. He took them with him?"

Crabbie nodded.

"So either a professional doing his job or a panicky son trying to cover his tracks," I said.

Silence descended.

I got to my feet.

"Well, folks, I can see you have this well in hand. I should go."

"Any parting words of wisdom, Inspector Duffy?" Crabbie asked.

"This professional killing angle is certainly interesting, but if I were you, Sergeant McCrabban, I would stress to our new arrivals that in your bog-standard criminal case in the greater Belfast area they'll find that Occam's razor is especially sharp; the simplest and most obvious explanation is almost always the correct one."

"Aye, but until we find the son and have a wee chat with him we'll keep our options open," McCrabban added.

I walked to the incident room door and gave Crabbie a little nod to let him know again that this really was his responsibility and I was not going to grab it from him. At least not for the moment. My own caseload wasn't half so exciting, but he had wanted this and if he solved it and somehow wangled a promotion out of it, good luck to him. Crabbie's undertakerish nod back was an equivalent of a high five from him.

I went to the personnel department and looked up the files on our two new detectives just to see if I'd missed anything. I hadn't, except for one thing; Lawson was Jewish rather than Protestant, which was a bit of a surprise. There were only a couple of hundred Jews left in Belfast. The community had been much larger before the Troubles, but now even Israel during the Intifada was a better bet than Northern Ireland.

I stuck the files back in the cabinet.

I read the *Sun* in the bog.

Coffee machine, office, feet on desk. Looking out the window, pretending to be interested in a series of unsolved muggings at Carrick train station.

Eventually the clock got its sorry arse round to five o'clock.

"Sean?"

The office door was open, Chief Inspector McArthur was standing there all uniformed up and rosy cheeked. He was wearing a Tyrol hat with a feather in it, and in case you didn't get the message, the hat had been placed at a jaunty thirty-degree angle on his head. He'd worn this hat before and you could see that he wanted desperately to be asked about it, which is why all the senior officers had made a silent pact never to bring it up.

"Yes, sir?"

"You want a quick one?"

"Well, I was on my way out."

"Have a seat. I'm buying."

We retreated to his office, which he had painted a sort of citrusy yellow. He'd moved in several palms and potted plants, and there were arty black and white photographs of boats on beaches and kids at country fares and so forth.

"Your photos?" I asked, pointing at the pictures.

"I dabble," he said.

It was my place to be encouraging. "They're really good," I said, and in truth they were good. Good enough to make into a calendar for American tourists, not like Diane Arbus good or anything.

He gave me a glass of whiskey. I sat.

"What are you working on at the moment, Sean?"

"Me, nothing much. Crabbie's got himself a double murder. I'll be assisting him on that one, no doubt, in due course."

"I want to thank you for last night; you were very helpful under the circumstances."

"Last night? Oh, that? Yeah."

McArthur took a gulp of his whiskey and I did the same. Twelve-year-old Islay. Good stuff if you liked peat, smoke, earth, rain, despair, and the Atlantic Ocean, and who doesn't like that?

McArthur smiled. "You've had quite a wee career, haven't you, Sean?"

"Have I?"

"Oh yes. You certainly have."

His eyes were twinkling. There was something he wasn't telling me. He looked at me significantly. "What are you not telling me, er, sir?"

"I'm just off the phone talking about you," he said.

"You were talking to someone on the phone about me?"

"Yes."

"What did you say?"

"Refill?"

"Sure."

He poured us each another healthy measure.

"What were you saying about me?" I persisted.

He laughed. "Oh, don't worry, it was all good stuff. I told them I've hardly had a chance to know you, but even in my limited experience I saw that you were a first-class officer."

"Am I getting a promotion or something?"

"Better than that, I think."

"Better than a promotion?"

"I'm afraid I can't tell you any more, Sean. My lips are sealed."

"You can't do that to me, sir," I said.

He shook his head. "Nope, sorry, I can't breathe a word."

"Come on, sir," I protested.

"*Vulpes, vulpes*, Duffy," he said with a wink.

"The common fox?"

"Actually, the not so common fox," he insisted.

I'd been neutral on McArthur before, but last night's shenanigans and now this confirmed in my mind that I actively disliked the wee shite. I knew I wasn't going to get any more out of him so I pushed the chair back, stood, and gave him a nod.

"I have to get on, sir," I said.

"OK. Go if you must."

I had a slash and went to see Crabbie, who was typing up his case notes in the incident room. He was smoking his pipe and the blue tobacco smoke and a mug of bergamot tea on his desk gave the room a very pleasant odor.

He looked up at me. "Sean?"

"Crabbie, has anyone been asking about me?" I wondered.

"About you?"

"Aye."

"Asking what?"

"Questions."

"Not to me. Why, what's going on?"

"I don't know. A couple of oblique references from the new Chief Inspector."

"You're not in trouble with the anti-corruption unit, are you?"

I gave him a hard look. "No, why would I be?"

"You wouldn't."

I leaned closer. "You'd tell me, wouldn't you, Crabbie?"

"Of course. But you're not in trouble."

"Aye," I said dubiously.

"Sean, come on, you're untouchable with your record."

"OK, mate. Look, I can see I'm keeping you from your work, I'll let you get back to it," I said, and didn't move.

A half-smile crept on to his face. "You're bored, aren't you? That's what it is."

"Not I."

"You want a piece of this Kelly case, don't you?"

"I am not going to interfere."

"Look, nothing's going to break until someone pulls in the son. And since they haven't, it probably means that he's already slipped across the water—"

"Have you alerted—"

"Yes, yes, but that's not what I was driving at. I have to type this up, so if you want to do me a favor you could take Lawson and Fletcher down to the crime scene."

"You think they'll be able to help find something?"

"No."

"So why bring them?"

"It's our, er, pedagogical duty if nothing else. And you never know, *you* might come up with something."

"You're taking pity on me, aren't you?"

He grinned. "A little."

"I appreciate the thought, but I can't do it, mate. I have a thing at six o'clock. I have to go home and shower."

"What thing?"

"A personal thing."

He gave me a slant-eyed, suspicious look.

Anybody else would have said, "What? You? A date with a real live woman?" but not the Crabman.

"All right, see you tomorrow," he said.

"Ok . . . and listen, mate, if anyone starts asking questions about me, you lemme know, OK?"

"I wouldn't worry about it, Sean, everybody knows you're a company man now through and through."

"Yeah."

5: A SUPPOSEDLY FUN THING THAT I'LL NEVER DO AGAIN

Home. The music on the turntable was classic Zep, and I let the plagiarizing bastards take me through a shower and a shave. I tied my tie, brushed my hair. More grey now on the ears and one or two little strands in the middle too. Yeah, in contrast to our fair-faced, behatted Chief Inspector, the smokes and the stress made me look every inch of thirty-five, but still, I was a reasonably presentable wee mucker who had a steady job and owned his house and his car, which presumably counted for something, right?

I put on a wool raincoat and then rummaged in the cloakroom for the fedora my parents had got me for Christmas. I checked my reflection in the hall mirror.

I looked ridiculous. I lost the hat. I still didn't look like me, but that was probably a good thing.

I went outside. A filthy-looking cloud hanging over Belfast like an evil djinn. The first raindrops.

I checked under the BMW for bombs and got inside.

I drove down Coronation Road, past a gaggle of sodden children and an emaciated horse being ridden by Dominic Mulvenna, the malevolent, demon child from the last house on the street.

The rain had become a biblical scourge.

On Kennedy Drive the surface was liquid and I slowed to a crawl. Frogs and even small fish were spilling out from the Mill Stream on to the road. The wipers on the BMW were going max but I could still hardly see anything at all.

I turned left on the North Road, swerving slowly around a band of tinkers going through a skip at the railway bridge and a goat—which may have been with them, or not—happily eating what appeared to be a box of candles.

Five glum backpackers were standing under the overhang at Carrick train station, no doubt wondering why *Lonely Planet* had told them to get off the train at this benighted destination.

I parked the Beemer outside the church hall and sat in the vehicle for a few minutes. The rain pounded off the roof and made a film on the windscreen. It was 6:15 and I was running late.

"Fuck it," I said, then opened the door and ran for the entrance.

Mrs. Beggs was, apparently, delighted to see me. "So glad you could make it, Mr. Duffy. Here's your badge."

She took my coat and hat and gave me a stick-on badge which declared: "Hello, my name is Sean!"

I put it on the lapel of my jacket. I could hear music coming from inside the hall and it sounded disconcertingly like Glenn Miller.

"The crowd's not all over forty, is it?"

Mrs. Beggs shook her head. "No, no. Have no fear, there are plenty of women your age, Mr. Duffy, and . . ." she lowered her voice "there are even a few Catholics."

"That's not important, as long as there—"

"You didn't come to chit-chat with me. Get in there, Mr. Duffy," she said, taking me by the arm and leading me into the hall.

"I think I left my cigarette lighter in the car, I have to go—"

"No you don't," she said, opening the door and frog-marching me into the room.

The church hall had been cleared of chairs and the lights dimmed to suggest intrigue. A table had been set up at one end of the room for soft drinks, and at the other end, a rather elderly DJ was spinning records on a twin deck. The music was indeed Glenn Miller, but I could foresee Acker Bilk and Benny Goodman in the immediate future.

The crowd was pretty substantial for a wet weeknight. About sixty all together with women representing a hefty majority. It was true that it skewed to an older demographic, but there were at least a dozen women my age or younger. Some people were dancing in a grim Northern Irish way, and off the dance floor there were several intense one-on-one conversations taking place. A large mixed-gender group had gathered at the drinks table, and a party of forlorn single men was pressed against the west wall, huddling in the shadows for their own protection.

"How does this work?" I hissed at Mrs. Beggs.

"Everyone has a name and everyone's here for the same reason. You just go and introduce yourself."

"I really need to get my lighter, I—"

"Say hello to Orla O'Neill. She'd love you. Thirty. Red hair. Divorced. Gorgeous. Worth a fortune. That's her in the green miniskirt."

"What? Where? Which one is—"

She gave me another little shove and closed the door behind me.

"In The Mood" ended and "Moonlight Serenade" began in waltz time. The men and women began pairing off.

Before I had the opportunity to register the full measure of my panic a tall, brightly dressed woman offered me her hand. Her fingers were powerful, with nails like those of an itinerant sheet metal worker. Her hair was red and her dress had a greenish tinge. Surely this couldn't be Ms. O'Neill?

"Aren't you going to ask me to dance?" she said.

"I don't really know how to dance. Not as such. Not formal—"

"A gentleman should know how to dance," she replied indignantly.

"I never really got around to it."

"What do you do for a living, *Sean*?" she asked, reading my name badge.

"I'm a policeman."

She pursed her lips. "Ah, well, please excuse me, Sean, I really must find a partner."

"Christ," I muttered under my breath, and got a fag lit with my emergency matches.

Unfriendly eyeballs. Strange homeopathic smells. The vast indeterminate space dominated by an ancient swaying chandelier that seemed to have homicidal intent.

A generously hipped woman with a reindeer-motifed cardigan made a beeline for me. I inhaled the wrong way, and, prompted by my coughing fit, she slapped me heartily on the back. She turned out to be a widow who ran a dairy farm.

"And you?" she asked.

"I'm in the police," I told her.

She nodded, looked into the middle distance, made an excuse, and went to meet someone/anyone else.

I fought a strong urge to flee and introduced myself to a girl called Sandra who looked a bit like Janice from *The Muppet Show* band. She was an estate agent who sold houses all over East Antrim.

"We've got something in common. I'm a peeler," I said.

"What do we have in common?"

"Well, uh, both of us are at home to a certain amount of moral ambiguity in our work."

No hesitant buyer ever got up Sandra's nose the way I instantly did, and she told me coldly that she had to mingle. Later I saw her dancing with a very tall man whose face was like a Landsat image of the Mojave.

I retreated to the west wall, joining the group of terrified blokes there who were avoiding all eye contact and presumably wondering why they had agreed to come here in the first place.

"I don't think you're allowed to smoke," a jealous fellow victim hissed at me as I lit another. I ignored him and inhaled deep.

Occasionally a bold woman or a pair of bold women would make a foray into these wallflowers and sometimes our herd would be reduced by one. The quarry dragged off to the dance floor or the drinks table.

"That was the late great Glenn Miller and now for your entertainment the swinging tunes of Mr. Acker Bilk," the DJ said.

A man with a comb-over who appeared to be in the midst of a nervous breakdown begged me for a cigarette. I lit him one.

"You're the peeler, right?" he asked me.

"Yeah."

"You wouldn't consider lending me your revolver for a minute, would you?" he said, miming putting the gun in his mouth.

"Sorry, mate."

A very pretty brown-haired woman with huge, radiant blue eyes began making her way through the wallflowers like an assassin in a Bruce Lee flick.

When she got to me she asked whether Jesus Christ was my personal savior in a Derry accent that sounded like a cement mixer with gearbox issues.

I told her that he wasn't.

She asked me whether I had heard of the Church of the Nazarene.

I told her that I had. A dozen of the massive American evangelical churches had sprung up in the greater Belfast area in the last year, their complicated blueprints and speedy construction bamboozling many a local planning officer into abject submission.

She asked me what I thought of the Church of the Nazarene.

I told her that I thought that it was an easily won trench religion, completely to be expected in a country with unending civil war and sky-high unemployment.

She said that I sounded interesting. I told her that she was the most beautiful woman I had talked to this evening, which was a dodgy thing to say, but her mind-set was seventeenth-century colonial America and she lapped up the compliment.

She asked me if I would be willing to let Christ into my heart.

"Anything's possible," I said, and told her that she had a gorgeous smile.

She asked what I did for a living.

I told her I was in the RUC.

She said that she had to go.

"No, wait . . ."

"I have to go."

The word went round and none of the other women came close. I didn't blame them. If you were a single lady, getting on in years, or worse, a widow, the last thing you wanted to do was marry a policeman who could be killed next week. It certainly didn't help that I was a Catholic. A Catholic in Carrickfergus was bad enough, but a Catholic policeman? My life expectancy could be measured in dog years.

Someone handed me a program and I saw that after the dancing the orchestrated jollity was to include musical chairs. *Must get out before musical chairs*, I told myself.

"I'm Sigourney," a bubbly, green-eyed, dark-haired girl with round glasses said to my left.

"I'm Sean," I said, and offered her my hand.

We shook nervously. She was pretty, and not pretty-for-a-wet-Tuesday-in-greater-Belfast kind of way, but objectively good looking.

"I don't think you're allowed to smoke in here," she whispered.

"So they tell me. I'm sorry, I, uh—"

"Oh, I don't mind at all, but if Mrs. Callaghan catches you she'll sling your hook."

"I'd better find this Mrs. Callaghan, then. I need to get out of here."

She laughed. "It's not that bad, is it?"

I nodded. "It is."

"Why'd you come?"

"Desperation. How do you meet members of the opposite sex in Ireland? The human race is somehow propagating in this island, isn't it? How are all these people getting together?"

"Discos."

"I can't do discos. I'm too cynical about the music."

"The music's not important. It's about the bopping!"

"I expect you're right. Hey, anyway, nice meeting you, I gotta run."

"Stay. Have some punch at least. They've put enough cheap gin in there to stun an elephant."

"I thought it was all soft drinks. Where is this punch of which you speak?"

She led me to the punch, which indeed had been cut with something the Russian soldiers in Afghanistan might have distilled from antifreeze. "Jesus. That is nasty," I said, putting down my plastic cup.

"The base is grapefruit juice but you can barely taste it. I emptied my flask of Bacardi in there to give it some body, but the hooch is so strong that it just swallowed it up."

"You brought a flask of rum to a church singles event?" I said with admiration.

"Can you think of better place to bring a flask of rum to?"

She had me there. She looked me over and smiled. "So you're the cop."

"Who told you that?"

"A couple of people."

"Have I been the subject of gossip?"

"No, just a few 'Watch out for him. He's a policeman,' sort of things."

I nodded. "Downtown Carrick is not the place to tease out really quality gossip, is it?"

"No. Although you see that guy with the hairpiece that looks like porridge?"

"Yeah?"

"Wife left him for another woman. You don't get that much round these parts."

"No."

"And you see that old geezer with the moustache over there? Divorced twice but still loaded. Owns half the land between here and Ballycarry," she said, pointing at a doppelganger of the gloomy General Sternwood from *The Big Sleep*.

"So, *Sean*, why does no one want to date a policeman?"

"There's the whole death thing. People get touchy about that."

"I don't see why. Isn't there a big compensation package if you get killed? And a nice widow's pension on top of that too? And then there's the black. I look fabulous in black. Brings out my eyes."

"Who are you?" I said with a laugh.

She pointed at her badge. "Sigourney," I read again.

She shook her head. "Actually . . ."

"Actually what?"

"Actually I wrote a fake name," she said in a whisper.

"Why would you do that?"

"I didn't want these creeps to know my real name. Have you looked at the quality of the men in this room. Yikes."

"I was sort of focusing on the women."

"Oh, the quality of the women is quite high, considering. And in terms of quantity women win out too. Have you met that alleged millionairess yet?"

"No, not yet."

"A bit of a fraud if you ask me. But the men! What a joke. Half of them are obvious alcoholics and the other half are born again Christians who probably found Jesus at the bottom of a whiskey bottle. I don't mind if a man drinks. It's the hypocrisy I can't stand."

"You're living on the wrong island, then, love."

"Indeed," she agreed. "I was talking to that tall, good-looking, slightly geeky guy over there, but I think that he could sense that I was faking my interest in his alien abduction stories."

"Sounds fascinating to me."

"You talk to him, then."

"What do you do for a living?" I asked.

"I'm one of your natural enemies."

"You make car bombs?"

"Worse. I'm a reporter."

"Who for?"

"The *Belfast Telegraph*."

"Ooh, fancy, like," I said in my Vera Duckworth.

She took the cigarette packet out of my jacket pocket and lit herself one.

"So are you at Carrick police station?" she asked.

"Yeah."

"Fascinating work?"

"It has its moments."

"What do you do there?"

"I'm a detective."

"A detective?" she said, almost sounding impressed. "Solving murder cases and missing diamonds and all that stuff?"

"Yup . . . Well, not so many missing diamonds."

"That's Nancy Drew's influence."

"What sort of things do you write about?"

She groaned. "I'm on the Wednesday Woman's Page. It's all 'Are You Wearing the Right Bra Size for You,' 'Are Stockings and Suspenders Making a Comeback' kind of thing."

My head was suddenly packed with lascivious images that I had to expunge before I could reply. "Not fun?" I managed.

"No, not fun. Our crack staff of two spend the week ripping off hot issues from women's mags and making them palatable for the *Bel Tel*."

"That sounds all right, reading magazines all week."

"Nah, it does your head in."

My beeper started going like the clappers. "Sorry about that," I said, and turned it off.

"Shouldn't you get to a phone or something?" she asked.

"It's probably nothing."

We stood there in silence for an awkward ten seconds.

"You want to get to a phone, don't you?"

I nodded.

"This way. I saw one as I came in through the vestry."

She grabbed her coat from a chair and I followed her to the vestry. She turned the light on and out of the dimly lit hall. I could see that she was indeed very attractive. No trouble finding men, I would have thought. Her coat was a wool duffel she'd clearly had since schooldays, which weren't that long ago. She was maybe twenty-four or twenty-five?

I called the station. "Duffy."

"Hold for Sergeant McCrabban."

"Sean, is that you?"

"Aye."

"I'm sorry to call you when you're off, but I thought you'd want to know that we found the son."

"The sun at last! So the blight of perpetual rain has finally been lifted from this cursèd island, then, has it?"

"What are you talking about?"

"What are *you* talking about?"

"Kelly."

The penny dropped.

"The murder case. The boy who offed his parents," McCrabban said.

"Yeah, I get it. He's confessed, has he?"

"In a manner of speaking."

"I'm intrigued . . ."

"He left a suicide note in his car and, apparently, jumped off the cliff at Blackhead."

"Oh dear."

"Aye."

"Are you there now?"

"Yes."

"And you want me to come down?"

"If you want to."

I looked at "Sigourney" and smiled. "In fact, Crabbie, I'm sort of talking to a charming young lady at the moment. I mean, mate, it's your case, the training wheels are off, you know?"

Crabbie sighed. Clearly he was still a bit nervous about running a high-profile investigation like this. But you had to get stuck in sooner or later. "All right, Sean, I just thought you might want to know. I'll fill you in tomorrow."

"Cheers, mate. See ya."

I hung up.

"What was that all about?" "Sigourney" asked, putting on her coat.

"A double murder. A kid killed his parents last night and felt bad about it and did a Wiley Coyote off Blackhead cliff."

"A double murder?"

"Yup."

"And they want you to investigate it?"

"No, my colleague, Detective Sergeant McCrabban, is investigating it. He just wanted my input . . . but it's a pretty straightforward one."

"And not a terrorist-related thing?"

"Doesn't look like it."

"I couldn't, uh—" she began and her voice trailed off.

"What?"

"I couldn't possibly beg you to go and take me with you, could I?"

"Why?"

"A scoop's a scoop, isn't it? One day assistant editor on the women's page, next day front-page leader writer."

"Steady on, Lady Macbeth, what do I get out of this arrangement?"

"I'll tell you my real name."

"I already know your real name."

"What is it?"

"Sara," I said. "Sara Prentice."

"How did you do that?" she asked, astonished.

"Maybe I read the *Belfast Telegraph* and because of my brilliant photographic memory I recalled your byline."

"Is that what you did?" she asked, her almond-green eyes still wide with amazement.

"No. It's written on the inside of your duffel coat."

"Ah. Yes. Embarrassing."

"What is?"

"Well, you know, still using the same coat you got in sixth form. Not cool for a fashion-conscious women's page reporter."

"I'm wearing an old trench coat."

"That is cool."

"Is it?"

"Yeah. So I can come with you?"

"Uhm, OK, if you want to."

"How about I cook you dinner or something?"

"I already said yes."

We went outside and ran through the rain to the Beemer. She put on her seat belt and smiled at me. "This is exciting."

"Ah, speaking of exciting . . . hold on a minute."

I got out of the car and looked underneath it for mercury tilt bombs.

I got back inside.

"What was that all about?" she asked naively.

"Nothing. Can you really cook? I mean, this is in return for a scoop on a murder-suicide," I said to distract her from the fact that there had been a possibility—slim, yes, but still a possibility—that we could have been blown up if I'd driven off without checking.

"You won't regret it. I did domestic science to O-level."

"So did I and I can't open a tin of beans."

"Well, I can."

I turned on the engine and my newly installed police radio. I called the station.

"This is Detective Inspector Duffy, can you tell Detective Sergeant McCrabban that I'll meet him at the crime scene?" I said.

"Will do, Inspector," one of the constables said back at the barracks. I turned off the radio and slipped in the clutch.

"A detective inspector," Sara said, sounding impressed. "Do you have a gun and everything?"

"Yup," I said as I turned right on to the Albert Road.

"Ever kill anyone?"

"On purpose, you mean? Who can keep track?"

"How do you know I'm not one of those IRA honey traps I'm always seeing ads for on late-night TV?" she asked with a charming little smile.

I had seen those ads too. An off-duty policeman or soldier meets a girl and goes off with her only to be kidnapped, interrogated, tortured, and shot by a terrorist group. The honey-trap girl in the ads was always a glamorous blonde, not a mousy little thing with brown hair.

"A honey-trap girl wouldn't actually bring up those honey-trap ads, would she?"

"It could be a clever double bluff."

"I'll have to keep my eye on you, then, won't I?"

"Always a good policy in this day and age."

At the bottom of the Albert Road I turned left at the four-way junction. We drove out past the rain-slicked lights of the Marine Highway. Herring buses were chugging away from the little stone harbor, and behind us in the rear-view mirror the castle lurked grey and black in the gathering dark. And ahead of us? Who knew what lay ahead of us, waiting at the bottom of a cliff up the Antrim coast.

6: TIDE BURIAL

We parked the Beemer in Whitehead car park, where a glum young constable standing next to a damp police dog headed us in the right direction. We walked along the seafront path to Blackhead cliff.

"Over there . . . that used to be Sting's house," Sara said, pointing to one of the big houses on the seafront.

"Sting from the Police?" I asked skeptically.

"Yes."

"I thought he was a Geordie."

"He was married to a local girl when he was still a teacher. Divorced her now. Seriously, they lived over there. Everybody knows that."

"My ignorance of local knowledge has been widely remarked on."

"And I'm a mine of useless information."

We reached the crime scene, which lay rather dramatically on the rocky path a hundred feet below Blackhead Lighthouse.

Quite a few peelers, ambulance men, and lookie-loos there, already getting soaked by the drizzle and sea spray.

I raised the POLICE CRIME SCENE DO NOT CROSS tape to let myself and Sara into the inner cordon (not exactly professionalism at its finest there, but the lass was growing on me).

DC Lawson saw me and came over with his hands up to stop me approaching the crumpled mass that was presumably the corpse.

"The forensic officers are at their task, sir, they've asked us to keep clear," he warned.

Lawson was wearing a dark blue suit and a cream raincoat, which was fine, but he had gelled his hair into spiky blond tips like a member of a boy band or a football player newly in the money. He saw that I wasn't pleased and assumed it was some sort of impatience with the FOs going about their slow, methodical business in their latex gloves and white boiler suits. "I'm sure they'll be done soon, sir, I—"

I cut him off. "What's that on your hair, Lawson?"

"My hair? Gel, sir."

"Why?"

"Why? Uhm, because it looks good, sir?"

"Do you think it's an appropriate look for a trainee detective constable in the RUC?"

"It's what people are doing, sir."

"Well, I don't like it. Peelers aren't supposed to be trendy. Peelers are supposed to be old fashioned and conservative and behind the times. It's reassuring for the general public to see coppers with bad haircuts and cheap suits."

Lawson nodded. "Yes, sir," he said meekly, avoiding the obvious "so that's why you dress the way you do, is it?"

"Now, what's the situation here?" I asked.

"Detective Sergeant McCrabban is up there on the top of the cliff at the lighthouse car park with DC Fletcher. Apparently that's where the boy jumped and, uh, landed in the rocks. He left a note, in his car, sir. Apologizing."

"A suicide note?"

"Yes, sir."

"What did it say?"

Lawson flipped open his notebook and read: "'I lost my head. I'm really sorry.'"

"Any signs that he was coerced or pushed?"

"None."

"What does Sergeant McCrabban think?"

"Suicide."

"Hmmmm. All right, very good, Constable, go about your business."

Lawson nodded again and went back to whatever it was he had been doing before I showed up.

"You were pretty hard on him, no?" Sara said.

"About the hair?"

"Well, we're here to replace you and that's bound to annoy you on some level."

"Who's *we*? Alien clones?"

"The younger generation."

"Jesus, how old do you think I am, love?"

"Forty?"

Shit, did I look forty?

"Maybe I was too rough on him," I conceded.

"Do you mind if I take some photographs?" Sara asked.

"No! No photographs. You can make notes, but definitely no snaps."

"We've probably got a stock photograph of the lighthouse anyway."

"Wait here for a second," I said, and went over to the place where the FOs were examining the body.

I knew the lead guy, an old stager called Jim McMurtry.

"Hey, Jim," I said.

"I was wondering if you'd show up, Duffy," Jim replied. "Where's that thirty quid you owe me for the Derby?"

"You don't forget, do you?" I said, reaching for my wallet. When I opened it there was only a tenner in there.

"Will you take a tenner?" I said, holding it out to him.

"I knew you wouldn't have all my money!" he said, and with a mirthless cackle grabbed the cash.

"What's your ESP say about our victim here?"

"How come you're late? Not like you, Duffy."

"I'm not late. It's not my show, Jim. Sergeant McCrabban's lead on this one."

"Oh, I see. Are you on your way out of the force, then?"

"Not to my knowledge," I said suspiciously. "Why, have you heard something?"

"No," he added quickly.

"Positive ID yet on our victim?" I asked him.

"We'll need to use dental. The lad landed head first on the rocks just under the water. It was low tide, but even if it had been high tide it wouldn't have made any difference. You want to take a look?"

The body was crumpled up under a white blanket.

"No thanks. Time of death?"

"It might be difficult to determine. Like I say, he's pretty smashed up. But the birds hadn't been at him, and there's no decay or advanced rigor, so my uneducated guess would be sometime early this morning."

"Anything else you can tell me?"

"We can tell you how he died."

"How did he die?"

"Blunt force trauma caused by jumping off a cliff."

"Thanks, Jim, always a pleasure."

I walked back to Sara, who was scribbling in her reporter's notebook.

"You want to take a wee dander up to the lighthouse with me?"

"Of course," she said enthusiastically.

"Let's go, then. Cause of death, by the way, was gravity."

She wrote that down in her book.

We followed the winding cliff path up to the lighthouse, where another group of cops and forensic officers were taking photographs and dusting for prints.

I found Crabbie and introduced him to Sara.

"This is Sara Prentice from the *Belfast Telegraph*," I said.

She offered him her hand and he shook it. He looked at me with bafflement. I had never previously expressed any desire to cooperate with a reporter. Why the change of heart?

"Sara's a, uh, friend. You don't mind if she makes a few notes, do you? The story's going to break sooner or later. We might as well have the media on our side for once," I explained rather lamely.

"No, I don't mind," he said dourly, utterly unconvinced by the cover story.

"Thank you," Sara said, and went off to look at the black Mercedes parked near the cliff edge.

When she'd gone Crabbie raised an eyebrow.

"I met her at a church social; she was there when I got your call and she asked if she could tag along. I was getting on well with her, I didn't want to kill the thing then and there," I explained.

He shook his head. "A reporter, Sean . . ."

"I know, I know . . ."

I took out my cigarettes and lit one. Not so easy a task up here on the windy cliff edge.

"So what's the story with our boy?" I asked.

Crabbie shrugged. "It looks like he tops his parents, drove here, parked his car, had a cigarette, had a think, wrote a quick suicide note and jumped."

"Any evidence in the car apart from the note?"

"We're dusting. Nothing so far."

"Can I see this note?"

"Sure. It's bagged and tagged."

He had Constable Fletcher bring me the note. I read it, and it was as Constable Lawson had reported: quick and not containing much information. It was written in script, not block capitals, on lined notebook paper. Blue biro. It didn't look written under duress to me, not that I was an expert. I read it out loud:

I lost my head. I'm really sorry.

That was all.

I flipped the piece of paper over. Nothing.

"Does it match with his handwriting?" I asked Crabbie.

Crabbie smiled. "Funny you should ask that, Sean. I had Lawson go over to the house and hunt me down a sample."

"Very professional of you. And?"

"We eventually found one of his notebooks from his university days."

"And?"

"It looks pretty similar to me. Constable Lawson, can you get me Bag 4 from the Land Rover?"

Lawson, who'd followed us up the cliff path and who'd been lurking in the background, went off and came back with the university notebook.

It was marked "PPE year 3: Philosophy. Hilary Term."

I flipped it open:

How then to balance the interests of liberty and democracy? Mill feared the "tyranny of the majority" and wanted a zone of personal liberty for all people, a zone that the majority could not impose its values upon . . .

"Pretty fancy stuff he was studying," I said.

"He was a student at Oxford," Lawson said. "Studying PPE."

"Yeah, I see that. And what's PPE when it's at home?"

"Politics, philosophy, and economics. It's basically three degrees in one, in three years. Oxford is the only place in the world that offers the subject. Very tough. A good chunk of the prime ministers of the twentieth century did PPE at Oxford. I, uhm . . ."

"You what exactly?"

"I applied there, but I, uhm, didn't get in . . . stuffed up the interview . . . sort of froze."

"Oxford's loss is the RUC's gain, though, eh?"

"Yes, sir."

I passed Lawson the notebook and pointed at the cover. "What's 'Hilary Term'?" I don't know that expression."

"Hilary is what they call Spring Term at Oxford," Lawson said.

"So he's in the penultimate term of his last year at Oxford, studying for an extremely prestigious degree, and he just drops out? There must be a story there, eh?" I mused aloud.

"It is a bit strange," Lawson said. "Even if a candidate does no work at all, they usually give them what at Oxford is called a 'gentleman's third.' If he'd hung in there for another couple of months, he would have got some kind of degree."

I could see that Crabbie was getting irritated. "If I could bring you gentlemen back to the task on hand, we're trying to focus on the handwriting here," he said.

I took the notebook back from Lawson and compared notebook and suicide note.

"I can't say with the confidence of a specialist, but it looks like the same hand to me."

"And me," Lawson offered.

"We'll need to get an expert in to compare them," I said.

"I'm already on it, Sean," McCrabban said.

I nodded. "I'm sure you are. Of course, the note could have been written under duress . . . Did we ever find that gun he used to top his parents?"

"No."

"I wonder what he did with it?"

"Tossed it in a panic before guilt took him over?"

"Aye, maybe." I rubbed my chin. "No witnesses, I suppose?"

"None that's come forward."

"Who found the body?"

"Several people reported seeing something floating in the water. A fisherman by the name of Wilson got him out with a boathook. Do you want to talk to him? We have him over at the incident van."

"Get Lawson to take a statement."

"We were lucky to find the body. The tide was on the turn, and if no one had seen the body tonight, it might have been carried out to sea and lost forever."

"I wonder why he didn't just shoot himself?"

"Not so easy after he's seen what a gun did to his parents."

"Hmmm."

I walked over to the FOs dusting the car.

"Keep an eye open for anything peculiar," I said.

"What like?" one of the FOs said behind his mask.

"You know, anything strange. Cocaine, used rubbers, evidence of violence. Anything."

"In this kind of posh fucking motor you'll find all that," the FO muttered.

"Try and keep the class war in check too, mate, yeah?"

I caught Crabbie's eye and smiled at him. We were both thinking the same thing.

"A rather neat end to the case," Crabbie said.

"Too neat?" I asked.

"Maybe." Crabbie took me to one side. "What would *you* do next?"

"I'd canvass for witnesses and I'd eliminate the other possibilities such as threats against the Kelly family and so forth . . ."

"Well, we're doing that, of course . . . But failing some unforeseen development I'd say that this one looks reasonably straightforward, wouldn't you say, Sean?" McCrabban asked hopefully.

I shook my head. Something didn't feel quite right.

"Did you see any of those family photographs of young Michael Kelly back at the homestead in Whitehead?" I said.

"Aye, I saw them. Couldn't miss them."

"He was a good-looking boy before a bunch of rocks rearranged his face."

"So?"

"Handsome lad like that with lots of money and a flash car? He's probably got a girlfriend. Wouldn't you think?"

"Could be."

I took a final puff on my ciggie and threw it over the cliff.

"Well?"

"You're thinking he might have called her after he did the dirty deed?" McCrabban said.

"Wouldn't you?"

"I wouldn't top me mum and dad."

"But if you did, you'd call your girl, wouldn't ya?"

"Aye, I would."

"So check it out."

"I shall."

"And find out why he dropped out of university, will ya? Probably a dead end, but you never know . . ."

"Maybe I'll put the new blood on it. Anything else you can think of?"

"Apart from eliminating the usual terrorist/paramilitary angles?"

"Aye."

"No, nothing else that comes to mind. How are the trainees getting on?"

"Fletcher's terrific. Does as she's told, keeps her mouth shut."

"And Lawson?"

"You saw . . ."

"A royal pain in the arse?"

"I wouldn't go that far."

"I'll have a wee word with him. He's a bit overfamiliar for someone who's been on the job less than a fortnight."

"Did you notice his hair?" Crabbie asked.

"I did. I already had a word."

Just then Sara came back from her wanderings, still scribbling madly in her notebook.

"Get what you needed?" I asked.

She gave me a little grin of satisfaction. "It looks like Michael Kelly killed his parents and committed suicide," she said.

"We couldn't possibly speculate at this early stage of the investigation," I replied cautiously.

"But wouldn't you say that this is an open-and-shut case, Detective Sergeant McCrabban?" Sara asked Crabbie.

"Detective Sergeant McCrabban has no official comment at this stage, Miss Prentice, and, off the record, we hate that bloody expression in the RUC."

"What expression?"

"Open-and-shut case."

Sara grinned and snapped her notebook shut.

"Can you give me a lift to a phone box? I think I'm the only reporter here at the moment, but I won't be for long."

I drove us back to Coronation Road and five minutes later Sara was unpacking her scoop *His Girl Friday* fashion to the copy desk at the *Belfast Telegraph* from the phone in my hall; I made sure she spelled McCrabban's name correctly; he might not like the attention of the media but his missus would be pleased as punch.

While Sara was at her task, Mr. Marks and Mr. Spencer and myself contrived to make a spag carbonara. We ate it with a bottle of Italian red that had gotten a 92 in the *Sunday Times* wine guide.

We talked Italy and wine and her career.

"This is really going to set me up. You've been a huge help," she said happily.

"My pleasure."

"No, really," she said, and gave my hand a squeeze.

We took our wine glasses and moved to the living room.

"Wow, you've quite the record collection," she said, amazed.

"Er, yeah."

"What do you listen to? A lot of jazz and stuff?"

Another old geezer crack. I put on *Reckoning* by REM, which had exactly two good songs on it but which I hoped would show her that I was in touch with the kids. I sat next to her on the sofa. "I had a nice time, tonight," she said.

"You did?"

I held her gaze longer than was normal for two people brought up in the arctic psychological environment of post-war Ulster.

That was all it took.

"Yes," she said, and then added, "I suppose you think one thing is going to lead to another?"

"Not necessarily," I said, and leaned across the sofa and kissed her.

"I'm not easy. Don't think that," she said as she followed me up the stairs. "It's just the circumstances."

"I can't promise you a corpse on every date."

"I think I can live with that," she said.

I laid her down on the bed. And one thing led to another.

7: THE GIRL IN INTERVIEW ROOM 1

Through the office window rain falling on coal boats, slag barges, dredgers. Ugly ships on an ugly lough. Melancholy thoughts. Low-level Masefield-style epiphanies. Outside the office door Lawson talking loudly to Fletcher about some crackpot theory he thought he'd invented about The Beatles.

Eyes heavy. Ciggie burning finger. Can of Coke with a nip of Jack in it.

Sleep for a minute.

McCrabban's big mug in the doorway. "Sean . . . Sean . . . Sean!"

"I wasn't asleep."

"Didn't say you were."

"What is it?"

"Are you busy?"

"I'm doing the CID overtime claims."

"So, er . . ."

"It can wait," I told him, pushing the confusing pile of forms away from me.

"Do you want to come down to observe Interview Room 1, Sean?"

"It depends who or what is in Interview Room 1."

"Sylvie McNichol," he explained.

"And she is . . ."

"Michael Kelly's girlfriend."

"So he did have a girlfriend."

"Yes."

"I'm waiting for it . . ."

"For what?"

"The 'you were right, Sean.' Validation, mate. We all need it. Pope, president, detective inspector."

"You were right, Sean."

"Come on, you don't need to say that, mate. Have you talked to her already?"

"Yes. I interviewed her this morning at her flat in Whitehead."

"Does she know anything about the night of the murder?"

"She says Kelly didn't phone her or see her that night, and true enough there are no records of any call from the Kelly house to anyone on the night of the murders."

"What about before that?"

"She hadn't seen him for a few days before that."

"Any hints of any trouble between them?"

"Nope. She said it was all giggles. They'd only been going out about a month. It seemed to be one of those on-and-off things that the kids get into these days."

"Where did he meet her originally?"

"The Whitecliff. She's a barmaid there."

"Big tall girl with ginger hair?"

"No."

"The wee mousy black-haired one?"

"Nope."

"I thought I knew all the . . . oh, wait, the sort of Greek-looking one."

"She doesn't look Greek. What does Greek look like?"

"Dark eyes. That kind of thing."

"She's a blonde. Platinum, dyed, skinny. Lots of denim."

"Oh, yeah, I know her. Never gives you a full pint. Always half an inch missing from the top of your glass. She was Kelly's girlfriend?"

"Apparently."

"And he didn't call her the night of the murders?"

"Nope."

"So we're looking at a newish girlfriend that Kelly wasn't particularly attached to, someone he didn't think to call on the night he murdered his parents."

"Something like that."

"At this interview at her flat did she provide you with any other insights into the case?"

"None at all."

I give him the old Spock raised eyebrow. "Then why bring her in for questioning? Do you not believe her?"

"Oh, I believe her, but I was thinking that it might be good practice for the new detective constables. Let them question a witness by themselves. A witness in a homicide investigation . . . You know?"

"They question her. We observe them?"

"Yes."

"Sounds good. Sounds like the sort of thing I should have thought of."

"They've already started. Do you wanna come see how they're doing?"

I followed him along the corridor to Interview Room 1's observation suite, which was a small office on the other side of the one-way mirror that looked into the main CID interrogation room.

Lawson and Fletcher had indeed already begun their questioning of Sylvie McNichol, who had come as a clone of early Madonna: bangles, denim, Daisy Dukes, ripped fishnets, scarves in her hair, massive hooped earrings . . . I got myself a coffee and a cigarette. McCrabban lit his pipe. Lawson was asking the questions and Fletcher was writing down notes as if she was his secretary, which was utterly unnecessary because we were taping the interview anyway.

"Where did you meet Michael Kelly?" Lawson asked.

"He come in the Whitecliff. Seen him in there a couple of times, so I did," Sylvie replied.

"And when did he ask you out?"

"Beginning of October, he asked me if I wanted to go see Van Morrison at the Ulster Hall."

"And you said?"

"Aye, why not. Bit of a laugh."

"And?"

"I went there. Seen him before. He was better the last time. Bob

Dylan did a surprise encore last time. This time it was just Van. Course neither of them is really my cup of tea . . . that old-man music."

"And after the concert?"

"What do you mean, after the concert?"

"Did you sleep with him? After the concert?"

"Don't be cheeky! That's my business."

"If I can remind you that this is a murder investigation . . ."

"I'm here cos Sergeant McCrabban asked me to come in. I don't have to tell you nothing, so I don't!"

"I'm just trying to find out how intimately you knew the late Mr. Kelly?" Lawson said.

Sylvie stood up. "Never been so insulted in my life."

Lawson had to spend the next five minutes calming her down.

"How many times did you see Mr. Kelly?"

"I don't know. Half a dozen?"

"Six in a month doesn't sound like a lot."

"Aye, it wasn't serious. It was just a bit of laugh, like I said."

"When did you hear about his death?"

"Radio. Next morning. Seen it coming."

"Seen it coming, how?"

"Well, Whitehead was full of the news about what happened with his parents . . ."

"And you thought he did it?"

"That's what all the gossip said anyway."

"But you had no inkling at all that his mind was disturbed or that he was in any kind of trouble?"

"Look, when we went out it was just a geg. He'd plenty of money and he knew how to treat a girl right, you know?"

"He didn't seem depressed or unhappy? Anxious?"

"Well . . ."

"Well what?"

"Ach, he was fine. Levelheaded you know. That was why it was all so amazing that he lost the rag and topped his ma and da."

"Because he wasn't the type?"

"Exactly. But people are strange, aren't they? And I suppose if he did it, he did it."

Sylvie lit herself a fag. Lawson looked at the two-way mirror and gave a little shrug.

"What do you think?" McCrabban said to me between puffs of blue pipe smoke.

"He's not as smart as he thinks he is."

"And the witness?"

"She's not lying but she's not telling the whole truth. She knows something she's not being forthcoming about," I said.

"What?"

"I don't know. She's not being forthcoming about it."

"You wanna do a tag team and go in there?" Crabbie asked.

I lit a Marlboro. "Tell me about the forensics."

"Forensics came up with very little. A nine-millimeter. The same gun shot both parents but this gun hadn't been used in the commission of a previous crime."

"Mr. Kelly's business was doing OK? Threatening phone calls, letters . . . ?"

"I had Lawson and Fletcher canvass the neighbors and go through the phone logs. Nothing unusual."

"And no threats on any of his bookie shops?"

"I talked to a bloke called Derek Cole, Ray Kelly's business manager. He says that things have been running smoothly."

"They must pay protection money."

"That's the point, Sean. They do. They've got four bookies in UDA territory and three in IRA territory and they pay through the nose. Five per cent of the gross. Not five per cent of the profit. Five per cent of the gross revenue. Kelly was safe as houses, protected from both sides."

"Had he missed any payments or anything like that?"

"Not a one. He hadn't a problem in years."

"Why did he have that gun?"

"The gun was a hangover from the dark days of the late seventies when you couldn't even rely on a decent protection racket."

"Dark days indeed."

Crabbie relit his pipe. "Young Lawson says to me that foul play makes no sense from a *Ciceronian standpoint* . . . I didn't like to ask . . ."

"In his early career Cicero was a defense lawyer. He was always asking *cui bono*? Which means *who benefits*," I explained.

"Ah, I see," Crabbie said, and puffed thoughtfully. "I suppose in the Kelly case no one benefits if the bookie shops are thrown into chaos and the protection racket money gets disrupted. It's killing the goose that lays the golden egg."

"On the face of it nobody profits from the death of the Kellys. Unless there was a will?"

"Michael Kelly was the sole beneficiary."

"And now that Michael Kelly's dead?"

"Relatives in Australia. Who, you won't be surprised to learn, have pretty good alibis."

"Which are?"

"They were in Australia at the time of the killing."

"All right. Let's talk to young Sylvie."

Tag team. Fletcher and Lawson out. Ageing Wunderkind and the Crabman in.

Crabbie sucked on the end of his pipe. "Miss McNichol, can you account for your whereabouts the night Michael Kelly's parents were murdered?"

"I certainly can. Double shift at the Whitecliff until midnight and then home to me bed, exhausted. Me housemate Deirdre was waiting up for me. She made me toast."

"And what time did you go to bed, exactly?"

"Don't know about exactly but maybe about one o'clock."

"And you didn't get any phone calls at all that night?"

"Not one."

"And when did you hear the news about the murders at the Kelly house?"

"The next morning. Everyone was talking about it. Everyone was saying Michael did it."

"Who's everyone?"

"Everyone! Deirdre. All the people in the street, all the people down the newsagent's, everyone down the pub."

"Everyone was saying your boyfriend killed his parents and you didn't think to go to the police."

"The peelers? What do you take me for? I'm no grass."

Crabbie looked. Yup, there was something she was hiding, but I couldn't figure out what that something was.

"Miss McNichol, where did you think Michael had gone after the murder of his parents?" I asked.

"Scotland."

"Why Scotland?"

"Well, he's not going to be stupid enough to go to the airport, is he? But he can just hop on one of the ferries to Scotland, can't he?" she said, and stubbed the remains of her cigarette out in the big, black, glass ashtray.

"Did he ever talk to you about going to Scotland?"

"Nope."

"Did he have an affinity for Scotland?"

"Well, he liked shortbread."

McCrabban looked away. I stifled a grin.

"Did you meet Michael's parents?"

"Met his ma, briefly, while Michael was looking for his car keys."

"You talked?"

"Yeah."

"What about?"

"She asked me if I was a Pisces."

"What?"

"She said that I looked like a Pisces. But I'm not. I'm a Virgo."

"And you told her that?"

"Aye."

"And what did she say to that?"

"She said that that would have been her second guess. But it's easy to say that after I told her, you know? She said she was a Leo but she didn't look like a Leo to me. She was an older lady, though. Maybe her hormones were playing up. Speaking of hormones, do youse want to hear a joke?"

"No. We don't. Do you have anything to add to your statement that can help us get to the bottom of this case?" McCrabban asked.

"And please remember that Michael has passed on, you can't grass up a dead man. The only thing you'll be doing is helping us close this sorry chapter and let the Kellys' kin move on with their lives," I added.

"I understand all that. I'm not an eejit. But Michael didn't tell me nothing and he certainly didn't call me after he topped his ma and da."

"Any jealous boyfriends in your past we should know about?"

She shook her head. "Me? Nah, I only get the love-'em-and-leave-'em type, don't I?" she said with a cynical little laugh. Hard as nails was Sylvie, but there was a vulnerability behind those heavily made-up eyes.

"Parents alive?" I asked her.

"Me ma, yeah."

"And your dad?"

She shook her head. "They done him in," she said after a pause.

"Who did?"

"The usual." She sniffed.

"Who's the usual?"

"They said he was an informer . . . Maybe he *was* an informer. I don't know. I was only a wee bairn."

She sniffed again, took a hanky from her bag, and dabbed her eyes.

"I'm really sorry, Sylvie," I said, and, reaching across the desk, gave her arm a little squeeze.

"It's all right, it was a long time ago. A very long time ago," she said, recovering herself.

I tried a couple more questions, but the barriers that briefly had come down had firmly gone back up. After another fifteen minutes Crabbie gave me his *I think this is getting us nowhere* look.

I nodded.

"Give us a minute, will you, Sylvie?" I asked. Crabbie and I retreated to the CID incident room and I looked up the case file on Kevin McNichol.

Shot in the head on the Antrim Road, North Belfast, 1974. Suspected police informer. No clues. No suspects. A case that would never be solved, like so many cases from that time. I showed the file to Crabbie.

"Even if she knows something, unlikely that she would tell us with that family history," I said.

"But I don't think she knows anything," Crabbie said.

I sighed. "Might as well finish it, then."

Back into Interview Room 1.

"OK, Sylvie, what's your hormone joke?" I asked.

"Hormone joke? Oh yeah: how do you make a hormone?"

I sighed. "I don't know, Sylvie, how do you make a hormone?"

"You kick her in the cunt."

I heard Lawson laugh behind the two-way mirror, but I was getting fed up with all this now. "OK, Miss McNichol, let me ask you just one more question and I want you to think very carefully about the answer," I said.

"OK."

"Do you really think, in your heart of hearts, that Michael, the boy you knew, killed his parents, in cold blood, the way everyone is saying that he did?"

It was tiny.

A blink.

That's all.

A momentary look away.

A flutter in her eyelids.

"How am I supposed to know? You're the police!"

"He was your boyfriend."

"Well, look, I wouldn't be shocked. He said that his da was always winding him up and I suppose it's like everyone says . . . he just snapped."

"He was a levelheaded kid who just snapped?"

"He just snapped."

We tried several more lines of attack but she wasn't giving us anything else. We went out.

"She *is* a Leo," Lawson said.

"What?"

"Mrs. Kelly. She wasn't lying about that."

I nodded. "Good work," I said, and rolled my eyes at McCrabban.

We tag-teamed Fletcher and Lawson back in again while Crabbie and I went down to my office.

I poured Crabbie a whiskey and told him about the eyelid flutter.

He hadn't seen it.

He didn't believe it.

"I think she knows something," I insisted. "And not just about Michael's love of shortbread."

"As you say, Sean, even if she does, she'll never cooperate with the police."

"That's what makes this such a fun job."

Crabbie sighed, tipped out his pipe. He looked at me. I looked at him. We sipped the Jura sixteen-year-old single malt. Outside, through the rain and wind, the afternoon was withering like a piece of fruit in an Ulster pantry.

"We serve shortbread at communion, sometimes," Crabbie said dolefully.

I was not going to have a conversation with him about shortbread's Eucharistic qualities. I drained my glass and got to my feet.

"It's still your case, mate, but before I went and told Chief Inspector McArthur that you were closing it, I'd let it sit for a bit. Maybe bring the wee lassie in again, next week. A second time can't hurt and we might get some inconsistencies in her story."

"Let it sit. Bring her in in a few days or a week or so," he repeated dutifully, but I could tell he didn't like it.

"Sound good?"

"Can I at least tell the Chief Inspector that we're close to closing the book on this one?"

"Tell him that when you hand in the written progress report."

"And Lawson and Fletcher?"

"Tell Lawson to dial it down, tell Fletcher to dial it up. She's a police officer not a bloody secretary."

"OK, cheers, Sean."

"Cheers, Crabbie, and well done. Case number one nearly under your belt. And it's a murder. Whew. I see Chief Constable in your future."

And he touched wood to ward off a jinx that might possibly have been impressed by my oracular abilities.

8: POLICE STATION BLUES

Rain and cold. Boredom. And then . . . 180. The pancake flipped. The pancake fell on the fucking floor.

Thatcher. Thatcher, like Stalin, was making a Five Year Plan . . . Northern Ireland had been too quiet. *This is the mid-eighties, love. Time to get your handbag swinging and shake things up.*

Sara Prentice gave me the news.

Brriinng. Brriinng.

Office phone. The direct line.

"Hello, Sean Duffy, Carrickfergus CID."

"I love hearing you say that. You sound so sexy and official."

"Sara? What's up? You're not canceling dinner for tonight, are you?"

"No way. I'm cooking. That's a rarity. That's Halley's Comet. And besides we have to go out tonight. We're both going to be busy in the coming weeks."

"Oh God. What have you heard?"

"It's going to be called the Anglo-Irish Agreement. Cross-border cooperation, devolved powers going back to the Province, groundwork for a new Assembly. Thatcher has cooked it up with the Irish prime minister."

"Jesus! When is this going to happen?"

"*Belfast Telegraph* sources say tomorrow afternoon."

"No consultation with the Unionists?"

"No consultation with anyone. It's just going to be announced as a fait accompli by the Secretary of State . . . so you know . . ."

"It's going to be trouble."

"Yup. A lot of work for both of us."

"Thanks, Sara, I'll see you later."

She gave me a kiss down the phone and I hung up.

I closed the office door, found an emergency joint, rummaged in the bottom-drawer cassette box, stuck in "Police Station Blues" by Peetie Wheatstraw. It didn't quite take, so I fast forwarded the tape to "Stack O' Lee" by Mississippi John Hurt, which worked a little better.

Emotionally righted, I went to see the Chief Inspector. He was white faced, shaking, and he'd already broken out the Black Label.

"Have a drink with me, Duffy."

Didn't need to be told twice. "You look as if you've seen a ghost, sir."

"I was at a pow-wow in Belfast."

"What have the Brits cooked up for us now?"

"Is it that obvious?"

"Yeah."

"New Assembly, devolved powers, the Irish government to have a say in Northern Irish affairs."

"Sounds reasonable."

"It's completely reasonable. In a normal society all the political parties would welcome this."

I poured myself a modest measure of the Black Label. He opened his filing cabinet and gave me a folder marked "Secret."

"All the station chiefs got a copy a day early. Read it here. In my office. Don't make any notes, just read it. I'll go get some grub and come back in ten minutes."

He exited and left me with the whiskey and a photocopy of the Anglo-Irish Agreement.

I read it.

It was a deal between the Thatcher and FitzGerald governments aimed at generating political progress in Ulster. McArthur was right. It was harmless stuff. A benign, innocuous series of cross-border panels and task forces, and an attempt to get a regional assembly off the ground. In theory, Nationalists would like it because of the cross-border dimensions and the nuanced notion that the views of the Irish government had to be taken into account when discussing Northern Irish affairs. Unionists would like it (the civil servants must have thought) because it guaranteed the union of Northern Ireland with the rest of the UK until a majority of its population wanted a change in its sovereign status.

McArthur came back in with a packet of Mr. Kipling's French Fancies.

I took one of the pink ones.

"Your assessment, Duffy?"

"You're right, sir. In a normal country this bold attempt to seize the middle ground would be met with polite agreement by all sides of the political divide."

"But not here."

"Here the politics are centrifugal not centrist. Extreme Nationalists and extreme Unionists will condemn the Agreement as a sell-out of their principles, and the moderates in the middle who support it will look like fools."

"Special Branch reckons the Unionists will give us the most trouble."

"I expect so, sir."

For seventy-five years, ever since Winston Churchill's promise to send Dreadnoughts to bombard Belfast during the Third Home Rule Crisis, the Unionists had suspected some sort of treachery from Albion Perfide. It was obvious to everyone that Britain's political class wanted to get out of Northern Ireland just as they had got out of India, Malaya, Aden, Rhodesia, and all the other nasty post-imperial trouble spots. Few Unionist politicians had the ability to parse the subtleties of Whitehall's actions—yes, the Brits were leaving, but they were going to take fifty years to do it, and they weren't going to run out with their tail between their legs as they did in, say, Palestine. The Anglo-Irish Agreement was not Albion Perfide.

McArthur and I finished the bottle of whiskey between us.

"I suppose we're just unlucky, sir, to have this on your watch."

"Or lucky. Depends on your point of view."

"What do you mean, sir?"

"Back where I'm from—across the water—people do what, exactly? Go to the shopping mall, go to the garden center, watch the fucking football? Eighty years of that until you die in a hospital bed, fat and alone, suffering from cancer or congestive heart failure. Our ancestors were hunters, Duffy. Survival of the fittest! A thousand generations of hunters. Hunters not bloody shoppers! And at least here we're fighting for a better tomorrow."

"Er, that's not the speech you're going to give to the men, is it?" I said anxiously.

"Why shouldn't I?"

I thought about McCrabban. "Well, for one thing most of them are quite religious, sir."

"Look, Duffy, maybe the forces of chaos will win, probably they will win, but we'll give them a hell of a fight of it, eh, Sean, eh?"

He yawned heavily and I was relieved to see that it was just the whiskey talking. "Yes, sir," I replied in a monotone.

He stared at me, his eyes like Elmer Fudd's in *Hare-Brained Hypnotist*.

"Sir, if you don't mind, I have a dinner engagement with a young lady."

"What? A young lady? Lucky you. Yeah, you should go. Go to your dinner and then go to bed, Duffy. For sleep, mind you! Get some sleep in, now. I don't think we're going to get much of it over the next few weeks."

9: CONTACT HIGH

The morning of November 15, 1985. Gentle rain falling over Ulster, falling over a country on the verge of the biggest crisis since the Hunger Strikes. How can you police a society facing a general uprising? How can you investigate a murder in a time of incipient civil war?

The beeper, of course, was going in the living room, but I didn't want to go downstairs and get it.

I wanted to stay here in bed. With her.

Sara Prentice's sleeping face. Strange and intelligent and beautiful in the blue flame of the paraffin heater.

Her green eyes opened. She smiled.

"What are you doing, Sean?"

"Looking at you."

"Why?"

"Why not?"

She shook her head. "Have you got any ciggies?"

I lit her one.

She sat up in the bed and stared at me. "Two can play at that game," she said. She stared at me and tapped me on the forehead. "So, what is it that makes Sean Duffy tick?"

"This isn't for a story, is it?"

She laughed. "Ha! Don't flatter yourself . . . Although you were in the papers a couple of years back, weren't you, Sean? Around the time of the DeLorean scandal. Your name was in the index."

I said nothing.

"Don't worry, though. You're old news now. In a place with a slower news cycle you might be a story, but here? That's ancient history."

"That's a relief."

"But *I'm* curious. For me. What makes Sean Duffy tick? What's a nice Catholic boy doing in the Protestant RUC?"

"I ask myself the same question."

"And what's the answer?"

She was looking at me with unfeigned interest. Not professional interest. Just boyfriend—girlfriend interest. At least I hoped it was that. It was an uncomfortable question. A metaphysical question. I'd been avoiding those kinds of questions for a long time now.

"Well, initially, I thought I could make a difference . . . Ten years ago now. I thought I could maybe help put an end to the madness."

"And now?"

"Now I realize that one man can do very little."

She nodded. "You look so sad, Sean. Stay there. I'll go make you some breakfast."

She came back with coffee and burnt toast. I ate it. I was grateful for the effort.

"So, what do you think is going to happen today?" she asked.

"I don't know. I really don't know."

What happened was: riots, strikes, rallies, demonstrations. And over the coming days: power cuts, graffiti on police station walls, Loyalist youths attacking peelers in safe Protestant districts.

Operation Black was instituted for CID; all investigations were suspended and detectives were seconded to riot duty.

"Hard-working senior and junior detectives seconded to riot duty!" I heard myself saying to McCrabban in the office one morning. But we all understood. The threat was existential. Northern Ireland had always been a place that was born bristling with paradox. All countries are illusions, but in the six counties of the north of Ireland the magic act had never been very convincing.

The first full day of Operation Black we spent on riot duty in North Belfast, standing like eejits in the rain under our Perspex shields while weans from the surrounding streets threw stones and half-bricks at us. Lawson and Fletcher were terrified. Crabbie and I didn't like it. And it would only get worse when the Protestant kids learned how to make

Molotov cocktails and petrol bombs. A riot was a frost fair, a jubilee, an escape from the dreariness of everyday life.

The second day of Operation Black we spent on riot duty in West Belfast, going to the Shankill Road in the morning and the Falls Road in the afternoon and night. Attacked by Protestant kids and then Catholic kids on the same day. Nice.

It didn't help that no one came forward to defend the Agreement at all. The Irish ran from it. The British were quickly embarrassed by it. One brave local Unionist politician, John Cranston, did quote from Bernard Williams' *Which Slopes Are Slippery?* but Cranston was howled down by colleagues who preferred to quote from the books of Ezekiel, Isaiah, and Jeremiah. Ulster Protestants were a dour, undemonstrative people, and it was the word on the street and in the pulpit that counted, and that word was that the Brits were going to withdraw from Northern Ireland and pass on the job of keeping the peace between the Protestants and Catholics to the US Marines or the UN or, God save us, the two undermanned regiments of the Irish Army . . .

I went home after the third day of rioting to find Mrs. Bridewell standing in her front garden with her arms folded. She was a looker was Mrs. Bridewell, recently divorced, today wearing a little miniskirt and heels with muck-covered gardening gloves. A loose brown hair was hanging fetchingly over her rosy left cheek.

"I'm awful sorry, Mr. Duffy. We're all awful sorry," she said.

"Sorry about what?" I began, and then I saw it. Someone had sprayed-painted a swastika on my front door, and underneath it they'd scrawled "SS RUC."

I nodded to Mrs. Bridewell, turned right, and walked down the street to Bobby Cameron's house.

I knocked on his door and saw him peering at me through the fisheye security lens.

He opened the door in a white tank top holding an Airfix 1:16 scale Hawker Hurricane. He was still channeling Brian Clough, but this time it was after a home win and a favorable write-up by Hugh McIlvanney in the *Daily Express*.

"What is it, Duffy? I'm in the middle of doing me models."

"Someone's painted a swastika on my front door."

"Have they? Well, that's what you get for being part of a fascist organization hell-bent on repressing the Protestant people of Ulster."

"Did you know one of my new trainees is Jewish? What if I'd had him over for dinner tonight and he'd seen that? Or what if I'd had my girl over? Eh?"

"You make your bed, you lie in it, Duffy. You were out of the RUC and now you're back in, and you have to take the fucking consequences."

"I want that swastika off my door tonight, and if anyone ever fucks with my house again, I guarantee you a police raid on *your* house every night until the end of time."

"Or until someone murders you."

"Or until some mad, pissed-off, rogue peeler with nothing much to lose murders you, Bobby."

"A raid on my house won't find anything."

"I'm sure your wife will love seeing all the family valuables in the street. And anyway, by the sixth or seventh raid the forensics boys will be so fed up not finding anything that they will find something . . . do you know what I mean?"

Bobby sighed. "I know what you mean," he grunted.

"We understand each other, then?"

"Aye."

"And tell them kids if there's a repeat of this incident I'll be keeping Mickey Burke's lioness in my back garden from now on."

I went home and put my dinner on. Not too long after that a group of three boys appeared at the front door with paint remover and set to work getting rid of the graffiti.

There would, I knew, be no recurrence of that particular piece of shite, but the Anglo-Irish Agreement shitstorm was only just beginning.

The very next day the Reverend Ian Paisley went on the radio and called for all the young men of Ulster to rise up against "Barry's Lackeys." Peter Barry was the Irish foreign minister and we were thus cast as his demonic agents. The nickname stuck and it appeared on graffiti all over Belfast.

The Protestant people were being told by their leaders to rise up against us, the Catholic community didn't trust us, and the IRA still wanted to kill every last one of us. Perfect.

I pulled the Beemer into the police station car park.

The Chief Inspector was waiting for me at the front desk.

"Sorry, Duffy, need your CID boys and girls again. Riot duty. Rathcoole. You don't mind?"

"Would it make a difference if I did mind?"

"No."

"Well then, I don't mind at all, sir."

I went into the CID incident room. Fletcher was passing out tea and Jaffa Cakes.

"The bad news is you're going to have to put down the tea and biscuits. The good news is we're going to get riot pay!"

"Where?" Crabbie asked.

"Rathcoole."

"Could be worse," McCrabban said.

Lawson and Fletcher, however, looked banjaxed. This was only the first week of the crisis and they were exhausted.

"Come on, lads, let's go show these regular coppers that the CID can hold a riot shield and get pelted like the best of them."

Fletcher sniffled but got up. Lawson, however, just kept sitting there, dazed. I patted him on the shoulder. "You too, Young Lochinvar, come on, suit up!"

"It'll be OK. These things are never as bad as they sound," Crabbie said with a big friendly grin that would have horrified them if they'd known him as well as I did.

The four of us piled in the back of a Land Rover with two regular peelers up front.

"Who saw the football on the telly last night?" I asked to take our minds off the riot.

"A good performance from Liverpool," Lawson said mechanically.

"They're an ageing side," Crabbie said. "The future belongs to Man U."

"What do you think, Fletcher?" I asked.

"I don't care."

"You don't care?"

"Why *do* men care about football?"

"Cos football's important. Football is war without the blood," Lawson said.

"And sometimes with the blood," I said, but I changed the conversation to the movies, a subject that would engage both of them.

We reached Rathcoole Estate in North Belfast. I had done riot duty here before many times. It wasn't just familiarity that bred contempt. There was actual contempt contempt. This was a pretty scary estate with some clever, old-school hoods running things.

We piled out of the Land Rover, and a Divisional Mobile Support Unit chief inspector gave us helmets and the new rectangular riot shields which worked better than the old round ones.

We stood in the Thin Green Line for an hour while the local kids pelted us with stones and milk bottles. I kept our little band on the flank of the line, and when it was our turn to rotate off I checked that none of my lads had been hurt.

Lawson had copped a Molotov on his shield but no one else had got a scratch.

Eventually the order was given to fire plastic bullets and a couple of eager, experienced peelers picked out the ringleaders, aimed, and shot the fuckers with baton rounds. The rain came down after that and the rioters dispersed.

It was a successful little operation and my unit acquitted itself well.

"Well done, everyone," I said, patting Fletcher and Lawson on the back. "You did very well. We're going home now and you'll get good reports from me."

We piled back into the Rover drenched with sweat and stinking of fear and petrol.

"So where are you from, Fletcher?"

"I was born in Armagh, but I grew up in Enniskillen. My dad moved there for work."

"I've heard it's nice in Enniskillen."

"Yes, our house is on the lake."

"Uh, boss, radio call, we've been diverted to another riot in the Ardoyne," one of the guys from up front said.

"Who's diverting us?"

"Chief Inspector McArthur."

"Dammit."

Up into the twisty streets of the Ardoyne in West Belfast. A much bigger riot involving dozens of Land Rovers and hundreds of people.

Another two hours on the Thin Green Line getting pelted with rocks and bottles and fireworks. Lawson breaking formation and chasing after a kid who'd chucked a brick at his head. Crabbie and I pulling the eejit back into formation.

"Take it easy there, Batman! You've done enough for today," I said.

"Sorry, sir, got carried away there," he said.

"Be more like Fletcher, son, keep your head down, don't get baited, don't get too worked up," McCrabban instructed him.

Darkness fell. Rotated off the line. Back in the Land Rover.

Too tired for conversation. The four of us in the rear just staring into space.

The Land Rover stopped suddenly.

"What's happening?" Crabbie asked the men up front.

"I think I'm lost," our driver said. "I followed the diversion signs but this road is a dead end."

"Diversion signs?" Crabbie wondered, an ominous note in his voice.

"What diversion signs?" I asked.

"Oh shit! Muzzle flash!"

"Incoming!" I yelled.

"Brace! Brace! Brace!"

"Fuck that, take evasive—"

. . .

. . .

White light.

An almighty bang.

A momentary suspension of the laws of gravity.

A crash against the metal roof that might have done for me if I hadn't been wearing my riot helmet.

A metallic taste in my mouth.

Blood.

Crabbie taking charge. The back doors opening. Belfast's crocodile skyline rotating into view.

"Are you OK, Sean?"

Ping, ping, ping off the armor plate of the Land Rover.

"I'm OK. Are we under fire?"

"Stay where you are, Sean; backup is on the way."

Crabbie with his sidearm out, shooting at gunfire from a ruined block of flats. I crawled toward him, pulled out my Glock.

"Where?" I asked.

"The abandoned building on the corner. Second floor."

Two more quick muzzle flashes.

I pulled the trigger on the semiautomatic and Crabbie and I shot at the target together.

I emptied my clip, the smell of cordite and blood choking my nostrils.

I blinked slowly and lost consciousness.

Cops.

Soldiers.

"He's awake."

"Where am I?"

Where I was was an ambulance being transferred to Belfast City Hospital. They'd hooked me to a drip, but after a minute checking myself I knew that I was fine. No bones broken. No puncture wounds. Just a concussion.

In the hospital car park I told the medics I'd see myself into Casualty.

Instead I scored some painkillers and Valium from a sympathetic nurse and called a bloke I knew at Queen Street RUC who sent a Land Rover to take me back to Carrick.

Crabbie was surprised to see me.

"What are you doing here? You should be in the hospital. Did you—"

"How is everyone?"

"Everyone's OK except for you and Fletcher."

"What happened to her?"

"Same as you. Banged her head. They took her to the RVH."

"She OK?"

"The last I heard she was fine. She wasn't completely out like you. A little concussed, though. And very badly shaken."

"Everyone else?"

"Few scrapes, cuts. A story to bore the grandkids with."

"So I was the worst?"

"You took the prize."

"What hit us?"

"Rocket-propelled grenade. Got the Land Rover above the wheel-base, knocked us over on one side."

"Who did it?"

"Who knows?"

"Any chance of catching them?"

"I doubt it."

"You or I hit anyone?"

"Nope."

"Did they at least leave the grenade launcher? Get prints off it?"

"They took it with them. Go home, Sean."

"I think I will."

Home to Coronation Road with a splitting headache.

Aspirin and gin. Valium and codeine.

I called Sara but she was busy and couldn't come over.

I made a vodka gimlet and put on the news. There had been half a dozen riots in Belfast that day. Twelve hijackings. Nineteen separate attacks on police officers. The attack on our Land Rover didn't even merit a passing mention.

The next day Lawson, McArthur, Crabbie, and myself went to see

Fletcher in the Royal Victoria Hospital. She was sitting up in bed. Her fiancé, Ted, was with her. He was a building contractor from Omagh. Big guy, moustache, ruddy cheeks, red hair. He was wearing Wellington boots with corduroys and a checked sports coat, which was the look of an older man although Teddy was only about twenty-five.

We introduced ourselves, asked how the patient was doing.

The patient was on the mend. A sprained wrist, a mild concussion, two stitches on her upper lip.

We gave her flowers. Chocolates. A card that showed Snoopy covered with bandages.

We told her that everyone in the station was asking about her.

She smiled at the card.

The kicker came at the end of the obligatory five minutes of small talk.

Big Ted took Fletcher's hand and, turning to McArthur, said: "She's got something she wants to say, don't you, love?"

"I do," Fletcher muttered a little reluctantly.

"Go on, then," Ted urged her.

"Well, it's like this. I really appreciate everything everyone's done for me, and to get into the CID was a dream come true, and Sergeant McCrabban has been nothing but kind and patient . . . I mean, I know I've had an amazing opportunity here and I don't want to let the side down or anything, but . . . it's just that . . . and I don't want you to think to yourself, oh God, this is what happens when the higher-ups make us take a woman . . . it's not like that at all. It's just me, you know?"

I looked at Crabbie but he was none the wiser either. Was she angling for a transfer already? She'd only been with us a fortnight.

"I'm sorry, what are you—"

"She's resigning. We want to have kids. And how are we going to have kids if she's getting thrown about in a Land Rover? Look at her face. It's fucking ridiculous, isn't it?" Ted said.

"You're resigning?" I asked.

"Yes. But don't think I'm not really grateful that you would take me on and I might not be resigning completely, you know? Maybe I'll put in for the part-time reserve. A couple of days a month . . ."

"You can't be a detective in the part-time reserve," I said, annoyed by what she was saying. Sure she'd just had the bejesus scared out of her, but even so, you don't resign because of a little thing like that.

"Maybe you should take a couple of days to think things over," Lawson attempted.

"I know I should, but—"

"She's resigning and that's the end of it! We're getting married. We're settling down and we're having kids. We don't need the money and as far as I can see Helen's done her part now. Done and done," Teddy insisted.

On the ride back to the station McArthur wondered whether there was any way we could spin Fletcher's resignation so it didn't reflect badly on Carrick RUC. "The higher-ups will criticize us for losing a new recruit who has gone through a lot of expensive training programs. They'll probably take the huff too and not send us a replacement. Carrick CID will be stuck with an embarrassingly top-heavy department: a detective inspector, a detective sergeant and you, Lawson, the sole detective constable."

"Aye, it is a bit silly," I agreed.

"And you, Duffy," he said with an accusatory tone. "You'll probably be getting out too, won't ya?"

"What do you mean, sir?"

"You'll see, my lad, you'll see."

10: THE OFFER

McArthur's cryptic remark and his mysterious hints over the pre-vious few weeks were clarified the very next day. It was an off day, and it was a good day to have off as there was a big "Ulster Says No" rally planned in Belfast, and the chances were that, if the rain held off, the rally would descend into yet another riot.

Cornflakes, hot milk, sugar. Coffee. *The Open University* on BBC 2. *Out of the Blues: The Best of David Bromberg* on the stereo.

I called Sara at the *Belfast Telegraph*.

"Whatcha doing?"

"Working. You?"

"My off day. Wanna do something?"

"I can't. Working. Working all the time now."

"It's an ill wind . . ."

"Exactly. Any developments on our case?"

"Our case?"

"Michael Kelly."

"Oh, no. I think it's done and done that one."

Awkward silence.

"I got a dog," she said. "Temporarily. My sister's actually. Her hus-band's allergic."

"Is that so?"

"A poodle."

"Do you want to do something tonight?"

"I really can't."

"Tomorrow?"

"I'll call you, Sean."

"OK."

I hung up the phone. Looked at it. Sipped my coffee.

A knock at the front door.

"Who is it?"

"Would your honor be home at all?"

I opened the door. It was a tramp. I listened to his story. He just needed some money to catch the boat train. He had a job in Scotland on the oil rigs, had a wife and child, and he would pay me back as soon as he got to Aberdeen. It was compelling fiction, and he was going great guns until he strayed into weirdo territory and started talking about the Book of Revelation.

I gave him a quid to get rid of him.

Back to the kitchen.

Bromberg. Cocaine. Cornflakes.

Another knock at the door.

"You're not getting any more money!" I yelled from the kitchen.

"We don't want any money. We want to talk to you," a woman's voice replied.

I retrieved my service revolver from the kitchen counter, decided against it, got my new Glock from the hall cupboard, and went outside into the back garden. I opened the back gate and went down the entry between the houses on the terrace. From the mouth of this shared entryway I had an excellent view of my front door. I saw who it was and put the nine-millimeter back in my dressing-gown pocket.

"Hello, Kate," I said.

"Hello, Sean," she said.

Kate hadn't changed a lot in the year and a half since I'd seen her last. She was still attractive, thin, weather beaten. Definitely no grey in her hair, but perhaps she no longer looked quite so youthful. Aloof and beautiful in a mannish, austere kind of way. Her blonde hair was a little lighter, her face had no trace of a tan. No holidays in the sun for Kate Albright, the MI5 head of station in Belfast.

She was wearing brown trousers over boots, a white Aran sweater over a T-shirt. She had no coat and she wasn't that wet, so there must be a car and a—

Yeah, there it was. A silver Jag with a driver wearing sunglasses. And someone in the back seat also wearing sunglasses, sitting there like an eejit.

Not another shiny Jag like that in all of Victoria Estate. Subtle. MI5 all over.

"Were you in a fight, Sean?"

"A fight? What? No. Land Rover rolled over. Just one of those things. Do you want to come in?" I asked.

"I'd love to."

"You'll have to come round the back, didn't bring a front door key."

"But you did bring a gun, I see."

I nudged the Glock handle back into my dressing-gown pocket. "Well, you never know who it might be."

"Would you mind if I invited Miss Kendrick to join us?"

"More the merrier. I'll go round the back and let you both in."

Back door. Kitchen. Kettle on. Through the hall. Front door.

Kendrick was a plump redhead with a frumpy peasant quality to her that no doubt endeared her to Kate. Thin lips, blue dress, sensible shoes.

"Tea, coffee, something a little stronger? Sixteen-year-old Ardbeg just waiting for an occasion."

"A little early for that. Coffee would be fine," Kate said.

"Coffee's fine," Kendrick agreed.

"Have a seat. I'll bring it."

I showed Kendrick to the chair by the fire so I could steal a look at both of them in the angle of the hall mirror.

Kate Albright. Kate fucking Albright, who had caused me much grief over the last couple of years. She'd pushed me to go to America to investigate a murder, and when that had blown up in my face and I'd been demoted, she'd promised to help me resurrect my career if I found my old school friend and IRA mastermind Dermot McCann.

I'd killed Dermot for her. In return I'd got my old job back. This job. This fucking shitty job.

For Dermot, too, an idealist, a dreamer, a poet—a fucking sociopath, yeah, but still, those other things as well . . .

Kendrick I'd never seen before. She had a clutch bag long enough
to hold a silenced nine-millimeter pistol. She was not someone you'd
suspect of wet work, which was perfect if you wanted her to do wet
work. On me? Sure, why not. I knew a lot, I was a drinker, I was morose
and unpredictable . . . Why not silence me and end a potentially embarrassing complication—I was just a dumb Paddy after all, wasn't I? A
Fenian Paddy at that . . .

This would be the moment to come in and whack me, with my
back turned, as the kettle boiled.

Death, judgment, heaven and hell. Bean grinder, French press,
where's the Hobnobs?

"What are you listening to?" Kate asked as I brought in the coffee
and biscuits and the possibly dodgy milk.

"The best of David Bromberg," I said shamefacedly. Shamefacedly,
of course, because compilation albums are always slightly embarrassing
to the serious record collector. *Legend: The Best of Bob Marley* and *The
Beatles 1967–1970* were piled high in every record shop in the land,
but I wouldn't be seen dead exiting HMV with either of those.

"I see," she said.

She pulled the ashtray toward her and lit up a Silk Cut—that was
new, she hadn't been a smoker before.

"Stress getting to you?" I asked.

"We all need our little vices."

Aye, we do. In the last fourteen hours I'd had tea, coffee, pharma
cocaine, hashish, tobacco, codeine, whiskey, bourbon, beer, and as a
sleep aid: Valium and vodka and lime. Nice combo if you could swing
it all. Could I swing it? Well, I was still standing, wasn't I?

Ms. Kendrick helped herself to a coffee and Hobnob.

Kate stubbed out her cigarette and grabbed a cup of joe.

"So, ladies, what brings you to sunny Carrickfergus?" I asked,
adjusting the fold of my dressing gown so I didn't accidentally expose
myself. "Am I in some kind of trouble?"

Kate took a sip of coffee and cleared her throat. "No, Sean, no
trouble, quite the reverse."

"Oh?"

"We were wondering if you were quite happy with the way your career is panning out in the RUC?"

"Because . . ."

"We . . . I . . . would like to offer you a job."

Now there's a phrase to send chills down your spine.

"In MI5?"

"In the Security Service, yes."

"Quit the police and join MI5?"

"Yes."

"Why would I do that, Kate?"

"For several reasons. I don't know if you've seen your personnel file at the RUC . . ."

"I've seen my file. Been through it with HR many times."

"Ah, yes, there's the file HR shows you and then there's the other file, isn't there?" she said.

"Go on."

"Well, for a start there's a promotion hold on you, Sean. I had to pull every string I could to get you bumped back up to inspector, but that's as far as you're ever going to go."

"Why? I'm good at my job. Better than most."

"They just don't like you, Sean. They feel that you bit the hand that fed, that you're a loose cannon, that you're more trouble than you're worth. You were being groomed for the top, for the very top, and they feel that you put your individual caseload ahead of your loyalty to the RUC."

I nodded. It wasn't an unfair assessment. I'd disobeyed orders by continuing an investigation into a supposed gay serial killer when the case had been taken from me and given to Special Branch. And then there was the trip to America where I'd really fucked up by making a deal with the FBI to ignore everything connected with John DeLorean, and then, idiotically, getting myself mixed up in the DeLorean case again within days of returning home.

"So I'll be a lowly detective inspector for the rest of my days; that's not such a bad life. Columbo has been stuck at lieutenant for the last fifteen years . . ."

"We believe that keeping you as a junior detective is not a good use of your talents and abilities. You're still young, Sean. We believe that you have potential to really make a difference in the Province over the next five or ten years as the Troubles begin to wind down."

"Wind down? I don't see any evidence of anything winding down."

"That's because you don't know what we know," Kendrick said.

I raised an eyebrow. "What do you know?"

"And of course your pay would rise substantially. With your years in, you'd be beginning at Civil Service Grade 5 with the usual Northern Ireland allowances," Kate said. "Which could mean up to an extra ten thousand pounds a year . . . You could move out of this . . . house."

"I like it here," I said quickly, trying to conceal my surprise. *An extra ten grand a year? Shit. I'd be bringing in serious money. I could buy a cottage in Donegal. I could go to America a couple of times a year . . . if I could make it through US Customs and Immigration.*

"We might require you to move, Mr. Duffy, but there would also be a moving allowance," Kendrick said.

"We'd quite like you in a house where they don't paint swastikas on your front door," Kate said.

"Ah, you saw that? That was just kids, no big deal; they took it off when I asked them to," I said, feeling oddly defensive about Coronation Road and its occupants.

Kate sipped her tea and said nothing.

"What would my job be, exactly? An analyst? That sort of thing?" I asked.

"We've got a lot of analysts, but we don't have experienced field men. We need agent handlers."

"I'd be running informers?" I said with distaste.

"You don't like informers?" Kate asked.

"Who does?"

"We do. We like them very much."

"The ones I've met have been the scum of the earth," I said, which was a high-horse line and she knew it—the RUC would grind to a halt without paid informers and the Confidential Telephone.

"Would it surprise you to learn that one in four IRA volunteers now works for us in some capacity?" Kate said, deadpan.

"One in four! You're joking!"

"One in four. Actually in terms of percentages it's around twenty-seven per cent."

"A quarter of the IRA are actually British agents? Bollocks!" I said, utterly shocked.

"It's true," Kendrick said. "One in four IRA volunteers work for us in some capacity as fully paid informers, as petty touts, or occasionally as active agents."

I was struggling to take this in. "But, but . . . but if that's true, why haven't you shut them down completely?"

"The cell structure," Kendrick explained.

"Some commands have entirely resisted infiltration. The South Armagh Brigade, for example. The sleeper cells in England and Germany. And there's also the fact that we're playing the long game with many of these agents and informers. Letting them rise as far as they can . . ."

"So you let them commit the odd murder here and there so they can prove their bona fides and move up the ranks?" I said with disgust.

"If it's any comfort, Sean, our guidelines, though flexible, don't usually permit us to sanction mass atrocities. Usually our sins are ones of omission," Kate said.

"I don't know what that means. And I don't want to know."

Kate could see that she was losing me. "What you do in the police is, of course, very valuable. You can pick up the odd enforcer or murderer or extortionist. But what we do . . . what we are doing is damaging entire networks. We are working at ending this insurgency from within."

"By placing your men at the top of the terrorist organizations?"

"And women. Let's not be all 1970s about this," Kendrick said.

"We need experienced, competent agent handlers, people who

know Northern Ireland. People who understand the nuances. People who are smart."

"I'm not as smart as you think."

"We think you are, Sean. We think you've got a great career ahead of you if you are with the right people. The RUC believes that you're not worth the trouble. The RUC would love you to stay in a backwater and keep your head down and make no waves until you're finally killed, or invalided out, or take early retirement. We like the fact that you have ambition; we like the fact that you're willing to take chances. I've seen your work, Sean. I've seen what you can do. Your skill with people, your insight. Even just by living here—a Catholic policeman on Coronation Road in Victoria Estate, Carrickfergus—you're demonstrating that you walk where others cannot. You've made mistakes, of course, but I'm willing to overlook those mistakes. I appreciate and understand you in a way that your bosses in the RUC do not."

"All this love's making my head spin."

"Let it spin."

"But the fact remains, I've put in ten years and—"

"Don't say no. Not now. Mull it over. Consider everything I've said. Think about the way you've been treated. Think about what we could do for you. We'd let you finish that PhD of yours. You'd like that, wouldn't you?"

I hadn't thought about my aborted PhD in years.

"We value your intellect. You wouldn't have to hide it."

"You have a very low opinion of the RUC," I said.

Kate shrugged and said nothing. She saw that no good would come of her piling on.

"Think about the difference you could make if you came to work for us," she said.

"Well, it's certainly food for thought," I said.

Kate stood. Kendrick got up too.

I saw them to the door.

Kendrick went to get the car started. Kate held my gaze.

"We need you, Sean. And we need fifty more like you."

"I don't really have the mind-set of a civil servant, Kate."

"To be honest, I don't think you have the mind-set of a policeman."

"Fair point."

"You'll consider it?"

I nodded.

She walked down the path.

Turned.

"Oh, and Sean?" she said in a half-whisper.

"Yeah?"

"Your house stinks of marijuana and Scotch, and there's what appears to be cocaine on the lapel of your dressing gown. Even if you don't join us, you could do with getting your act together, yes?"

"Yes."

11: THE SUICIDES ARE PILING UP

The Jag slipped away from its mooring and drove round the bend in Coronation Road. I picked up the milk bottles feeling what . . . ? Shell-shocked? Excited? Kate and Kendrick were those rare English bureaucrats who lived in the future not the past, something that no one in Ireland ever did. "But, Jesus, a job with MI5?" I muttered to myself.

I looked at the ever so faint swastika stain on the front door. Kate missed nothing. She was good.

The phone was ringing in the hall. I put down the milk, picked it up. "Yeah?"

"Sean, sorry to bother you on your off day."

It was Crabbie.

"What's up, mate?"

"You know that open-and-shut case of mine . . ."

"Not so shut, eh?"

"I could do with your help, Sean. I know it's my responsibility and all that jazz, but things are starting to spiral away from me a bit."

"Say no more, mate. Where do you want me? The station?"

"Bannockburn Street, Whitehead."

"Who lives there?"

"Sylvie McNichol."

"She's got new information? I told ya she was holding back."

"She killed herself, Sean."

"Killed herself?"

"Aye."

"Because she couldn't live without Michael Kelly?"

"That's what we're expected to believe."

"I'm getting chills."

110

"Me too."

"Does it stink?"

"Nothing obvious but . . ."

"I'll be right over."

"And can you please tell the Chief Inspector that we can't possibly do riot duty today with a murder investigation on our hands again."

"I'll tell him."

Boots. Jumper. Raincoat. A quick check under the BMW for bombs. My distorted reflection in a puddle under the car. A tired old man's eyes staring back at me through the rainbow of petroleum coefficients.

Drizzle on the lonely A2 to Whitehead. I continued my love-hate affair with the Gillette electric razor while I looked out *Hex Induction Hour* by the Fall. I put it in the tape player and it came on at "Hip Priest." The Fall on repeat. Joy Division and the Happy Mondays on the sidelines in reserve. A future M60 triptych.

Bannockburn Street, Whitehead. Three Land Rovers and a few neighbors nosying over their fences.

Sergeant McCrabban in a sweater and an orange Peter Storm raincoat. Constable Lawson next to him in a suit and tie and a raincoat like mine. Both of them pale as match factory girls.

McCrabban led me to the garage next to the house.

The door had been jacked open from the outside by boiler-suited FOs who were milling around waiting for the go-ahead from Sergeant McCrabban. They had set up floodlights in the garage so we could see everything, and the lights were so bright one of the FOs was taking photographs without the aid of a flash.

"Will we go in?" Crabbie asked.

"It's a nasty scene," a leery old forensic officer said with satisfaction.

I hid my genuine reluctance to look at the girl's body in a comic pretense of reluctance, but I had no choice, not in front of McCrabban and Lawson.

The car was a blue 1960s-model Volkswagen Beetle. A hosepipe had been run from the exhaust to the front driver's-side window. The door had been opened so that I could see Sylvie McNichol dead in the driver's seat. Lips blue, eyes bulging from the sockets, vomit on her chin. No handcuffs, no restraints, no sign of a struggle. A thick blue jumper was lying on the ground next to her, obviously the thing she'd used to stuff in the top of the car window in the gap made by the hosepipe.

Residual carbon monoxide. Urine smell.

I coughed.

"Are you OK?" Crabbie asked.

I nodded and examined her closely. Her hands were in her lap, her nails unbroken. She hadn't been trying to claw her way out. Her face was blank. Resigned?

Everything was as it should be. What was I missing? And I was missing something, something my two colleagues had seen.

"The first thing we should tell you is that the garage light doesn't work," Lawson said. "The bulb's been out for weeks. Neither girl could be bothered to replace it."

Why was that important?

"OK," I replied.

"There's a suicide note," Crabbie said, and handed it to me in a plastic bag.

I read it.

"I can't go on without him," it said.

"Her handwriting?"

"It's block capitals but Deirdre Ferris, the housemate, says that sometimes that's how she wrote," Lawson said.

"Where is this Deirdre Ferris?"

"Upstairs with a WPC."

"She find the body?"

"She found the note first. She'd come home from a visit to her mum's. The note was on the kitchen table and then she heard the engine going in the garage. The garage connects to the house through the washroom," Crabbie explained.

A suicide note, no sign of a struggle, and a possible motive.

"Apart from the fact that she didn't seem that cut up when we interviewed her, what makes you think murder rather than suicide?" I asked McCrabban.

"Tell him," Crabbie said to Lawson.

Ah, so Lawson had spotted it, had he? Got to watch out for that one.

"She ran a hosepipe from the exhaust to the driver's-side window."

"I can see that."

"She wound the window up as tight as she could and then stuffed a jumper into the gap that the hosepipe made at the top of the window," Lawson explained.

"OK, I'm with you. I'm still not seeing a problem."

"The problem is the passenger's-side window."

"What about it?" I asked.

"It doesn't wind all the way up," Lawson explained.

"What?"

"It's broken."

I examined the window and he was right about that. It went to about a quarter of an inch from the top and left a gap.

"So?"

"It's never worked since Sylvie bought the car a year ago. She always complained to Deirdre about how the passenger's-side seat got wet in the rain."

I understood it now.

"She didn't stuff anything in the passenger's-side window," I said.

"No. She didn't."

"So we're expected to believe that she meticulously put a jumper in the driver's-side window but forgot to put something in the passenger's-side window," I said.

Crabbie nodded.

"But a killer wouldn't have known about the tiny gap in the passenger's-side window, would they?" Crabbie said. "Not in a dark garage through which he was navigating by torch."

"The fumes killed her, but by not stuffing the passenger's-side window she gave herself a longer and more lingering death," I said.

Crabbie shook his head. "It doesn't add up."

"Suicide's not impossible, sir," Lawson said, covering himself. "But it is very strange that she would carefully block one window and not the other."

"And then add in the fact of her interview at the police station that we all got to witness," Crabbie added.

"She didn't seem the suicidal type to me," Lawson said.

"Or me," Crabbie agreed.

"Or me," I concurred.

We looked at the car and the victim and the cold, concrete garage floor.

"Careless of him, wasn't it?" Crabbie said.

"Him?" Lawson asked.

"The killer."

"Or killers," Lawson said.

"Come on, let's get out of here and let the forensic boys do their work," I said.

Crabbie nodded and we went to the mobile incident van where mugs of tea were waiting for us. I ordered out the reservists and closed the van door to get some privacy.

"It doesn't have to be related to the Kelly case, you know. There could be new boyfriend trouble, threats against her, stalkers, something like that. She was a good-looking lass under all that make-up; she could have stirred some passions," I said.

Crabbie nodded. "We're checking on that. But the similarities are worth considering, aren't they?"

"Two suicides. One of which was possibly staged," I agreed. "What are you Brains of Britain cooking up between you?"

"We're thinking what you're thinking, Sean. That Sylvie knew something about the Kelly case and they killed her before she blabbed . . ."

I rubbed my chin. "It's certainly a possibility."

"Think she was blackmailing the killer?" Crabbie asked.

"Nah, she's not the blackmailing type. She was the *whatever you say, say nothing* type. They probably weren't going to kill her, originally, but it was gnawing at them. And I suppose last night they just decided better safe than sorry."

"Crime of opportunity, maybe? With Deirdre away?" McCrabban asked.

"And of course it calls into question Michael Kelly's suicide too," Lawson said, stating the bleedin' obvious.

"It calls into question the whole Kelly case," Crabbie underlined. "If Michael was abducted and then murdered, the death of his parents would be a lot more explicable with the known facts. The professional nature of the shooting. The fact that both parents were killed within a matter of seconds of one another. The lack of defensive wounds . . ."

"Could be that the parents were simply in the way. They had to be taken care of first before the murderer or murderers went upstairs and grabbed Michael," Lawson suggested.

"Michael was then abducted and killed and the death made to look like a suicide," Crabbie said.

"For what motive?" I asked.

Crabbie shrugged. "I have no idea. I thought we'd closed . . . well, you know what I thought. Should have known it was too good to be true. My first murder . . ."

"Someone wants to kill Michael. They abduct him from his home, killing his parents in the process. They kill him by throwing him off a cliff. Then, a week later, they murder his girlfriend because they think she might know too much."

"Maybe she was a witness; maybe Michael told her something," Lawson said.

"Or it could be unrelated. We'll have to rule that out. As well as suicide, obviously," Crabbie said.

"If, Crabbie, *if* we rule out your actual lovesick suicide or a non-related murder, then yes, it all comes back to Michael Kelly. What was he doing? What enemies had that wee lad made in his twenty-odd years on planet Earth?"

Lawson cleared his throat and looked around cautiously as if the van might be bugged or something.

"Yes, Constable Lawson? Do you have something to contribute?"

"There's something I've been working on in my own time ... It's probably nothing ..."

I gazed at Crabbie. This was news to him too.

"In your free time between riots?" I asked.

"Yes."

"Go on," I said.

"Well, that thing you said, Inspector, about Michael leaving college just before his graduation. About how he only had a few weeks left and he quit ..."

"Yeah?"

"Well, it got me thinking. I looked into Michael's university history and something very interesting cropped up."

"What?"

"Do you remember when Anastasia Coleman died?"

"No."

"It was in the *Daily Mail*, the *News of the World*, the tabs were all over it."

"I rarely read the *News of the World*," I lied.

"I never get the chance," Crabbie added. "Missus won't have it in the house."

Lawson sighed. "Anastasia Coleman was the daughter of the minister for agriculture. Five months ago she took a heroin overdose at a house in Oxford. She was a student there studying English. It was at a big party being held by the Round Table Club."

"The what club?" Crabbie wondered.

"The Round Table is an exclusive Oxford University student club. Only the rich and connected are invited to join. They're famous for their parties. Apparently they eat at restaurants, drink all the most expensive wines, smash the place up, and then leave a huge bag of money to hush the owners up."

"Charming bunch of kids," Crabbie said.

"Anyway, at this party there was a lot of heroin and cocaine and booze. Everyone passed out, and when they woke up next morning Anastasia was dead. The house was owned by this guy called Gottfried

Habsburg, so he's the fall guy. Obviously Habsburg has to leave the university because it happened in his home. But here's the interesting part. A certain Michael Kelly, *our Michael Kelly*, is in the house with Habsburg the next morning and he's caught up in the scandal too."

"Shit."

Lawson flipped open his notebook. "Some of the tabloids make the suggestion that Kelly is the one who supplied her with the drugs or that he was her boyfriend. It's all just speculation. But they make Michael's life miserable, so he quits the university too before he gets thrown out."

"Michael Kelly and this Habsburg guy are the only ones left in the house with the dead girl?"

"There's another guy there that neither of them know. He scarpers after they find the body and call the cops."

"Sensible chap. Maybe he was the dealer?"

"Maybe."

"They never find out who this third guy is?" Crabbie asked.

"Nope. The papers look for him. The Oxford police look for him, but they don't find him and obviously he doesn't testify at the inquest."

"So the focus is on Kelly and Habsburg?"

"Yeah. But from what I've read Michael Kelly gets off pretty easily. By leaving when he does and going back to Northern Ireland, most of the heat falls on this Gottfried Habsburg guy. He's the perfect fall guy for the tabs: rich, gay, German."

"That's the trifecta," I said.

"Yeah. They really go after him too. Front page of the *News of the World*. Front page of the *Sunday People*."

"Michael must have been dragged through the mud over here to some extent. The *Sunday World*?"

"Not as much as you'd think. Habsburg's eccentric lifestyle and notorious reputation captured most of the ink even here. It was his party. His house."

"Were there criminal charges against Michael or this Habsburg bloke?" Crabbie asked.

"No criminal charges in the end, but Habsburg was rusticated and his reputation was destroyed. By leaving quietly and going home Kelly got the heat off himself. It was the smart move. Michael became a footnote. It was Habsburg the tabloids wanted," Lawson explained.

"Michael must have had to go back for the inquest," I said.

"Yes. But he testified the same day as Count Habsburg, so again the next day's papers were devoted to the German."

Crabbie had grown silent and reflective. "It sounds like quite the scandal, but I don't see how it has anything to do with all of this," he said at last.

"I looked through Michael's effects and sure enough he had a Round Table Club tie and membership card," Lawson said.

"So?"

"Maybe he knew the identity of the mystery man? Maybe he knew who supplied Anastasia with the heroin?"

"But he was a good boy. He was quiet. Why kill him now?" I asked.

Lawson shrugged. "Because he knew too much? Because he was blackmailing someone? We're dealing with the elite here. The Round Table Club is the future establishment. Future prime ministers. Future foreign secretaries..."

I looked at Crabbie, but he seemed dubious. "There's no evidence of a conspiracy," he said.

"The complete lack of evidence is the sure sign that the conspiracy is working," I offered.

"That's what the nutters say," Crabbie said.

"Sometimes the nutters can be right."

"I suppose it's not impossible," Crabbie conceded.

12: OVER THE WATER

Lawson, McCrabban, and myself attended Sylvie McNichol's autopsy in Belfast where the ME found a tiny piece of cotton wool in Sylvie's throat. He admitted that he might have missed it if he hadn't been looking for it. The cotton wool had been dipped in chloroform. Ergo Sylvie McNichol *had* been murdered, and murdered by a professional who had attempted to make it look like a suicide, but who had just got a little unlucky with the passengers'-side car window.

The next job at hand was to interview Deirdre Ferris, Sylvie's flatmate.

Deirdre was also a barmaid at the Whitecliff: twenty, fake tan, dyed black hair, five foot nothing, and not quite as sharp or as pretty as Sylvie. Deirdre was adamant that she knew zilch about Michael Kelly's death or what had happened to her flatmate.

We canvassed Sylvie's friends and neighbors. Sylvie had no debts, had not pissed off the paramilitaries, and had no suspicious ex-boyfriends. No stalkers, nothing in the RUC files.

Under further interrogation at the station Deirdre admitted that Sylvie had acted a little strangely after Michael Kelly's death. She'd made a couple of phone calls from random call boxes, she'd double-checked that the doors were locked at night.

I explained the whole situation to Chief Inspector McArthur and got Carrick CID excused from further riot duty until we had got to the bottom of the Michael Kelly/Sylvie McNichol case.

McCrabban didn't want to travel in "cattle round-up" season so I left him to pursue any local developments while Lawson and I travelled to Oxford to see whether there really could be some kind of conspiracy.

I picked up Lawson at his home and drove to Belfast Harbor

Airport. I left the Beemer in the long-term car park and we got the British Midland flight to Birmingham International.

When we got through Arrivals a constable from Thames Valley Police CID was standing there holding up a sign that said "Daffy."

"That'll be me," I said.

"Constable Atkins. Thomas Atkins, Thames Valley Constabulary," he replied.

"Tommy Atkins? You're having us on."

"No."

He looked all of nineteen. Younger than Lawson maybe. Skinny, tall, blond, with lifeless but not unintelligent blue eyes.

We shook hands. "Oh!" he cried. "Oh, hold on, I've got a present for you, from the Super, inter-service cooperation and all that. I left it in the café. Shit. Hang about. Hold on."

He ran to the café and came back with a paper bag with a box in it.

"From the Super," he said again.

It was a twenty-five-year-old bottle of Macallan.

"Nineteen sixty," Atkins said appreciatively, and doing an awful Scottish accent he added: "If I was a drinker I'd definitely have a wee dram of that."

"Tell the Superintendent thanks," I said.

"Oh, I will. He knew you'd like it. 'Those RUC boys will love this,' his very words."

While we waited at the luggage carousel Atkins went off to find a pay phone and let the station know we'd arrived.

"They think we're eejits. Drunken Paddy eejits," I said to Lawson.

"I see that, sir."

Atkins came back.

The bags.

The exit.

A police Ford Sierra. Me in the front. Lawson sprawled out over the back.

The M42 to the M40. England racing past at 80 mph.

"We've put you up in a little B&B on the Banbury Road. Lovely little spot. We use it all the time. Get a police rate. Although I'm not really sure if the RUC's paying for it or us. I'm not privy to all the details . . . Actually they haven't told me much of anything. I'm just your liaison. It's your case, Inspector Duffy. The Super will sort you out I'm sure."

"Were you on the team working on Anastasia Coleman's death?"

"Me? No. It was hardly a team, Inspector, if I remember correctly. I think it was a fairly straightforward affair, no?"

"If you say so."

"Oh yes, I think so."

"You get a lot of cabinet ministers' daughters taking overdoses around here?"

He smiled. "No, can't say that we do. But fortunately for us, if I'm remembering correctly, there was no hint of foul play, so we—the investigating officers—dealt with it fairly quickly."

I caught Lawson's eye in the rear-view.

This had been a major tabloid story for nearly a week. Surely it must have been all hands on deck at Oxford Police HQ. I mean, what else did they have to deal with around here? Stolen bikes?

"Have either of you gentlemen been to Oxford before?" Atkins asked.

We hadn't.

"I think you'll have a lovely time. You're right next to one of the best pubs in the city. And London's only forty minutes away on the train. Suppose you're not into clubbing at all?"

"We're here to investigate a murder," I grumbled.

"Oh yes, sure, of course, mate."

Mate. Not *sir.*

Green fields. Woods. Church spires. The names of the exits: Horton-cum-Studley, Weston-on-the-Green. This wasn't England, this was bloody Trumpton.

"Nah, I only meant that once you have your investigation wrapped up, there will be plenty of time for sightseeing and a spot of R&R. London's close and Oxford has some wonderful old pubs, as I'm sure you'll find out."

He drove us into the city down Headington Hill. He gave us a tour. The full Waugh, the full Morse: Magdalen Bridge, the High Street, All Souls, and then by a complicated series of cop-car-only routes: Broad Street, Trinity College, the Sheldonian, Balliol . . .

Atkins ran a commentary which I tuned in and out. "Christopher Wren . . . Bridge of Sighs . . . of course 'new' really means five hundred years old . . . And this is where they burned Cranmer, Latimer, and Ridley, the Oxford Martyrs."

"Where is this B&B?" I asked.

"Nearly there."

Atkins drove up the Banbury Road and dropped us at a red-bricked Victorian with tubs of plastic flowers, twee ornamental gargoyles obstructing the work of the gutters, and an ornate cast-iron sign that said, "Mrs. Brown's Family Guest House."

"The Superintendent thought you'd like to meet at eleven o'clock tomorrow morning, Inspector Duffy?"

"Aye, eleven sounds fine for a meeting. But we'll want to get an early start. We'll need an office for nine."

"An office?"

"Of course an office. We can't read the case files at the B&B."

Constable Atkins shook his head. "I don't know anything about any case files. I was told you were having a meeting with the Super. He's going to clear everything up for you."

I looked at Lawson in the mirror. Your turn, son.

"We'll need to read the case files, if we're to determine if a crime's been committed here," he said.

Atkins smiled, apparently unperturbed. "Oh, I see. No, I think you fellows may have got the wrong end of the stick. Thames Valley Police has already conducted a thorough investigation into Anastasia Coleman's tragic death. As you know, Miss Coleman died of an accidental overdose of heroin. There was an inquest. A coroner's inquest. The coroner returned a verdict of death by misadventure . . . you may even, ha, ha, have read about it in one or two national newspapers."

He could see by the look in my eye that he had overplayed the pH level that I was willing to tolerate in a constable from the Thames Valley Police.

"But if you'd like, I'll make sure you get a full copy of the coroner's report and the inquest transcripts."

"Not enough?"

"And I'll get a WPC to get you a photocopy of the CID final report on Miss Coleman's death."

"That's all very good, Constable Atkins, but we'll still need the actual case files. And the office. And the full cooperation of Thames Valley Police which I'm sure will be forthcoming. None of us wants this to get kicked upstairs to Chief Constable level, eh?"

"Chief Constable level? No! No, of course not! I was merely pointing out that there's no point in both of you wasting your time wading through a bunch of old dusty box files. We've already, uh, solved this case. The coroner has already returned a verdict."

Lawson and I exchanged another look. Was he being condescending or obstructionist, or was he merely a lazy functionary in a department that had become complacent? And which of those was the more interesting answer?

"I'm sure your work has been exemplary, but we all have masters to serve and our boss wouldn't like us to come back without turning over every stone," I said diplomatically.

"Yes, I understand. For the sake of form. Yes, of course. But those files . . . they might not even be here. They might be in the records office in Reading. I know it's your right, Inspector, but if you insist upon it, it might take a while and it's going to put a lot of people out."

He was starting to grow on me, this Atkins. He'd been playing his part quite well for the last two hours. That "Daffy" sign at the airport. The inane chatter. But he had mettle. They had picked a good one when they selected him for the delicate operation of dealing with the invading Paddies.

I nodded at Lawson, *Your turn again, son.*

"Constable Atkins, even if it was an accidental overdose there's still the question of who supplied Miss Coleman with the heroin. Was anyone with her when she injected herself? Did she really inject herself? Who were the witnesses? Who were her roommates? What did her parents know? We will definitely need to see the case files. We can't possibly just go on the coroner's report and what we've read in the *News of the World*, can we?"

Good job, Lawson.

"Well, I shall certainly pass your request on to the CID. Like I say, the records may be in Reading."

Like fuck they are, son, I almost blurted out.

"But if they're not we'll need them by tomorrow morning in an office," Lawson said.

"I shall endeavor to do my best."

"Excellent."

I got out of the car and we got our bags from the boot.

"And once the business end of your trip is out of the way you lads should really avail yourselves of the opportunity to enjoy a couple of days off from what must be a very stressful job over there. If, uh, half of what we see on the news is true. Like I say, London is very close."

"If we get the time," I said.

"Do you want me to help you in with your bags?"

"No, we'll manage."

"Until tomorrow, then. A pleasure to meet you both."

"The pleasure's ours, I'm sure."

He drove off.

"What do you think, Lawson?"

"Seems like a nice place."

"Of Atkins."

"Oh, I don't know. A bit of a fool?"

"You think so?"

"You don't, Inspector Duffy?"

"I'm not so sure they would have sent an idiot to liaise with us on such a sensitive matter."

"Perhaps not."

"Not unless they consider us to be even bigger fools. But he was nervous, though, wasn't he? And he wasn't telling us everything."

"How do you know that, sir?"

"Because nobody ever tells you *everything*. We'll go deeper tomorrow. The German gets kicked out of the university and his name is in the papers, the Mick gets kicked out of the university and his name is in the papers, but the third man gets to keep his anonymity and presumably continues with his brilliant career. A lot at stake for that bloke, eh?" I said.

"Yes, sir."

"I've never been terribly fond of conspiracy theories, but even if a crime hasn't been committed, even if this is a wild goose chase, the last thing Thames Valley want are a couple of Mick detectives blundering in and digging up God knows what, eh, Lawson?"

Up the steps to the B&B.

If there was a theme to the place then the theme would have been Claustrophobic Edwardian: chintzy carpets, uncomfortable chairs, lace, porcelain cats, real cats, Hummel figurines, clocks, ornate candle-holders, scented candles, gloomy portraits of severe young women.

In through the hallway to a little desk with a bell. *The Archers* coming from enormous stereo speakers mounted over William Morris–style wallpaper.

I dinged the bell and a little old woman and her pointy-headed son appeared Mr. Benn-like from a side room. She was dressed in a blue cardigan and an apron that said Martini on it. He was got up like a 1950s teddy boy. "A pair of lovable eccentrics," someone had written in the guest book. I didn't like the sound of that.

I introduced myself and Lawson. She looked us up and told us that we were expected and that all expenses had been paid. That board included breakfast but not lunch or dinner. That there were to be no guests after 10 p.m. That we had to be in no later than 11:15; otherwise we would be forced to pay an unspecified penalty. That all local and UK phone calls had to be paid for. That international calls were not allowed except in emergencies.

"That sounds reasonable," I said.

She held out a pen.

"Inspector Sean Duffy," I wrote in the book. She didn't notice the

"Inspector," but the name and the accent gave her a fond memory: "Of course, in my late husband's time we had a strict rule about Irishmen. He was very particular. Do you remember that, Jeffrey?"

"No Irish, no West Indians," Jeffrey said.

"Oh yes, he was very particular was my Kenneth. You knew where he stood."

"He was stood over there at the old bar, mostly," Jeffrey said, and he and his mother both chuckled.

"Now, Mr. Duffy, it's the off-season at present, of course, so I can let you have the two rooms overlooking the garden—213, 214," she said. "Keep the windows closed, mind. The squirrels will come in. We had a shocking incident two years ago with a gentleman from Norway."

"Windows closed to keep out the squirrels. I'll remember that," I said, and, resisting the urge to inquire further about the "shocking incident," took the keys.

Mrs. Brown gave me a smile and in a confidential tone added: "These days, of course, it's the Pakistanis who are the real trouble-makers, God love them. You wouldn't think it, but they are. It's the drink. They're not used to it. Oh dearie me no."

"I don't think you'll have any problem with us," I said, picking up my suitcase and putting the bottle of whiskey under one arm.

We went upstairs to a narrow landing.

"Half an hour to freshen up and then we'll get some food, OK, Lawson?" I said.

The lad nodded.

I put the key in the lock and went into the room. More faux William Morris wallpaper, a thick, dirty-looking, red carpet, an old-fashioned, uncomfortable-looking bed. Thick, mahogany dresser. New TV. Ancient radio. Push-up window that overlooked a rather lovely garden.

I undid the swivel lock and opened the window. An oak tree. A square of lawn. A tabby cat walking along a wall. An innocent-seeming squirrel sitting on a tree branch looking at me. I took in the autumnal air and, remembering to close the window, lay down on the heaving, springy bed.

I called Sara at the *Belfast Telegraph*. She answered on the third ring.

"Sara Prentice, Women's Page."

"Guess where I am?"

"Who is this?"

"It's Sean."

"Where are you?"

"I'm in England."

"What are you doing over there?"

"I'm on a case. The same case actually. Michael Kelly."

"Really? I thought that was a suicide?"

"There may be further developments."

"You'll keep me abreast of those developments, though, right?"

"Well, I've got to keep a lid on everything at the moment, but if something big's going to happen, you'll be the first to know."

"Definitely keep me informed. You can call me any time . . . Look, Sean, I'm a bit swamped—"

"I'll let you go. I'll see you when I get back, yeah?"

"Sure."

Phone in cradle.

She couldn't have got rid of me quicker.

Bathroom.

Reflection.

Cadaverous cheeks, pale complexion, grey hairs, dull-witted, sleep-deprived eyes.

TV on. Carol's numbers: 25, 50, 75, 100, 3, 6. The target was 952.

No point in even trying.

Cold shower.

Walkman. Fast-forwarding through a Pogues knock-off band mix tape until I got the exact song I wanted:

> *Like the six men in Birmingham or the four in Guilford town,*
> *The Old Bill will lift you and beat your knackers down,*
> *The filth will get promotion and you'll be up the farm,*
> *Your crime was being Irish, tho' you've done no one any harm . . .*

Yeah, I know. A little on the nose. A little obvious. But you had to be there lying on the chintzy bed with that dick Atkins' smug smile still in your cerebral cortex.

I flipped on the TV and put the news on mute. The pictures were of young men in masks throwing stones and Molotovs in Belfast. I turned it off.

The phone was ringing. Sara? Push-back from Oxford CID? Neither.

"Hello?"

"Sean, you're in Oxford!" It was Kate Albright from MI5.

"Yes."

"What are you doing over here?"

"A case. I still work for the RUC, you know."

"But you're thinking about our offer?"

"How did you find me? Are you watching me?"

"No! Of course not! . . . Well, maybe a little. Do you want to have dinner tonight?"

"Are you over here too?"

"Naturally. I'm at Chicksands. A little conference I'm running."

"What's Chicksands?"

"Oh . . . you don't want to know. It's only up the road, though. Not a million miles away. Shall I treat you?"

"It's awkward . . . I'm with one of my trainee detective constables."

"Is the redoubtable Sergeant McCrabban with you?"

"How do you even know about him?"

"I know a surprising amount about you and your colleagues, Sean."

"That doesn't fill me with comfort."

"It shouldn't. Are you on a per diem?"

"No, not really, it's . . ."

"That settles it. I know this wonderful little brasserie in North Oxford. I'll meet you all at the Eagle at seven."

"No, really—"

"Bye, Sean!" and with that she hung up.

"Bugger," I said, and, smiling, I put the phone back in its cradle.

13: GUN STREET GIRL

The front room of the Eagle and Child. A pint for Lawson, a vodka tonic for me. A sour, sawdusty smell. Obnoxious, good-looking male students. Ridiculously pretty female students.

With a pint of Theakston's already in him Lawson was displaying a not completely lovable chatty streak. "Big fan of Tolkien, actually," he was saying. "Not so much for your man Lewis though. Bit too heavy on the God stuff for me . . . Same again, Inspector?"

"Why not."

When he came he was carrying two pints and two packets of crisps and no vodka tonic. He took a big hungry gulp of his beer and launched straight back in: "Both of them were in the trenches—1917. Explains a lot. The violence, obviously. Lewis liked allegory. Aslan is Jesus, you know? Tolkien hated the form. He wanted to write an alternative mythology of Europe. People thought he was talking about the Nazis but he wasn't, he wasn't."

"Fascinating. You're a smart lad. How come you never went to uni, Lawson?" I asked.

"Well, as I explained, sir, my heart was set on getting in here, and, uhm, I screwed up the interview. A-levels were coming up . . . and then the RUC recruitment officers came round the school and they said if I got an A and two Bs I could be inducted straight into the CID after the usual training and stuff."

"And what did you get in your A-levels?" I asked, pretending that I hadn't already read his personnel file.

"I got three As. Four actually. Bit of a cheat, though, as I did maths and further maths. So, you know, it was a job and money and if I put in ten years I reckon I can always go back to uni as a mature student."

I shook my head. "Nah, once you're hooked you're hooked, mate. You'll do twenty and at the end of that you'll be too burned out to do anything else. Spend the rest of your days fishing or playing golf. Either that or become a promotion junkie and try to make your way up the greasy pole: Chief Superintendent, Assistant Chief Constable, Chief Constable, knighthood."

"I'm not interested in promotion. I just want to do good for the community."

"Doing good, eh? I used to think like that. First month I'm on the job old Dickie Bently takes me aside to explain what 'emotional leverage' is. Have you heard of that term, Lawson?"

"No, sir."

"It's where you arrest a family member for a minor outstanding warrant to get information on your real suspect. Dickie explained by showing. Arrested a widowed father with four kids for a bum check he'd passed three years earlier. The dad was climbing the walls. Youngest was two years old and in the house alone. Course, Dickie arrested him under the Prevention of Terrorism Act: no phone call, no lawyer. We broke the dad and he told us all about his brother-in-law who was fencing stolen goods for the Provos. Dickie schooled me pretty quick in the ways of getting things done. It's not just 'doing good'; sometimes it's doing bad too for the greater good, Lawson. It's a bastard of a job."

"Yes, sir," Lawson agreed glumly.

"And it's not just—" I began, but at that moment Kate waltzed into the Eagle and Child bringing an autumnal breeze, golden leaves, and a slight hint of perfume. She was wearing a tartan skirt and a sweater. Her hair was tightly coiffured. She kissed me on the cheek and introduced herself as an old friend. Lawson bought it but Crabbie would have been more dubious.

I gave Lawson a tenner and told him to get another round in. Kate wanted a gin and tonic—easy on the tonic.

When he'd gone Kate patted me on the knee.

"This is a nice surprise," she said affectionately.

"Surprise I don't think."

"He seems like a pleasant young man."

"Lawson? He's the one you should be trying to recruit. Pretty sharp and green enough to be malleable."

"It's lovely, isn't it, Oxford? Such a small world too. Last time I was here I was behind Iris Murdoch at Tesco."

"She doesn't seem the Tesco type," I said skeptically.

"So, what's this case you're working on?"

"As if you don't know that too."

She smiled coyly. "Well, I did poke around a little bit. I hope you're not going to make waves over here, Sean."

"Are there waves to make?"

"There are always waves to make."

"Young Lawson thinks that the Thames Valley Police may be protecting an important member of the British establishment in the Anastasia Coleman case."

"And you? What do you think?"

"As usual, Kate, I have an open mind."

"Well, you're the detectives, not me, but frankly it sounds preposterous. The tabloids were all over that case."

Lawson returned with the drinks.

"Were your ears burning, sweetie? We were just talking about you," Kate said.

"You were?" he said, coloring quickly.

"Sean tells me that you think that the Thames Valley Constabulary may be conspiring to keep the truth from the public in the tragic case of Anastasia Coleman."

Lawson looked at me to see whether it was OK to say anything.

"Kate works in, uh, law enforcement; you can speak freely in front of her," I assured him.

Lawson told her his theory about Count Habsburg and Michael Kelly being the fall guys, but the mysterious "third man" getting off scot-free. A third man who, as a member of the Round Table Club, was a future mover and shaker or the son of a current mover and shaker.

Kate smiled and took a generous sip of her G&T. "Nothing would shock me about the Thames Valley Constabulary, but how they would have pulled the wool over the eyes of the coroner in the Anastasia Coleman affair is beyond me. Sir Bradford Wells was in Colditz, so I doubt very much whether he would have been successfully intimidated by a few bobbies in the Oxford police."

Was that the reason for our little rendezvous tonight? To warn us off officially? Or was she speaking *obiter dicta*? Simply giving her own opinion. She was a very difficult woman to read.

She smiled and finished her drink. "I'll get the next one, lads."

We finished the next round and Kate led us outside. The light rain had stopped and the street was full of people. That feeling again. That this was the normal world. A world without bombs and terrorists and suspicious packages. All these young people out having a good time. Carefree. Happy. No undercurrent. No tension. No sectarian cold war. It felt weird.

"Do we need a taxi?" I asked, spotting a black cab.

"No, no. We'll walk."

We hoofed it up the Banbury Road to a place called Andre's.

It was quite exclusive, and Lawson and I felt underdressed in our sports jackets and shirts. No one actually offered to give us a tie, but we were the only men in the place without them.

Kate seemed to be well-known to Patrice, the elderly maître d'. She spoke to him in French, a tongue both Lawson and I knew well enough to understand our introduction as "her two gallant, handsome comrades in arms."

An aperitif was produced along with three menus. Kate did the ordering, and extravagant dish followed extravagant dish. The wine flowed freely too.

The waiters, who, as a species, customarily looked on me with neutrality or even veiled hostility, were positively nice.

"It's a fine old place, isn't it? I saw Benjamin Britten in here once when I was a girl. And my father told me that this is where Epstein took The Beatles after their audition with Decca. Stopped off on the way back from Liverpool," Kate said, winking at me.

"Look at you with the music references to get on my good side," I said to her appreciatively.

"Really, The Beatles? Here?" Lawson said, impressed.

"I have a bootleg of that Decca session. Couple of good Leiber and Stoller and Goffin and King numbers. You have a theory about The Beatles, don't you, Lawson?"

"Young Lawson seems to have theories about a lot of things," Kate murmured.

"Well, it's not so much a theory as an observation," he said.

"Go on."

"The *NME* had this piece about them being archetypes. You know? The funny one, the smart one, and so on, but it seems to me that people start off liking Paul, the nice, pretty one, but then as they mature they move on to the John stage—the thinker, the troublemaker; finally, as they get older, it's the George stage, the quest for spiritual meaning."

"There's no Ringo stage?" Kate asked.

"Maybe if they slip into dementia." Lawson said unkindly.

Booze. Good food. Convo. And by eleven o'clock we were the only customers left.

Lawson was hammered and I was swimming against the tide. Kate seemed unaffected. She paid with a check and complimented the staff on their discreet service. *"C'est une grande habileté que de savoir cacher son habileté,"* she said.

The waiter bowed.

"Come on, Sean, let's get your young friend home first."

With some difficulty we got Lawson back to the B&B. I expected trouble from Mrs. Brown or her son, but neither of them was anywhere to be found. The cats were on guard.

We carried Lawson to his room. I took his shoes off and put him in the recovery position.

He was groaning now.

Not surprising, really, since we had consumed nearly five bottles of wine between us.

"If you're gonna hurl try and make it to the bathroom, but if you really can't make it I've put a wastepaper basket next to your bed," I explained.

"Blurgh," he said.

We left him. "I'll see you out," I said.

Back downstairs through the feline minefield.

"My car's parked on Norham Gardens just round the corner. Walk with me."

"All right."

The cool night air was clearing my head now. Kate had taken off her shoes and was walking in her bare feet. She was happy, relaxed. She produced a little camera from a bag and asked a student to take a photograph of us to "commemorate the occasion."

I fake-smiled, she smiled for real, the shutter clicked, the moment was saved.

"This way," Kate said, and led me down a beautiful tree-lined street.

"You seem to know Oxford quite well. I suppose you went here for university?"

"I didn't go to this or to any other university."

"So how did you get into MI5?"

"I was recruited into the Security Service through a friend of my father's."

"They scooped you right up, like Lawson, after your A-levels?"

"I didn't do A-levels either, thank God. They sound like bloody awful things."

"Didn't you go to school at all?"

"I did the baccalaureate. In Switzerland."

"Oh, you're from money, then?" I said, trying to be ironic.

"Ah, here's my car. Hop in. We'll go for a spin."

The car was an ancient TR7. She skidded out of the parking spot and gassed it up the Banbury Road at 50 mph.

"Let's put our seat belts on, eh? When the inevitable crash comes I don't want to be the only survivor. The cops hate it when the man survives and the woman dies."

"I'm not sure this thing has a seat belt."

"Where are we going anyway?"

"Home."

"I don't think that's a good idea, do you?"

"Don't worry. Daddy won't be there. He hates England in November."

"Is it nearby? I'm supposed to be making an early start tomorrow. It'll make a bad impression if I show up late and hung over."

"It's nearby."

We drove out of Oxford along the Woodstock Road and then along the A4095 past Blenheim. This was really the middle of nowhere: no street lamps, just two narrow lanes of country road with tall hedgerows and catseyes down the middle of the tarmac.

"What are you doing over here, Kate?" I asked.

"I told you. I'm running a little conference at Chicksands."

"About Northern Ireland?"

"As a matter of fact, yes. Things are very finely balanced at the moment."

"Things are totally chaotic at the moment."

"Not really. On the surface, perhaps. But underneath . . ."

"Underneath, what exactly?"

"Movement. But it's fragile, delicate. We have to be cautious. We can't go blundering around stirring things up, can we?"

I looked at her. Was that another hint about me and this case?

We turned right down a single-lane road called Gun Street.

"Gun Street?" I asked.

"Used to be an old arsenal. Daddy's family owned it, fast friends with the Dukes of Marlborough, dontcha know."

"Nice."

"Not really. The Churchills, with one exception, have always been crashing bores."

Daddy's house turned out to be a fairly large pile in the country.

It wasn't exactly Brideshead, but it wasn't a cottage in the Cotswolds either: an eclectic, almost eccentric Victorian mansion with Indian red sandstone bricks, large Gothic windows, and a ridiculous mansard roof. There was a formal garden, a bit of woodland, and a classical folly that you could just make out in the moonlight.

"Hideous, ain't it?" Kate said.

"Well—"

"Daddy's great-uncle built it. A pastiche of something certainly, but we never could figure out what exactly."

"Your father's great-uncle?"

"Great-great-uncle Max. He made a lot of money in India. Please don't ask how."

"How?"

"Sean, whenever someone says don't ask how their antecedents made their money in the colonies, it's always either opium or slavery . . . Come on, this way."

We walked over a freshly tarred driveway and pushed the doorbell.

"Jesus, don't you have a key? We'll wake everyone up."

"There is no everyone. I told you, Daddy's in Italy."

She rang the doorbell again. A light went on in one of the downstairs rooms and a plump, elderly, dark-haired woman in a housecoat opened the door.

"Kate!" the woman said, and she and Kate embraced.

"Bea, this is my friend, Sean. Sean, this is my dearest friend in all the world, Bea!"

"Nice to meet you," I said.

"I'll put the kettle on and turn out your room, Miss Kate," Bea said.

"Don't put yourself to any trouble," Kate insisted.

"Are you hungry at all?" Bea asked.

"Not remotely. We've stuffed ourselves like pigs."

"Lovely."

"This way, Sean," Kate said, and led me through a chilly, portrait-lined hall into a large but rather squalid kitchen. Dishes swam in a sink of brown water, bread and cheese crumbs littered an enormous oak table. Black pans hung from hooks on the sooty brickwork. I sat down on a chair that had been worn smooth and comfortable over the generations while Bea and Kate busied themselves making a pot of tea.

"I'll take it from here, Bea," Kate said when the boiling water finally made it into the teapot.

"I'll sort out your room," Bea said, and then added in a lower cadence, "or should that be rooms?"

"Room," Kate said firmly.

"Very good," Bea replied, and scuttled off upstairs.

The tea was ridiculously strong, and although the biscuits came from a tin marked Fortnum and Mason, they were soggy and tasteless.

"Have you got any milk?" I asked.

"I doubt it," Kate said without looking.

"Sugar?"

"Somewhere, I'm sure. Come on, drink up."

I put some of the foul brew to my lips and pretended to drink.

A little bell rang next to the fireplace.

"All right, let's go up," Kate said.

I put down the teacup and followed her up a dimly lit staircase to the second floor. It was freezing up here and damp. Draughty windows, bare bulbs, more gloomy portraits in the shadows.

"How do you like the old place? I'm hardly ever here now that I've relocated to Rathlin Island. Not as cozy, but it has its own charms, don't you think?"

"Well—"

"I always feel that it's a bit like something from an M. R. James story. And there is a ghost too. Bea's seen her. And Willis, who used to do the garden, said she was a right shocker . . . Ah, this is my room."

We went into a large bedroom with a high ceiling painted with blue stars and walls painted a deep, pillar-box red. There were ancient rugs on the floor, a small library filled with books, a beautiful old dressing table, a gorgeous secretary-style writing desk, and a walk-in clothes cupboard. An ancient, comfortable-looking, four-poster bed dominated the rear of the room.

"Bathroom's along the landing. Bea will have turned the bulb on so you can see the light under the door."

"I think I'll make use of . . ."

"I'll go after you. If you see her, the ghost is called Margaret."

I went along the spooky corridor, had a slash in the flush toilet, came back.

"See her?" Kate asked.

"No."

"That's good. Wait here. I'll be back in a sec . . . you can take your clothes off if you like."

"Are we sleeping in the same—"

But she was gone.

I took my kit off and got under the covers.

Kate came back and started taking her own clothes off.

"Good. Now listen to me, Sean. This is highly unprofessional, I hope you realize that. I'm not encouraging this sort of behavior at all. We're not cowboys. We have an HR department and rules just like everyone else," she said.

"I understand."

"Good. Kiss me, then."

"All right."

We made love in the cold bed.

It was hurried and desperate and *good*.

It was something we had both wanted for a long time, and she had realized this before I had.

She opened an antique cigarette case and fished out a couple of ancient Gauloises. The traditional short, wide, unfiltered Gauloises made with dark tobaccos from Syria and Turkey.

"I'm so glad we've got that out of the way, aren't you?" she said.

"Well, I wouldn't put it quite like—"

"You speak Irish, don't you, Sean?"

"Yes."

"I've been trying to learn but I have no aptitude for languages. Give me a quick burst."

"*Tá gile na dtonn, is uaigneas an domhain i ngleic*, says Louis de Paor."

"Meaning?"

"The brightness of the sea and the loneliness of the world grappling in my father's green eyes."

"Hmmm. The lingo may come in useful when you come to work for us."

"If I come to work for you."

She smiled and kissed me and lay in my arms. We finished our ciggies and lay in the big bed and fell asleep to a strange, far-off sound.

The icy leak of the future into the present.

The *thud, thud, thud, thud* of Chinook helicopter blades . . .

14: EVEN THE WASPS CANNOT FIND MY EYES

*ee me running. Running through the woods of the high bog. See me in
*the snow. In the Woodburn Forest, a dog barking, the body of a hanged
girl swaying in the wind. Those rolled-back-in-head eyes. Those blue lips.
The smell of piss and shit. Dog barking. Silent cops. Stuff of nightmares.
Stuff of night—*
"Wake up, Sean, it's a quarter to seven."
"What?"
"Come on! Breakfast is on the table."
"Where am I?"
"Daddy's house. Near Blenheim."
"Yeah. Jesus."
The dream was an old case. A girl who was murdered by an MI5
agent, a man who I went all the way to Italy to kill. That's the sort of
person I'd be dealing with if I took her job.
I rubbed the sleep out of my eyes.
"Breakfast, yes."
Downstairs.
Breakfast was toast and marmalade and cornflakes. Bea fussing
about us. Kate reading a stack of her father's correspondence. The
kitchen fireplace burning coal.
Two unread copies of the *Daily Telegraph* and the *Times*.
We said good-bye to Bea and thanked her. Back along the country
road to Oxford. Kate listening to Radio 3. Not talking because we were
both hung over.
"Here you are, Sean."
The B&B.
"Thank you. For everything."

A smile. "Good luck with your investigation. Word of advice. Don't rock the bloody boat."

Upstairs. Cat maze. Lawson still asleep. The worse for wear.

I led him to the shower.

"Shower, get dressed, meet me downstairs."

I got a coffee down his neck.

Nine o'clock now.

I asked for directions to the Oxford City Police HQ.

Mrs. Brown got me a tourist map. It was all the way at the other end of town next to the Crown Court.

The walk would do us good.

Cold out. Freezing. Wind cutting through us like a knife through pie crust.

Students. School kids. Civilians.

Everyone on bikes.

We finally made it to the police HQ on St Aldate's. Lawson looked slightly less green.

A quiet little police station. No one wearing body armor, no one wearing side arms, no stench of fear. This was what policing was like over the water. This was policing in civilization. These guys didn't know how lucky they had it. Burglaries, stolen bicycles, the odd rape, a murder every five or ten years—the real Morse World.

Atkins was there to meet us alongside a detective chief inspector called Boyson.

"We came in early and looked out all the files and documents you might possibly need, Inspector Duffy. We've set you up with your own office. Coffee and sandwiches will be on hand. Constable Atkins is at your disposal," Boyson said.

"Thank you very much. That's great."

"If you've any questions at all, please don't hesitate to ask."

Handshakes. Smiles. Atkins led us to the room. And sure enough, everything: Case files, case notes, the coroner's report, evidence bags, the ME report, individual police officer logs, the desk sergeant's blotter,

interview tapes. My little crack about the Chief Constable had scared
the bejesus out of them.

After Atkins and Boyson had gone I poured more coffee down
Lawson's throat.

He was finally in the land of the living.

"You see what they've done to us, Lawson?"

"No."

"They don't want to be accused of withholding evidence, of starting
an inter-force scandal, so they've given us absolutely everything. Do
you see?"

"Uhm . . ."

"It could be they're trying to bury the relevant info in a blizzard of
detail."

"Yes, sir."

"This lot will take us all morning."

It did, and much of the afternoon.

We conference-called McCrabban with our results. What came
out at the inquest appeared to be more or less the truth. Anastasia
Coleman had died of a heroin overdose in the rented North Oxford
home of Count Habsburg after a party given by the Round Table Club.
Also in the home that morning were Michael Kelly and an unidenti-
fied male who, according to Kelly and Habsburg, "slipped out after
the body was found but before the police arrived." Neither Kelly nor
Habsburg knew who the male was, but Habsburg had given a description to the police of a white male, about 11 stone, 5 foot 10 inches tall,
black wavy hair, rounded face, public-school English accent. The police
had circulated an artist's sketch of the male and canvassed partygoers,
the Round Table Club, and the Oxford colleges, but there had been no
takers. Or rather, a lot of false alarms but no leads that had panned out.

In the Oxford CID report the third man seemed to be a red
herring anyway. The third man was almost certainly not the person
who had either supplied or injected her with heroin. There were multiple eyewitness testimonies that Anastasia was an adept and experienced junkie: a smack cook from her very first year at Oxford. She was

an established intravenous user and had injected friends and boyfriends on several occasions; a skill she had presumably learned during a gap year that she had spent mostly in South-East Asia.

The ME, crime scene, and autopsy photographs showed an emaciated, hollow-eyed girl covered with track lines. Anastasia was racing toward her rendezvous with death, and even if she'd survived that particular night and that particular party, you didn't fancy her chances of making old bones.

Still, none of that was our concern.

Our concern was Michael Kelly and his role in the affair.

The Michaelmas term was ending so we had to move fast before the students left college. We tracked down Anastasia's classmates, friends, and her college tutor. We showed our warrant cards, and everyone answered our questions even though we had no *de jure* authority.

Didn't matter. People wanted to talk. Lovely girl. Shame. So quiet. So gentle. Lovely. Dreamy. Off in her own world. Not much of a student. Not really a party girl as a matter of fact. Not wild. Reflective. Wrote poems. Big fan of Sylvia Plath and Anne Sexton.

Interview with Colin Prenderghast, the chief inspector who ran the local drug squad. "Where would a girl like Anastasia get heroin around here?"

"Not so easy around here. But London is only sixty minutes away by express bus."

"You ever find Anastasia's dealer?"

"No. But she was rich. She had contacts. We found trace amounts of heroin and cocaine in her car, and in her rooms at Somerville she had an ounce of Turkish brown tar heroin stashed away in a hollowed-out economics book."

"Who doesn't?"

My joke not appreciated. My jokes seldom appreciated.

And it wasn't really a joke anyway, more of a confession.

Michael Kelly's mates had mostly graduated, but several people remembered him with affection. A good egg. Not such a brilliant student, "but a total waster."

We got a list of names of the secretive Round Table Club, but the interviews with them were unproductive. Most of the club were freshers who hadn't been at Oxford when Anastasia had died, and for the remaining members *omertà* was the order of the day. They hadn't been at the party that night, they had alibis, they didn't know who was there. It was not a completely officially sanctioned Round Table Club event, so there were no records . . .

Michael's college tutor spoke well of him. Not terribly hard working, not what you'd call brilliant, but applied himself and was pleasant enough.

"Popular?"

"Indeed. Yes. Didn't row but was in the right clubs. He was charming and a little bit dangerous. He was always one step ahead of the proctors. Until, of course, the fateful party . . ."

We spent the next day chasing down leads, conducting interviews, looking at angles, but there was nothing new. No signs of conspiracy. Oxford CID and the Thames Valley Constabulary depressingly competent.

Third day. Breakfast at the B&B. Toast and marmalade. Silver-top milk and cornflakes. Terry Wogan on in the background. Mrs. Brown hovering. A squirrel looking in the window.

Morning going through files.

Lawson found a meticulously photocopied copy of Anastasia's personal diary. Initial excitement as we read it together. But there was nothing of real interest. A few hasty entries. Lecture notes. Tutorial times. On the day before her death she had copied a few lines from Anne Sexton, but there were no revelations from the gates of death.

Doors open. Visitors. Superintendent Smith, Chief Inspector Boyson, Constable Atkins.

"How is everything, gentlemen?" asked Superintendent Smith, a tall Basil Fawltyish man in a grey suit.

"Good, thanks," I replied.

"Everything up to the high standards of the RUC?"

No attempt to hide the sarcasm.

Grins.

Sniggers.

Even some outright laughter in our faces.

Gave Lawson the afternoon off. Walked up Norham Gardens to the house Gottfried Habsburg had rented on Fyfield Road—his pad while he was at the university. Bikes outside, students going in and out. Followed one of the students in. A communal living room. TV chairs, bean-bag chairs. No aura. No feel. Nothing to see here.

Back downtown. Martyrs' Memorial. Roman emperors' heads. Blackwell's bookshop. Michael Foot peering in the bookshop window. That stick, that haircut: unmistakable.

Inside. "Where's the poetry section?"

"Just over there to the left. All the way against the wall. There's new stuff by Christopher Logue and Geoffrey Hill. A display."

"Oh yeah?"

"And of course we're stocking up on Philip Larkin in light of . . ." sotto voce "you know, on his last legs . . . cancer . . . no chance."

I looked under S and found *The Complete Poems* of Anne Sexton. I flipped to the back cover and discovered that she was a glamorous, intelligent, good-looking brunette. It was ten quid but I bought it anyway and walked to the Bear Inn off the High Street. I ordered a pint of Fullers and sat down by the window. Rummaged in my briefcase, took out a picture of Anastasia Coleman in her sixth-form uniform. Before the gap year. Before the H. Bright girl, clever eyes, dimples. A good daughter. Destined to go far.

I opened the Sexton book in the middle. A nice line about suicides having a special language: "like carpenters" they want to know which tools, "they never ask why build . . ." As the book went on the poems about death and the methods of achieving death grew thicker. A poem entitled "Sylvia's Death" seethed with anger at Sylvia Plath managing to escape life first. A poem called "Suicide Note" spoke of taking an elevator into hell where "even the wasps cannot find my eyes." It was heady stuff. Comforting, perhaps, if you were a junkie on a nightly elevator ride down into the depths unsure if you were ever coming back.

I closed the book, left the pint half drunk. I found Lawson at the B&B listening to The Archers with the Browns, a cat purring on his lap.

"Let's get out of this town," I said.

"Home?" he asked hopefully.

"Not yet. Let's go to London. Let's interview the German."

"OK," he said.

15: GOTTFRIED HABSBURG

He had a reputation as a louche aristocrat, but we found Habsburg working as a stockbroker at a respectable City firm and living with an elderly uncle at a nice, large but rather run-down house by Hampstead Heath. I called to make an appointment and Gottfried said that he would take the day off to talk to us.

He was a slight young man with blond hair, blue-grey eyes, and high cheekbones. He was dressed in a dark, formal suit. His English was excellent, his manners impeccable. A valet brought us coffee in a large sitting room stuffed with books.

I told him about the suspicions that had arisen after Michael Kelly's supposed suicide and explained why we were looking into Anastasia Coleman's death again. I laid it all on the line for him: a conspiracy, the third man, police incompetence, Michael Kelly as the fall guy who knew too much . . .

Lawson looked horrified as I spilled all of our pet theories to this stranger/material witness/potential conspirator. Sometimes it's best to keep all the pertinent information from an interview subject, sometimes it's better to tell them everything you know or suspect, and most of the time you follow Aristotle and take the middle road between these poles. Each case is a discrete entity. With the pleasant young Gottfried I felt that candor and forthrightness would get the job done. With the past behind him, our presence would be an unpleasant shock, but if we were ingratiating and explained that he was a tangential element in a wider investigation, it might be enough to get his lips moving. And if it wasn't, well, you could always dial it up. RUC men were experts at dialing it up . . .

"So you can see why we'd appreciate your cooperation in this matter, Mr., er, Herr—"

"Gottfried, please."

"Gottfried. The last thing we want to do is drag up painful memories. I know you've cooperated with Thames Valley Police and the coroner, but you can see that what happened with Anastasia might have some bearing on Michael Kelly's tragic death. Perhaps Michael knew the identity of the third man at your party. Perhaps he was being blackmailed into revealing this individual's identity. Perhaps he was the one doing the blackmailing. Maybe this has nothing at all to do with his death. There are many potential variables which we will need to eliminate from our inquiries."

Gottfried stroked his chin and stubbed out his cigarette.

"You think Michael may have been killed to keep this man's identity a secret?"

"Who knows? If there was a blackmail scheme, someone may have killed Michael to keep him silent," Lawson said.

"It's baroque, I'll grant you, but not beyond the realms of possibility," I added.

"Then I too may be in danger?" Gottfried asked, his eyes widening slightly.

Lawson and I exchanged a glance. "Only if you know the man's name. Do you know the man's name?"

Gottfried looked at the floor.

"Sir? Do you know the man's name?"

Gottfried closed his eyes and shook his head, but there was no reeling it back in now.

"Let me make myself perfectly clear, sir. I am asking you if you know the name of the man who was with you and Michael Kelly the morning Anastasia Coleman died? Do you understand what I'm asking?"

Gottfried nodded.

"Well?"

"Am I being compelled to tell you?" Gottfried asked.

"It is a murder inquiry, Gottfried. Michael Kelly is dead; you are required to cooperate with us," I said, although, of course, this wasn't strictly true.

Gottfried lit another cigarette.

"Sir, if we have to, we'll arrest you and bring you to Northern Ireland and interview you there," Lawson said, his powers of invention impressing me no end.

Gottfried blew out a line of cigarette smoke.

He sighed.

Silence.

One beat, two, three.

"Sir?"

"But you see, there is still the question of honor," Habsburg said.

"Is the man you are protecting an honorable man? Would the gentleman you are protecting do the same for you?"

Habsburg considered it. "I do not know."

"When the newspapers were attacking you, did he speak up? Did he offer to help you?"

"No."

"Has he offered to help you since?"

"No."

"Has he done one thing to help you clear your reputation?"

"No."

"What is his name?"

"You already know his name. Why must you make me confirm it?"

"What do you mean *we* already know his name?" I asked.

"You, the police."

"What police?"

"At the Oxford police station I was shown his picture and asked if this was the man."

Lawson and I exchanged another look.

"Oxford CID showed you a picture of the man who was in your house the morning of Anastasia Coleman's death?" I said.

"Yes."

"And you confirmed that it was him?"

"Yes."

"So Oxford CID already knows who he is?"

"Yes."

"And they kept this name out of the papers and kept him away from the inquest?"

"Naturally. He is very well connected."

"But how did it not come up at the inquest?" Lawson asked.

"The inquest was an extremely interesting experience. That too was a matter of honor. I had decided that if I was asked a direct question under oath about this person's identity I would tell the truth. But the situation never arose. The coroner was very careful not to ask me any direct questions about him."

"The whole thing was rigged!" Lawson said, shocked. "That Colditz guy was in on it."

Habsburg shrugged. "What difference could it make to have an innocent man's name dragged through the newspapers?"

"How do you know he was innocent?" I asked.

"Of course he was innocent. We all know what happened to Anna."

"What happened to her?"

"Anna died of a self-administered, heroin-cocaine speedball."

"Why self-administered?"

"She was the only one capable of injecting anyone with heroin at that party. Besides, everyone else was drinking champagne. My champagne. She was the only one who had heroin."

"Is that why you invited her to the party? Because she had heroin?"

"I didn't invite her. She came with this third person. They were old friends."

"Boyfriend and girlfriend?"

"No. I don't think so. Merely old friends."

I opened my notebook. "The name, sir," I said, dialing it up to maximum Scary West Belfast.

Habsburg took a long draw on his cigarette, sighed. "His name is Alan Osbourne."

Both Lawson and I wrote down the name in our books.

"What can you tell us about this Alan Osbourne?"

Gottfried sighed heavily and fiddled with the ashtray. I lit him another cigarette and pressed it between his fingers. "He was a third-year student. PPE. Brasenose. He has graduated now of course."

"How did you know him?"

"I knew him through the Round Table Club."

"British?"

"Yes."

"You don't happen to know where he is now, do you?"

"I do. He works for the government."

"The government?"

"He works for Conservative Central Office as a researcher. I saw him about two months ago in the Reform Club. One of the few clubs in London where I have not been blackballed. He did not acknowledge me."

Lawson and I were scribbling like mad.

"Did Michael Kelly know Alan Osbourne's name?" Lawson asked.

"I believe so. Although as far as I know he never told anyone."

Not surprising. Michael was from Belfast where the rule was: whatever you say, say nothing.

I scratched my head and lit another fag.

Lawson was still reeling. "Let me get this straight, Herr Habsburg. Are you suggesting that the Thames Valley Police told the coroner at the Anastasia Coleman inquest not to ask you or Michael Kelly any direct questions about the 'third man's' name?"

"I am not claiming anything. I am merely stating what happened. I was not upset about this. This is how things are done in a civilized country. My reputation was damaged as was that of Michael Kelly, but why damage the reputation of someone else?"

"But couldn't Mr. Osbourne have provided some insight into Anastasia's death?" Lawson asked.

"I doubt it. He must have been asleep when Anna injected herself."

"You actually saw her do it?" I asked.

"No, but as I have attempted to explain no one else was capable of such an action. At that stage of the party everyone had gone but Alan, Michael, and myself. Alan was asleep upstairs. He had drunk quite a bit."

"And then she went off to inject herself alone?" I ventured.

"Not quite."

"Please explain."

"She was . . . what is the word? An evangelist. An evangelist for the drug. She offered to inject Michael and myself but we declined. Both of us, however, were persuaded into smoking some of the heroin she cooked for us over tinfoil."

I flipped through my notebook and read back my careful notes from the last few days.

"Neither you nor Michael said any of this at the inquest."

"We weren't asked," Gottfried replied mechanically.

"So Miss Coleman gave you and Michael heroin before injecting herself?" Lawson asked.

"Yes."

"And Alan was there, but he didn't take the heroin because he was asleep?"

"Asleep or passed out."

"How did the subject of heroin come up?"

"Anna told us what she was going to do and Michael and I were curious. The way she described it: she said it was the greatest experience in the world. More beautiful than sex or anything else. She told us that she was going to inject herself with a speedball and offered us the experience, but with the caution that it might be dangerous for the novice. Michael had a fear of needles, and perhaps I was nervous too, so she showed us how to 'chase the dragon' off a piece of tinfoil. I tried it. I fell into a beautiful dream. In the morning when I awoke Anna was lying on the living-room sofa, dead."

"And then what happened?"

"I called 999 immediately, but it was obvious that Anna was beyond saving. She was cold. She had died some hours before. Relatively peacefully, I hope. I woke Alan and Michael and told them to get out of the house before the police came. Alan pulled on his clothes and left, but Michael said that he would stay and help me deal with the situation," Gottfried said with emotion.

"Alan left but Michael stayed," Lawson said, writing furiously.

"I told him not to be a bloody fool, but he insisted on 'facing the music'? Is that the expression?"

"Yes," I said absently. "Yes it is. Why would he do that, do you think?"

"He followed his own code of honor. He was an interesting fellow. He came from some money in Ireland, new money, I think, but he wasn't embarrassed about that. He did exactly as he pleased. He was very well liked . . ."

"Was there anyone else in the house that we don't know about?" I asked.

"No. That was it. Alan, Michael, and myself."

"When did you tell Oxford CID Alan's name?" I asked.

"I'm afraid I was not able to keep it a secret for very long. They questioned me for the entire day and night before my father found out what was happening and sent a solicitor from London."

"You told them Alan's name that day?"

"Not quite. I believe it was the early morning of the next day. I was very tired and quite emotional. I gave them the description first. A description which was all too accurate. The artist's rendering was uncanny. Have you seen it?"

"Yes."

"I was just so tired. And they kept asking the same questions again and again. And then they showed me Alan's photograph and I confirmed that he was indeed the third person in the house."

"So Oxford CID knew Alan's name from very early on in the investigation?" Lawson asked.

"Yes."

"A decision must have been taken at the highest levels of Oxford CID to protect Alan Osbourne," Lawson said, thinking aloud.

"Protection which worked and which has lasted a long time," I echoed.

Gottfried shrugged solemnly. "I wish I could have kept Michael out of it too. Poor chap. And now he is dead."

"Has anyone ever warned you about keeping Alan Osbourne's identity secret?"

"No."

"An implied threat. A direct threat. A warning?" Lawson asked.

"No, nothing like that. Ah, the coffee has grown cold. Would you gentlemen care for another pot?"

"No thank you. Just a few more questions, Herr Habsburg, and then we will need to get going. We've got a busy day ahead of us, I feel."

Half an hour later we were done. I told Gottfried to be careful and if he saw anything suspicious or felt himself in any danger he was to call the local police.

Gottfried told us that he had private security guards sent by his father who kept a very good watch on him. We thanked him for his cooperation and walked up the Highgate Road to hail a taxi.

16: THE THIRD MAN

Conservative Central Office was only a short twenty-minute taxi ride away from Hampstead Heath.

"How do you feel about conspiracy theories now, sir?" Lawson said a little too cheekily for my liking. But he was right to be cheeky and I didn't have an answer for him. Thames Valley had snowed the coroner and had attempted to snow us. Although it posed the obvious question, if Michael Kelly was murdered for what he knew, how come Gottfried had been allowed to live? How come no one had even put the fear of God in him? He'd told us about Alan Osbourne with almost no prompting at all. No rubber hose. No physical pressure.

"This is you, gov. I can't take you into Smith Square, proper, cos of the Old Bill," the taxi driver said. "You'll have to walk from here."

"I'm sure this will be fine."

We got out and paid and the taxi drove off.

I had absolutely no idea which building it was so I had to stop a passing policeman. "Excuse me, sir," I said, "we're looking for Conservative Central Office?"

The peeler looked at Lawson and myself with a jaundiced eye. I gave him the look right back. I noticed from his strange helmet that he was actually City of London Police, not Met.

"Conservative Central Office?" I asked again.

"And what would you two gentlemen want with Conservative Central Office?" he said with a suspicious tone.

It took me a beat or two to realize what his problem was.

His problem was my Belfast accent.

The IRA had almost killed Mrs. Thatcher and her cabinet the year before and here were a couple of Micks in a hurry looking for Conservative Central Office.

I showed him my warrant card but he still wasn't entirely convinced as he walked us through the security cordon to Smith Square.

Conservative Central Office was a charming, almost quaint, three-story, Georgian building. There was another bobby standing outside. We showed him our warrants and he let us in.

A receptionist paged Alan Osbourne for us and we waited in a pastel lobby under twin portraits of Mrs. Thatcher and the Queen.

Music was bubbling from concealed loudspeakers.

"Elgar?" Lawson guessed correctly.

"Yeah."

"It's nice."

I nodded. Elgar's all very well, but you wouldn't want to hear the bastard on a loop from nine to five every day.

"Look at those portraits," Lawson said. "Do you notice something funny about them?"

I looked first at the Queen and then Mrs. T. The Queen's picture was a copy of a portrait presumably done in the early seventies. Mrs. T.'s was a recent sitting and looked to be an original, but other than that I couldn't see anything odd about them.

"Thatcher's bigger by about three inches vertically and about six inches horizontally," Lawson said.

Observant wee shite.

"Oh yeah."

"He's keeping us waiting, isn't he?" Lawson said, looking at his watch.

My pager started to ring and I went up to the reception desk and asked to use the telephone.

I called Crabbie at Carrickfergus RUC.

"Detective Sergeant McCrabban."

"It's me. You paged me."

"Sean, where are you?"

"London."

"London? Look, mate, we really need you back here. There's been a development in the case."

"What development?"

"Remember Deirdre Ferris?"

"Who?"

"Sylvie McNichol's roommate."

"Oh, her. Oh God. Let me guess, now she's turned up dead, too."

"No. *She's* fine."

"What, then?"

"She got herself arrested for assault."

"Who'd she hit?"

"She went after some wee girl in Lavery's in Belfast. Glassed her in the face because the wee girl was supposedly flirting with her boyfriend. The girl's messed up. Plastic surgery, broken jaw, the whole bowling match."

"All very seedy, I'm sure, but what's this got to do with us?"

"So the cops at Queen Street RUC are telling her that she's looking at four years in prison and she says she doesn't want to do four years in prison. She says that she can help solve a murder and she asks to speak to detectives from Carrick RUC."

"This is getting interesting."

"It gets better. So they call me and I go up there and she says if I can grant her immunity she'll give me an important lead in the investigation. So I tell her to give me the lead first and I'll see what I can do . . ."

"Wise move. And? Come on, Crabbie, I'm on the edge of my seat here . . ."

"She tells me that she 'might have eyewitness testimony that could help the investigation.'"

"Very interesting."

"I didn't have the authority to offer her any kind of immunity deal, Sean, but I'm arranging to have her transferred here to Carrick RUC tonight, so you can question her and see if it's legit."

"Good work. We'll be back this evening. Make sure this young lady is not granted a bail hearing and is kept under your beady eye in your protective custody, OK?"

"OK. Any progress at your end?"

"A few things. I'll fill you in tonight."

"OK, Sean."

"See you later, mate."

I put down the phone and in a whisper told Lawson everything that McCrabban had told me.

Deirdre Ferris seemed to be on the verge of breaking the sacred Belfast code of silence, and if you were gonna sing, the only reason to sing was to save your own skin. Thank you, Deirdre Ferris's cheating boyfriend.

"So what do we do now?" Lawson asked.

"Well, we'll brace Mr. Osbourne for all we're worth. If there's no play here, we go back to Oxford, get our stuff, get back up to Birmingham International, and fly home."

"What do you think Osbourne will tell us?"

"I think we're about to find out."

A breathless, grinning, slightly chubby young man with longish black hair came confidently down the stairs. He was in his shirtsleeves, a blue tie, and black suit trousers. Future PM? Future foreign secretary? Future day trader who destroys an entire city bank and causes a mini-recession because of bad investments? Maybe all three.

He offered us his hand. "Alan Osbourne," he said. "Are you the gents from the *Mail on Sunday*?"

"No, we're not. We're detectives from the Royal Ulster Constabulary. I'm Detective Inspector Duffy and this is Detective Constable Lawson."

Alan looked confused.

He let his hand drop to his side.

"What's this about?" he asked.

"Is there somewhere we can talk privately?"

"Uhm. Sure. Yah. Conference room. Follow me. Sheena, will you bring us in some coffee?" he said to the receptionist in a very posh voice.

We sat down and showed him our warrant cards. He inspected them gravely and gave them back.

"So how I can help?" he asked.

"We're investigating the death under suspicious circumstances of one Michael Kelly. I believe he's known to you?"

Osbourne shook his head. "Michael Kelly, uhm, the . . . the, uhm, name doesn't ring a bell."

The tips of his ears were turning red as he spoke and he was sweating bullets. Osbourne was not an accomplished liar.

"He was at Oxford with you."

"Michael Kelly? Uhm, was he at my college?"

"He wasn't. But you were with him on at least one occasion. The night Anastasia Coleman died. On Fyfield Road in North Oxford at Gottfried Habsburg's rented home. There was a party there for the Round Table Club. Apparently most of the partygoers went back to their own digs and colleges, so only you and Gottfried Habsburg and Michael Kelly were left in the house that morning. All three of you found Anastasia Coleman's body, apparently with a needle still in her arm. Gottfried called the authorities and he and Michael decided to stay there and, quote, 'face the music,' unquote, but you thought that discretion was the better part of valor and hightailed it home. Is that an accurate depiction of events?"

The color had drained from his cheeks, his grin had become fixed and his eyes were glassy, almost teary.

"Mr. Osbourne?" I said softly.

He put his face in his hands.

"I'll be ruined! Father will be ruined."

"Oh no, Lawson, *Father* will be ruined," I said.

Osbourne looked at us like a hunted animal. "Oh my God! Gottfried, he must have . . . The Reform Club . . . I should have . . . I'll need a solicitor, won't I?"

"Sir, if you could just calm down and—"

"Wait a minute, wait a minute! I'm not under arrest! You haven't arrested me. I don't have to tell you anything, do I?"

"Mr. Osbourne, you are not under arrest. You are under no legal obligation to tell us anything. However, your cooperation in this matter would greatly benefit our inquiries. At the moment you are tangential to the Michael Kelly murder investigation. But, depending upon your level of cooperation in the next few minutes, you could instead become a major focus of our investigation. It would not at all be difficult to come back here this afternoon with several detectives from the Metropolitan Police and maybe even a few reporters from the *Mail on Sunday* or the *News of the World*," I said.

Osbourne was sweating now and he took out a large polka-dot handkerchief and mopped his forehead.

"My name won't necessarily have to come up at all, will it? If I tell you everything I know."

"If you tell us everything you know," I insisted.

"Whew. Well, then I suppose . . . well, I suppose I should say first of all how sorry I am to hear about Michael's death. I had no idea. I've been very busy."

"I'll be sure and tell Michael's next of kin how moved you were. Oh, wait, his next of kin got murdered too," I said.

"You were the 'third man' in the house on Fyfield Road that morning, then?" Lawson said.

"Yes . . . I was there. It was a Round Table Club—sanctioned event so I had to go."

"And Anastasia, she was your girlfriend?" I asked.

"Christ, no! Who told you that? She was trouble! Everybody knew that. She asked me to take her and I knew it would be less hassle to take her than to leave her, so I brought her along."

"How did you know her?"

"Her father and my father are friends. Known her since forever."

"What does your father do?"

"He's a banker. But . . . he's also a wheel in the party. Behind the scenes. Chairman of the constituency groups. You wouldn't have heard of him."

"Did he get you your present job here?" Lawson asked.

"I got a first in PPE. That's a pretty strong recommendation," Osbourne said defensively.

"If I could bring you back to the night of Anastasia Coleman's death. Tell me in your own words what happened," I said.

"I don't know what happened. I went to the party. It was up in North Oxford. I had a lot to drink. I didn't want to walk all the way back to Brasenose. Char— uhm, a friend of mine offered to drive me home but he was so plastered I thought it was safer to just crash at Habby's . . . Gottfried's, I mean."

"What happened then?"

"I fell asleep. Next thing I know Habby's waking me up and telling me that Anastasia is dead. I told him to call an ambulance but he'd already done that. He told me and Michael to make ourselves scarce. I took his advice and got out of there."

"And then what?"

"I left. Michael stayed to help Gottfried deal with everything. I don't know why he did that. I assumed it was some kind of Irish thing."

"And then?"

"Well, then . . . nothing."

"Did you ever get contacted by the Thames Valley Police?"

"No."

"The coroner's office? Reporters?"

"Couple of tabloid hacks were sniffing around the Round Table Club looking for gossip, but no one told them anything."

"You must have seen the artist's impression of yourself in the papers?"

"Yeah, all that third man stuff. I was shitting myself for a week or two."

"Did you have any contact with Michael or Gottfried after the party?"

"I never saw Michael again. I saw Gottfried at the Reform Club a couple of months ago. We didn't talk. I sort of avoided him."

"Do you have any idea why someone would have wanted to murder Michael Kelly?"

"No. I don't."

"Think about it for a minute or two before you answer."

He thought about it and shook his head.

"Has anyone tried to blackmail you about your involvement in Anastasia Coleman's death?"

"To tell you the truth, until you two came along I'd barely thought about it since I started here in September."

I looked at Lawson. He gave me a little nod. He was thinking the same thing: Osbourne was a scumbag, but an honest scumbag. Unless we were very much mistaken those chubby, boyish chops were the chubby, boyish chops of verisimilitude.

"So why do you think someone might have killed Michael Kelly?"

"I have no idea. I mean, it's Northern Ireland, isn't it? People are getting killed over there all the time."

"Michael's death was not a random act of violence. We believe it was a very deliberate murder concealed to look like a suicide."

Osbourne shook his head, horrified.

"Are you sure *he* wasn't blackmailing you about Miss Coleman?"

"Michael wouldn't do anything like that. Michael could have left that morning but he didn't. He stayed to help Gottfried. That was the kind of guy he was. How do you think he got into the Round Table Club? Those are old-money clubs and Michael was Irish and new money, but people liked him. And then there was the whole gun thing. Everybody loved that. He was charming and—"

"Sorry, what gun thing?" I asked.

"The AGC. The Antiquarian Gun Club. Michael was president. All the Round Table guys loved it. Everyone in the Dangerous Sports Club too. We all went to the AGC events."

Osbourne explained that the AGC liked to shoot old shotguns, muskets, arquebuses and the like. They were enthusiasts, collectors; some of them were also re-enactors of ancient battles.

"Michael even got us permits to fire old cannons on Christchurch Meadow. Apparently there's an old university law that allows you to do that. We did it on May morning! That shook everyone up!"

"So, in fact, you knew Michael quite well?" Lawson asked.

Osbourne nodded sadly. "He was a good chap."

"Tell us more about the guns," I said, intrigued by this turn in the inquiry.

"He really knew his weapons. He had a great eye for a gun. The AGC was dying until he took it over. He became a very active club president and treasurer."

"Any financial irregularities?"

"Quite the reverse, actually. The best treasurer they ever had. It became one of the wealthiest non-dining clubs in Oxford. Under Michael's stewardship it had become *the* club to be in. Some clubs just become *the* club and that's what happened to the AGC. It had always been the club for people wanting to go into the MoD, British Aerospace, and so forth, but under Michael it became positively *trendy*. In the end he had to start turning people down for membership."

Lawson and I were scribbling furiously now. Oxford CID had discovered none of this. But was it relevant?

"So how would it work? You would all just meet up and fire old guns?"

"And new guns too. So exciting. Pistols, rifles. I suppose in Northern Ireland you're around guns all the time?"

"You don't remember if Michael was a good shot, do you?" I asked.

"Yes, he was actually. An excellent shot. Some of us thought he could have competed at club or even international level."

"And this was modern weaponry as well?"

"Oh yes. Michael's friend Nigel got us access to the government range at Dartmoor. That was a trip we'll never forget. Machine guns, grenade launchers. Boris even got to shoot a Blowpipe missile!"

"Who was this Nigel?"

"Oh, a lad from Belfast. An old friend of Michael's."

"An old friend of Michael's from Belfast?"

"Yes."

"Second name?"

"I didn't catch it actually. Really."

"And he got you access to the government range at Dartmoor?"

"Yes. Nigel was connected to some factory in Belfast that made missiles. They always needed the range for testing."

"Short Brothers?"

"I don't know."

Lawson looked at me. *Yes, this was a very interesting development indeed.* I wrote "Nigel..." in my notebook. Old school friend called Nigel, possibly connected to Shorts, had once used his pull to get access to the MoD range at Dartmoor—shouldn't be that hard to find out a surname with a little old-fashioned legwork.

"This all must have cost a fortune?" I suggested.

"Michael made the AGC a very profitable enterprise."

"Through membership fees?" Lawson asked.

"Not just that. Like I say, he had a great eye for a gun. He would go to auctions and estate sales. Always came back with a bargain or two. He found an old Ottoman matchlock for my father. Pride of place in our living room."

"He bought guns for the club?"

"And for the collectors."

"Would he sell guns as well?"

"Of course, yes. It was all perfectly legal, Inspector. There was no suggestion of wrongdoing."

"But it wouldn't be unfair to say that by the time he, er, left Oxford he was well established in the network of gun dealers and buyers?"

"Well, yes."

We asked him a few more questions about the gun club and his relationship with Michael and the mysterious Nigel: a tall, thin man with long blond hair and a Belfast accent.

I asked Osbourne to give us the room for a minute so Lawson and I could talk privately.

"Just wait outside the door, sir. We'll let you know when we need you again."

He exited nervously.

"Thoughts?" I asked Lawson.

"Arms dealing. Quite the growth industry. Legal and illegal, especially in Ulster. Maybe he made some enemies? And we'll definitely have to find this Nigel guy."

"What else jumped out at you?"

Lawson looked at his notes. "Michael, apparently, was an excellent shot."

"So he could have murdered his parents after all. Fast, like a pro."

We called Osbourne back in.

"Mr. Osbourne, where were you on the night of November 11, 1985?"

"Uhm . . ."

"Working late here at the office with lots of witnesses?" I suggested.

"Uhm, well, actually we had the week off. Post-conference lull, you know? We all worked really hard for the conferences. I mean after last year. You remember what happened last year?"

I remember it only too well, son. I was fucking there.

"So what were you doing if you weren't working?"

"Oh, you know, just hanging out at the flat. At the weekend I went home, saw a whole bunch of friends."

"By the weekend Michael Kelly and his parents were dead."

"Look, I've never been to Northern Ireland in my life. I don't think I even have a current passport!"

"You don't need a passport," I said.

I got to my feet.

"Thank you for your cooperation, Mr. Osbourne. And if I were you I'd try and think of an alibi for the night of the eleventh."

A smile creased his chubby cheeks. "So that's it for now?" he asked hopefully.

"For the moment that's it. We're going back to Northern Ireland tonight, Mr. Osbourne."

"And, and what about . . . what about my name? It won't get in the papers?"

"We have no interest in releasing your name to the press, Mr. Osbourne, and it seems that Thames Valley Police and Gottfried Habsburg are of like mind. Today is your lucky day in what seems to have been a life filled with lucky days."

"Well, it's not quite all—"

"We may want to interview you again, sir, so please don't leave the country and please give Constable Lawson here your address and home phone number."

"And that alibi would be very helpful if you can come up with one, sir," Lawson said, giving him the Carrickfergus CID phone number.

17: INTERROGATING DEIRDRE FERRIS

We asked the receptionist at Conservative Central Office to call us a taxi which we took to Paddington, where we caught the Oxford train. There was no point staying in England now.

When we pulled into Oxford station I told Lawson to pack our stuff, pay the bill, get a receipt, get two bus tickets to Birmingham International airport, and meet me at the Eagle and Child.

"Yes, sir."

"Good. Don't forget the receipt. Sergeant Dalglish is a stickler for receipts."

"I won't. Sir?"

"Yes?"

"You don't suspect Osbourne, do you?"

"No. But you never know, do you? We'll make sure we call him and follow up with him on that alibi."

"Yes, sir. Uhm, sir?"

"Yes?"

"What are you going to do while I'm packing?"

"I'm going to go back to Oxford CID and raise just a little bit of holy hell."

Back through the streets of Oxford again.

The same girls on bikes, the same boys rowing on the river, the same red sandstone ... but a more sinister aspect to it all now. The Round Table Club. The AGC. This is where the elite cemented their connections, this is where deals got done, this is where you got inducted into the secret world of men with money and power. Through the looking glass indeed.

Oxford Police HQ. Piped music. Natural light. Georgian windows uncovered by grilles. Flowers on the incident desk. This was a station without armor, a station that anyone could just walk right into. The same thought: these bloody peelers didn't know how lucky they were.

What did they know about policing in a crisis zone? What did they know about fucking anything?

I went upstairs to the CID offices.

The big back room overlooking Christchurch Meadow.

The big back room overlooking one of the most beautiful places in all of Europe. Yellow wood, aurulent leaves, Jersey cows . . .

The CID officers were gawping at me.

I asked for a meeting with Superintendent Smith, Chief Inspector Boyson, Constable Atkins. I played it low key, dropped my voice half an octave and got it low and growly like those slab-faced goons who come to your door late on foggy December nights asking whether you want to "contribute something for the prisoners."

I told them what Habsburg had told me. Let it sink in. *Let it bloody sink.*

They had committed serious professional wrongdoing and they bloody knew it. I could end their careers if I wanted to. Even if that would entail grassing up a fellow peeler.

White faces. Panic. *Yeah, that's right, you underestimated the Paddy cop.* Either that or you overestimated Gottfried Habsburg's ability to keep his mouth shut. Either way: serious fucking mistake. Career-ending mistake. Front page of the fucking *Daily Mirror* mistake.

"You don't understand, Duffy. There was nothing in it for us; we just wanted to protect an innocent young man. It was nothing untoward. No one told us to do it or paid us or—"

"If that's true you're even stupider than you look."

"Please, Inspector Duffy, you can see our side of it, can't you?"

"Falsifying reports. Concealing information from the Crown Prosecution Service? Concealing information from a county coroner? That's not just your career, lads, that's jail time . . ."

"No, Duffy, wait a minute—"

"That's Inspector Duffy to you."

But I had already begun to lose interest. Busting chops was never my scene. And I wasn't going to do anything anyway. Just fuck with them. Leave the possibility of action hanging over them . . . That was the ticket. That was the way of ulcers.

"I'm going," I said.

"No! Wait, Duffy! What are you going to do?"

They followed me downstairs.

Out into the street.

"What are you going to do?"

"Do I look like a bloody informer?"

I walked up St Aldate's, up the Cornmarket, up St Giles'.

Good-bye, English girls on bikes. Good-bye, Christopher Wren. Good-bye, Morse World.

Lawson had packed our stuff and was waiting for me at the Eagle and Child.

There was a bus to Birmingham International leaving Oxford coach station in half an hour.

Airport.

British Midland 737.

Belfast.

Crabbie met us at the gate.

"You didn't have to meet us at the airport!" I said.

"I was in the neighborhood," he lied. "How was the trip?"

"It wasn't a total loss. Turns out our Michael Kelly was starting to become a big-time gun dealer. Networking, meeting people. And we got a name: Nigel something, possible connection to Shorts Brothers in Belfast. Oh, and Lawson was right about the conspiracy."

"A conspiracy?"

"Aye, a conspiracy of fools to protect an idiot."

"They always are."

Crabbie drove me back to 113 Coronation Road.

Boys playing football. Girls pushing prams. Neighbors chatting over fences. Why is it so comforting here? I'll tell you why: poverty and a rumbling, low-level war have engendered a blitz spirit.

Vodka gimlet. Converse sneakers. Sweatpants. Ramones T-shirt. Put in a cassette I bought at the airport. The *Z and Two Noughts* soundtrack album by Michael Nyman. Bit samey. Not up to his usual standard.

At nine I called Sara but her phone just rang and rang.

I called her at the *Telegraph* offices.

"What is it, Sean?"

She sounded irritated. I asked her whether she wanted to do something after work. She said she couldn't. There'd been rioting in Belfast and the photo editor wanted to build a big story around an arc of petrol bombs sailing through the air . . .

I called my parents and told them I'd been over the water on a case. They showed polite and rather touching interest. I made another vodka gimlet. Easy on the lime.

Phone call. The Crabman. "Deirdre's been transferred down from Queen Street cop shop. We can interrogate her now if you want. Or tomorrow if you want to settle in."

"I'll be right over. Get Lawson in for this one too. I think it's going to be good."

The tape recorder running in Interview Room 2, Deirdre Ferris sitting there in white stilettos, leopard-print top, and a red miniskirt. She was sipping a tea with four sugars and smoking Embassy Kings.

Did I describe Deirdre before? You know the type: fake tan, dyed, straightened black hair, green eyes, chubby, pretty. There was a bruise under her right eye but you should see the other girl . . .

"So you're the one that can get me off my assault charge?" she said, blowing smoke at me.

"Only if you've got something pertinent to offer us," I replied.

"*Pertinent*. Pertinent, eh? That's a good word, that pertinent."

"Well, what do you know?"

"I might have seen somebody *pertinent* to the case."

"Who?"

"What do I get in return?"

"It depends who you saw."

"What if I seen someone going up our garden path the night Sylvie died."

I looked at McCrabban and Lawson.

"Tell us what you saw, Deirdre," I said.

Deirdre shook her head. "If I tell you'll have to guarantee me no charges from them peelers at Queen Street station. They're not nice up there. Not nice like youse down here."

"If you can give us Sylvie's murderer I'll get you off the GBH."

She shook her head, puffed on her ciggie. "Nah, nah, nah, I'll tell you what I seen and then it's *your* job to get the fucking murderer. I get off the GBH in return for what I seen, even if you don't catch the killer."

"All right, that's the deal, then," I said. "I'll get them to drop the assault charge in return for what you saw."

"And if I'm going to be blabbing to the cops about a bloody maniac who goes round topping barmaids I'll need to be somewhere safe, so I will."

"You're safe in here."

"I'm not spending the next six months in fucking jail while you look for the lad who might have done Sylvie in."

I sighed. "So what do you want, Deirdre?"

"Charges dropped for that wee bitch Angela McCorey who fucking had it coming if anyone ever had it coming. And then outta here. One of them safe houses. Well away. Over the water."

"I think we could do that," McCrabban said. "We have a reciprocal arrangement with Strathclyde Police."

Deirdre nodded. "Aye, Scotland would be all right. Like it over there."

"So what did you see, Deirdre?" I said, starting to lose my patience.

She stubbed out her fag, took a drink of water. "So anyway, the night Sylvie supposedly topped herself I was away to see me ma. Wee drink at the Whitecliff and then train to Carrick, you know? Anyways, I left the house and I was walking down the street but then I realized I'd forgotten the twenty quid I owed Darren for the acid tabs, right? Wait, you're not Drugs Squad, are you?"

"We're not interested in the acid tabs. Carry on, Deirdre," I said.

"Now Darren's UVF and if you don't pay when you owe it's double the next week, so I was going back to borrow the money off Sylvie, but then I seen someone outside our house, you know? Oh, thinks I, a gentleman caller. I knew better than to bother her. You know? All cut up after Michael's death and all. Wee bit of comfort, and anyway, Darren'll take a hand job in lieu so to speak. See what I mean?"

"So you think that someone was outside your house that night and you think that they were going to see Sylvie?"

"Aye."

"Did you actually see this person go to your front door?"

"No, I'm not a nosy parker, so I'm not, and the rain was on so I just turned and went on to the Whitecliff."

"How do you know it wasn't someone just out walking their dog—dog stops in front of your place to take a piss?" I asked.

"There was no dog. Let me think ... no, if there was a dog it was a wee small dog ... No, there was definitely no dog. He was going to see Sylvie, I know it."

"You didn't think to tell us any of this before!" Lawson exclaimed.

"I'm no squealer, so I'm not!"

"You think you can describe this person?" I asked.

"Only seen him from the back and the side but he was pretty tall, wearing a leather jacket, wee baseball cap or a flat cap, something like that for the rain, you know."

"I'll get the sketch artist," McCrabban said, and left the interview room.

Deirdre and the sketch artist drew the profile of a nasty-looking, hatchet-faced man with hollow cheeks and narrow slits for eyes. You wouldn't want to meet him on a dark night. Or indeed on a sunlit morning.

"Are you sure this is the man?" I asked.

"Look, like I said, it was dark and I was on the other side of the street, but it's not a bad likeness."

"You're not just making all this up to get off the GBH, are you?"

"No. I seen that man. Sleekit-looking fella and no mistake," she said.

"This is good stuff, Deirdre, very good stuff," McCrabban said.

"I told youse. It's enough to get me off my GBH, right?"

I smiled at her. "I'll have a word with the Queen Street detectives in the morning."

"And I'll be across the water until you catch him?"

"I'll arrange that too."

"Ach, you're awful good, Detective Duffy. You know, for a Fenian, like."

"Thank you."

I was about to leave the interview room when I had one final thought.

"You don't know someone called Nigel by any chance? Maybe a friend of Michael's?"

"Oh, aye. Nigel Vardon. Seen him with Michael a few times down the Whitecliff. Good friend of his, I think. Lives up Ballycarry way. In the country. That any help?"

"Yes, Deirdre. That's very helpful indeed."

18: NIGEL VARDON

Home. Bed. Sleep on the sofa. Awake at 4 a.m. Car alarm going on the BMW. Grabbed my revolver. Outside into the freezing rain. Coming down in buckets. Something wrong with the car. Closer look.

"Wee shites! Fucking wee shites! If I catch you!"

Both rear tires of the Beemer had been let down.

Back inside. I huddled in front of the electric fire, turned on the World Service, lay there listening to bad news until eight when the phone rang. Whoever it was was going to cop it because I was in a foul mood. "Yeah?"

"Sean, please tell me you weren't at Conservative Party Central Office yesterday threatening one of the young Treasury researchers."

"Complained about me, did he?"

"Sean, why don't you just drop this ridiculous case you're working on, resign from the RUC, and come and work for me."

"Even if I do resign, Kate, Sergeant McCrabban will still pursue every bloody lead in this case, or are you going to offer him a career in MI5 to keep him quiet too?"

"What are you talking about, Sean?"

"What are *you* talking about, Kate? Your Colditz coroner didn't do his job. Oxford CID didn't do their job. We, however, we plodding Paddies in the RUC, we did do our bloody jobs. We found your little Conservative Party Central Office researcher and he told us he was the one who took Anastasia Coleman to the party where she died. He was the third man in Gottfried Habsburg's house."

"Oh."

"Yeah, well, don't worry, if he's tangential to the inquiry his name won't come up again, but if he's not I don't give a shit who's protecting him."

"Sean, I wasn't suggesting—"

"If your little friend in Conservative Party Central Office wants to complain about me, let him fucking complain, he's got more to lose than I do."

"Sean, please. No one's complained about you. Not officially. I'm just concerned that you've bitten off more than you can chew here. In the big scheme of things your little murder investigation is a drop in the ocean. It's not worth making waves for."

"When I make waves you'll fucking know it," I said, and slammed down the phone. I went into the kitchen and put the kettle on.

"Fucking wee Tory shite," I muttered.

I went outside to get the milk and saw the sad state of my Beemer resting on its wheel rims.

Mrs. Campbell was bringing in her milk. Hair askew, fag end dangling out of mouth, nightgown slightly ajar.

"Is there something wrong with your car, Mr. Duffy?"

"Who lets down a man's tires? A mercury tilt switch bomb under the driver's seat I can understand. That's an assassination, I get it, but who lets down a man's tires? I ask you."

"Probably weans."

"Aye, weans. They better not let me catch them."

"I've never seen you so upset."

"You don't mess with a man's wheels, Mrs. Campbell."

Inside. Shower. Shave. *Walk* to Carrick. Grey sky, boarded-up shops. Tarkovskian dystopia. Mean, damp, menacing.

Into the station. No one around. Just a couple of reservists I didn't know.

Dawn over the lough. Coppers filtering in. A stack of paperwork. I fictionalized the CID overtime claims, signed off on McCrabban's hardship allowance, put in a request for a new dress uniform, and made up a whole bunch of bullshit for Lawson's performance review.

Chief Inspector McArthur came in with blow-dried hair, a pink shirt, and a police college tie.

"Hello, Duffy, you're in early."

"To catch the worm, sir."

"How was your England trip?"

"Extremely productive. We were able to more or less eliminate an entire wing from our inquiry, and we established an excellent rapport and working relationship with Thames Valley CID. We also liaised with a representative of the City of London Police and even with Conservative Party Central Office."

His face beamed. "That's terrific, Sean. I look forward to reading your report."

"Interesting fact about the City of London Police. Lawson tells me they're the reigning Olympic tug-of-war champions, and speaking of Lawson, here's his performance review. I gave him a superior grade. He's shaping up to be a very capable detective."

McArthur took the performance review and frowned.

"Don't make him sound too brilliant, Duffy, or he'll get noticed by the higher-ups and they'll steal him from us. Tone this down a bit."

"Will do, sir."

"And what's this about a safe house for one of your witnesses, Duffy?"

"Deirdre Ferris asked for protection in a safe house over the water. I had to give it to her. I took it out of discretionary CID budget, but we'll split the cost with the host force."

"Who's the host force?"

"Strathclyde Police. We have a good reciprocal relationship with them."

"Good thinking. Where will you put her?"

"Ayr. Near Glasgow."

"And the Kelly case is proceeding well?"

"We've several very good leads. An artist's impression that I'm going to circulate."

"Ooh, an artist's impression. Will you try and get us on the news?"

"I'll try, sir."

"Very good, Duffy, don't let me keep you . . . And I'm very glad to see that you're still with us; we need experienced officers at a time like this."

"I don't know what you've heard, sir, but I'll be staying with Carrick CID for as long as I'll be needed."

He smiled. "Glad to hear it."

I looked up Nigel Vardon in the electoral register, and when McCrabban and Lawson came in we signed out a Land Rover and I drove us to his house, which was in wild back country of County Antrim near Ballycarry.

Radio 3 was playing an unknown Haydn symphony—at least unknown to me—Symphony no. 34 in D minor, which turned out to be a masterpiece; the courtly third movement so ingeniously constructed that I found my mood lifting a little.

Vardon's house was a turn-of-the-century farmhouse that had been much expanded upon and "improved" to include a semi-enclosed patio, a double floor extension, and a glass conservatory. It was a thing a lot of people around here did, taking a beautiful little farmhouse and progressively fucking with it until it wasn't a farmhouse or beautiful anymore. There were tiles missing from the roof and the walls hadn't been painted in a long time. The renovation had been done a few years ago, but recently money had been tight chez Vardon. Interesting . . .

"OK, lads, game faces on. Let's see what Mr. Vardon has to say for himself, eh? Nice and gentle with him at first."

Out of the Land Rover. Doorbell. Doorbell again.

Two vicious Alsatians bounding round the back of the house toward us.

"Bloody hell!"

Back into the Land Rover. Sharpish.

The dogs snapping and snarling, slobber coming from their mouths.

The front door opened.

Vardon standing there with a coffee cup in a light blue dressing gown, white underpants, one foot in a slipper, one not. Very long blond hair, two-day growth of beard, blue eyes, tan. He was a handsome lad, but possibly not as handsome as he thought he was.

"What do you want?" he said with a sniff.

"Mr. Vardon?"

"Who wants to know?"

"Who else pulls up to your front door in a police Land Rover, Mr. Vardon?"

"Oh, is that a police Land Rover? I haven't got my lenses in."

"Can you control your dogs, please, Mr. Vardon?"

"Look, there's no need for this. I've told you everything I know. It's got nothing to do with me."

"Can we come in and talk, please, sir?"

"I've told you everything a million times already! I didn't do anything. I've never done anything in my life."

"Mr. Vardon, there must be some mistake you've never talked to us before about—"

"I'm the victim here. I'm the fall guy. Somebody in senior management fucked up big time, but of course nobody in senior management is going to take responsibility so they get rid of me. I did nothing. And what about Tommy Moony, eh? I'll bet you brave boys in the RUC don't go around asking him questions non-stop. Nah, only yours truly. Everybody's afraid of Moony, afraid of the union, but no one's afraid of me, are they?"

One of the Alsatians tried to jump in the open window of the Land Rover.

"Control your dogs or I'll fucking shoot them both. I'm in no mood for this today," I said.

He ordered his dogs inside and we got out of the Land Rover.

"We just want to ask you some questions, Mr. Vardon," I said. "Just to establish a few facts about your whereabouts."

"Facts? Facts, is it? I'll tell you the bloody facts! I'm suing Shorts for wrongful dismissal! I've done nothing wrong. Those are the facts."

"If we can come in and talk . . ."

"I'm done talking with the bloody peelers! You can talk to my solicitor," he said, and attempted to close the door on McCrabban's size-twelve foot.

"Mr. Vardon, we're here to talk about Michael Kelly," I said, pulling the door wide open.

"Michael Kelly?"

"Yes."

"Who's that?"

"You don't know who Michael Kelly is?"

"It doesn't ring a bell."

"That's odd, isn't it, Sergeant McCrabban?"

"Very odd," McCrabban agreed.

"Why is it odd?" Vardon asked.

"It's odd because you went to school with him. You were in the sixth form together. Good friends by all accounts. And it's odd because he called you on the telephone quite regularly. It's odd because you went over to Oxford and took some friends of his to the MoD range at Dartmoor."

Vardon looked at the ground, shuffled his feet, sighed. "All right. Big deal. So I know him. So what?"

"You do know that he was murdered?"

"Heard it was suicide. Heard he jumped off a cliff."

"We think it's possible that someone pushed him off the cliff."

"Oh, you think I did it, do you? Yeah, pin that one on me too."

"May we come in, Mr. Vardon?"

He sighed again. "If you must . . ."

I looked at Crabbie. "Oh, I think we must."

The interior of the house was relatively unspoiled: original stone walls, nice original fireplace and chimney equipment, wood floors, Persian rugs, comfortable sofa, a very impressive quadrophonic sound system, and a high-end CD player.

"Where are the dogs?" Lawson asked nervously.

"Locked in the back kitchen," Vardon said.

"What's your relationship to Michael Kelly, Mr. Vardon?" I asked, sitting down on the sofa.

"Not much of a relationship. Friends at school but we drifted apart. I went into Shorts management program after my A-levels and he went off to Oxford."

"You went over to visit him?"

"It wasn't really like that. We'd lost contact for a while and then he calls me up out of the blue asking if I could get him a pass to the MoD range in Dartmoor for a corporate hospitality thing."

"That's a very unusual request," McCrabban said.

"Not that unusual. He knew I worked at the Shorts Missile Division and he knew we did all our range testing at Dartmoor."

"So you organized a little trip for his Oxford pals."

"Good PR for Shorts. Those lads are the future movers and shakers. The future buyers of missile systems for the Ministry of Defense."

"How long did you spend with Michael?"

"Oh, that was just a long weekend. December of last year."

"But after that you and Michael had re-established contact and remained friends?"

"Yeah. Not close friends to tell the truth. But friendly enough."

"So why deny him to us?" McCrabban asked.

"Are you kidding? Last thing I need is to be mixed up with the Michael Kelly story at a time like this."

"What exactly is going on with you? What's all this talk about Shorts and unions and the like?" I asked.

"As if you don't know," he said skeptically.

"We don't know."

"I've been interviewed by RUC Special Branch no less than three times. Twice at the station. Once here."

"About what?" Lawson asked.

"The stolen missiles. The *allegedly* stolen missiles," he explained.

"What stolen missiles?" McCrabban asked.

"What stolen . . . All right. For the hundredth time. They did an internal audit and they found that six Javelin missile systems had gone missing."

"That sounds pretty serious!" McCrabban said.

"I think I heard about this on the news." I vaguely remembered. "So what happened to you, Mr. Vardon?"

"I was in charge of plant security at the Missiles Division, so naturally they gave me the sack. Except there's only one problem. I've only been in that particular job two months and the missiles could have gone missing at any time since the last inventory, which was fourteen months ago! And you can't fire Harry Tapper because he's dead, and you can't fire Tommy Moony on the shop floor because he's union. So what do you do? You get rid of me. The new guy on the totem pole. Junior manager. Expendable."

"Plant security was your job," Lawson said.

"I've done a great job over there. I've tightened security. The missiles did not go missing on my watch! And I'll tell you something else, I'll bet you they're not even missing. Have you actually been over there? They don't know their arse from their elbow. They have a pre-war system of accounts, the shipping isn't even done on computer; it's all in these big black double-entry books. And you think when the missiles do show up in wooden crates in some corner of the factory à la Indiana Jones, you think I'm going to get my job back? Will I, fuck? I'll still be out on my ear with my reputation ruined!"

He seemed genuinely upset by this, as you would be if you'd got the can for someone else's mistake.

"And you've told all this to Special Branch?" McCrabban asked.

"I have. Three times."

"And what have they said?"

"No criminal charges. They think I'm innocent. And you know why?"

"Why?"

"Because I am innocent! What would I do with half a dozen Javelin missile systems?"

"Get rid of them through your friend Michael Kelly, a growing presence in the international weapons market?" I suggested.

"Rubbish! Stuff like that is far too hot to move and you know it!" he scoffed.

"What was your reaction to the murders at the Kelly home, Mr. Vardon?" I asked.

"Honestly? I saw it coming. He was always rowing with his da back when I knew him. Don't want to speak ill of the dead but his da was a bit of a fucking head case. Old-school hard man. You don't get to run a chain of bookies without bashing a few skulls."

"Did he bash Michael's skull?" Crabbie asked.

"Oh yeah. When he was younger. Smacked him about quite a bit."

"What about Michael's mum?"

"What about her?"

"Usually the mother steps in to stop the violence," I said.

"She didn't do shit. She was too far gone in the drink by lunchtime to do much of anything."

"So you think years of simmering resentment finally spilled over and Michael killed his parents?" I suggested.

"I do. Stands to reason, doesn't it?"

"And then what?"

"Well, then Michael tops himself."

"Because?"

"He's grief-stricken. You don't go round killing your ma and da and not feel something."

"You do if you're a psychopath."

"Michael was no psychopath. He just snapped is all . . . That's my theory, anyway."

He'd blinked a hundred times since we'd started this conversation and he'd sniffed half a dozen times. His pupils were dilated and he had the jitters. Evidently he and me and our actor buddy, Mr. Dwyer, all enjoyed the Peruvian marching powder. But how did you pay for a cocaine problem on the dole? Could a cocaine problem make you risk everything by stealing a bunch of missiles? Nah. Heroin I could see fucking with you like that, but not coke. And he was right—where in the name of God would you unload a bunch of missile systems? It would be too hot even for the paramilitaries, wouldn't it? Even for someone as connected as Michael Kelly?

"Where were you on the night of November 11, 1985?"

"What happened then?"

"That was the night Michael Kelly's parents were murdered," I said.

"Here more than likely. Maybe down the Whitecliff pub for a bit."

"Here with a helpful alibi?"

"Do the dogs count?"

"No."

"No, then."

"Where were you on the evening of the twelfth?"

"The night Michael went off the cliff? Here," he said dolefully.

"Where were you on Wednesday of last week?"

"What happened then?"

"That was the night Sylvie McNichol was murdered. You know who she is?"

"Yeah, barmaid down the Whitecliff. Michael's girlfriend supposedly. But I, uhm, I heard that that was a suicide too."

"We're still investigating the circumstances surrounding her death, Mr. Vardon," I said. "Where were you?"

"I was here as well."

"So you've no alibi for the evening Michael was killed or the night Sylvic was killed."

"No."

"And the night Michael's parents were killed?"

"I was here . . . Look, I've been here every night since I got dismissed from Shorts. I can't afford to go out, can I?"

"Do you have family around here?"

"Parents have emigrated to South Africa. Can't take the winters."

"Pretty fancy stereo system. How do you like being part of the CD revolution?" I asked, gazing at the expensive bit of kit.

"CDs are the future, mate. And if you must know I paid for the stereo system and the CDs out of my own money."

"You'll always stick with vinyl, won't you, sir, it's got more character," Lawson said to butter me up.

I grinned at him.

"Character my arse. CDs will last forever," Vardon said.

"Was Michael into music? What did you talk about when he called here?" I asked.

"He was only ever over here a couple of times. We just shat the shit. You know?"

"He ever talk to you about guns?"

"Guns?"

"Guns, firearms, weapons. I heard he was fascinated. Quite the collector, apparently. Dealer too."

He thought for a second or two and ran his hand back through his long hair.

"Guns? Nope, we didn't talk about guns. Not really. Still he was always, well, he was always one of those wee boys, but he could tell I wasn't interested."

"One of what wee boys?"

"One of those wee lads fascinated by guns. You know the type. He showed me his dad's gun more than once. To tell the truth I thought he was going to go in the army. Oxford and Sandhurst, you know? Up that chain."

"He ever talk about getting kicked out of Oxford?"

"I did mention it a couple of times but he didn't want to talk about it."

"So what did you chat about?"

"Football. Friends. You know."

"Girls?"

"Occasionally."

"What girls did he mention?" I asked.

"Oh, you know, just local girls."

"Sylvie McNichol?"

"Yeah."

"What did he say about her?"

"Nothing much. Just, you know. He liked her, I think. He was pretty cagey about that stuff."

"Did you know Sylvie?"

"I told you I knew her from down the Whitecliff."

"Did you, she, and Michael ever go out together?"

"No . . . I think you're getting the wrong end of the stick here, Inspector."

"Oh yeah? What's the right end of the stick?"

"After Michael came back from England I only saw him half a dozen times. Chatted on the phone a few times. He'd moved on, you know?"

"Moved on from what?"

"From me. From Northern Ireland. He was just getting his bearings here. If he hadn't gone nuts, he would have moved away."

"Where to?"

"He always talked about America or the Continent . . . If he could have just stuck out his old man's constant crap for a few more months he would have been OK, I think."

"Did you ever talk to Deirdre Ferris?"

"From the Whitecliff?"

"Yeah."

"I don't think so."

"Look, Mr. Vardon, we have it on good authority that Michael was something of an entrepreneur in the arms dealing business. Do you think it's possible that that's how he tried to make his living on his return to Northern Ireland?"

Vardon shook his head. "Anything's possible. But he never mentioned anything like that to me."

"Is it possible that you and Michael went into business together to conspire to steal missiles from Shorts, Mr. Vardon?" I said.

All three of us peelers carefully noted his reaction.

Outrage and annoyance or, perhaps, well-feigned outrage and annoyance.

"You're as bad as Special Branch! What the fuck would we do with half a dozen Javelin missiles? Me and Michael! Jesus Christ!"

"Sell them?" Lawson suggested.

"Who to?"

"The IRA?" Crabbie said.

"I'm a Prod. How do you think I got into Shorts in the first place? Michael's a Prod too. Neither of us are selling any missiles to the IRA."

Crabbie asked if it was OK to smoke.

"Yeah, go ahead."

He lit his pipe and I lit a Marlboro. Nigel produced a large ashtray and shoved it in front of me on the coffee table. I took out the photocopy of the artist's impression based on Deirdre's description.

"Ever seen this man?" I asked, handing him the picture.

"Nope."

"Anyone like that in the Whitecliff or hanging around with Michael?"

"No."

"He looks a little bit like you, doesn't he?" I offered.

Nigel shook his head. "I don't think so. What's this bloke supposed to have done?"

"He's someone we'd like to help us with our inquiries into Sylvie's death."

He handed the picture back. "Yeah, well, I never saw him about."

"Those are some vicious dogs you have, Mr. Vardon. What are you afraid of out here in the Irish countryside?"

"Anything. Burglars . . . you know."

"You're not afraid of anyone in particular?"

"No."

I took a long draw on my cigarette and looked at Crabbie. He shrugged.

"So in summary you don't know anything about any missing missiles, you have been wrongfully dismissed from Shorts, and you don't know anything about the deaths of Michael Kelly's parents or Michael Kelly or Sylvie McNichol?"

"That's about it," Nigel said.

I looked over at Lawson but he had nothing more for now either.

In the Land Rover back to Carrick we digested the convo.

"I don't like the lack of alibis," I said.

"But there's also a lack of motive. Why kill Michael and his parents and Sylvie?" Lawson said.

"Why indeed?" I agreed.

"There's something untrustworthy about him, but I don't see Mr. Vardon as the murdering type," McCrabban muttered.

"No. Or the missile-stealing type. But this connection to Michael Kelly is pretty interesting. Michael Kelly, the proto arms dealer, hanging out with Nigel Vardon, who works in a place that has just lost a bunch of missiles."

We spent the rest of the afternoon circulating Deirdre's artist's-impression picture in the Whitecliff pub in Whitehead, on the notice-board at the post office, on the telegraph pole outside the station, and we even got it on the UTV lunchtime news with the suggestion that "anyone who may have seen this man call the Confidential Telephone."

The Confidential Telephone passed on a couple of leads, but when Crabbie followed up on them they were dead ends. We got the forensic report back on Sylvie McNichol's death, and, surprisingly, the chief FO ruled that the "foreign body in Miss McNichol's mouth may not have been a contribution to her death. The presence of chloroform may have been a false positive due to cross-contamination at the lab."

"So maybe it was suicide after all?" Lawson suggested. "Maybe she just forgot about the car window."

"You're the one that got us thinking about murder in the first place!" Crabbie said.

"Maybe I was wrong."

"And the person Deirdre saw lurking outside their gate?" McCrabban countered.

"Someone walking their dog, dog stops to take a piss, like Inspector Duffy says. It was dark and it was raining."

"Or maybe Deirdre made the whole thing up to get off the GBH rap?" I said.

"Two murders and two suicides would close the case," Crabbie said reflectively.

"I can't believe they were incompetent at the lab," Lawson groaned.

"I can't believe they admitted it," Crabbie said.

"Incompetence. Better get used to that, Lawson. Bright lad like you. You should have gone over the water and joined the bloody Met," I grumbled.

I went to my office, brought back a bottle of Jura, and poured three glasses of the good stuff. We took a healthy sip each and I lit a ciggie. Marlboro and sixteen-year-old Jura go very well together . . .

"And Nigel Vardon and his missiles?" I said after a pause.

"Unrelated to our investigation," Crabbie replied.

I sighed. "This false positive bullshit is going to make a conviction almost impossible anyway. Forensics have fucked us if this was a murder."

I went home that night, exhausted.

Bobby Cameron saw me walking up Coronation Road and came out of his garden where he had been trimming the rose bushes.

"Saw someone messed with your car, Duffy," he said.

"Yeah," I replied sourly.

"It won't happen again," he said. "Trying to murder you is one thing, but fucking with a man's wheels is quite another."

"That's what I said," I replied.

"Well, it won't happen again. Not on my street."

When I got back to the house I saw that the tires had been replaced and I saw Sara's car parked in front of mine.

Things were looking up.

"I was waiting for you," she said, getting out and kissing me.

"I should give you a key."

She shook her head. "Oh, no, I don't think we're at the key-giving stage just yet," she said. "How was England?"

"It was fine. Nice actually. Safe, you know?"

"I know," she said. "Boring in other words. No stories. Whereas here: murder and mayhem every day."

"Must keep your editor happy."

"It does. What's the latest on the Kelly case, if you're allowed to tell me?"

We went inside and I told her that Sylvie's death might be a suicide again, but I kept the Vardon angle to myself.

I made pasta for dinner and Sara thumbed through my record collection looking for something that "wasn't a million years old."

The rain came down and we went to bed.

I woke up in the middle of the night with her snuggled in beside me. She was cold and fragile and lying innocently in my arms, but I could think only about Kate. Kate—that girl from Gun Street, Kate who had resurrected my RUC career and who was offering me a way out of this lost province, to a place where the newspapers were dull and the world wasn't quite so violent and black.

I slipped out from under the covers and lit the paraffin heater to warm the house.

I put on an Elmore James record and watched the indigo paraffin flame flicker in the draught from the bedroom window.

I climbed back under the duvet, and eventually the distant sound of "Every Day I Have The Blues" carried me off to a weary, broken, melancholy sleep.

19: SPECIAL BRANCH MAKE A SCENE

The next morning at the station we kept chasing down the Confidential Telephone reports on Deirdre's supposed mystery man, but none of them went anywhere. Even if someone had recognized the picture no one was going to shop their friends and neighbors to the RUC. *Omertà* held sway. The oldest Belfast rule there was: never ever tell the police anything. And of course, if Deirdre had just invented the man it was a waste of everyone's time.

We were in the middle of a case conference when the door burst open and two detectives burst in.

They were mightily pissed off about something, and initially I thought it was that blowback from Larne RUC I'd been expecting for weeks, but it wasn't that at all.

DI Billy Spencer was a short, skinny, ginger bap, with a little, pointy, elven beard I quite liked as it made him resemble Richard Stillgoe from off the telly. DCI Martin McCreen was a lean, sleekit-looking, bald guy with dark eyes and a menacing robotic grey tinge to his skin.

"Which one of you is Duffy?" McCreen said.

"I'm Duffy. What's your problem?"

"The problem is Carrick CID poaching on our case. The problem is you, Duffy. You've got a reputation for poaching other people's cases. You want to solve every crime in Ulster? Is that it? You want to be Chief Constable by the time you're forty? First Fenian Chief Constable, eh?"

McCrabban got between McCreen and me. "How about explaining yourselves, gents."

McCreen explained that they were detectives from Special Branch who had been assigned to the case of the missing missiles from the

Shorts factory. Apparently they had been conducting a surveillance operation on Nigel Vardon and we'd blundered into it.

"We've got Vardon nice and quiet. Thinks we're off his case, and then you lads show up and get him all riled up again. Asking him questions about a murder inquiry, which everybody knows is really a murder-suicide, with the suicide at the bottom of a fucking cliff," McCreen snarled.

"How were we supposed to know Special Branch was surveilling Nigel Vardon?" I asked.

"You could have asked somebody, couldn't you, Duffy? Use your fucking common sense, if you've got any. If a bunch of missiles really have disappeared it would be a pretty fucking big deal, wouldn't it? Special Branch, Customs, the MoD, Military Intelligence . . . you know? Use your fucking head! Fucking yokel PC fucking plod. Typical," Billy Spencer said, poking me in the left front shoulder of my sports jacket.

I was seething at the pair of them. Bursting in here, screaming at us, saying the word "Fenian," poking me . . . and doing all this in front of Lawson. Who did they think they were?

I pushed Billy violently backward. He tripped over himself and went down on to the incident room floor. "Touch me again and I'll put you in the fucking hospital," I snarled.

I turned my attention to McCreen.

"And you. Call me a Fenian again. I fucking dare you. I fucking dare you!"

McCreen saw that I was right on the verge of knocking seven bells out of him. He took a step away from me.

Crabbie put his hand on my shoulder.

"Easy, Sean, easy does it."

"Tell them to take it fucking easy."

"I think an apology is in order, gents," McCrabban rumbled.

McCreen nodded and attempted a smile. "No offense meant, I'm sure," he said.

He offered me his hand.

I looked at Crabbie. *Come on, Sean,* his eyes were pleading.

I breathed out, nodded at him, took the proffered hand.

"Why don't we discuss this at the pub? Was that a pub next door I saw? Special Branch will be buying," McCreen said.

"Pub. Yeah. OK," I agreed.

McCrabban pulled Spencer off the floor. "No hard feelings," he said.

Half an hour and a couple of pints later things were better. We weren't exactly all pals now, but if I carried a vendetta against every bastard who had called me a Fenian in Northern Ireland there would be a lot of gits out there who were looking a hiding . . .

McCreen and Spencer explained the whole missile situation to us.

Short Brothers were the last engineering film left in Belfast, which had once been the greatest shipbuilding and heavy engineering city in the British Empire. The Troubles and a lack of government support had put paid to the shipbuilding, but Shorts had managed to survive various crises by building nippy little cargo planes and diversifying into missile manufacture.

Shorts was now virtually the only employer left in East Belfast, and although they were subsidized by the British government, they were so good at what they did they very nearly turned a profit, something of a minor miracle in the Northern Ireland of 1985.

"All the current problems occurred in the Missile Division. Half a dozen completed Blowpipe replacement missile systems—known as the Javelin Mark 1—had disappeared from the factory's inventory," McCreen said.

"But not necessarily stolen?"

"Shorts aren't sure whether it's an inventory failure and the missiles have in fact been legitimately shipped out to various customers, or whether the missiles are in a different part of the factory complex, or whether the missile systems have in fact been stolen."

"Quite the world-class cock up. Heads had to roll, I suppose?"

"One of the first to go was Nigel Vardon, who had been the manager in charge of site security. I think the head of inventory also got sacked, and the vice-president of the Missile Division has been put on unpaid leave."

"And they called in you guys."

"Not just us. Internal inquiry and an MoD Procurement Office inquiry," McCreen said.

He was a lot calmer than I'd be if I thought that the IRA might just have got its greedy paws on a half-dozen anti-tank or anti-aircraft missiles. Police and army Land Rovers got hit by petrol bombs all the time without much effect, but rocket-propelled grenades could do serious damage, and a Javelin missile? That would just about kill everyone inside, wouldn't it?

I said as much to him over another pint of Guinness and a double whiskey chaser.

"Well, if they have, in fact, been stolen, they've been stolen by Loyalist paramilitaries. Shorts is in hard-core Loyalist territory in East Belfast," Spencer said.

"And the Loyalists won't sell them to the IRA?"

"No chance. If the IRA took down an army helicopter with a missile they got from the Loyalists there would be holy hell to pay. A bloody internal Loyalist feud to say the least. And the Loyalists can't use them against a Republican target cos even they know it would be disproportionate force and would set off a war with the IRA. Despite all the killings there's an uneasy truce between the IRA and the Loyalist paramilitaries. As you probably know only too well, Inspector, Belfast is divided up between IRA and Loyalist zones of control for the distribution of drugs and for so-called protection rackets," McCreen said.

"So what can they do with the missiles?" McCrabban asked. "Sounds like it's a bloody stupid thing to steal. High risk. Low reward."

Spencer finished his whiskey and asked the barman to bring us another round. Lawson was looking green so I put him on shandy Bass.

Spencer lowered his voice to a gravelly burr. "See, just between us, we've got some intelligence that international buyers have been looking to get their hands on Javelin missile technology."

"What international buyers?"

"Well, it's only speculation but as you may be aware the South African government is in the midst of a struggle against Cuban forces in Angola . . ."

"Cubans? Angola? What?"

"The details aren't important. The upshot is that the South African government may be looking to acquire foreign weapons systems so that they can reverse-engineer them. We've also heard rumors about the Iranians and the Libyans too," Spencer said. "If indeed the missiles really did get nicked and this whole thing isn't the usual Northern Ireland bullshit."

"Who was that bloke Vardon was blaming? Moony?"

"Tommy Moony? He mentioned him?" Spencer asked, becoming a little more interested.

"He said that everyone blamed him and was questioning him but nobody was blaming Tommy Moony. Tommy Moony didn't get the sack."

Spencer looked at McCreen. McCreen shrugged so Spencer continued.

"Moony's definitely one of our suspects. He's a player, or at least he was in the seventies. Ulster Freedom Fighters, we think. Rare birds, whole family immigrated here from Birmingham in the sixties to work in the yards. But they certainly bought into the local culture. His brother, Davy, is doing twenty to life for murder. His uncle, Jack Moony, is a UFF commander in South Belfast. Tommy's never been so much as arrested for anything but got a rep as a killer in the late seventies. An iceman, the guy you went to for big hits, not random sectarian bullshit."

"Sounds interesting," I said. "Michael Kelly's parents were probably murdered by a pro."

"He's retired from all that now, though, it seems. He's a shop steward at Shorts. Big guy in the Shorts Transport Workers' Union. That's enough power for anyone. In theory nothing goes in and out of the Shorts factory without either him or his men knowing about it."

"So why didn't he get fired in the internal review?" Crabbie asked.

"You fire Moony and the whole plant goes out on strike. Production stops, orders are missed, Shorts loses millions of pounds a week and pretty soon Thatcher says fuck the lot of them—like she did to the miners—withdraws the government contracts and the place goes out of business," Spencer said, sipping his beer and beginning to look as green as Lawson—*bit of a lightweight, this one*, I thought, filing away the info for later use.

"Six thousand men out of work, just like that!" McCreen added, and clicked his fingers. "Belfast's last major employer gone forever."

"So you see, Inspector, they can sack our boy Vardon, but no one's going to fuck with the Transport Workers' Union or the UFF or Tommy Moony," Spencer said.

"It sounds like Moony could be the one who pulled all this off," I thought out loud. "Management guys aren't going to be hauling missiles out of boxes and shipping them through the gate. That's hands-on stuff. You'll need the blue-collar workers for that."

"Don't worry, Inspector, we're on top of this. We've got our eye on the key players. If either Moony or Vardon is involved in any of this, we'll find out, eventually," McCreen said.

"We wouldn't be doing our due diligence on the Michael Kelly murders if we didn't at least interview this Moony character, if only to eliminate Vardon and him from our inquiry. If that's OK?" I said. I gave him a friendly smile and not only got another round in but four packets of Tayto cheese and onion crisps.

When I got back with the drinks and the crisps, McCreen nodded. "I'll let you do that, Duffy, but we'll have to go with you. This is a Special Branch case."

"That's OK with me. Crabbie?" I asked, remembering that technically he was still lead detective.

"Fine with me, Sean."

"When do you want to go?" McCreen asked.

"No time like the present."

"Fuck it, aye, let's go!" McCreen said.

We signed out a Land Rover and drove to the massive, sprawling Short Brothers plant over the river in East Belfast.

In through the factory gates, past an impressive display of parked aircraft including an enormous WW2-era Shorts Sunderland flying boat.

McCreen drove us straight to the Transport Union headquarters, which was a green Portakabin next to one of the aircraft hangars. McCreen and Spencer led us past a secretary straight into Moony's cramped little office. They entered without knocking or being announced, which, I supposed, was how you did things in Special Branch, but something you couldn't get away with in the regular RUC.

Moony was behind a desk stacked with paperwork and books. The office had one little dirty window that barely let in any light, and on the plywood Portakabin walls there was a Short Brothers calendar, a Harland and Wolff calendar, and a big red Union flag.

Moony was on the phone when we came in. He had a Brummie accent that had been softened a little by Ulster.

"Hard hats are compulsory everywhere on the worksite, if they ask you to take them off that is a breach of . . . oh shit, it's the fuzz."

He slammed down the phone and stood up. He was a tall, skinny, lupine character with a shaved head and deep-set, brown eyes. He was wearing a grey boilersuit that accentuated his leanness. He had big, hairy hands with a fading UFF tattoo on three fingers of his right hand. He had indeed been a player at some point . . .

Both Moony and Vardon looked a little bit like Deirdre's artists-impression pic but only a little. Moony was older than the man in the pic and Nigel had softer features.

He stared at McCrabban, Lawson, and myself, and then at McCreen and Spencer.

"This is harassment. That's what this is. Police harassment. You were warned, Inspector McCreen. You'll be hearing from my solicitor this afternoon!" he said.

"This isn't harassment. I'm not here to ask you any questions, Tommy. I was just showing Inspector Duffy where your office is. He's conducting an entirely separate investigation. A murder inquiry. I won't be asking you anything today. So you can tell that to your solicitor," McCreen said.

"I will, don't worry," Moony said, and turned his attention to me. "Now what do you want?"

"I'm Inspector Sean Duffy from Carrick RUC. We're conducting a murder investigation into the deaths of Michael Kelly, his parents, and his girlfriend Sylvie McNichol."

He nodded. "I read about that. Some bloke kills his mum and dad and jumps off a cliff . . . Don't know the woman. Never heard of her," Moony said.

I explained the circumstances surrounding Sylvie's death.

Moony nodded impatiently. "Any road, all very interesting, I'm sure, but what's this got to do with me?"

"Did you ever meet Michael Kelly?" I asked.

"No."

"Did you ever meet Sylvie McNichol or Michael's parents?"

"I doubt it. Never been to Whitehead in my life and I've been saved by the Lord Jesus Christ, so I wouldn't go into any of those Kelly's Bookie Shops either."

"But you do know Nigel Vardon."

"Of course."

"What was your relationship to him?"

"He was a manager here but they got rid of him after the whole missing missile bollocks. What's he got to do with anything?"

"Nigel was one of Michael's good friends. We think Michael was becoming a bit of a mover and shaker in the arms dealing business," I explained.

Moony nodded. "Oh, I get it. Vardon steals the missiles, Michael is the conduit for some sort of international arms deal. It goes wrong and Vardon kills Michael. Is that it?"

"Well, that's one possibility," I admitted.

"Have you met that Vardon guy? That plonker's not killing anyone. Why do you think he has them dogs? He's frightened of his own shadow. Him a killer? No chance."

"How do you know about his dogs?" I asked.

"Pictures of them in his office."

"So you *were* in his office, then."

"Of course I was. And he was in mine. That's how a factory works.

Ever had a real job, Inspector?" Moony said, rolling his eyes. "And besides, your whole theory rests on the fact that somebody did indeed steal a bunch of missiles from under our noses, which I can assure you, Inspector Duffy, they did not."

"How do you know? If the inventory is as messed up as everyone says—"

"As I have very patiently been trying to explain to Chief Inspector McCreen here, nothing goes in or out of this plant without me or the union knowing about it. I don't care what the inventory says or doesn't say; if none of our boys moved it, it didn't leave here. And none of our boys moved any missile systems out of here without a work order. If there's one thing I school into my men it's never do anything without a work order. If you're injured on the job, we go straight to the work order to see who the foreman was, who the manager was, how many men were supposed to be on the job, who the safety inspector was . . . But if they do a job without a work order it's chaos. No, no, no. No work order, no job. And there was no work order for those missiles. Ergo, Inspector, they're still here. Somewhere."

"Nothing can move in and out of here without you knowing about it?" I reiterated.

"That's right."

"What about at night? After dark, after the plant's closed."

He shook his head. "Dubious. You'd have to know exactly where the crates were, you'd have to somehow ship them out without the proper equipment, past half a dozen different security guards into the middle of Belfast. Without any alarms getting tripped or anyone ever seeing it. No way."

"So if they didn't steal the missiles at night, they would have had to do it during the day and you're saying that's impossible because your men weren't involved."

"No such work order was issued. Simple as that."

"So how do you explain this whole scandal, then?" I asked.

"Management screw-up."

"That's all there is to it?"

"Yes. Everybody on the shop floor here goes through a six-year apprenticeship scheme. One of the longest in the world. But the managers? Those blooming idiots? They just hire them right out of university. They don't know anything. Yampy cobs, the lot of them. My men have to teach them on the job."

"So you don't think this is serious?" I asked.

"Oh, it's serious all right! Thatcher is just looking for an opportunity to close us down. Save a few million from the Treasury purse and turf thousands of men on the dole. Butcher us like they did with Harland and Wolff and what they're doing on the Clyde. Ever been to Germany?"

"No, I can't say that—"

"The Germans support their shipyards and heavy industry. They've got the right idea. When all the British yards will have closed the only people left in the world to build warships and cruise ships and tankers will be the Germans and the South Koreans. We can't all be bloody stockbrokers, can we! This country has to make things, you know? We can't all be on the government shilling like you, Inspector Duffy, and you, Chief Inspector McCreen. Oh, it's serious all right, Inspector Duffy. If Shorts goes that's it for Belfast. First Harland and Wolff, and then DeLorean, and us too? The city will be finished!"

"You're not suggesting a conspiracy, are you, Mr. Moony?"

He smiled. "Nah, not a conspiracy, just a common or garden management screw-up."

"Tell me about your brother and your uncle, Mr. Moony," I said, changing tack.

His eyes darkened. "What about them?"

"Players. Your brother's doing twenty years. Your uncle is a UFF commander."

He nodded and looked at McCreen. "Special Branch tell you that, did they?"

"It's common knowledge," I said.

"Well, that's them and they're family and I love them. But it's not me. Look up my charge sheet. Clean."

"It's also common knowledge you were a UFF iceman in the seventies. One of the best, every—"

Moony was on his feet. "That's enough!" he said angrily. "What you're saying is slander. Slander on my reputation. Guilt by association. I never did anything like that."

"Your knuckles tell a different story," I said.

He ran his hand over his bald head.

"When I was a very young man, innocent Protestants were being murdered every day by the IRA and the police were doing nothing to stop it. I did join the UDA and the UFF to protect our streets—1968, inspector, a long, long time ago. We'd just moved here as a family. I didn't know any better. I am a very different man now. I have been born again in the Blood of Christ, Inspector Duffy. I was saved by the Reverend Graham in person, Villa Park, Birmingham, July 7, 1984. I'm a family man. I have two boys and a girl. I know Jonty is doing life for murder. And Toby, well, I'm not going to talk about him in front of police officers, but Toby has, shall we say, chosen the path of violence. But that's not me."

It was a convincing speech. In fact the whole spiel was convincing. When he got breathy and worked up he sounded like Enoch Powell, another lad from the Midlands whose strange stars had taken him to darkest Ulster.

I looked at Lawson and Crabbie to see whether they had anything.

Crabbie asked him about the timeline and Moony claimed to have an alibi for the night of the Kelly murders, for Sylvie's death, and for the night Michael went off the cliff. He was at home with his family. They would all vouch for him. Wife, four kids.

"So the first murder would have been on the night of November 11, 1985," I reiterated.

"Home watching the box. The eleventh of the eleventh . . . always a good war film on the TV."

"Remember the film?"

"*The Great Escape.*"

"And the evening of November twelfth?"

"Work and then home with the family. I don't go out much. Not on a weeknight. Call up the missus and ask her."

"And November nineteenth?"

"Same deal."

We thanked Mr. Moony for his time and drove back to Carrick RUC.

I looked in the Moony family RUC files and I did a quick newspaper index search on whether Billy Graham had indeed come to England in 1984. He had. Everything Moony said checked out. We called up his wife to check on the alibi, and as we suspected she backed her husband all the way.

All five of us went down to Ownies Bar, where the food was good and the black stuff was the best in County Antrim.

"What did you think of Moony?" Spencer asked me over my second pint.

"I thought he was sincere," I said.

Spencer and McCreen laughed bitterly. "He's got you fooled as well, then, I see," McCreen said. "Special Branch intel says he's a player. Big-time player."

"But he found God," Crabbie said. "The Reverend Billy Graham himself. At Villa Park. I looked it up. Cliff Richard sang that day."

"Is this the same Reverend Graham who told President Nixon he was doing the Lord's work when he bombed the shit out of the Chinks?" Spencer said.

"I think you mean the Vietnamese," Lawson said.

"Chinks, Slopes, what's the difference? Point is, I don't believe this phony God number, and I don't believe his bullshit about the work orders, or that he's clear of the UFF."

Spencer looked at McCreen and some secret communication seemed to pass between them.

"I mean, maybe there are no stolen missiles," Spencer continued. "But if there are he's in on the scheme up to his fucking neck."

"So you've Moony under tight surveillance too?" I asked.

"We might have," McCreen said cagily.

"I'm asking because you might be able to verify the alibis of both Vardon and Moony."

McCreen shook his head. "We can't do that. We only got approval for a full-time surveillance operation seventy-two hours ago. Bureaucracy/limited resources, you know how it works."

"But let us assure you, Inspector Duffy, if either Vardon or Moony make a move in the next couple of weeks, we'll know about it and you'll know about it," Spencer said.

"Phone taps?" I asked.

"We're not supposed to tell you," McCreen said. "But I assure you that if either of them mentions anything pertaining to your investigation we will let you know."

I smiled. "See, this is what I like. Special Branch and CID working together."

McCreen stood up to get the next round in. "Sorry about that Fenian crack earlier, really, no offense meant, you know? I actually heard you were a good peeler."

"No offense taken."

Another round.

And another.

Beers. Whiskey. Ciggies.

Improvised pub crawl through Carrick in the drizzle. The Dobbins Inn. The Central Bar. The North Gate. The Borough Arms. The Railway Tavern. The latter three sour, vinegary, paramilitary pubs, filled with dour men in denim jackets looking for trouble but knowing they were out of their depth with the five of us.

Home through the rain to Coronation Road.

Telly, a can of Bass, a late-night call to Kate.

"Sean? Is there anything wrong?"

"Sorry I snapped at you."

"It's OK. Are you all right?"

"I'm fine. I just got worked up. You know? The Tories. That guy in Conservative Central Office rubbed me the wrong way. Bloody Thatcher closing down all the bloody factories. The

Germans are still building ships, aren't they?" I said, slurring my words a little.

"Uhm, look, Sean, I think maybe you've had a little too much to drink."

"I have. I just wanted to apologize. Apologize for everything. I saved her. I saved her and now look what she's doing."

"Are you talking about Mrs. Thatcher? Sean, you've signed the Official Secrets Act; you're not supposed to—"

"Sara wants to get to the real Sean Duffy? Who is the real Sean Duffy? What if there is no real Sean Duffy, eh?"

"Sean, look, it's a quarter to one . . ."

"Sorry, didn't realize the hour. Call you another time."

"All right . . . Look after yourself, Sean, now, won't you?"

"I will."

She was right. Too much booze.

Kitchen sink, dry heaves, room spins, before finally the darkness came and I fell asleep on the unjudgemental ceramic tiles of the chilly, kitchen floor.

20: IS THAT ALL THERE IS TO A FIRE?

Rain. Sleet. A grey, half-hearted dawn.

Phone bleating in the hall.

"Hello?"

"Inspector Duffy?"

"Aye."

"This is Billy Spencer."

"Who?"

"From yesterday. Inspector Billy Spencer. Special Branch."

"Oh yeah. Jesus, you're up early. What's going on?"

"Someone attacked Nigel Vardon's house a couple of hours ago. Our man was parked on the road but they came over the fields so we missed the incident itself."

"What happened?"

"Arson. Brigade boys say it was a petrol bomb."

"Shit."

"And someone's shot his dogs with a crossbow."

"Where are you now?"

"We're here, but I thought you'd want to know. Now that we're all lovey-dovey and everything. Cooperation between our departments."

"What about Moony? Where did he go last night? You've been watching him too, right?"

"We certainly have. He went home after work and didn't leave. No suspicious phone calls either. Listen, are you coming here or not? This is a good development for us. It means Vardon's pissed off somebody, somehow."

"I'll be over."

I called McCrabban and Lawson and filled them in. I pulled on jeans, a jumper and my leather jacket and went outside. My God it was cold.

I looked under the Beemer for bombs, didn't find any, got inside and put on the radio.

A bad night in Ulster for trouble. Riots, demonstrations, sporadic power cuts. The Reverend Ian Paisley, MP, MEP, had held a torch-lit rally at the top of Slemish Mountain telling a crowd of concerned local farmers and excited British journalists that a deal had been struck between Mrs. Thatcher and Satan himself to sell out the good honest people of Ulster. Paisley called for a general strike, noncooperation with the police, and the setting up of a "Third Force" of licensed gun owners who could police Protestant districts instead of the RUC. It wasn't subtle. It was overcooked. It reeked of melodrama. But in Northern Ireland there wasn't much emotional space for subtlety or nuance.

Dolly shot along the seafront. Me in the BMW, grim faced, window wipers on max, listening to all this on the radio.

Up the Tongue Loanen Road toward Ballycarry.

Nigel Vardon's house.

Ex-house.

The fire had brought out a few locals and a journo or two. I met Crabbie and Lawson and DI Spencer, and I talked to the mustachioed, grim-faced fire inspector. Arson, yes. Most definitely. A petrol bomb chucked onto the back porch.

I went and had a chat with the crack Special Branch surveillance team, who hadn't exactly done a quality job here, but the pair of them sitting in a car on the Tongue Loanen Road hadn't seen anyone approach the house.

I examined the two dead Alsatian dogs.

"Who kills a dog?" Crabbie said, visibly upset.

Nigel was sitting in a fire engine cab with a blanket around his shoulders and a cup of tea in his hands.

"Let's talk to him, see what he has to say," I said to the lads.

"Our case, Duffy, I'll do the talking," Spencer said.

"How about we both do the talking?" I suggested.

"OK."

"Mr. Vardon?"

"Yes?"

"Do you remember me? Inspector Duffy, Carrick RUC? We talked the other day. This is DI Spencer from Special Branch whom I think you already know."

"I remember both of youse."

"You want to tell us what happened here tonight?" Spencer asked.

"Someone tried to burn me out. That's all I know."

"You must have an idea about who did this."

He didn't reply.

"Come on, Mr. Vardon, if you help us, we'll help you catch these people," I said.

He looked at me with contempt. "You? You'll catch these people? How are you going to do that?"

"If you help us, we can do it," Spencer insisted.

"No thanks."

"You're refusing to cooperate?" I asked.

"I am cooperating. I just don't know anything. OK?"

"You must have some idea. Enemies. Threatening letters? Phone calls?"

"They killed my dogs!"

"I see that. Tell us who might have done it," I said.

"Well, if it wasn't . . . look, I don't know. Your man Lawrence one field over said my dogs were always worrying his sheep . . . Maybe him?"

"What's his name?"

"Sam Lawrence. That's his house over there. On the other side of the stream."

"You think this bloke Lawrence did this because your dogs were worrying his sheep? Bit excessive, no?"

"Look. Fuck off. OK? I have no idea. Why don't you question him and leave me the fuck alone."

Maybe now wasn't the time.

"Maybe now's not the time," I said to Spencer.

He nodded. "Give him a day or two."

We walked over to the burning house and warmed our hands against the flames. A few local kids were dancing about happily in silhouette.

"Nothing like a fire," I said to McCrabban.

"Nope," he agreed.

"What do you make of the dead dogs, Lawson?" I asked our young recruit.

"The dogs went for the fire starters and they shot them?"

"What else does it tell you?"

"Uhm . . ."

"Think, lad."

"They must have known he had dogs, cos otherwise why come here with a crossbow. So they scouted the place or they knew him."

"Or they saw the photographs in his office. What does it tell you about numbers, Lawson?"

"I'd guess that there were at least two men, possibly three. They probably had a driver, parked on the B road on the other side of the field."

"And three men implies?"

"Organization? Paramilitary involvement?"

I gave McCrabban a nudge. "He's good, isn't he? But still, we'd better go question Farmer Lawrence just to be on the safe side, eh?"

Lawrence was awake looking at the fire with his wife and kids. He was about fifty-five but very fit and strong. We told him about the Alsatians.

"I can't say that I'm sorry. Those dogs got out half a dozen times and ran wild. Worried my sheep, Mr. Finnegan's sheep, and frightened the weans too."

"You wouldn't have killed the dogs and set fire to Mr. Vardon's house, would you?" Spencer asked.

"I would not. I've already got a suit against him in small claims court. As if I'm stupid enough to sue him and then go after his dogs."

I let McCrabban and Lawson continue the questioning while I walked back to Vardon's with Spencer.

"So what do you reckon this was all about, then?" I asked.

"I reckon it's you, Duffy. You went to Moony yesterday and mentioned Vardon to him and Moony sent some lads out here to warn Vardon to keep his fucking mouth shut."

"Why not just kill Vardon?"

"Well, murder brings a lot of heat, doesn't it? And if they have stolen the missiles and are trying to get rid of them . . ."

"I thought you boys were of the school of thought that possibly the missiles hadn't been stolen at all. Open mind and all that?"

Spencer shook his head. "There's things I can't tell you, Duffy, OK? It's surely obvious to you that you've spooked somebody. A certain somebody that used to be a player."

"So you're not buying the God-bothering, then, are you?"

Spencer laughed. "In his younger days he was supposed to be one of the best Loyalist icemen in Belfast. Not street stuff. Political hits. Assassinations. Clever stuff, you know? Tommy was a rare breed. Smart and ruthless. Him getting convinced by Cliff bloody Richard to turn over a new leaf? I don't buy it."

"And crossbowing a couple of dogs would be pretty easy for someone of that ilk," I said.

Spencer groaned. "It would be, except that this little episode wasn't Tommy Moony. Our team has got him under close surveillance and he didn't leave his house last night."

"And another one of your teams had Vardon under surveillance too," I said.

I could feel Spencer bristling in the grey mist.

"Listen, Duffy, I know the quality of policemen that you're used to dealing with in fucking Carrick and Larne, but we're the cream of the crop in Special Branch. University educated. Young. Smart. Good morale. So just watch your lip, OK?"

"Take it easy, Spencer. I'm just saying you'd better keep a good watch on both of them," I said.

"We do," he growled.

"And *we'll* need to talk to Vardon again. Presumably you'll kick up a stink if we come back here alone?"

"I'll come with you. When do you want to do it?"

"Tomorrow?"

"Tomorrow it is."

The next day Spencer met us at the station. I'd been on the late shift and I'd had a horrible night's sleep. It was a frosty morning that was threatening snow so I took the Beemer, which didn't sway around as much as the Land Rovers on the country roads.

We drove up the Tongue Loanen to chez Vardon. A caravan was parked in front of the place where his house used to stand. The building was a twisted abstract of blackened beams, embers, and scorched stone walls. The roof had fallen in, crushing the furniture. In a study at the back of the house tropical fish had been boiled in their tank.

"Monsters, killing his dogs and his fish," McCrabban said, shaking his head.

We knocked on the caravan door.

"Who is it?"

"Carrickfergus RUC."

"And Special Branch."

"Oh, fer fucksake. I've told you peelers I've got nothing to say. I don't know who started the fire."

"Or what happened to Michael Kelly?"

"Or who stole the missiles?" Spencer said.

Nigel opened the caravan door. He was wearing a dirty black hoodie, flared jeans, and he was holding a fluffy white cat.

"How stupid are you guys? I've told you: I don't know shit about missiles! I was wrongfully terminated."

"We're trying to help you here, Mr. Vardon," Spencer said.

"If you want to help me why don't you go arrest that guy, Lawrence," Vardon snarled.

"Mr. Lawrence didn't burn you out. You know who burned you out," I said.

"Who?"

"The Ulster Freedom Fighters."

"Oh yeah, why's that?"

"A wee reminder from Tommy Moony to keep your gob shut," I said.

"About what?" Vardon asked.

"Why don't you tell us what this is all about? We can protect you, Mr. Vardon, we can get you into protective custody over the water. We could get you a new life over the water."

Vardon shook his head.

"I've done nothing wrong. I've got nothing to say to the police. I don't know anything about any stolen missiles or what happened to Michael Kelly, OK?"

Snow began to fall. The now unworried sheep in the field next door began to bleat. Nice up here in the countryside, surrounded by farms and woods with the Irish Sea a hazy, blue-grey line at the eastern horizon.

"Could you leave, please, I've had a very stressful couple of days," Nigel said sniffing and rubbing his nose.

"Was your house insured?" I asked.

"Yes. Of course it was. And before your evil peeler brain kicks into gear, no I didn't shoot my own dogs and burn my own house down."

"They'll come back, you know," I said.

"Who will?" Nigel asked.

"I know how they think. They'll be saying to themselves: 'OK, lads, no worries, we've put the fear of God in Vardon, he'll not say anything.' But then a week or two will go by and they'll be out drinking and one of them will say, 'Maybe we should have finished the job. I mean, why scare him when we can just top him? Dead men tell no tales, right? We were too lenient with that big useless fuck.' They'll be back, Nigel. Sooner or later. You know they will. But we can protect you. We can get you over the water. England. Australia. Wherever . . .'"

"In exchange for what?"

"For what you know about the stolen missiles, for what you know about Michael Kelly's murder."

"I don't know anything about any stolen missiles. And I don't know anything about Michael's death . . . and, even if I did know something, I still wouldn't fucking tell youse. I trust the RUC as far as I could bloody throw ya, and that isn't far," he said, stepped back inside, and slammed shut the caravan door.

"Any ideas, Spencer?"

He shook his head.

"Lawson, McCrabban?"

Nope, nothing from them either.

"Back to the station, then," I said.

"Or a wee country pub," Spencer said. "For breakfast, like."

We found a bar in Ballycarry that was open and had Irish coffees and Ulster fries.

The whiskey in the coffee was loosening Spencer up so I got him another with a double in it.

"You're not a bad sort, Duffy," Spencer said.

"You're not a bad sort, yourself, Spencey, me old mucker. Oi, Sergeant McCrabban, a round of whiskies, eh?" I said and gave Crabbie the minutest of head shakes, which meant a double for Spencer, brown lemonade in a whiskey glass for the rest of us.

A few more rounds like that.

"Don't see why we can't just cooperate, you know? Youse and us. We're all on the same side," Spencer said, red eyed, starting to go.

"That we are. That we are, Spencey, old son. Is there something you're not telling us, mate? Something McCreen doesn't want us cut in on?"

"McCreen? What does he know? You know where he went to school?"

"Lemme guess. Inst?"

Spencer laughed. "You're spot on! You are spot on, Duffy. The Royal Belfast Academical Institution. The bloody establishment."

"Another round, mate?"

"Why not?"

Another double whiskey for Spencer, double brown lemonade for the rest of us.

"So what is it that McCreen doesn't want us to know?" I asked after drawing him out a little more.

"What?" Spencer said sleepily.

"What did Vardon do that McCreen doesn't want us to know about?" I asked.

"Oh aye, that? You really want to know?"

"We really want to know."

"All right. We're all on the same side, eh? We're all going in one direction."

"It's us against the world, mate."

"It is . . . So after the fire . . . After we've all gone, like, Vardon goes to the payphone here in Ballycarry. A payphone that I told McCreen to tap. *Me.* My initiative, not his. He would never have thought of it."

"Who does he call, Spencer?"

"He only calls the private line for the guest house at the US consul's home. Not the Consulate General in Queen Street, mind you, the US consul's private residence out near Holywood," Spencer said.

"That's strange," I said. "Any idea what he talked about?"

"He didn't get through to anyone. The phone just rang and rang."

"Did he call again?"

"No, I think he rumbled it. One of our boys was watching him. Got a little too close."

"Any idea who is staying at this guest house in the US consul's home?"

"Nope. DCI McCreen did ask if we could interview the consul general but we were warned away by the Northern Ireland Office."

"So you just left it there?" I asked.

"Had to. But if he calls again and we get an actual lead the NIO will have to let us proceed. It's all very touchy stuff, you know, Duffy. Diplomatic immunity. Intergovernmental cooperation. You wouldn't want to upset the Americans."

"No, of course not," I agreed. "We wouldn't want to upset the Americans."

21: THE QUIET AMERICAN

We drove Spencer home and I went back to Coronation Road for a nap.

Paraffin heater. Bed. Sleep of the just.

Sara's smell on the pillow, but no Sara. High times for her, busy days. Mustn't come over all heavy with her, give her space, don't appear desperate, Duffy, ya hear me lad?

Downstairs to the kitchen. Coffee. Starlings at the milk bottles. A nasty-looking crow staring at me from the drooping curve of the telegraph wire. A dusting of snow in the garden. A dusting of snow up my left nostril.

I stuck on the lunchtime news. More riots. Tedious now. Depressing. You ever read Thucydides? I'll boil him down for you into one easy moral: *intergenerational civil war is a very bad thing.*

I dressed in my jeans, black DM's, Che T-shirt, black polo-neck sweater, leather jacket. Checked under the Beemer. No bombs today, chum. Drove to the police station, where I encountered a protest by a score of DUP councilors, UVF proxy councilors, and other assorted riff-raff.

A man called Jimmy Harlan, an "Independent Unionist" councilor from Sunnylands, got in front of the car. "Police scum! You're all Lundies! You're all traitors! You're all in it together!" he yelled, and for good measure smacked his ULSTER SAYS NO placard off my windscreen.

I put the Beemer in neutral and got out, grabbed the placard from his hand, and broke it over my knee. "You'd better not touch my fucking car again. Any of you!" I said.

"Aye, the car you got with blood money, traitor's gold. You're all in on it," Harlan persisted.

"You're in on it too, Jimmy, don't deny it," I said, and turned to address the mob. "You think *they* would let Councilor Harlan speak freely, if *they* hadn't already sanctioned it? He's part of it and he fucking knows it. He's only here to give you the illusion of freedom and dissent. He's the worst of the fucking lot of us!"

It was Marcusian pearls before swine, but it made me feel better. Maybe give them food for thought. I got in the Beemer and drove into the station. When I got out of my space I saw that someone had thrown eggs at the back window.

I went up to Chief Inspector McArthur's office seething.

"Listen, mate, you can't have a protest right in front of the station like this. It's bad for morale."

"What can I do?" McArthur said.

"Disperse them."

"There's councilors out there."

"So?"

"What about free speech?"

"Fuck free speech. Get those eejits away from the station entrance. That's your fucking job, pal."

"I'll have to consult with my superiors," he said.

"Yeah, do that and do it now. You're making us all look bad, McArthur."

I went into CID. Crabbie was already there. He let me blow off steam about the protests and McArthur. When Lawson arrived I told him to sign out a Land Rover.

"Where are we going?" Crabbie asked.

"The US consul's private residence, Holywood, County Down."

I drove past the demo avoiding the temptation to run them all over and I put the radio on Radio 3. Mercifully they were playing Toru Takemitsu's "Rain Coming," a hidden gem that almost nobody in the UK apart from myself and the Radio 3 music selector knew about. I could see that McCrabban and Lawson hated the fuck out of it, so I turned it up out of spite.

Light snow. Heavy traffic on the A2.

The US consul general lived in a cul de sac on the water in Holy-wood, County Down, which was known as Northern Ireland's most exclusive community. It was a big old Edwardian house that originally had been built as one of the Belfast residences of the Marquess of Lon-donderry. Sturdy stone walls. Three storeys. Nicely kept lawns. Palm trees. Private beach.

There were uniformed and armed US Marines outside the gates who checked our IDs thoroughly before letting us through.

The guesthouse was on the same grounds as the main house. A small, two-story, neo-Georgian, manse-style structure almost right on the beach.

The door was already open for us when I parked the Beemer in the gravel driveway and walked up the steps of the main house. At the top of the steps a bespectacled, tanned, nervous young American woman with a clipboard was waiting for us.

"I'm very sorry, Officers, but there must be some misunder-standing; the consul is already at his office in Belfast—"

"We're not here to see the consul. We're here to see the person staying in the guesthouse."

"Mr. Connolly?" she asked, very surprised indeed.

"Yes, Mr. Connolly."

She looked at her clipboard and then at us. She swallowed, pushed her glasses up her nose. She was about Lawson's age. A bit of a looker. "Do you, do you, uh, do you have an appointment?" she asked.

"We don't need an appointment; we're the police."

"Oh. Yes. Well, uhm, look, I'll ask him, but I don't know if he'll agree to talk to you. Mr. Connolly isn't part of the official delegation. I don't know if he'll speak to you."

"We'll cross that bridge when we come to it. What's Mr. Connolly's first name again?"

"John."

"That's right. John Connolly. That's who we're here to see. May we wait for him inside?"

It was, of course, extremely important to get permission implied or explicit to enter the residence as it was considered US territory and thus beyond the remit of our authority. Vampires and cops had to be invited in.

"Oh yes, of course, uhm, follow me, can I get you gentlemen a cup of coffee?"

She led us into a large, conference-style room with a long hardwood table and chairs, and portraits not only of American worthies but also originals of the Marquess of Londonderry's diverse clan of wasters and ne'er-do-wells. Probably been hanging on these walls since the First World War.

"Sorry, what's your name, miss?" I asked the young woman.

"Melanie Ford," she said.

"Miss Ford, mine's black, two sugars, if you don't mind," I said.

"White, two sugars," Crabbie said.

"White, no sugar," Lawson said.

"And if you've got any biscuits that would be brilliant," I added.

She went off. The distant sound of a heated conversation. No coffee. No biscuits. A man came into the room. About forty, greying black hair, craggy, curiously simian ears. He was wearing a civilian black suit, but over the left breast he was sporting a series of medal ribbons. The full scrambled egg. I recognized two of them: one was a Purple Heart, the other was the flag of South Vietnam. He'd also been decorated with some kind of US military cross.

"You were looking for me?" he asked in a boyish, middle-American accent with a slight Southern lilt.

"You are Mr. John Connolly?"

"That's me." He smiled and sat down at the table.

I introduced myself, Crabbie, and Lawson, and explained that we were investigating the suspected murder of Sylvie McNichol, Michael Kelly, and Michael Kelly's parents.

Connolly cocked an eyebrow. "I don't know who those people are," he said.

"Michael Kelly's best friend was one Nigel Vardon. Name ring a bell?" I said.

"Nope."

"There was an arson attack on Mr. Vardon's home two nights ago, and very soon thereafter he called you at your residence here. Any idea why he would do a thing like that?"

"None at all," Connolly said cheerfully.

"You can't offer any explanation?" I asked.

"No."

"Could you have met Mr. Vardon in a social setting?"

Connolly rubbed his all-American, clean-shaven, square jaw. "I doubt it. I haven't done much socializing since coming here to Belfast."

"What are you doing here in Northern Ireland, Mr. Connolly?" I asked.

He shook his head. "Ah, now that I can't tell you, Inspector. Classified government work."

"Can I ask which US government department you're working for?"

"You can ask, but I am not at liberty to tell you, Inspector Duffy." He gave me what he must have thought of as a reassuring smile. "I will say that what we're attempting to do will benefit citizens of both the government of the United States and that of the United Kingdom."

What the fuck did that mean?

"Let me see if I understand you, Mr. Connolly. You're working for the US government on a classified mission that will mutually benefit the governments of the US and the UK?"

"You have it in a nutshell. I couldn't have said it better myself."

He leaned back in the chair, thoroughly satisfied now. He grinned a gap-toothed, monkey grin and Miss Ford finally came in with the coffee and the cookies.

"Mr. Vardon was sacked from his job at Short Brothers," I said.

"Was he? So?"

"He worked in the Missile Division. Developing the new Javelin system. He was sacked after some of the missiles allegedly went missing. Could that possibly have something to do with why you are here in Northern Ireland?"

"I'm not at liberty to say, Inspector," he replied.

"The RUC has cooperated with the FBI on a number of occasions. Inter-agency cooperation is mutually beneficial, sir," I said.

Connolly frowned before he understood what I was suggesting.

"Ah, no, Inspector Duffy, I am not with the FBI. That I *can* tell you."

"Which department of the United States government do you work for? Can you tell me that?"

"No."

"You were a soldier, though, weren't you?"

He gave a half-shake of his head before saying: "I can't confirm that information either, Inspector Duffy."

"Are you still a serving officer in the United States Army?"

"I am not in the United States Army."

"Are you in the Navy? Or the Marine Corps?"

"I am not at liberty to tell you my current position or job title within the administration. That's classified information," he said sharply.

I stared at the dull eyes, the rock-hard posture, the curious, bland, thin, chimp-like face. He looked at his watch.

"Gentlemen, I'm a very busy man, as I'm sure you are too. I'm sorry that I couldn't have provided more assistance to you in this matter."

"We just have a few more questions," I said.

"Be that as it may, I'm afraid I'm going to have to ask you to leave. We are really very busy around here."

He got to his feet. Lawson and McCrabban got up but I didn't move. I took a sip of the rather good coffee.

"Is it a special occasion for American service personnel today?" I asked.

"No."

"So you wear those medal ribbons all the time on your civilian clothes?"

He could see that I was fucking with him now and he didn't like it one bit.

"As I say, I'm a very busy man, Mr. Duffy, I'm sure you can see yourself out from here."

"One more question, Mr. Connolly: where were you on the night of November eleventh of this year?"

"Where was I on November eleventh? I'd have to consult my datebook."

"Please do so."

"Oh, wait, I probably have it here in my diary," he said, taking a little book from his inside pocket.

"On November eleventh I was in Switzerland," Connolly announced triumphantly.

"Whereabouts in Switzerland?"

"Zurich."

"What were you doing in Switzerland?"

"United States government business. I was there from November eighth until November fifteenth. Then I flew back to Belfast, via London. What happened on November eleventh?"

"That was the night Michael Kelly's parents were killed and he was possibly abducted."

"I didn't know the gentleman and, as I say, I was out of the country," Connolly said.

"Can you prove that you were out of Ireland from November eighth to November fifteenth?"

"I'm sure that someone in my office can supply you with credit card receipts, hotel and airplane reservation information, that kind of thing."

"What hotel were you staying at in Zurich?"

He looked in his diary. "The Dolder Grand, 65 Kurhausstrasse Street."

"Strasse means street," Lawson said.

"Excuse me?" Connolly said.

"Constable Lawson was pointing out that Kurhausstrasse means Kurhaus Street; you don't need to say the word street twice," I said. I showed him the photocopy of the artist's impression. "Ever seen this man?"

"No. Now I really must be—"

"Where were you on the evening of November nineteenth?"

He flipped through his diary again. "November nineteenth?"

"Yes." The nineteenth was the night of Sylvia McNichol's supposed suicide.

"Ah, I'm afraid I can't tell you where I was on the nineteenth," Connolly said.

"You don't remember?"

"I know where I was but I am not prepared to give you an answer as to my movements on the nineteenth."

"You'd rather not say?" I asked incredulously.

"I exercise my Fifth Amendment rights to refuse to answer that question."

"Your Fifth Amendment rights?"

"Exactly. And I believe I can also exercise executive and diplomatic privilege."

"Be that as it may, Mr. Connolly, I'm conducting a murder investigation and it seems to me that you're withholding evidence that may be pertinent to our inquiries."

"Believe me, Duffy, I've got nothing to do with your little murder investigation. I'm working at a level far above your pay grade. And you might want to think twice before accusing a United States government official of being mixed up in some kind of local homicide. Now I think perhaps it's time that you left . . . Steven!"

A functionary saw us to the front door and ushered us outside. We walked across the gravel to the Land Rover in a reflective mood.

"Thoughts?" I said.

"Why did you ask him about his whereabouts? Surely he's not a suspect in the Kelly murders?" McCrabban said.

"You heard what he said. Government agency. Maybe he's CIA? He was tall, wasn't he? Didn't Deirdre say the person outside her house was tall and thin?"

"Tommy Moony is tall and thin. So's Nigel Vardon come to that," Crabbie said.

"So's Alan Osbourne . . . well, maybe not the thin part, but he is tall," Lawson said.

"All four of them aren't that far off the artist's-impression picture," I said.

"But this guy had an alibi for the night of the Kelly murders," McCrabban said.

"Yes. So he says. We'll have to check it out."

"What were you asking him about the ribbons for?" McCrabban wondered.

"You don't normally wear medal ribbons on a civvy suit except on special occasions. He's a vain man. But he did serve in Vietnam. He's no coward."

We got back in the Land Rover and drove into Belfast.

"So what happens now, sir?" Lawson asked.

"We'll formally ask the consul general's office for information about John Connolly, but based on past experience of dealing with the Americans I think two things will happen. First, they won't tell us anything. Second, we'll never bloody see John Connolly again. If he's a spook he knows he's been blown. He'll be spirited out of the country."

"What about Special Branch? They're going to be livid," McCrabban said.

"I'll call them when we get home. Better they hear from me than through channels. I'll send them over a bottle of Islay as an apology. Maybe two bottles."

"Isn't that why you got so angry at Oxford CID? A whiskey bribe to an Irishman?" Lawson said.

"It worked, didn't it? I didn't throw the book at them."

We went back to Carrick RUC. Lawson checked the Swiss hotel and a Mr. Connolly had indeed stayed there on the nights in question under an Irish passport, which was very interesting. A lot of Americans had Irish passports. But American diplomats?

The consulate told us nothing about Connolly, as I'd been expecting. They refused to confirm whether he was with the mission in Belfast and forwarded our inquiries to the embassy in London, who told us they would get back to us but never did. If that kept up I could always turn to my good friend Kate Albright from MI5.

Lawson found a flight from Zurich to Belfast that left at 9 p.m. on the night of November fifteenth. There was no John Connolly on that flight, but if the man was a spook with multiple passports . . .

I poured myself a stiff drink and called Special Branch. They were indeed livid about our interview with Mr. Connolly, but when the two bottles of eighteen-year-old Islay arrived they soothed the savage breast as eighteen-year-old single-malt Islay whiskey is wont to do.

22: DAVENPORT BLUES

Sara had decided to come over. Hadn't seen much of her. Her hair was shorter and blonder. She looked good. She was happy. She'd had four front-page stories since the Anglo-Irish Agreement riots had begun. It's an ill wind . . .

She was in the kitchen making a casserole, one of her "specialties," she claimed. I was in the living room listening to more Toru Takemitsu. His early percussion work—all John Cage meets Japanese trad music meets Carl Orff's post-Nazi stuff for kids. Acquired taste to say the least.

I put down the *Belfast Telegraph*. Page two said that Philip Larkin was dead, aged sixty-three. I went to the book case upstairs and looked out the *Selected Poems* and his jazz criticism.

The phone rang.

"Duffy here."

"Sean, it's me."

"What's up, Crabbie?"

"Are you OK, Sean. I didn't bother you? I know it's your night off."

"No, I'm fine. Just reading."

"Anything good?"

"Philip Larkin's jazz criticism. He wishes the world had stopped in 1950."

"Amen to that . . . Listen, Sean, Strathclyde Police have been on the blower. Two bits of bad news. One pretty serious, I'm afraid."

"Tell me," I groaned.

"Well, first of all, as instructed, they showed Deirdre Ferris pictures of Moony, Vardon, Osbourne, and Connolly, and she can't say for certain if it was any of them outside her house that night."

"Is that the really bad news?"

"No. The really bad news is that apparently Deirdre has blown the safe house. They want to move her now and they want us to pay for the move. I ran it by Sergeant Dalziel and he said it'll have to come out of the CID budget, not the station budget."

"Blown how?"

"She told her ma where she was staying, so her ma could forward all her Christmas presents to her."

"Where is she staying again?"

"Some flat in Ayr, just south of Glasgow."

"She gave her ma that address?"

"Aye, and her ma's told all her friends and relations where to send the presents too. Strathclyde Police are having kittens. They think some goon's gonna come over and murder her."

"Yeah, it's OK to move her, then. We'll pay for it. I'll find the money somehow."

"Thanks, Sean, I'll give them the go-ahead."

"And tell them to keep that wee doll away from the telephone."

Sara called me into the kitchen, handed me a can of Bass and a dish of casserole, which I had to admit looked pretty good.

"What's the matter, Sean? I heard you on the phone. Bad news?"

I told her about Deirdre Ferris's big mouth.

"Strathclyde Police think that someone's going to come over from Belfast and murder her."

"Why wouldn't they come over and murder her?" Sara said.

"Well, she might not even be telling the truth about seeing someone outside her flat that night."

"But if she is telling the truth and she's just blabbed the location of her safe house, why wouldn't the killer come over and clean up that loose end? He's ruthless. He killed Sylvie. He killed Michael and his parents. What's one more murder to him?"

I put down the can of Bass. "You might have something here. We get Deirdre to a different safe house, then we stake out the old safe house to see if anyone shows up."

"And I get the story if you catch the killer!"

I called Crabbie back and ran the scapegoat idea past him. He liked it. I ran the Ayr trip past the Chief Inspector and he didn't give a damn what we did as long as it didn't involve the higher-ups and was within our budget.

I phoned Lawson. "Stranraer ferry tomorrow morning. Six a.m. boat. Be there for five thirty. Don't be late."

"What?"

"Be at Larne harbor for five thirty, pack a change of clothes, don't be late."

Larne to Stranraer on the ferry.

Alone on the freezing stern deck smoking grass, looking back at the County Antrim coast in the pre-dawn light.

Crabbie inside eating egg and sausages, Lawson sitting next to Crabbie looking peaky.

Arrival at the unpretentious Scottish port of Stranraer.

We drove the Beemer off the boat and up the really quite lovely A719 to Ayr. DI Cyril Bullock from the local CID met us at Ayr police station. A chubby, curly-haired, wee character with glasses and an elbow-patched, corduroy jacket that made him seem like the new maths teacher. He told us that Deirdre was gone, rushed away in the middle of the night for her own safety.

"She's to be allowed no access to the telephone. For all intents and purposes she's still here," I explained to Bullock.

"Aye. That makes sense," he agreed.

We set up the stake-out between us. Bullock reckoned that the three of us and a rotating team of four Strathclyde CID officers would be sufficient for the job. A bigger team would have been better, but Ayr was a small cop shop and we didn't want to overburden them for what would probably amount to nothing.

"How long do ye think we'll have to do this?" Bullock asked.

I shrugged and looked at McCrabban.

"A week?" he suggested.

"A week tops; we can't really afford the man hours for longer."

We followed Bullock to the safe house, which actually was a rather nice flat overlooking the water, the strand, and Goat Fell on the Isle of Arran.

We staggered the watches between the two forces.

Two men outside the flat, two inside at all times.

First night stake-out—zilch.

In the morning we found a little café on the seafront which did the full Scottish breakfast, which consisted of bacon, eggs, pancakes, toast, black pudding, white pudding, and haggis.

Washed down the breakfast with oily coffee and smokes.

Downtime walking around Ayr. Crabbie found a Presbyterian church where John Knox had given a sermon. We all made our way sooner or later to the Robbie Burns Cottage. I ran my fingers along Burns's thatching and a passing lady motorist stopped her car, wound down her window, and said, "Please don't touch the thatching," in Maggie Smith's Jean Brodie voice.

The sun setting over the Firth of Clyde.

Darkness.

Shifts again. Strathclyde CID outside in a patrol car. Carrick RUC inside the flat.

Midnight came and went. I let Lawson get a kip. Crabbie was up reading the New Testament. I lay on the living-room sofa reading Philip Larkin's essay on Django Reinhardt.

In a way it is the jazzman who, in this century, has lived the life of the artist. At a time when the established arts are generally accepted and subsidized with unenthusiastic reverence, he has to suffer from prejudice or neglect to get the unique emotional language of our age recognized. And he has been able to do this by the intensity of his devotion to the art. It is hard to think of the career of say Bix Beiderbecke or Charlie Parker without sensing something of the emotion of Wordsworth's "We poets in our youth began in gladness/But thereof come in the end despondency and madness."

I put down the book. Father McGuire, that melancholy Cumbrian sadist, had beaten more stanzas of Wordsworth into my slender frame than I cared to think about. I was certain that the line in Wordsworth actually read "We poets in our youth *begin* in gladness."

I was about to ask the Crabman whether he knew any Wordsworth when the radio crackled into life.

"Duffy, there's someone coming up to the fourth floor that we don't recognize from the building. Big lad, jeans. Parka," Bullock said.

Crabbie put down his Bible.

I went to the bedroom and woke up Lawson.

"Wassa—"

I put my hand over his mouth.

"Ssshhh. Someone coming."

I tiptoed across the flat to the bedroom.

"Keep the lights off," I whispered to Crabbie.

Lawson was nervously holding his revolver.

"For God's sake don't point that thing at us," Crabbie whispered.

I advanced carefully across the apartment.

There was someone right outside the door.

I put my fingers to my lips and nodded to the lads.

We heard the jangle of a keychain. Skeleton key, no doubt.

No voices. No whispers. Solo job.

A metallic scraping at the lock?

I had a good view of the door handle in the moon and ambient street light. If it began turning I'd see.

The radio crackled. "Has he come up yet, Duffy?" Bullock said.

The scraping noise stopped.

I turned the radio off but it was too late. I heard running down the corridor.

I turned the radio back on. "He's coming back down. Grab him!"

I opened the flat door but there was no one there. I ran along the hallway and sprinted down the stairs. When I got to the lobby Bullock was standing there looking at me.

"He didn't come out this way!" he said.

"Who's out the back?" I asked.

"DC McGrath."

We ran out the back. McGrath had been barreled into a metal bin and knocked unconscious.

"Sean!" McCrabban said. "On the street!"

I looked to where he was pointing. A figure in a balaclava was sprinting along the Esplanade.

We drew our sidearms and bolted after him.

"Stop! Armed police!" I yelled.

He kept running.

"Get after him, Lawson!" I screamed at the kid, and he took off like he was on fire.

"Halt! Police!" Lawson yelled as he gained on the man.

Balaclava Man darted across Cromwell Road and into a car park.

Lawson had halved the distance to him.

"Go on, son!" I yelled.

The man turned and shot at Lawson twice with a semi-automatic pistol. Lawson dived for cover. The man shot at him again and ran on.

I pulled out my Glock and fired three rounds at him, but in the dark at that distance I had no chance.

I reached Lawson. "Are you OK, lad?"

"Yes, sir."

He'd twisted an ankle but otherwise was unhurt.

"Stop! Armed police!" I yelled again and fired three more rounds at the man as he skidded to a halt next to a Porsche 944. He jumped in the passenger-side door and the car screamed off down Montgomerie Terrace.

I narrowed the angle and almost got level with the car at Arran Terrace.

The passenger-side window opened and the man shot his entire clip at me. I hit the deck and crawled behind a Volvo 240.

The big old Volvo was clobbered numerous times. Engine block, door, door, door. Thud, thud, thud, thud. Good grouping. Hell of a shot.

When I got to my feet the Porsche was a hundred yards away and doing 80 mph.

Two beats later and it was gone down Montgomerie Terrace to the A719 or the A70, and from there to basically anywhere in Ayrshire. At that speed they could be in Glasgow in twenty minutes, but if they were smart they'd ditch the vehicle as soon as they could and either hijack another, or wait somewhere safe until the manhunt was over.

As I caught my breath I could hear the Porsche's throaty 170-horsepower engine tear up the quiet evening air. I heard them hit fifth gear on the manual gearbox and then I heard them no more.

"I didn't know you had guns!" a shocked Bullock said to me.

"Of course we have guns; we're the RUC," I said.

"I dinnae think you're allowed to bring your guns over here! This is going to cause us a whole mountain of paperwork," he said, visibly upset.

"Fuck the paperwork, get on to Traffic and get a fucking roadblock set up sharpish!"

Bullock notified Traffic. Traffic set up a roadblock on the slip road to the motorway.

We went to the station to await developments.

The Porsche was found burned out in East Kilbride two hours later. No sign of the men. No usable forensics.

"They won't be back to the flat," Crabbie said.

"Nope. We blew it."

"Couldn't be helped, Sean. We did all we could."

"Did we?"

"'Course we did. Try not to be so hard on yourself," McCrabban said, and patted me on the shoulder, which, for him, was a bold foray into interpersonal contact.

"All right," I said.

"He wasn't that tall a man," Lawson said. "Five ten maybe. And he had a partner. So maybe the paramilitaries?"

"Nevertheless we'll check the alibis on all our suspects," I said.

Unfortunately for us both Nigel Vardon and Tommy Moony were, according to Special Branch, safe at home in their beds. I made them check for us just to be on the safe side. They knocked at the door and woke them both up. John Connolly wasn't answering his phone and the consulate staff refused to say whether he was still in Ireland or not. Alan Osbourne was home in his London flat.

Back to Ulster on the ferry. The stink of diesel. The grey water. The boat chugging unenthusiastically into Larne Harbor. Ports are places of beauty and mystery but Larne, as always, was the exception to the rule.

"I don't think we'll even bother going into the station today. The Troubles will continue on their merry way without us," I informed the men.

"I could do with a day on the farm," McCrabban said.

"Take it. And you could do with getting that ankle looked at, Lawson."

"Yes, sir."

"And don't worry about Scotland. I'll type up a report for McArthur that will make us all look good."

BMW to Coronation Road. A bread van in my parking space. No sign of the owner. I had to park two doors down in front of Bobby Cameron's place. Sort of thing that would piss him off, so I walked down the path and rang his doorbell.

He came to the door holding a baby and a tin of Heinz beans.

"What's the matter, Duffy?" he asked suspiciously.

"I'm in your parking spot is all," I said. "Just wanted to let you know."

"What's wrong with yours?"

"Bread van's in it."

"Oh. Right. You wanna know why that is?"

"Does it involve the bread man having a torrid affair with one of the chronically lonely housewives on this street?"

"Maybe."

"Then I definitely do not want to know."

I said good-bye to Bobby and went home. I kipped for a couple of hours, checked the cinema listings in the *Belfast Telegraph*, called Sara at work.

"You wanna go to the flicks tonight?"

"You finally caught me on a slow day! What'll we see?"

"How about *When Father Was Away on Business* at the QFT?"

"What's that about?"

"It's about a kid growing up in Yugoslavia after the war."

"Yikes! What about *Out of Africa*? It's an early screener. Tickets are going round the office; they're like Gold dust."

"Sure. Yeah. Heard good things. Read the book. She's an interesting character. Starved herself to death. Like Bobby Sands."

"What? I don't think it's about that. It's about Africa. Robert Redford's in it."

"I'll pick you up at six."

I shaved, showered, dressed in a suit, checked under the Beemer, and drove to the office. I sat in my office, typed a report on our Ayr adventure, emphasizing the "excellent inter-force cooperation with the Strathclyde Police."

After lunch I got back in the Beemer and drove to the Shorts factory in East Belfast.

I flashed the warrant card and got passed through a couple of low-level flunkies before a very senior manager agreed to see me. I could tell he was a very senior manager because he was from Ballymena and he was wearing a wig. No junior manager could have survived both of those handicaps.

We shook hands and sat in an empty conference room overlooking the Harbor Airport.

"So you're here about the missiles? Are you with Special Branch?" Mr. Williams asked me.

I explained where I was from and my interest in the case.

"Has there been any progress in finding out what exactly happened?" I asked.

"I'm afraid not. We still don't know who stole them."

"But you know that they were stolen? That's a development, surely?" I said.

"We've known that all along. The inventory thing was a cover story the government made us put out for national security reasons."

I was surprised. "Do Special Branch know that?"

"Oh yes."

"They never told us! They were always humming and hawing about it."

"I assume it was on a need-to-know basis only."

I flipped open my notebook. "So what exactly got nicked?"

"Six Javelin Mark 1 missile systems."

"What's a missile *system*?"

"The missile and the launching mechanism and the radar control."

"Bulky?"

"In its original box, yes. But it could be broken down."

"Do a lot of damage with six Javelin missiles?"

"Yes. But the tech is even more valuable."

"How so?"

"If you got access to the technology you could reverse-engineer it. And with six different rockets to play with you really could get to the guts of the system pretty quickly."

"Who'd want to do a thing like that?" I asked.

"Oh, I don't know. Your guess is as good as mine. The South Africans? The Russians? The Iranians?"

"Would the Americans be involved by any chance?" I asked.

"The Americans? Irish Americans? Terrorists, you mean? IRA?"

"No. The government."

"Oh no, I don't think so. The Americans have their own missile systems that are as good as the Javelin, superior in many ways. There are no intellectual property or proprietary patents that they'd be interested in that I can see."

"Special Branch seem to be focusing their attention on Nigel Vardon and Tommy Moony."

"That's who I'd look at."

"Why?"

"Nigel was the manager in charge of security and Moony runs the Transport Union. Nothing moves in here without Moony's say-so."

"Nigel got the sack but Moony's still in his job."

"We can't sack Moony. The whole plant would come out on strike. Or worse."

"Worse?"

"He's paramilitary, isn't he?"

"So they say. Have you heard of a man called John Connolly?"

"No. The name doesn't ring a bell."

"Are you sure?"

"Yes."

"Could terrorists in Northern Ireland use these missiles?"

"I'm sure they could. But that would mean a transaction between the Loyalists and the IRA."

"Because it was an inside job?"

"Exactly! The missiles were almost certainly stolen by workers in this factory who, I'm sorry to say, are overwhelmingly from East Belfast and therefore ..."

"Overwhelmingly Protestant and if thus connected to a terrorist group it would have to be a Loyalist one."

"Indeed."

"Ever seen this guy?" I asked, and handed him the artist's impression.

"No, and I wouldn't want to."

"Thank you, Mr. Williams, you've been very helpful. You don't need to tell Special Branch that we had this little chat. They're ridiculously overprotective about their turf."

I drove back to Belfast and called in at the American consulate. I showed my warrant card and asked whether I could possibly see a Mr. John Connolly.

An extremely pretty red-headed secretary told me to wait.

She made a phone call, smiled, wrote something on a pad and hung up.

"I'm afraid Mr. Connolly is unavailable today," she said in a pleasant Southern accent.

"Unavailable today? So he's still in Belfast, then?"

"Yes."

"Do you know when he might be available?" I asked.

"No. Can I take a message?"

"No message, thank you. You've been very helpful. Love your accent. Where in the States are you from?"

"Little Rock."

On principle I like to be as chatty to secretaries and assistants as I can possibly be, but the only thing that came to mind when she said Little Rock was an image of some fat redneck sheriff beating some black kids, so I said nothing, exited the consulate, and took the short walk to the *Telegraph* offices.

I was puzzled.

John Connolly was still "in country." He hadn't flown the coop. He was still here. We'd clearly blown him, which meant that he was either sloppy or desperate . . .

Sara was pleased to see me.

"You're a man," she said.

"I am," I agreed.

"Can I ask you one of the survey questions for the women's page? It'll only take a minute."

"OK, fire away."

"Dogs or cats?"

"Dogs."

"Boxers or briefs?"

"Marks and Spencer whips."

"I'll write briefs. Panties or knickers?"

"What's the difference?"

"There is no difference. It's about the word. Which word sounds sexier?"

"Knickers sounds like something you'd wear in a 1950s' Carry On film."

The survey continued in similar vein.

We went out to dinner at an adequate Italian place. We saw *Out of Africa*. It was nothing like the book but Sara loved it. Crying at the end and I knew I was well in. I drove her back to Coronation Road.

Gin and tonics and in tribute to Philip Larkin: Bix Beiderbecke.

"That was so sad," she said.

"Wasn't it, though?"

"It was so sad when he died. She'll never find love. That was her one true love, wasn't it?"

"Redford?"

"Yes."

"In real life he was English."

"And did she have VD in real life?"

"Syphilis. Funny that he didn't even try to do an English accent. Probably couldn't do it. Knew Streep would act him off the screen."

Sara paused in mid-drink and looked at me. "You're always nit-picking. Have you ever noticed that?"

Dodgy situation this. Agree with her. "Yeah, you're right. It's not important."

"You didn't even like it, did you?"

"No. It was good. Beautifully shot and the music was great and she was terrific, and the guy who was the villain in that Bond film was pretty good."

Sara had put her glass on the coffee table.

She wiped the tears from her face.

"Tell the truth. Did you even like it?"

"Yes."

"You're lying to me."

"What's the big deal? It's *Out of* fucking *Africa*."

"You didn't like it."

"It was fine."

"Can you take me home, please?"

"Are you kidding?"

"I'd like to go home. Will you take me or shall I walk?"

"Wait here while I go and check under the car for bombs."

"Very dramatic."

"Very necessary."

"I'm sure."

I went outside, checked under the Beemer.

"OK," I said.

I drove her home. We didn't speak. Outside her house I tried to make up. "Look, Sara, I'm really sorry if I—"

"Oh, Sean," she said. "It's not really . . . This isn't about . . . My life is just so complicated right now."

She gave me a kiss on the cheek and got out of the car.

"Do you want me to walk you to your door?" I asked.

"No. Thank you . . . Bye."

"Bye."

I drove down to the castle car park and rolled a joint. I walked to the radar station at the end of the harbor pier to smoke in peace.

There were no stars. Or wind. Light snow was falling into the calm black sea à la Basho.

The joint was too loosely rolled and kept going out. I finally tossed it.

I walked back to the car along the steep-sided harbor wall.

When I got home Bix Beiderbecke was still playing. Poor sod. Died at twenty-eight of overwork and the booze. Jazz's "number 1 saint," Benny Green sarcastically called him. He was good, though, you couldn't deny that. Good on horn and piano.

I played "Davenport Blues" three times in a row. Tommy Dorsey on trombone, Don Murray on clarinet.

Sublime. Fucking sublime. And there was no one else on this street, or in this town, or in this fucking country to share it with.

"Fuck it," I said, took the record off and went to bed.

23: STASIS

Case conference. No dice with forensics. No dice with eyewitnesses. No dice with tips from the Confidential Telephone or on our artist's-impression pic or anything else relating to the case.

This was how all murder cases in Ulster died. No one knew anything. No one would tell you anything. And if forensics couldn't deliver a hat trick then the only way to bring in your suspect was to fit him up or beat him up.

But those were the old ways of the RUC. The seventies ways. This was the mid-1980s. This was the brave new world.

Crabbie was stumped. I was stumped. Even bright young Lawson was stumped. We asked Glasgow CID to show Deirdre Ferris pictures of Nigel Vardon, Alan Osbourne, John Connolly, and Tommy Moony again, but she still insisted that she couldn't tell whether any of them was the man she *claimed* to have seen outside her house the night Sylvie was *allegedly* murdered.

I called Inspector Spencer at Special Branch, asked about the latest updates. Fanny Adams on the missiles, Shorts still conducting an internal review, SB pursuing every lead but no one was talking and the lines were cold.

No leads forthcoming there. No leads forthcoming anywhere.

The three of us sat in the CID incident room looking at one another.

"Either of you think of anything to do?"

Lawson shrugged.

"There's good money to be made if we volunteer for riot duty," Crabbie said.

He was right. The Prods were rioting every night and the cops were getting stretched very thin. It wasn't just about the Anglo-Irish Agreement now. It was about the future. The Prods could read the demography. The Prods could see the writing on the wall. In November 1985 it was a benign, toothless document called the Anglo-Irish Agreement, but if population trends continued the Prods would become a minority in the six counties and the whole *raison d'être* for Northern Ireland would cease to exist. Northern Ireland was becoming Algeria, and everyone was worried that Mrs. Thatcher was becoming De Gaulle.

But riot duty? Not for me. I didn't need the money or the aggravation.

Case conference over. Back to my office. Whiskey in the coffee, staring at the lough. Black, sleekit, greasy water; grubby, little boats. The world was mean and damp. The music was Peggy Lee's *Greatest Hits*. Leiber and Stoller's existential classic "Is That All There Is?" on a loop.

Revolver sitting on desk. Well oiled. Six .38 slugs. Was it ennui that killed all those RUC men who blew their brains out every year? As Peggy Lee warned in the song, death was sure to be just another in a series of great disappointments.

Knock on the door.

"Come in."

The Crabman. "What if we brought Nigel Vardon in for a formal interview, here at the station. We haven't done that yet."

"We'll have to clear it with Special Branch."

"Aye."

I nodded. "All right, let's go get the arson-surviving, missile-stealing, long-haired fuck."

Interview room 2.

Crabbie and me and the missile-stealing, long-haired fuck. Lawson and DI Spencer observing through the glass. A notebook, a wee jug of water, the tape recorder running precisely as required by the Police and Criminal Evidence Act (Northern Ireland Order).

"Mr. Vardon, where were you on the night of November 11, 1985?"

"I was at home watching TV."

"Where were you on the evening of November 12, 1985?"

"Home watching TV."

"Where were you on the night of November 19, 1985?"

"Ditto."

"Who do you think burned your house down, Mr. Vardon?"

"I don't know."

"Who do you think killed your dogs?"

"I don't know."

"Who killed Michael Kelly?"

"I heard he topped himself."

"Why have you been calling the US consulate?"

"I got the wrong number. I was trying to call my solicitor."

"Do you know a man called John Connolly?"

"Never heard of him."

"Did Michael Kelly know John Connolly?"

"No idea."

"The number you called at the US consulate was the number for the guest house where Mr. Connolly is staying."

"Like I said, that was a wrong number."

Two hours of this. The guy was jumpy, upper lip sweat, dilated pupils. Aye, the guy was a user too. Big time. Try to crack him.

Three hours.

Four.

But it was no good.

The incident room. Coffee and biscuits. "He knows something, but he is more afraid of them than he is of us," I said.

"Afraid of whom?" Lawson wanted to know.

"Afraid of the Loyalists. Afraid of the men who killed Kelly and his family," Spencer said.

"Is that who killed Kelly and his family?" Lawson said.

Spencer shrugged.

"So what now?" Crabbie asked.

"Anybody know any jokes?" Spencer asked.

"A barman says, 'We don't serve time travelers in here.' A little later a time traveler walks into a bar," Lawson said.

"I don't get it," Spencer muttered.

"Lawson, go in there and tell Vardon he's free to go."

Days. Nights. Rain. Bomb scares. Bombs. Riots.

December. Christmas lights in Carrick. Season of Good Will. Black Santa. Cops taking regular hits from both sides now. Assassination attempts from the Republicans. Death threats and drive-bys from the Prods. Bricks through policemen's windows. Kids to other kids at school: "Your dad's a peeler!"

Sleepless nights. Bad news. Exhausted men at the morning briefings.

A theft case took me and McCrabban into Belfast. Driving up in the Land Rover to arrest a man called Kevin Banville who'd been the wheelman on a post office robbery. Of course, he'd been tipped off and was long gone. To Manchester, everyone said. Normally neighbors didn't tell you stuff like that but Kevin was a hated wife-beater. We passed on the tip.

Time to spare in Belfast.

"You fancy a run out to East Belfast?"

"Who lives there?"

"Moony."

Crabbie's jaundiced eye.

"Don't worry, I'll fix it with the specials."

A run over the Lagan to Larkfield Avenue. A red-bricked terrace in solid Prod working-class territory. Curbstones painted red, white, and blue; pictures of King Billy on gable walls.

Knock on Moony's door.

Mrs. Moony standing there large as life and twice as scary. Younger than Tommy by a decade and a half. Five foot two, rollers in hair, gunmetal-grey face tempered by violet eyes à la Liz Taylor.

"Lord have mercy, I think that it's the cops," she said, quoting Van Morrison at us.

"Mrs. Moony, could we have a word with your—"

"Tommy, love, it's the peelers for ya!"

Tommy's living room. Crockery in a cupboard. Piano bedecked

with pictures of the shipyard and dour men in flat caps. Transport and General Workers' Union regalia. Another red flag. A picture of Che. Jesus, Tommy knew how to get on my good side: lefty, working-class, union guy, Brummie accent . . . if only he hadn't done all those murders. If only this family that had immigrated to Belfast to work in the shipyards hadn't been radicalized by the violence of the early seventies . . .

If only . . .

Mrs. Moony bringing tea and biscuits.

Tommy not well pleased by our presence. "What is the meaning of this? My solicitor has warned you lot before!"

I waited until the wife had gone before beginning the unpleasantness.

"Listen, Tommy, we know you did it. Michael Kelly, his parents. Killed that wee girl in cold blood. Had to be you. Only *you* had the organization. Only you could have sent men to Scotland after Deirdre Ferris."

Not a flinch. Not an eye-twitch out of place. Just a sad, silent shake of the head. He took a sip of his tea. "I have been born again in the blood of Christ, Inspector Duffy, something you as a Roman Catholic would never understand."

"I wonder how Christ feels about the man who murdered little Sylvie McNichol," McCrabban said.

"I wouldn't know anything about that."

"Tell you something you didn't know. Sylvie's dad was an alleged police informer. They killed him when she was a wean. Her family got the message. *She* got the message. She would *never* have talked. She would never have told us anything. Her death was completely unnecessary," I added.

"Are you going to ask me any actual questions, or are you just going to hurl accusations at me, gentlemen?"

"No one else has to die, Tommy, if the missiles just show up. A tip to the Confidential Telephone, that's all it would take," I suggested.

"I don't know anything about any bloody missiles!"

"I'm not asking for a confession, a tip to the Confidential Telephone, that's all, OK?"

"I've had enough of this. You two must be a couple of Bennies. Now could you please get out of my home?"

Back outside the house.

Rain on Larkfield Avenue.

We got in the BMW.

"Where to now?" McCrabban asked.

"Falls Road."

"I don't like the sound of that."

"Due diligence, mate. If I'm warning one side I've got to warn the other."

We drove to the Sinn Fein advice center on the Falls Road. I parked outside and immediately showed my warrant card to the half-dozen concerned security people who were rightly fearful of assassination attempts on the IRA leadership.

We went inside and I asked to see Gerry Adams.

"Are you one of his constituents?" a secretary asked.

"No, but we've met a couple of times before. He might remember me," I said, showing her my police ID.

Half an hour later Crabbie and I got shown into a crammed little upstairs office stuffed with papers and books overlooking the Falls Road and West Belfast. There were many framed photographs on the wall: Adams meeting Ted Kennedy, Adams meeting Rosa Parks, Adams with Winnie Mandela, Adams with Arafat. You got the message . . .

Adams came in through a side door dressed in a tweedy jacket and brown cords.

"Yes, I do remember you, Inspector Duffy," he said.

"And this is my coll—" I began, but I saw McCrabban giving me a panicky *no names* look.

"And this is my colleague from Carrickfergus CID. We're investigating the murder of Michael Kelly and his parents in Whitehead. And the subsequent murder of Sylvie McNichol," I said.

"What can I do for you?" Adams asked, sitting down behind his desk.

"I want to warn you about a man called Connolly. An American.

He's here to conduct some kind of arms deal. He's got a lot of money, but he doesn't know what he's doing. He's trouble. He is not someone with whom you want to do business."

"Me?" Adams said, surprised.

"Your friends in the IRA. I think they've already made the call that Mr. Connolly is a clown, but just to be on the safe side I thought I'd pass on the message. Special Branch are all over him. He's bad news."

"I don't know what you're talking about," Adams said.

"I've been to see Tommy Moony and told him too. If you or your friends know anything about any stolen missiles from Shorts they should contact the Confidential Telephone. Four people have been murdered already. No one else has to die because of this."

Adams gave the slightest of nods before adding, "I don't know anything about the IRA or any stolen missiles."

I got to my feet. "I think we understand each other, Mr. Adams," I said.

"I think we do, Inspector Duffy."

Back outside to the Beemer.

Rain on the Falls Road. Men with guns watching us from many angles.

"Home?" Crabbie asked nervously.

"Do you mind if I just pop into the *Belfast Telegraph* offices first?"

"What for?" Crabbie asked.

"See a friend of mine."

"Is this your, er, your . . ."

"Girlfriend?"

"Yes."

"I don't know."

"I'll wait for you at the Crown Bar."

The *Belfast Telegraph* offices were in a prime location on Royal Avenue that got a lot of foot traffic. In the ground-floor office windows they often displayed provocative headlines and photographs. The first edition went to press at one in the afternoon, and if the headlines caught your interest there were newspaper boys outside selling the papers right off the pavement. In other parts of the city the newsies attracted customers by shouting "Teleyo!" and yelling the headline that seemed the most dramatic. The Troubles had been a boon for journalists in what was really a rather dull, provincial city well outside the mainstream of British and Irish culture.

The *Belfast Telegraph* offices were buzzing.

I showed my warrant card to the old-stager security guard at the front desk and asked him where Sara Prentice might be.

"First floor. News," he said, looking her up in the directory.

I went up the steps and saw her immediately, poring over a layout at a huge work desk. She was wearing jeans and gutties with a white blouse. She looked good. Couple of hacks with her. One older, curly hair, beard, checked shirt, brown cloth tie, round glasses—passing resemblance to Peter Sutcliffe, the Yorkshire Ripper. The other was her age, skinny, black hair, pale, handsome if you liked thin and Byronic, and these days who didn't?

She saw me out of the corner of her eye.

"Hello, stranger," she said.

"Gonna introduce me?"

"Martin—Sean, Sean—Martin," she said, introducing me to the older man. He had a bold handshake and he looked me in the eye.

"Nice to meet you," I said.

"Likewise."

"And this is Justin. Justin—Sean, Sean—Justin."

Justin didn't look at me and his handshake was limp, but also kinda condescending and dickish. "Are you in the press?" Justin asked.

"I'm Sara's spiritual coach," I said.

"What's a spiritual coach?" Justin asked.

"It's sort of like a guru," I explained.

"He's only joking. He's a policeman."

"A policeman? We love policemen around here," Martin said. "They've always got the most interesting stories."

"I don't have any stories."

"Everyone's got a story," Martin insisted.

"Except me. Nothing ever happens to me," I said, and taking Sara gently by the arm, I added: "Can we talk for a sec?"

"Of course we can."

Her office. Little more than a news division cupboard but it smelled of paint and was freshly moved into. She was going up in the world.

"So, what's happening? Are we done?" I asked.

"What? No. We're not done."

"I haven't seen you in ages."

"Sean, the whole city's going mad. Riots. Bombs. They're out every night making copy for us. This is our busy time."

"Ours too."

Silence. Fifteen seconds of it. Hostility creeping in. Tension. I'd blown this again somehow. Maybe it was my face. Jealousy. That dude Justin giving me the limp finger-shake. *Who do you think you are, peeler, compared to us movers and shakers of the fourth estate?*

I cleared my throat. "Hey, listen, I'd better go. Work to do. I'll be in the Dobbins tonight about eight, if you want to join me."

A momentary pause. "Tonight?"

"Tonight not good?"

Look at those eyes. Eyes so green they hurt.

"I'd love to, Sean, but it's my deadline night. You know how it is."

"Of course, I forgot. Some other time, then."

"Absolutely. Some other time."

Downstairs. A pack of Marlboros from a cigarette machine. I found McCrabban nursing a pint of the black stuff at the Crown Bar.

"Come on, mate, time to head."

"How did it go with, uh . . ."

"Swimmingly. Let's go."

On the way back to Carrick we popped into an off-license and I got a bottle of Smirnoff Blue Label.

I went to the Dobbins at eight. Sara didn't show. I ordered a bowl of Irish stew, and when Martin brought it he lit the pile of turf logs in the big sixteenth-century stone fireplace. In this all too brief world of tears you have to take your pleasures where you can find them, and a bowl of mutton stew, a pint of plain, and a pack of Marlboros were rare comfort for the soul.

I finished my meal and walked home via the Albert Road, where there was a riot going on. Two dozen kids with scarves over their faces throwing milk bottles, snowballs, and ripped-up cobblestones at a dozen RUC officers in body armor.

I walked behind the peeler lines, where I found Sergeant Jackie Gillespie in charge. "Hello, Jackie."

"Hello, Sean."

"What's going on?"

"It's just kids blowing off steam. You on duty?"

"Just sightseeing."

A milk bottle filled with piss arced through the air and smashed six feet in front of us.

"You wanna get yourself a riot shield?"

"No thanks. I'll leave you to it, mate."

"Yeah, see you, Sean."

I walked home through the snow, lit the paraffin heater and rummaged in my singles collection for Ella Fitzgerald's recording of "Baby It's Cold Outside." I drank half the Smirnoff Blue Label through the vector of a series of increasingly diluted vodka gimlets and fell asleep on the sofa while Ella sang like an angel.

24: THE MYSTERIOUS MR. CONNOLLY

Another early morning. Another crisp day. Another idea. "Fuck it, Crabbie. Let's bring Connolly in. If he's here let's bring him in."

"He's protected."

"Is he? Does he actually have diplomatic immunity? Are we sure about that?"

Crabbie's pale eyes grew paler. "I'll have Lawson check."

Lawson in my office two minutes later.

"Sir, there's no Connolly registered at the US consulate in Belfast. There's no Connolly registered with the entire United States diplomatic mission to the UK or to Ireland, come to that."

"You checked Dublin too? That's good work, son." Lawson was growing on me. He was a thinker and a go-getter. "Get Sergeant McCrabban back in here, would you?"

McCrabban's dour, worried face.

"He's not official, Crabbie. The Yanks can't kick up a stink if he's not an official part of the delegation."

"I'm not so sure I'd agree with you there, Sean."

"He's a potential witness— Hell, he's a potential *suspect* in a murder inquiry. We have to bring him in. It's our duty."

"What about Special Branch?"

"I'll call Spencer after we've lifted him. Sign out a Land Rover for us, will ya?"

Back out along the seafront in a police Land Rover. Low tide. Shopping trolley sculpture art. Garbage. Raw sewage.

Sun coming up. Lens flare. Motorhead on the radio.

Gun the Rover up to 80.

"The ace of spades, the ace of spades . . ."

Through Belfast to what the locals unironically call the Gold Coast. Holywood, County Down. The "Surrey of Northern Ireland." Leafy lanes, golf courses, yacht clubs. You wouldn't think there was a war on.

The consul's house on a rise overlooking the water.

Park the Rover, get out. Light snow on the ground.

Crabbie: "Still time to change our minds."

"I'll take the heat, mate. It was my call, my fault."

Crabbie doesn't know what I know. That this is probably going to be my last case and it would be nice to see something—anything—come of it.

Up the gravelly drive. Doorbell. The consul's . . . what would you call him? Factotum? House manager? Butler?

"Can I help you?"

"We'd like to see Mr. Connolly, who I believe is still one of your guests."

"It's rather early, gentlemen, perhaps you could—"

"Perhaps nothing. We've come for Connolly," I said, showing my warrant card.

"Mr. Connolly's gone for a jog."

"Where?"

"Up Scrabo way, along Strangford Lough, I believe."

"Thanks."

Back in the Rover. The Lough Road. Woods to the right, the lough to the left. Morning so clear you could see all the way to the Mountains of Mourne.

"We'll never find him. He could be in Newtownards or Comber, God knows where," Lawson said.

But we did find him. Ten miles out from Holywood along the Ballydrain Road. Connolly running in a grey jogging suit and a red headband. Listening to a Walkman. With him, two big men also in grey jogging suits.

"Those boys with Connolly look like goons," I said to McCrabban. "I'll bet you they're packing heat."

"Aye."

"Look at the pace on Connolly. The way he runs. That haircut. He's military. There's no way he's State Department."

"Here and back to Holywood is practically a full marathon. The man's fit."

Flashing lights. Sirens.

I got out. Showed my warrant card.

"We'd like to bring you in for questioning, Mr. Connolly."

"You've got the wrong guy, pal."

"You're under arrest, Mr. Connolly."

"What for?"

"Material witness in a murder inquiry. Your men are going to have to give me their guns," I said.

"No they are not. These men are my personal protection. They are Secret Service agents and they have permission to carry weapons."

"Permission from whom?"

"Permission from Scotland Yard."

"You've been running for quite a while, lads, cos you're not in London any more. To carry weapons in Northern Ireland you'll need permission from the Chief Constable of the RUC," I said.

Back to Carrickfergus in the Land Rover. A cell for each man. Let them sweat.

"Who do you think first?" Crabbie asked.

"I think the goons first. Let Connolly get himself worked up some more."

The goons said that they were Secret Service agents. They gave badge numbers. IDs. Contact numbers. They were cool and professional and didn't raise their voices. This kind of thing had clearly happened before. They were trained for it.

They said that they had committed no crime. That under the United Kingdom's treaty, diplomatic, and courtesy arrangements, they were allowed to carry concealed weapons. It actually had the ring of truth but it would take a while to verify. I put the least competent officer in the station, a chubby young reservist called James Braithwaite, on the case. "It's up to you, Jim. If these men are legally allowed to carry firearms in Northern Ireland then we have no right to hold them. You must find out the true jurisprudential situation."

"Me?"

"Yes, you. Their freedom or otherwise depends on you. Now get cracking."

"But how?"

"You'll figure it out."

We gave Connolly a cup of tea and some biscuits and brought him down to Interview Room 1.

"Detective Inspector Duffy, Detective Sergeant McCrabban interviewing Mr. John Connolly at 10:23 a.m., December 2, 1985 . . ." I said into the microphone.

"I want a lawyer from the consulate. You have no right to hold me. This is false imprisonment."

"Mr. Connolly, where were you on the night of November 11, 1985?"

"You've asked me that before! Where was I? Switzerland. And I've got a dozen witnesses who can prove that."

"Where were you on the night of November 19, 1985?"

"I exercise my Fifth Amendment rights."

"Where were you on the night of November 19, 1985?" I repeated.

"I plead the Fifth."

"You seem to have some trouble understanding the remit of the United States Constitution, Mr. Connolly. The Fifth Amendment does not apply here. And just to let you know, neither does *Miranda* v. *Arizona*. There is no right to silence in this country. You are obliged to answer my questions. Where were you on the night of November 19, 1985?"

"No comment."

"I must warn you, Mr. Connolly, that a judge and jury may be entitled to take your silence on this matter as corroboration of wrongdoing."

"I'm not answering any more questions, Duffy. I'm exercising my Fifth Amendment rights," he said again.

"You don't have any Fifth Amendment rights."

A knock at the door. It was Lawson.

"Yeah?"

"Talk in private," Lawson whispered.

Outside into the corridor.

"What is it?"

"He doesn't exist."

"Who?"

"Connolly."

"What do you mean?"

"I ran his IDs all the way back to America. It's a fake name, fake passport."

"He must have left a paper trail."

"Oh yes. I've been on that with the British Airports Authority and Interpol."

"What did you find out?"

"In the last few months this so-called Mr. John Connolly made a couple of dozen flights from Washington, DC, to Shannon to Dublin to Zurich, back to DC. Before that—nothing. No record of Mr. Connolly anywhere. I checked the birth and parish records and he simply does not exist. It's a genuine Irish passport for a completely made-up individual."

I leaned my head against the cool, peach-painted, cinderblock corridor walls.

"What do you think this all means, Lawson?"

Lawson shrugged.

"The flights originated in DC, you say?"

"Yes, sir."

"And Connolly's staying at the American consul general's house in Belfast."

"Yes."

I took out my packet of Marlboro and lit one. It didn't help me think but it stopped my hand from shaking. "Connolly was invented in DC, by someone in the US government," I said.

"CIA?" Lawson suggested.

"Let's go ask him."

We went back inside the interview room.

"Your IDs are fake, Mr. Connolly. There is no Mr. John Connolly. You have entered this country illegally under false documents," I said.

"No comment."

"What are you doing in Ireland, Mr. Connolly?" McCrabban said.

"No comment."

"Who do you work for, Mr. Connolly?" I asked.

"No comment."

"Where were you on the night of November 19, 1985?"

"Jesus, what's the matter with you guys? I told you, I'm not going to answer your questions."

"Where were you on the night of November nineteenth?"

"No comment."

"How do you know Nigel Vardon?"

"Who?"

"Nigel Vardon tried to call you at your residence at the consul general's house."

"Never heard of him."

"Nigel Vardon worked for Short Brothers. Nigel Vardon may have been working with one Michael Kelly on an arms deal for stolen missile systems. Have you heard of Michael Kelly?"

"No, I have not heard of Michael Kelly."

"Michael Kelly, his parents, and his girlfriend were all murdered. And I want to know why," I said.

Connolly shook his head. "What's this got to do with me?"

"Michael Kelly's friend, Nigel Vardon, tried to call you."

"So?"

"Why would he try to call a person who doesn't exist? Who are you, Mr. Connolly?"

"No comment."

"What's your real name, Mr. Connolly?"

"I'm exercising my right to silence."

"And we've told you that there is no right to silence in UK law. Not anymore. I don't know if you appreciate the fact that we are detectives conducting a murder investigation. We're not interested in the stolen missiles. We're investigating the deaths of Michael Kelly, his parents, and Sylvie McNichol," I said.

He looked at me and shook his head. "I don't know anything about that."

"What's your connection to Nigel Vardon?"

"I've never heard of Nigel Vardon . . . Look, buddy, you're making a big mistake here. A career-ending mistake. Where's my fucking phone call? I have a right to a phone call, don't I?"

McCrabban bit his lip. Lawson looked at the floor. He had asked for his phone call and under the terms of the Police and Criminal Evidence Act (NI Order) we had to supply it to him.

"Get the man a telephone."

A reservist brought a telephone and plugged it into the wall. We left Connolly alone in the room for five minutes. Watched him through the glass. Made sure he dialed only one number.

Phone out, us back in.

The grin wider now.

"The cavalry's on its way, is it?" I asked.

He nodded. "And for you, zipppp . . . Russian front," he said in a comedic German accent.

"Well, we'd better be quick with our questions, then."

"You'd better be like the Flash."

But before I could begin again there was a knock on the interview room's glass window.

"I'll go see who that is. Keep at him, Sergeant McCrabban."

Behind the glass was Chief Inspector McArthur. Not exactly livid but if he were on a heart ward alarms would be ringing.

"Why have you brought these Americans in, Duffy?"

"Because I believe they have evidence relating to the Michael Kelly case."

"What evidence?"

"I don't know. That's what we're trying to find out."

"Please tell me in the name of Christ that these men were not dragged out of the US consul's house."

"They weren't dragged out of the US consul's house. We got them while they were out for a run along Strangford Lough."

"At least that's something," he said, still looking aghast.

"They've been well treated. We've followed procedure."

"You really think they know something about the Kelly case?"

"One of the suspects in the Kelly case, Nigel Vardon, attempted to call Mr. Connolly here. He knows something about either Michael Kelly's murder or the stolen missiles from Shorts."

"Jesus God, you'd better be right. Have you called Special Branch?"

"I was going to."

"Do it now!"

I called Spencer and informed him that I had brought Mr. Connolly in for questioning. Silence on the other end of the phone.

"Do you want to come down to Carrick and ask him some questions?" I asked.

"Uhm, I think we'll stay out of this one, Duffy," Spencer said. "But if you do get any information out of him, I'd appreciate it if you could pass it on."

I hung up. Clearly Spencer thought I was committing career suicide.

Back into Interview Room 1.

The questions again. Where were you on the night of November eleventh? Where were you on the night of November nineteenth? What do you know about the death of Michael Kelly? How do you know Nigel Vardon? Who are you really, Mr. Connolly? Who do you work for?

No comment. Silence. Right to silence. Boyish face. Monkey grin. Jug ears.

Half an hour of this. Tea break.

"He won't tell us anything. He's been well schooled," McCrabban said.

"We've been trained too, haven't we?" I said.

"If he's military he could go on like this for a long time," Lawson contributed.

"In the old days . . ." McCrabban said.

"In the old days . . ." I agreed.

Lawson's eyebrows rose.

Connolly was the perfect metaphor. The representation of a thing by another thing or even by its opposite. I wanted information and he was an information vacuum. And I couldn't hurt him or scare him. He was American. Holy. Precious. Untouchable.

A phone ringing in my office. "Better take this, lads.

"Hello?"

"Inspector Duffy?"

"Yes."

"Please hold for the Assistant Chief Constable."

Oh shit.

"Inspector Duffy?"

"Yes."

"This is Assistant Chief Constable Nutt."

"Yes, sir."

"Is it true that you've arrested an American consular official? A man called Connolly?"

"That's not strictly true, sir. 'Mr. Connolly' has traveled to the United Kingdom under a false Irish passport. We don't actually know who 'Mr. Connolly' is at this stage."

"He was in the consulate, though, wasn't he?"

"No. When we arrested him he was on the road jogging just outside of Newtownards."

"Thank fuck for that . . . What's this about, Duffy?"

"It's about a murder inquiry, sir."

"Details, fast."

"We're investigating the death of one Michael Kelly and his family. We strongly suspect that this Michael Kelly was an arms dealer, the arms dealer who may have helped to mastermind the theft of Javelin missile launchers from Shorts. We've informed Special Branch of our suspicions and they're looking into it."

"That's all very well but how does the Connolly chap fit into all this?"

I told him about Nigel Vardon's phone call.

"So you've arrested him because of some dismissed Shorts employee's phone call?"

"A Shorts manager who was connected to Michael Kelly."

"What else have you got on this case?"

"We do have a partial eyewitness sketch from Deirdre Ferris. She saw a man lurking outside her house the night Sylvie McNichol was murdered. It was pretty dark but if you allow me to hold Mr. Connolly for twenty-four hours I could have our eyewitness brought in from protective custody to see if she can identify him in person."

"Presumably you've already shown her a picture of Mr. Connolly?"

"Yes, sir."

"And?"

"She couldn't tell if he was the man who was outside her house, sir."

"Is this Connolly fellow an American citizen?" ACC Nutt asked.

"It looks that way, sir, but because of the false passport there's no way of knowing for sure. He has an American accent and he was jogging with American Secret Service agents, and I'm pretty sure he served in Vietnam with the United States Marine Corps, but Mr. Connolly has repeatedly refused to tell us his real name."

"Are you in your office right now?"

"Yes, sir."

"Wait there. I'll call you back in five minutes."

I sat on the edge of the desk. Snow fell out of the grey sky on to the Marine Highway and the choppy green lough. I lit a Marlboro. The phone rang. I picked it up.

"Duffy?"

"Yes, sir."

"You are to release 'Mr. Connolly' and his men immediately."

"But, sir, they are—"

"Do you have problems with your hearing, Duffy?"

"No, sir. It's just that—"

"You are to release them and you are to offer the RUC's pro-
foundest apologies. Do you understand my orders?"

"Yes, sir."

"That will be all, Duffy."

"Yes, sir."

The phone went dead. I put it back on its cradle. This job taught
you humility if nothing else. Shit from the public. Shit from your superiors. Pulling in a Yank? What was I thinking? I was nothing more than
a plodding peeler, stuck forever at a low rank in a mediocre station in
an out-of-the-way town.

Thank God for Kate and MI5 offering me an exit strategy.

The lesson here: stay away from Americans in Ireland. This was
their backyard, this was their playground.

Back down to the interview room.

"All right, Mr. Connolly, I'm sorry to have kept you here for so
long; you are free to go."

Connolly's grin stretched from monkey ear to monkey ear.

Lawson gave him back his documents.

"You think this is over for you, Duffy? Is that what you think? It
isn't over. You've fucked with the wrong guy," Connolly said.

"Is that a threat, sir?" I asked.

"A promise," he replied.

I went to my office and pulled down the blinds and closed the door.

I brought out the Jura and called Kate.

"What can do I for you, Sean?"

"You won't like it."

"I never do."

"You really won't like it."

"Go on."

"I need you to use those informers of yours. I need you to use your
Whitehall contacts."

"Is this still that Michael Kelly case you were working on?"

"It's got more complicated."

"Oh dear."

I told her everything. Michael Kelly. Nigel Vardon. Tommy Moony. John Connolly. Special Branch. The Secret Service. The Assistant Chief Constable. I asked her to dig into it. Informers. MI5. MI6. Friends of hers.

"This sounds like very bad news, Sean," she said.

"Will you help me or not?"

She called me back later that evening. She sounded breathy. Freaked.

"Sean, I'm afraid you've got yourself into some very deep waters."

"I'm listening."

"I haven't actually got much to tell you, which in itself is quite interesting. If MI5 are being kept in the dark then this is very bad."

"Did you find out who John Connolly is?"

"He's American. But he's not CIA. CIA would be fine. CIA would be manageable."

"Who *is* he working for?"

"He's working directly for the White House. He's working for the president's National Security team. Connolly must be a big wheel because the order to keep away from him has come not from MI5 or MI6, not the Home Office, not even the Foreign Office, but directly from Number Ten itself. Sean, Mr. Connolly is involved in something so secret that only Number Ten and the White House know about it."

"Sounds serious."

"This is serious's older, wiser, much more serious brother. These are deep, deep waters, Sean. Not waters any of us want you to be swimming in. I know you want to finish your RUC career on a high but this is not the case to do it on."

"A murder is a murder. We've got to follow the leads wherever they go."

"Solve your case but stay away from Connolly. The minefield around Connolly is coming from Number Ten and the White House. I don't know what they're doing, but I know it's not something that I want you to be involved with."

"Thanks for your concern, Kate, I'll take it under advisement," I said.

I poured myself a medicinal dose of Jura and went home.

Tomato soup for dinner. Terry Wogan on TV.

Doorbell.

Mrs. Campbell in a tight black jumper, black miniskirt, high heels, red lipstick. Curly red hair cascading down her back. She looked a knockout.

"Mr. Duffy, me and Ted are away to the pictures. You wouldn't take Tricksie for a walk if she starts howling, would you? I know she likes you."

"Who's Ted?"

"You know Ted. The pastor at the Church of the Nazarene. He has that bread van too. Very ambitious, so he is."

"What? What about your husband?"

She blushed. "Ach, Mr. Duffy, you must have heard that we've separated. He's away over the water with his fancy woman."

"Fancy woman?"

"She's colored, if you can believe it. Jamaican. And him voting for the National Front all them years. Saul to Paul, eh?"

"I'm sorry to hear that. I had no idea."

"You're right not to listen to the gossip. Sure it's wrong half the time. Will you walk Tricksie if she starts howling?"

Mrs. Campbell left with Ted, a long-nosed, meek little man who wasn't in the same league as a spitfire like Mrs. C.

Tricksie began to howl as soon as the front door closed.

I took her along the lough shore. Border collie but with none of the breed's reputation for intelligence.

An agitated sea. Surf folding over the granite levee on to the frost-bitten beach. The idiot dog barking at the seaweed.

"Come on, girl!"

Granite rocks. War of attrition. Sea on land.

A car following me. Biding its time. Waiting until I was away from prying eyes.

260 GUN STREET GIRL

Wet dog. Happy dog. Dog back on the leash. Up through Shaftesbury Park. Behind the leisure center. On to Kennedy Drive.

A black Mercedes screeched to a halt next to me. Men in balaclavas got out. Men with guns. I turned to run. Nowhere to run.

I reached for my sidearm but my Glock was back in the house.

Shit. Sort of thing that gets you killed.

"Get in the car, Duffy," a man with an American accent said.

They know my name?

"What is this?"

Two revolvers pointing at my head.

"Get in the car!"

I got in the car. Zip ties behind my back.

"What about the dog?" I asked.

"What about the dog?"

"You can't just leave it there. It'll get run over. It's my next-door neighbor's dog."

"We'll see the dog gets home."

Animal lovers. Can't be all bad. Along the coast. Past Kilroot. No hood for my head.

We drove up into the boglands. The high country. The forest. Miles from anywhere. It was wild up here. You could do anything to anybody.

The car stopped. I was kicked out.

More kicks.

A baseball bat to the shins and ribs.

No guns now. So they weren't actually going to kill me. Not the paramilitaries, then.

"Remember this, Duffy, you're nothing. You have no friends. No influence. To kill you would be to kill a cockroach. You don't even have sons or brothers who would come after us, if they could ever find us, which, we assure you, they never would," the American said.

"Who are you?" I groaned.

"You can fuck with people, Duffy, but you can't fuck with institutions."

"Jesus, pal, who writes your fucking dialogue for you?"

"Lippy bastard. Hit him some more."

Blows.

Kicks.

Kicks.

Blows.

Painful, yes, but all in the extremities: legs, arms, back. If they wanted to do real damage they'd be hitting me in the head.

"He's had enough . . . Can you hear me, Duffy?"

"I can hear you."

"Stay out of other people's business or else, OK?"

"I'm a difficult man to kill," I said.

"All men think that and all men die."

"Including you."

"The bastard's not fucking listening. Go get the boss."

Silence.

Footsteps.

A man bending down next to me.

Cigar breath. Brandy. Cologne.

"Can you hear my voice, Inspector Duffy?"

Another American accent. Southern. An older man.

"I can hear you."

"Look at me."

I opened my eyes and blinked through the blood. He wasn't wearing a balaclava. He didn't give a shit if he was ID'd. He was an old geezer. A tough old pro with grey hair and a face like a smashed crab.

"You've got to understand, boy. We're giving you a gift here tonight. We're giving you back your future. Your days and your nights. Your warm bed. And in return for this gift all you have to do is keep your nose out of other people's business. Do you get me?"

I spat the blood out of my mouth from where I'd bitten my tongue. "Are you always this much of a cunt or are you just making a special effort today?"

"I told you he was a lippy one, sir."

"Give him another taste of it."

More kicks and a punch right in the nose.

More punches.

And eventually, of course . . .

Nothing.

Nothing for a long time.

Snow on my face.

Pain.

Up on to my knees.

Head splitting. Blood in my mouth. Zip ties gone. Legs not broken. Nothing broken. Wait . . . maybe a rib. Still, a good job. Professionals.

Up on to my feet.

I staggered along a single-lane road next to a pine forest.

Up a hill. Lights on the next hill. A cottage.

One foot in front of another. Take a break. Kneel down. Up again.

No, not a cottage, a gospel hall.

Singing.

A couple of cars parked outside. A tractor.

Light in the window.

Singing over.

A man's voice: "He is slaughtered and cast out among the heathen, annihilated among his kin. And the years that curve in heaven. And the years that are warped by time are nothing to Him. He will come! He will come again! Praise the Lord!"

Door open. Light flooding in. Half a dozen heads turned to look at me.

"I'm so sorry to interrupt your service, but I find that I am in need of some assistance."

25: CONVINCING NIGEL VARDON

A night in Coleraine District Hospital. My rib was cracked, but nothing else. Bruises, sprains, but none of your actual broken bones. Yeah, they were pros. They probably thought I wouldn't report them because they took it easy on me, because they didn't kill me. Because we understood each other.

But fuck that.

The next morning I went into Coleraine RUC and told them the whole story. Gave them a photofit of the old geezer and everything. Didn't care if he was American. Didn't care if he was connected. If they found him I was bringing charges.

Not that they would ever find him.

I phoned work and told McCrabban I was taking a couple of "personal days."

He didn't mind. He and Lawson wanted to go on riot duty anyway (double time and overtime and danger money) and he knew I didn't approve of CID detectives pulling that kind of duty, especially after what had happened to Fletcher.

Coleraine CID drove me back to Carrick in a Land Rover.

I called Sara. "Hey, Girl Friday, pictures tonight?" I asked. "It'll go better than last time, I promise."

"What's playing?"

"*Back to the Future.*"

"I don't like the sound of that."

"Come on, let's do something. I'll pick you up. I'll drive you up the coast."

"Why?"

"For something to do."

"I don't think so, Sean. Another night maybe."

"Are you sure?"

"I'm sure."

I called Kate.

"Sean, how are you?"

"I've been better."

"What are you doing?"

"Taking the day off. You want to get dinner or something?"

"Dinner?"

"Yeah, dinner. People get dinner, don't they?"

"Oh, Sean, it's a lovely idea but we're just so busy here at the moment. Another time perhaps, OK?"

"OK."

Garden shed. Place of masculine retreat. Reliquary.

Cannabis resin. Virginia tobacco. Thick multi-tracked memories of girls and cars and music. Nice.

Back inside. A piece of toast, a cup of coffee. Out to the Beemer. I found myself driving on the top road. I found myself parking outside the Eagle's Nest Inn on Knockagh Mountain.

Rain. Moody cross-fades between mountain and cop. The detective looking rueful.

I walked to reception.

Mrs. Dunwoody remembered me.

"I knew you'd be back, Inspector Duffy," she said in low tones. "You don't look yourself. Were you in an accident?"

"Yes. Car accident."

"Dear oh dear. Well, what can we get for you today?"

"Uhm, not really sure why I'm here, I . . ."

"A nice girl? A nice young man?"

"Girl. Just a girl. Please. That good listener you were talking about."

"A good listener? Oh yes, I know the very person. Niamh. Spelled the Irish way. Not just a good listener but very, very discreet."

"Niamh? Does she speak Irish?"

Mrs. Dunwoody smiled. "You know what? I think she does."

She led me to a room on the ground floor. I lay on the big bed and closed my eyes. A hand on my chest. A plump, curly-haired redhead wearing a pink chemise. She was about twenty-five, pale, pretty with blue eyes. She kissed me on the lips and stroked my forehead.

"You look exhausted," she said in Irish.

"I feel exhausted," I answered in the same language.

"What do you do for a living?"

"Mrs. Dunwoody didn't tell you?"

"No."

"I'm a policeman."

"Ah, that explains it," she said sadly. She stroked my hair and I talked. I told her that I was lonely. I told her about Sara and I told her about Kate. I told her that I didn't know what the hell I was doing with my life anymore. I told her that when I joined the police I thought I could help keep back the anarchy, but that every day the chaos was worse.

"What does your girlfriend say when you tell her all this?"

"Sara wanted to know about the real Sean Duffy, but there is no real Sean Duffy. There was once, but there's not now. There's just a tired, broken, compromised wreck of a man."

Tell this to your girlfriend or your wife and at best she'll roll her eyes or nod impatiently or answer you with a platitude. Tell it to a professional and she'll gather you into her bosom and say "there, there."

"There, there," she said.

An hour later. Mrs. Dunwoody walking me to the car. I reached for my wallet. Mrs. Dunwoody shook her head.

"I've got money. I can pay," I said.

Mrs. Dunwoody looked hurt. "Your money's no good here, Inspector. Feel free to come back any time."

The BMW back to Coronation Road.

Late afternoon now. Blue sky and low winter sun burning off all the snow.

Garden shed.

Cocaine.

A neat little line of it on the workbench that I rolled inside a Rizla.

Back to the house. Two fingers of Glendfiddich to make the Rizla go down. This was called a snow bomb. The rolling paper dissolved in your stomach and the cocaine with it. The euphoria wasn't as intense as the cocaine crossed the blood/brain barrier, but it lasted much longer.

Upstairs office.

Windows open.

The Velvets on the tape deck. Bowie in reserve.

Mrs. Campbell in her back garden hanging up the washing. Yellow dress. No bra.

"Hello, Mrs. C. Did Tricksie get home safe yesterday?"

"Oh! Mr. Duffy, I didn't see you up there! I was just putting the washing out. What did you say?"

"Did Tricksie get home all right yesterday?"

"Mr. Duffy, what happened to your face?"

"Is it that noticeable?"

"Were you in a fight?"

"No. Nothing like that. Just an accident. Minor car accident. I'm fine. Did Tricksie get home OK?"

"Oh yes, your friends brought her back just fine."

"That's good. Did the old American guy leave her off?"

"Yes. What an old charmer, eh, Mr. Duffy? Is he a friend of your father's or something?"

"Or something," I muttered.

"Well, I'd better get back to this. These clothes won't hang themselves."

"No."

A wave. A flash of side boob.

Notepad. Pencil. Notes. Coke hitting. What to do? What to do? What to do? Cartoon of Connolly with big jug ears. Arrows radiating from Connolly to Michael Kelly to Sylvie McNichol to a crate of stolen missiles to Zurich.

Arrow radiating to Nigel Vardon.

Him. Has to be. He'll know. Or he'll know someone that knows.

Who does Nigel fear? Not us, not the police. Who does Nigel fear? The Loyalists. The Americans. Tommy Moony and his boys.

What does Nigel need? Nigel needs a golden parachute. Nigel needs exit money.

Does Nigel know anything? Maybe. Maybe not.

Shed. Emergency escape fund in the biscuit tin. Six bundles of fifty-pound notes. Half of it? Half of it. It was only money. What about the cocaine too? Yeah, that too.

Inside the house. Dress in character. Black jeans. DM boots. My old Dr. Ernesto Guevara T-shirt. Leather jacket. Scarf.

Out the front gate.

Quick check under the Beemer for mercury tilt bombs.

Radio 1. The Pet Shop Boys. Jesus, I'd rather have silence.

Down Victoria Road and along the A2 toward Whitehead.

Turn up the Tongue Loanen.

The back country.

Sheep. Cows. Nigel Vardon's burnt-out ruin of a house.

The Special Branch goon snoozing in the driver's seat of a Ford Sierra.

Drove past him and around the bend in the road. Parked the Beemer down an old cattle trail. Hopped the stone wall. Approached Vardon's house across the sheep field. From the back, where the snoozing Special Branch goon wouldn't be able to see me.

Crunch crunch crunch on the gravel.

Burned house. Caravan. Rap on the window.

Vardon lifted the door curtain and looked at me. He was skinny, unshaven with dark exhausted eyes.

"What do you want?"

I showed him the money. Three bundles of fifty-pound notes. I showed him the cocaine.

"What's that?"

"Pharma coke. Purest shit you've ever seen."

"What are you going to do, plant that on me?"

"This stuff? Are you joking? This is the business, brother. This is for using, not for planting. I should know. I've got a line of it dissolving in my stomach as we speak."

He opened the door, looked me in the eyes, saw that they were coke happy.

"Why don't you come in, Officer."

I went in.

Couple of cats. An old WW2 revolver sitting on a fold-out writing desk.

"License for that?"

"Was me granda's. You gonna bust me for it?"

"Nope."

"Show me this coke."

I opened the bag and let him try it. He dabbed a little coke on to his finger and ran it around his gums. His eyes widened.

I gave him the bag of cocaine and the roll of money. "Yours to keep."

"In exchange for what?" he snarled.

"Set us up a couple of lines," I said.

He expertly cut two lines of cocaine on his Formica table. I rolled up a fiver and sniffed a line. The shit all right. This stuff could take you into fucking orbit.

I gave him the fiver and he sniffed his line.

"Jesus Christ!" he said.

"Yeah, I know."

"I mean, Jesus Christ."

"Yeah, I know."

"Another?"

"You have one, Nigel, I'm OK."

He snorted another long rail of that beautiful German pharma cocaine. He grinned at me.

I leaned back in the little plastic chair and took one of the cats off my lap.

"As I see it, Nigel, it's all about the Americans," I said.

"What about the Americans?"

"Connolly."

"What about him?"

"For reasons I haven't figured out yet Connolly has been trying to get his hands on sophisticated missile systems that can be sold to rogue nations such as South Africa or Iran or Libya. Connolly needs to get the missile systems on the black market because the US Congress has an arms embargo against those nations."

"Interesting idea."

"It is, isn't it? Now I know what you're thinking, Nigel. What good are a couple of missiles to countries like South Africa or Iran that are fighting big-time wars? But here's the clever part: they only need half a dozen missile launchers. You know why? Because their scientists and technicians will be able to reverse-engineer the missiles and make more."

"That *is* a good idea," Nigel agreed.

"But where can Mr. Connolly get these missiles from, eh? He can't steal them from an American factory. FBI will be all over him. So he puts the word out, tentatively, quietly. There's a deal worth millions, maybe tens of millions, if someone can get him advanced missile systems."

"I like this story, very entertaining," Nigel said. "Another line?"

"Yeah, why not. Set it up, Nige."

"Into the tale pops Michael Kelly. Burgeoning player on the international arms market. A few small scores here and there. But Mr. Connolly would represent a huge score. Like I say, millions . . . tens of millions. Mr. Connolly would represent freedom. Away from his da, away from grubby little bookie shops, away from Ireland, up into the big time. And here's the good part. One of Michael's old school friends, Nigel Vardon, works at Short Brothers, where they make, guess what, advanced missile systems."

Vardon sniffed another line of coke and passed me the rolled-up fiver. I sniffed another line too. Vardon laughed. I laughed.

"Finish your story," Vardon said.

"Michael needs you, Nigel. But you know that nothing can move in and out of the factory without the say-so of Tommy Moony. Fortunately for all of you Tommy Moony is not the born-again Christian he claims to be. Tommy Moony is a player. Tommy Moony is UFF up to the eyeballs. Tommy Moony is an old-school iceman who has personally killed more walking bipeds than we've had hot dinners. Tommy Moony is one scary motherfucker."

"Go on."

"So Michael meets Mr. Connolly in England or Ireland or fucking Switzerland or wherever. Michael tells him about you. Mr. Connolly is interested. Very fucking interested. You talk to the terrifying Tommy Moony. Moony is also very interested. The dollar amount is just too big to fucking ignore. That's why I'm thinking tens of millions here. It's the US government, for crying out loud. They can afford it."

Nigel said nothing.

"The missiles get stolen. But something goes wrong. Before the missiles get to where they are supposed to go there's an internal audit at Shorts. Just a random security check out of the blue and Short Brothers discover to their horror that half a dozen Javelin missile systems have gone missing. They call in the Special Branch and launch an internal inquiry. You're immediately let go because you were the manager in charge of plant security. They'd love to fire Tommy Moony, too, because everybody knows that he's the one that arranged it. Tommy's the one who opened the gates and shipped the missiles out and is hiding them somewhere in deepest Ulster. But they can't fire Tommy because they're afraid of him. They're afraid of him because he's UFF and a fucking iceman, but also because he could call a strike and bring the whole plant to a halt and send Short Brothers on to Mrs. Thatcher's chopping block."

Nigel shook his head. "I'm not completely convinced by this tale, you know."

"Hold on, mate, I haven't finished it yet. So Michael and Moony fall out. Doesn't matter why. Maybe it's about the split, maybe it's about the delivery, maybe Special Branch has got Michael spooked. Maybe Michael doesn't trust Connolly. Maybe Michael has a big mouth. Doesn't matter why. Michael's getting to be a problem. Moony decides to take action. Decisive action. He drives down to Whitehead, kills Michael's parents, drags Michael out of the house. Gets Michael to tell him who he's been talking to, and when they're satisfied with Michael Kelly's answers they chuck him off a cliff."

"I still think Michael killed himself," Nigel said.

"No you don't. You know what happened. And you know what happened to Sylvie McNichol when Moony didn't trust her one hundred per cent to keep her mouth shut about Michael Kelly's various dealings over the previous few weeks. Little Sylvie didn't tell us a bloody thing, but that wasn't good enough for Moony, was it? Sylvie had to die. And when Deirdre Ferris thought she saw Moony or one of his boys outside her house, Deirdre had to die too."

Vardon was pale now, quiet.

"And just in case you got any ideas, one of Moony's boys burned your fucking house down. Just to show you that you could be got even with the Special Branch watching you like a fucking hawk. What do you think of my story now, Nigel?"

"I think it's bollocks, Duffy. You haven't told me why. What's in it for Mr. Connolly? What's in it for the Americans?"

I put my hand on his shoulder. Looked him in the eyes. "I don't know why, Nigel, but you do, don't you? You do and that information alone makes you vulnerable. What are you playing at here in this caravan, Nigel? Hiding here, waiting for the deal to be done. And maybe when Moony gets his payday he'll swing by the caravan and remember to give you your cut. Is that what you're thinking? This ruthless killer who murdered Michael Kelly and Michael Kelly's mum and da. And little Sylvie. And sent a team all the way to Scotland to kill Deirdre Ferris. You think he's going to let you live and give you your money?"

"I . . . I've got nothing to do with Moony," he said. He was very pale and very sweaty now and that wasn't just the coke working its white magic.

"It's the Americans who are calling the shots around here, isn't it? I've tangled with them myself. They almost did for me and I'm an RUC detective. An RUC detective with no evidence and a lot of wild guesses. Whereas you . . . you actually know the whole story. And once the deal is done, once the missiles are gone, they'll make sure all the loose ends are tidied up. And in case my figurative language has confused you, Nigel, by loose ends I mean you. You won't be getting any dough, Nigel. You won't be getting any love. But you'll probably be getting a bullet in the fucking head."

Nigel closed his eyes, breathed in and out, went to get a glass of water, drank it.

"Talk. Tell me, Nigel," I said.

He sat down again.

"What do you want, Duffy?" he asked.

"I want the killers. I'm a homicide detective. I don't give a fuck about the missiles. I want the men who threw Michael Kelly off a cliff. I want the men who murdered little Sylvie."

He shook his head. "I . . . I don't know what you're talking about. I don't know anything about that," he said in a monotone.

I grabbed his dressing gown by the lapels and pulled him close to my face.

"Can you deliver them to me, Nigel? Can you? If you can you can save your skin."

He shook his shaggy head. "I don't know who killed those people and I don't know anything about any missing missiles."

"We can go the official route: full confession, witness protection program, new identity for you anywhere you like," I said.

I took the roll of banknotes and held it in front of his nose.

"Or we could go the unofficial route. There's ten grand here. That pharma coke could be worth another ten. You just give me the proof I need and it's yours. Disappear. Vanish off the face of the earth until Moony's in jail or dead . . ."

Vardon shook his head.

"I want you to go now," he said.

"Are you sure?"

He nodded. I stood up. I had him on the hook and that was enough for now.

I wrote out my home phone number and my phone number at Carrick RUC and left them on the table. "Call me any time. Day or night. Just don't do it from the phone box in Ballycarry. Special Branch has tapped that one. Understand me, Nigel?"

He nodded sullenly. "I understand," he said.

I put the coke and money in my jacket pocket. I walked back across the muddy field to the BMW. I drove home as another snowstorm moved in from the north.

My whole body ached now just as the doctors in Coleraine predicted it would do. I stripped off in the bathroom and found that I was covered with yellow and purple bruises. I lay in the bath and drank neat vodka with aspirin and codeine.

Darkness fell on Ireland and I went downstairs and locked the doors.

I lit the paraffin heater and climbed into bed. I checked that my Glock nine-millimeter was under the pillow. I tested the action and checked the clip. All was well. If they came for me again tonight they'd pay a heavier price this time. I thought about Sara and I thought about Kate, and finally I thought about Niamh. "*Tá an tachrán ina shuan codlata*," a voice from the past said. *The child is fast asleep.* And some time after that he was.

26: THE CONFIDENTIAL TELEPHONE

Doorbell at eight in the morning. I looked through the peephole. Crabbie and Lawson.

I opened up.

"What's the *craic*, lads?"

"We got a report that you were in the hospital, Sean," Crabbie said, concerned.

"I'm fine. And they mostly avoided my pretty face."

"What happened? Someone lifted you?" Crabbie asked.

"Yup."

"Paramilitaries?"

"Hard to tell because they were wearing balaclavas. But here's the interesting part . . . they had American accents."

"Wait a second, what happened to you?" Lawson said.

"Someone gave him a hiding," Crabbie said.

Lawson was shocked. "How can this happen to a policeman?"

"It happens, and worse. Where do you think you're living, son?"

"Did you report it?" Lawson asked.

"I did. Not that that will ever do any good."

McCrabban's knuckles were white with fury. "If I ever catch them that's done that to you," he began.

"Forget it. Why don't you come in and have some coffee."

After the lads left I took another personal day. I stayed home because I couldn't face the office, but also because I was waiting for Vardon to call.

Waited there. Watched *Murder She Wrote* and *Countdown*. Solved the murder before Jessica, solved the numbers before Carol.

Vardon didn't call.

274

That was OK. Give him another day to stew.

I went to the wine shop in Carrick and bought a bottle of the expensive stuff that Sara liked.

Quick shower. Shave. Clean shirt. Sports coat. Tie.

Under the BMW.

Inside the BMW.

Sara's house.

Knock, knock, knock.

The door didn't open.

"Who is it?" she asked.

"Who do you think?"

"I told you I was busy, Sean."

Her voice . . . annoyed.

"I bought you some wine."

"Leave it on the doorstep, will you?"

"Can't I even come in?"

"No. I'm working."

"What are you doing?"

"Working! For fuck sake, Sean. I'm trying to do some work."

"Are you alone?"

"Of course I'm alone. I just don't want to be disturbed. All right?"

"I'll leave the wine on the doorstep, then."

"Yes, thank you."

I walked back to the Beemer and turned on my police radio. I ran the license plates of all the cars on the street.

The one on the other side of the street belonged to a certain Martin McConville, who was the deputy editor of the *Belfast Telegraph*. The man with the good handshake. The one that looked like the Yorkshire Ripper.

I moved the BMW to a more discreet location under a chestnut tree at the end of the road. Martin finally came out at nine. He almost tripped over the bottle of wine. He handed it back through the doorway. He leaned in for a kiss good-bye. It was lingering. Heartfelt.

"And that's the end of Sean Duffy and Sara Prentice," I said to myself. "Shame. I really thought we were on to something."

I didn't blame her. I was just as bad. Worse.

Back to Coronation Road.

Up the path, phone ringing.

"Yes?"

"Where were you? I tried you at your office. I tried you at your home number."

Vardon.

"Where are you?" I asked.

"I slipped over the fields to the James Orr pub in Ballycarry."

"Special Branch see you go?"

"No."

"Who's in the pub?"

"Couple of old farmers."

"Any strangers?"

"No."

"All right. I'll meet you there in twenty minutes."

I went to the shed and got the coke and the money. I looked under the BMW for bombs, didn't find any and drove to Ballycarry.

The James Orr was a sour-smelling country pub with a few old stagers in flat caps complaining about the price of wool and beef.

Nigel was in a corner hanging on to a pint of Harp and looking nervous.

I got a pair of double whiskies and brought them over.

"Speak," I said.

"You figured out most of it anyway."

"Tell it in your words. From the beginning. From Michael coming back from uni."

Vardon sighed. "Michael getting into uni in the first place. His da virtually building the school gym so Michael would get glowing letters of recommendation. Dad furious when Michael dropped out and got himself mixed up in a scandal with a homosexual. His da had got all respectable, you know? A long road to respectability. Rotary Club, charity work, MBE on the cards. He didn't even want to take Michael in. Said he was a bad 'un. Mikey told me that there was some doubt about whether Ray was even his real da . . ."

"Go on."

"So anyway, they do take him in. The ma insists. Mikey's living at home dealing with that lunatic old man and he's not happy, but he's OK because he's biding his time. He's done well at Oxford. No degree, but he didn't really give a shit about that. It's not the piece of paper. It's who you meet. And Michael met. He has all these contacts. Knows a million people. Contacts over the water. International contacts."

"Contacts for what?"

"Guns. Arms. You name it."

"So what was the score when he came to see you?"

"Big score. Massive score."

"What was it?"

"It was all his idea. He'd heard about these men who were interested in acquiring a modern surface-to-air missile system. And he knows I work at Shorts and, well . . . it was a match made in heaven, wasn't it?" Nigel said bitterly.

"Where were the men from?"

"He told me different stories."

"Like?"

"Israel, Iran, South Africa, all over . . ."

"Not Northern Ireland?"

"No! This was big money. This was oil money or something."

"He mention America?"

"Aye. He said some of them were American. The man he was dealing with was American."

"Connolly."

"Connolly came on board later."

"What did the men want?" I asked.

"At first it was only blueprints. Just blueprints. A million quid for blueprints. But that was just to hook me. They needed complete missile systems so they could reverse-engineer them."

"And you were the inside man?"

"Yeah."

"But you didn't do the stealing."

"Fuck, no! All I had to do was provide security passes and old Tommy Moony would do the rest."

"Michael met Tommy?"

"Oh yeah, all three of us met up before the operation."

"Then what happened?"

"They took the missiles. Everything went according to plan."

"And then?"

"The problem was the timing. The foreign partners were having problems moving the money. They were good for the cash but the problem was moving it. Scrutiny, you know?"

"Scrutiny from who?"

"Michael didn't say, but I assumed the cops."

"So what happened to the Javelins?"

"The missiles are hidden, wherever Tommy Moony has stashed them, waiting to get shipped out of Ireland."

"Why the murders? What went wrong, Nigel?"

"Moony was getting impatient. 'Where's the money?' 'We want to meet with the buyer.' Michael was the voice of reason. He knew how to deal with these sorts of people; he knew that Moony would fucking blow it."

"So no meet."

"No. But Moony's not happy. Getting more pissed off all the time. And then we hear Shorts has started an internal probe into the inventory. And Moony's fucking furious. He wants to change the split. He said that he'd done all the work and all we'd done is set up the deal between them and the foreigners. Moony said that we could split a ten per cent finder's fee between us."

"Michael didn't like that."

"No he didn't. Michael said it was his show. It was the old split or nothing. We were getting a third each."

"What was the original split?"

"Two million for him, two million for me, two million for Moony."

"So how did it escalate?"

"Michael threatens to call the whole thing off. He says that he's indispensable, that the international buyers will only deal with him . . . And you know what happened next?"

"What happened next?"

"Michael's parents are killed and Michael goes off a cliff."

I swallowed my whiskey and got another round in. "So Moony found a way of contacting the international buyers without Michael's assistance."

"Looks like it, doesn't it? And after you talked to me, someone fire-bombs my house, as if I haven't got the message before."

"The message to say nothing."

"Aye."

"Do you have any proof that Moony killed Michael and his parents and Sylvie?"

"No."

I nodded. "So will you a wear a wire?"

"No way!"

"We need proof. If you can get Moony to incriminate himself we can give you witness protection and—"

"No. I'm not doing any of that. Moony will kill me. He'll get to me somehow. Be my death warrant. No, I want your Plan B, Duffy. The money and the coke. You've brought it?"

I patted my jacket pocket. "What do I get for it, Nigel? All you've told me is what I already guessed."

"I know something you don't know, Duffy."

"What?"

"I know the date they're shipping the missiles out. My last conversation with Michael was in Whitehead car park. He was telling me not to worry about Moony or the investigation or anything else. He said that after December seventh we'd get our money as planned. That's when the boat's coming—December the seventh. That's when the missiles are leaving Ireland."

"Where?"

"I don't know where. Michael never told me that. Somewhere up the north coast, I think."

I shook my head. "But after he killed Michael, Moony must have made other arrangements with the foreign buyers."

"Other arrangements for the money, maybe, but the missiles are going out that night. It's been arranged for weeks. They can't leave it much longer. Every day they delay is a day closer to discovery."

"The night of December seventh? That's your tip?"

"Aye."

"That doesn't get me the murderers."

"No, but if Special Branch follow Moony on the night of December seventh, he'll lead them to the missiles and they get him for theft, espionage, whatever else you can throw at him."

"And he won't blame you."

"And he won't blame me. He'll think *he* fucked up. So I'll live."

He eyed the pile of cash. I showed him the bag of pharma coke.

"That's all you've got—December seventh?"

"That's all I know."

"Why did you call the consulate that time?"

"Panic. I thought Connolly might be able to help me with Moony. Mistake. If Moony found out I'd done that . . ."

"If you wear that wire and we get Moony for murder I can get you a new life in America or Australia."

"I'm not doing that. That's a death warrant. They'll find me. They always find you."

He took the money and the cocaine. "I'm leaving tonight," he said.

"Where will you go?"

"I'm not telling you, Inspector."

"Before you go, do me a favor and go to that payphone over there and say what you just told me to the Confidential Telephone and tell them it's a tip for DI Duffy of Carrickfergus RUC and for DI Spencer of Special Branch."

He nodded and got to this feet. "I will. I'll see you, Duffy. Or rather I won't see you."

"Take it easy, Nigel."

I drove to the station and waited for the tip to come in from the Confidential Telephone.

It came to Spencer first.

He called me at the office. "You won't believe this, Duffy! We got a real break in the case! A tip has come in from the Confidential Telephone."

"Yeah?"

"They say that our man Tommy Moony is moving the stolen Javelin missiles out of Northern Ireland on the night of December seventh! I'm telling you as a professional courtesy, Duffy. If he did steal the missiles, he might well be involved in the Michael Kelly murders."

"Thanks very much, Spencer. Any way we can help you, just let us know."

"We can include you on tailing duty if you want, Duffy. We're always short-staffed for that kind of thing."

"We'd be happy to help."

"Fine. But it's our bust. It's our score. You'll be under our direction. You'll have to do what we tell you, OK?"

"That's OK, Spencer. We'll just be happy to help in any way we can."

Spencer was not used to cooperative colleagues in the CID and he didn't trust it. "You won't be tailing Moony or arresting him. That'll be us. Our score, Duffy. Our pictures in the paper."

"Whatever you want, Spencer. We'll take reflected glory on this one. It'll make my boss very happy."

I hung up and when the tip came into Carrick CID I told Crabbie and Lawson.

"Just got a tip from the Confidential Telephone and from DI Spencer at Special Branch. Tommy Moony is moving the missiles on December seventh."

Crabbie was skeptical. "Anonymous tips are always rubbish."

I shook my head. "I have a feeling about this one, Crabbie, I really do."

27: OUR BUSINESS NOW IS NORTH

*M*idnight. *Midnight and all the agents . . .*

Yeah. That's right. An ironic echo.

December 7, 1985, Belfast.

A day of riots, roadblocks, burning buses, fires.

There had been a big Ulster Says No rally against the Anglo-Irish Agreement that afternoon. Three hundred thousand people had shown up at the City Hall to protest against Mrs. Thatcher's covert, pseudo-communist, anti-imperialist agenda. While most of them had gone home after a peaceful demonstration, several thousand had decided to stay in Belfast and demonstrate their moral seriousness by hijacking buses and throwing stones and petrol bombs at the police in West Belfast.

Over in East Belfast the Special Branch team were watching Tommy Moony's house. McCreen, Spencer and a dozen of their finest men watching the little, red-bricked terraced house off Larkfield Road.

As a bone to Carrick CID and inter-agency cooperation we'd be assigned the house of Barry (Mad Dog) Murphy on Yukon Street. Barry was a known associate of Moony, a player in the UFF, and also an employee of Short Brothers.

Several other RUC officers had been assigned to other Moony associates, but the real action was going to be over at Larkfield Avenue, where Moony was, at some point, going to take the Special Branch right to where the Javelin missiles had been hidden.

Or at least, that was the theory.

I looked at my watch and blew on to my hands.

"Midnight," I said. "Could be here for a while yet, lads," I said.

The lads were McCrabban and Lawson and a couple of Ulster Defence Regiment soldiers with us as backup in case we got caught in the riots. I didn't like working with soldiers as a rule, but the police were stretched so thin tonight that you took your help where you could find it.

We were sitting inside my BMW three doors down from Barry Murphy's house on Yukon Street. A Special Branch team was parked on Lewis Drive in case he snuck out the back way.

Crabbie next to me on the front seat took out his pipe.

"Mind if I smoke?" he asked.

"Any objections, lads?" I asked the three men squeezed into the back seat.

The soldiers shook their heads and Lawson knew better than to complain.

Crabbie smoking his pipe. Me sipping coffee from a Thermos. Radio playing Brahms. Nothing moving on Yukon Street.

"My bad knee is killing me," one of the soldiers said, adjusting himself so his rifle was poking into the front seat.

"Hey, watch the leather," I said, moving the gun back.

At one o'clock it began to drizzle. Crabbie was dozing off.

Lawson and the soldiers were in mid-conversation about football.

A light came on in the downstairs window of Barry Murphy's house. I nudged Crabbie.

"Whassa?"

I pointed through the windshield. He rubbed his eyes.

"You're missing my point," one of the soldiers was saying behind us. "If George Best had been fit in '82 we would have won the World Cup. Can you imagine George Best, Sammy McIlroy, Norman Whiteside, Gerry Armstrong, Pat Jennings, and Martin O'Neill all on the same team? All on rare form? Who would the opponents have marked? Two men on Best every time? That opens up the field for Whiteside and McIlroy. Even if he doesn't score he draws the heat. Do you see?"

"You're a dreamer, mate. George Best was ancient in 1982," Lawson said.

"He wasn't ancient. He was only thirty-five. In fact he was a year younger than Pat Jennings."

"Jesus, that's a different thing completely. A goalkeeper? You can't compare the two positions at all," Lawson insisted.

Murphy's hall light came on. McCrabban tensed and put out his pipe. I picked up the police radio. I turned to the boys in the back seat.

"Shut up, all of you. Murphy's coming out."

They shut their bakes. One of the UDR guys grabbed his rifle.

"Fingers away from triggers until you're out of my car," I reminded him.

Murphy's front door opened and a man in a duffel coat got into a Ford Cortina. I picked up the police radio.

"Magpie has left the nest," I said.

"Confirm," Spencer said.

"Magpie has left the nest and is getting in his car."

"Are you sure? Blackbird is still inside his house," Spencer said.

"Am following Magpie, over and out."

Murphy turned left on Mersey Street and drove down to a warehouse on Dee Street. The warehouse door opened and Murphy drove inside.

I picked up the radio again. "Magpie's at a warehouse," I said.

"Blackbird still hasn't moved. There's going to be no play without him."

"I think maybe you should get over here," I said.

"No. Magpie's the diversion. Blackbird still hasn't come out."

"I think you're wrong," I said.

"Jesus, stay off the bloody radio until something changes!" Spencer snapped.

"Touchy lad, isn't he?" McCrabban said.

I turned to the boys behind in the back seat.

"You lot stay alert, OK?"

Lawson nodded, but the two young squaddies suddenly looked very young and very afraid. A skinny, blond one and a spotty, ginger-bap one. Both of them were certainly in their teens.

"Are you lads from Carrick UDR?" I asked them.

They both nodded.

"What are your names?"

The blond was called Peterson, the ginger-haired kid was called Boyd.

"Heard you talking about the World Cup, earlier. George Best, eh? Think on this: what if Northern Ireland had got Liam Brady to play for them? Eh? Height of his career, just after being named PFA player of the year. Brady and McIlory and O'Neill in midfield . . ."

"OK," Peterson conceded. "But with Best and Whiteside up front."

"They still wouldn't have won the World Cup," Crabbie said dourly. "Not against that Brazil side."

"That was some side," I agreed.

"Aye. Zico, Socrates, Serginho, Junior—" and he might have named the entire squad had not the warehouse doors suddenly opened and a large black Mercedes van come speeding out.

I turned to McCrabban. "Shit! This is it, mate. Spencer and McCreen have to believe us now. Get them on the blower and tell them!"

I followed the van up toward the Sydenham bypass.

"Magpie's on the move, he's up on to the A2 in a big honking van," Crabbie said into the radio.

Silence.

I grabbed the radio. "Did you hear what he said? Magpie's driving a van west on the A2."

A pause and then Spencer came back on. "Follow him. Keep us abreast of developments."

"What are you going to do?"

"We're still waiting for Blackbird."

I turned to Crabbie. "They're still waiting for Moony!"

"He said Billy Graham saved him at Villa Park. Maybe he's changed his ways; maybe he's innocent," Crabbie said.

"Innocent my arse. He's got out of the house somehow. He knew he was being watched and he's got out," I said.

We followed the Mercedes van through Belfast. There were riots and paramilitary roadblocks on the Crumlin Road, but the local police had kept the A2 and the motorways clear of trouble.

The van made its way down the Westlink to the M2.

Five minutes later it was on the M5 heading north along the lough at a steady 70 mph.

We sped through Carrickfergus and continued north.

I picked up the radio again.

"Blackbird is either not involved in this operation or he's given you the slip. Magpie is in a black Mercedes van, registration SIA 8764, heading north on the A2! Request backup," I said.

"All right, Duffy, I'll send a car after you. Where are you now?" Spencer said.

"We're on the A2 just outside Carrickfergus. *Everybody* should get up here. This is the move, I'm sure of it."

"Maybe it is, Duffy, but my orders are to stick with Blackbird. I should have backup with you in about fifteen minutes unless they get caught up in the riots. Keep me appraised of your position, OK?"

"OK."

We followed the van at a safe distance up the A2 until it turned off onto the Slaughterford Road and then up the Ballystrudder Road just outside Whitehead. Then it vanished.

"Jesus, they've killed the lights!"

I slowed to a crawl so we didn't run into them, but there were dozens of sidetracks and lanes, easements and throughways they could have slipped down.

"They must be heading for a port," I said to McCrabban, trying to remain calm.

"Aye, a place far away from the army and the police. Somewhere a boat can get in and out. Brown's Bay, Portmuck, Millbay, any of those places."

"Which one?" I said, desperately scanning the myriad of country roads for a trace of the van. "Which one, Crabbie?"

"If it were me I'd go for Portmuck. The wee quay there. Good harbor and it's quiet. Go straight on and turn left over the hill."

I gunned the Beemer up to 75 and it roared up the hill. I turned it in a screaming third gear on to the Portmuck road.

I killed our lights and reduced speed as the sea loomed on the horizon and we approached Portmuck. Not a big place. Tiny little harbor, fewer than a dozen houses, and almost all of those seasonal summer rentals. Not that many spots to seek cover either. No trees. No big buildings. But on the plus side: no nosy civilians dandering around trying to get themselves topped. I parked the BMW on the hill outside the village, turned off the engine.

"Everyone out," I ordered. "No talking, no ciggies."

I fired up the radio. "We lost them on Islandmagee. We think they may be down at Portmuck; that's where we've gone," I said, but there was no response.

"Out of radio range?" McCrabban asked.

I tried again but all I got was static.

I turned to the men.

"OK, lads, follow me; we'll go over the fields and get behind that wee cottage there on the edge of the village. No shooting, no talking, no cigarettes. All right? If they're not here we'll pull out, OK?"

"All right," they agreed.

We climbed over a stone wall, made our way over a boggy field and stopped before a little cottage.

"Over the wall into the garden," I whispered. "Quietly does it now."

I edged my way over the wall and helped the others over too.

Cabbages, flower beds, and a rather sinister little line of red-hatted garden gnomes. I crawled to the wall facing the harbor. We were twenty yards from the Mercedes van that was sitting there in the harbor car park.

"It's them!" I hissed.

I remembered the lessons from the *Ship of Death* up in Derry.

"OK, lads, this is how it's going to go. No one is going to get hurt: not one of us, not one of them. We are going to use the presence of overwhelming force to make them surrender, OK?"

"OK," they said together.

"What do we do now?" Peterson asked.

"Now we stay alert, try and stay warm, and wait."

Five minutes.

Ten.

Clouds. Drizzle. A curling line of blue smoke coming from the Mercedes van.

"I'm freezing," Boyd said.

"Here," I said, giving him my driving gloves.

"Why don't youse just arrest them now?" Peterson asked.

"They're meeting somebody. We want to lift them and their contact," Lawson explained. "And if we arrest them as they're actually unloading the missiles we can charge them with espionage and smuggling as well as theft."

"He's a bright lad," McCrabban said.

"How did you end up in Carrick RUC, Lawson?" I asked.

"They said it was a good place for me to go learn."

"Who said that?"

"Superintendent Figgis. He said that I could learn a lot from you, Inspector Duffy."

I shook my head. "These young people, Crabbie, they look innocent enough but they're here to replace us."

"That they are," he agreed dourly. "Oh, I think I saw the back door of the van opening."

The back door of the van was indeed opening from the inside.

"Where's our bloody backup?" Private Peterson whined.

"We don't need backup. We've a good position here. We'll be OK," McCrabban said. I looked at him. That Vulcan coolness. That dour Presbyterian calm. That stiff upper lip that was invented in the Scottish kirk and the English public schools. He was a good man to have standing next to you in a pinch, or even when there wasn't a pinch.

The van door closed again.

"False alarm," Lawson said.

The harbor was quiet. The Irish Sea was glass. The evening was so clear that you could see headlights along the B738 over the water in Portpatrick.

Both rear doors of the van opened and two men got out. One of them was Mad Dog Murphy. Another man got out of the driver's cab. It was Moony. "How did he slip past Special Branch?" McCrabban said, amazed.

It wasn't so difficult. Basements, outhouses that led on to back alleys, and if you got access to the attic you could in theory exit from any of the houses on a connected terrace.

All three of the men were armed. Two with AK-47s and one with a shotgun.

I turned to Lawson and the two soldiers. "OK, lads. Remember, no one does anything without my say-so. We're going to make arrests here tonight. *Arrests*. There are going to be no shots fired. No gunplay. No cock-ups. There's only one road in and out of Portmuck. They'll see that and they'll give up quietly if they know what's good for them."

"Small fishing boat coming. One man in the cabin by the looks of it," Crabbie said. "Nope, it's going past the shore, not stopping."

He was right. The boat wasn't stopping. I scanned the horizon. No other vessels in sight, the sea empty for miles in every direction.

But there was something inherently cinematic about this place, something about it that screamed denouement.

Moony's men began unloading boxes from the Mercedes van.

"They're standing there like they haven't a care in the world," McCrabban said.

Suddenly one of the men lit a flare and dropped it in the middle of the empty car park. Red fire and bright yellow smoke pigtailing into the night air.

"It must be handover time," McCrabban said flatly.

"Aye," I agreed. "But handover to whom?"

"Maybe they're coming in a fucking submarine," Private Peterson suggested.

Suddenly we could hear the sound of an aircraft. But there was nowhere to land an aircraft. The car park wasn't nearly wide enough and the fields would be a death trap at night.

Cold sweat on the back of my neck as I began to sense that this operation was spiraling out of control.

I didn't want a balls-up. I wanted this to be clean. But how in the name of God did those jokers expect to land a light aircraft at night in the—

"It's a helicopter!" McCrabban said.

"Impossible!"

The only people allowed to fly helicopters anywhere near Northern Ireland airspace were the army and the RAF.

But helicopter it was, coming out of the night from the south-east. From England or possibly the Isle of Man. A Bell 206 painted black. No livery or markings, which gave it a sinister quality.

A helicopter? Who would have the bottle to fly a chopper into Ulster?

"Look at that bloody thing," Private Boyd said, unconsciously standing up to get a better look.

"Crabbie! Grab that eejit."

In slow motion McCrabban made a grab at Peterson.

His fingers reached the UDR man's belt and he pulled him down. *Too late.*

One of the Loyalists must have seen him because a second later the wall in front of our position was lit up by tracer and AK-47 fire. Boyd was lucky he didn't get plugged.

Before we even had a chance to return fire the Loyalists had tossed a hand grenade at us, which dropped just short and blew up in front of the stone wall protecting us. Kaboom!

Another hand grenade landed dead on the wall and bounced back five feet into the air before it exploded. The entire top half of the wall collapsed and we hit the deck.

"We are the police! You are surrounded! You must surrender immediately or we will return fire!" I screamed.

"Like fuck we will!" one of the gunmen screamed back, and tracer flew around us.

Shotgun blasts began pounding into the remains of the wall.

"We're sitting ducks here!" Private Peterson yelled.

"Return fire! Fire at will!" I ordered.

The two soldiers opened up with their SLRs on full automatic. McCrabban and I fired our Glock pistols and Lawson pulled out his sidearm and began plugging away with his .38. Crack! Crack! Crack!

The hail of bullets was enough to drive Murphy and Moony behind the van.

"Moony! Listen to me. You are totally surrounded! We've got the high ground. There are half a dozen Land Rovers on the hill filled with soldiers. There's no escape! Lay down your weapons and put your hands up!" I yelled.

"No surrender!" one of the Loyalists yelled back, and all three of them began firing their AKs again. Bullets bounced all around the garden, massacring the small army of garden gnomes behind us.

I put my hands over my head and hunkered for cover under the remains of the wall.

"You lads with Moony! There's no need for any of youse to die! Did he tell you this was for the cause? It's not for the cause, it's for the fucking money!" I yelled as everyone reloaded.

"Your peeler scum tricks won't work with us, Duffy!" Moony yelled back.

"You killed Michael Kelly and his parents to protect your money, Moony. You killed a twenty-year-old barmaid just so you could get a bigger cut of the loot! And now you're going to kill these two lads with you?"

This gambit was met by another round of shotgun and AK-47 fire.

I ducked behind the last scraps of the garden wall, the bullets whizzing inches above our heads.

"Someone's going to die all right and it won't be us!" Moony mocked.

"I have a kill shot," Private Peterson said coolly from a sniper's position.

"Take it!" I said.

Peterson shot his SLR once and his man went down.

"Ya shot Tommy! Ya fucking bastards!" Murphy yelled, and ran across the car park toward us with an AK-47 in both hands.

He didn't get fifteen feet. A hail of SLR bullets ripped through his upper chest and almost took his head off.

The final gunman was a bald guy with long sideburns and a comb-over. He was wearing jeans so tight that he could barely move in them. His shotgun had jammed and he was shooting at us wildly with a big .45 semiautomatic pistol.

"Put your hands up!" I yelled.

But he didn't put his hands up. Instead he climbed into the van and started it.

He accelerated across the car park while the two soldiers tried to take him out. He must have been wounded, or he simply panicked and lost control. He hit a speed ramp far too fast, the van shuddered, tipped over on its side, and the driver came out of the windscreen at thirty miles an hour straight into a telegraph pole.

It was over.

From first shot to last had been three minutes.

I looked for that incoming helicopter but of course it was now long gone.

We got up from our redoubt and walked down the little slope in front of the house and across the car park.

McCrabban checked for pulses on Murphy and Moony.

"Any hope?" I asked him.

He shook his head glumly. "Dead," he said. "And that other's fella's head's been caved in."

"I wanted a confession. I wanted to ask him how he coerced them into writing those suicide notes. Michael's suicide note anyway."

"Probably just common-or-garden torture."

"We did it!" Private Peterson was whooping until McCrabban shut him up.

"Find a telephone, Lawson, tell Carrick RUC what's happened," I said to the young detective.

The air smelled of cordite and blood and burning diesel. Moon-light was illuminating a little golden trail of spent shotgun shells.

We inspected the crates and they were indeed the stolen Javelin missiles from Shorts.

I walked down to the water.

Three dead men. Three more dead men to add to the grim toll of dead men and women killed in these Troubles.

I felt sick. Ashamed. This was my op. This was my fault.

"Hey, Sean!" Crabbie yelled.

"Gimme a minute, will you?" I said, and walked along the beach next to the little harbor.

I pushed back the tears and took a deep breath.

I looked out my picture of St Michael, the Archangel, the patron saint of policemen, kissed it, and closed my eyes.

"Bless me, Father, for I have sinned. It has been two years since my last confession," I said quietly, and told the water about my sins, but, as usual, the cold black sea lapping against the sand refused to give me absolution.

"Thank God I'm getting out," I muttered, and lit a cigarette.

When I got back up to the car park the Special Branch Land Rovers were arriving and cops were pouring out of them. I nodded to Spencer and McCreen.

Too late for you. Too late for all of you.

The police forensic team arrived from Belfast in white boiler suits. They set up arc lamps and began gathering blood samples and shell casings.

Chief Inspector McArthur appeared in his full dress greens. The press were with him.

"Yes, this was a joint operation between Carrick CID and Special Branch," he was saying.

Sara Prentice was holding a tape recorder mic up to his mouth. Our eyes met. I'd broken up with her two days before. She hadn't minded in the least. She smiled at me. I nodded and walked on.

While McArthur blathered away I looked into the dead face of Tommy Moony.

I wanted a confession, Tommy. I wanted to hear you say it. You killed Sylvie McNichol and Michael Kelly and his parents. You killed them all for the promise of a pile of Yankee gold.

I kneeled under one of the forensic team arc lamps and tried to read the truth in Tommy's cold blue eyes.

But there was no truth.
There was only death.
Always, there's only death.

28: BLUE TIGERS

Special Branch and the Ulster Defence Regiment took the credit and the headlines. The soldiers had done the killings and it was a Special Branch op. But who cares about headlines?

"Who cares about headlines?" I said to McCrabban as we sat in the incident room the next day.

"Headlines? Not me. All is vanity, saith the Lord."

"Very true. Any word on that helicopter?"

Crabbie shook his head. No helicopter with that description had taken off anywhere in the British Isles.

Why was I not surprised?

I smelled spook. I smelled America.

I called the US consulate in Belfast to ask to speak to John Connolly to find out what he had been doing last night, but I was told that Mr. Connolly had gone back to the States and would not be returning to Ireland again.

Of course, Special Branch questioned the families of the dead men in Portmuck, but none of them claimed to have any knowledge of the Kelly murders or indeed of the stolen Javelin missiles. We had no real proof that Tommy Moony had killed Michael Kelly, but the RUC intelligence file implicated him in the deaths of nine people in the 1970s, three of whom had been killed with a single shot from a nine-millimeter pistol . . .

We had no choice but to put the case in the yellow file for inquiries that had been suspended but were still open in case further evidence came to light.

"Just once I'd like one of our homicide investigations to end in a court case and a conviction," I said to Crabbie.

"You can't take it personally, sir," Lawson said, bringing in the tea. "At CID training school we were told that clearance rates for homicides have been on the decline since the 1970s."

"Is that so?"

"Yes, sir. The vast majority of murders in Northern Ireland are never solved. The clearance rate is under fifteen percent when there's a terrorist dimension," Lawson explained.

McCrabban could see that the kid was annoying me.

"Go and get some biscuits, Lawson," he told him. "How can you have tea without biscuits? That's the first thing they should have taught you in CID school."

"He's a good lad," Crabbie said when he was gone.

"Matty was funnier."

"He's not Matty, but he's a good lad."

Lawson came back with chocolate biscuits. We drank our tea and ate our biscuits, and then we stripped the incident room until it was bare. We put the two boxes of Kelly material on the cold case shelf.

My final case for the RUC ending the way so many of the others had done with no closure and no justice.

The story the papers invented was that the stolen missiles were being shipped to apartheid South Africa. Which made sense, but it wasn't true at all. If the missiles had been going to apartheid South Africa, Special Branch would have followed all the leads and eventually, I'm sure, there would have been some kind of international inquiry involving Interpol and the governments of several countries.

But the real destination of the missiles explained what in fact happened with the year-long Special Branch investigation: nothing. Two apprentices at Short Brothers were eventually charged with aiding and abetting the theft. Special Branch was seeking Nigel Vardon to assist them with their inquiries, but Mr. Vardon had mysteriously disappeared.

That evening gave me yet another reason to leave the RUC: the constant chickenshit. Literally days after surviving an epic gun battle on Muck Island without so much as a powder burn on my fingers, I was to break an ankle and an arm responding to a domestic violence call while I was actually off duty. This was typical. Typical of life as a detective in the RUC. Typical of the human comedy in general.

Wet weekday night. *Badlands* on the box. I'd just got to Terrence Malick's cameo as a neighbor knocking on his friend's door when not a minute later there was a knock at my door that became a persistent banging.

"Jesus Christ!"

Hallway. Peephole. Bobby Cameron. He was unshaven, his hair was wild, and there was a stain on his red lumberjack shirt that could be anything from barbecue sauce to human blood. He was wearing black jeans and big shit-kicker DM boots. In fact he looked a lot like Desperate Dan from the *Dandy* comic, which wasn't as reassuring an image as you would have thought.

I opened the door. "What's the matter?"

"Does something always have to be the matter?" he said.

"With you it does."

"Need your help, Duffy."

"If it's about the fucking lion, there's nothing I can do."

"It's not about the lion. It's a domestic. Artie McFall's giving his wife a hiding across the way. My missus and the neighbors on both sides can't stand it. Normally I'd take care of things, but obviously here I can't get involved."

"Why not?"

"Artie's a connected man."

"What do you mean?"

"Do I have to spell it out, Duffy? Artie's UVF. If I went over there and broke his door down and beat the living shit out of him there'd be a feud, wouldn't there?"

"Oh, because you're UDA."

"I'm not admitting that, Duffy. But we can't have a feud between paramilitary organizations, can we?"

"Look at you, Bobby, the Talleyrand of Coronation Road." I sighed. "But you're right, we can't have a feud, can we? A domestic, you say?"

"Yeah, don't bring your gun. Artie's pissed out of his mind. We don't want an escalation."

"Don't tell me how to do my job," I said, lifting the Glock off the phone table. For all I knew he was leading me to an ambush. However, as soon as I stepped outside I could hear Artie McFall's wife's screams.

"See?" Bobby said.

We crossed the street and made our way through a crowd of angry women. "Fucking finally. Our heroes," one of them said sarcastically.

Upstairs the screaming had become a quiet whimper between thumps.

I banged on the front door. "Police! Open up!"

"G'way and fuck yourself, this is none of your business!" came the reply from upstairs.

I looked at Bobby. "Gimme a hand with the door."

Bobby produced a sledgehammer. "I'll take care of this, but I can't go inside the house."

Swing hammer swing. The plywood council house front door disintegrated.

A hall full of broken things. A sobbing five-year-old girl.

More thumping from upstairs. Up the steps two at a time.

Artie McFall waiting for me on the landing with a cricket bat. He'd smashed the lights so I didn't even see him until it was too late. A cricket bat in the gut and I went backward down the stairs, breaking my arm and ankle.

McFall came down the stairs after me. I drew my Glock. "Take one more step and I swear to God it'll be your fucking last," I said.

He could see that I was dead serious.

He dropped the bat.

"Sit down where you are."

He sat.

A street posse held him until backup arrived from Carrick RUC. An ambulance took me to the Royal. Fractured fibula. Fractured calcaneus.

I was released after two days. Foot in a cast. Arm in a cast and a sling. I didn't know it then, but that was my Blue Tiger moment: Artie McFall was the blind beggar who, as in the Borges story, had given me back my days and nights. Had saved me from death, by preventing me riding in the Chinook . . .

Kate and Kendrick came to see me.

"Gosh! What happened to you, Sean?" Kate asked.

"I fell down some stairs."

"Your stairs?"

"What difference does it make whose stairs it was?"

"Good point. Are you still on for lunch?"

"I'll have to check my busy social calendar."

Kendrick drove the Jag. Kate sat in the back with me and talked. It was all business. I liked that. Kate talking. Kendrick smiling in the rear-view. Kate wearing jeans and a silk, polo-neck sweater. Kendrick wearing a red shirt and corduroys. Their ensemble calculated to disarm and relax me—it didn't, of course, but I admired the thought that had gone into it.

I'd made my decision but I wanted to hear her tell me I was doing the right thing. "So if I stayed in the RUC, what would my future be like?"

"Very dull. The RUC's patience has been worn thin. The feeling of the top brass is that there will be no more, quote, 'teaching moments for you,' unquote."

"I couldn't play by their rules."

"It's their feeling, Sean, that you couldn't play by *any* rules. It's their feeling that you again, quote, 'think you're special,' unquote."

"I never said that. Nor thought it. And none of this is news anyway. I know how they feel about me. I know that I'm no longer being groomed for the bigger and better. The future belongs to the Lawsons of this world."

"The best you can hope for, Sean, is that they let you stay a lowly detective in an out-of-the-way station where you can't cause too much trouble."

"Not a terrible life."

"But not a terribly productive one for someone of your abilities."

"Why doesn't my bad reputation scare you, Kate?" I asked.

"I can see that you have matured, Sean."

"Is that what you tell your bosses?"

"I am the boss. I can more or less recruit whomever I like."

Lunch was a place in Cultra, County Down, that had garnered a Michelin star. It was all "freshly sourced" this and "locally produced" that. I got the lamb chops and both Kendrick and Kate got the Strangford Lough trout.

With my injuries it was impossible to use a knife and fork so Kate was mother and cut up my chops and potatoes.

We were sitting on a balcony overlooking fields of cows and sheep and a little deserted beach.

"So what do you think, Sean? Would you like to come and work for us? We've been patient. We waited until your case was solved."

I looked at her. She was really very beautiful. How had I not seen that before? Beautiful and intelligent and, well, rich . . . And I liked her. I liked her very much. Although she had discounted in her mind the possibility of us ever getting together, you never knew what might happen, did you?

"My case wasn't really solved," I said.

"Resolved, then. We let you finish it without interference because we knew that it was important to you."

I didn't pick up on the tone then, but I should have. *We let you finish it . . .*

"The police, Sean. That's the tactical battle. The strategic battle is being fought by us."

I remembered something she'd told me a few years ago. About the long game the British were playing. *The strategic retreat from Empire.*

"What's the actual process?" I asked.

"You provisionally accept our offer of employment. You get vetted. You sign the Official Secrets Act. You join," Kendrick explained.

"And resign from the RUC."

"Naturally, yes," Kendrick said.

I wanted to say yes. I wanted to tell her that I'd already typed my resignation letter. But to leave the police after ten hard years? The words stuck in my throat.

"Why don't you say yes to the vetting process. Let us vet while you make your final decision," Kate said.

"OK, then," I agreed.

"And look, Sean, we're having a big intelligence pow-wow in Scotland next week. We're gathering together all the bigwigs from all the agencies. The C2 group, all N.I. Contact, us, our sister service, army intel, police, Special Branch. Even some Europeans and Americans," Kate said.

"You have conferences?"

"Like I say, Sean, it's about strategy, not tactics. Northern Ireland's next ten years. And the thirty after that. We're not going to make the same mistakes on our doorstep that we made in India. We'd like you to come, Sean. Meet some very bright, very interesting people. Come if your leg and arm can take it."

"My leg and arm will be fine," I said. "I'll come."

They drove me home to Coronation Road.

Kate walked me to the front door.

"They've blown you up. They've shot you. They've pushed you down stairs. I think it's time to come off the line and get behind a desk, eh? Move up an echelon. Be one of the thinkers, not the cannon fodder."

It was a revealing comment. For her this was the logical next step for me. Promotion to officer class.

The next morning the phone rang. I put down my coffee cup and answered it.

"Hello?"

"Sean, I'm sorry. This is a bit of an annoyance but the RAF won't let you come in the helicopter. They say that you and your injuries would be a hazard in the Chinook in any kind of emergency situation."

"Isn't part of their job to fly injured people?"

"Not these particular pilots. I'm afraid the flight lieutenant was very strict about it. I'm most dreadfully sorry."

"It doesn't matter. We'll talk when you get back."

"You passed your vetting, by the way. Don't be impressed. Almost everyone does. You'd be surprised by the people in the Northern Ireland Department who have passed their vetting."

"I don't think I would."

"No, I don't think you would either. After I get back from the conference I'll officially send you an application form and you'll officially have to resign."

"I've drafted my letter. Just have to type it up."

"I thought so. Will you be sad to go?"

"You've made a strong case for my continuing uselessness in the RUC. I'll only work for you, though, Kate. Only you. I trust you."

"Don't worry. I'm the only one that will have you!"

We both laughed. "I'll talk to you next week when I get back. Good-bye, Sean."

"Bye, Kate."

She hung up.

I didn't see her the next week.

I never saw her again.

29: FLOW MY TEARS THE POLICEMAN SAID

*S*ssssssssssssssssssssssssssssssssssssssssssssssssssssssssssssssssssssssssssssssssssssssssssssssssssssss
ssssssssssssssssssssssssssssssss . . .

And so on . . .

Et cetera . . .

Imagine a page of esses. Imagine it so we can save on ink. S after s after s. You know what that noise is? The primordial hiss from the Big Bang. From Deep Time. Static. That's all we are. Tiny blips of consciousness in a great grey ocean of static and entropy . . .

I have just finished yet another draft of my resignation letter, typing with one finger. I have praised McCrabban and Lawson. I have recommended that McCrabban be given my job and that Lawson be promoted from acting to full-time detective constable.

I reread the letter, sign it, and seal it up.

I make a cup of coffee and look for a stamp.

I hear a Chinook flying low over the town. The distinctive noise is the twin turbo shaft engines delivering 4,000 horsepower to the counter-rotating rotors.

I find a stamp and set the letter aside to post later.

Thud, thud, thud, thud goes the Chinook.

I go into the garden to see the chopper.

Onion sky.

Coral sky.

Black sky.

Disappearing rotor blades.

Back into 113 Coronation Road. On the living room hi-fi is *Rain Dogs* by Tom Waits. Side 2, the point where "Walking Spanish" bleeds into "Downtown Train."

The smell is Nestlé instant coffee, Virginia tobacco, and the molasses in the toasting veda bread.

Breakfast over, I put on the radio. "We are getting reports of a helicopter crash in the Mull of Kintyre ..."

Later there will be an inquest. And later still a public inquiry. Pilot error, the inquest will say. Institutional failures that led to overwork and pilot exhaustion, the inquiry will say.

There will be skeptics who suspect foul play. It would have been quite the coup for the IRA if they'd done it. But of course the intelligence agencies would have known if the IRA were planning something like that because of their mole within the IRA Army Council.

No, it isn't an act of terrorism.

Merely an accident. An RAF Chinook filled with all the top MI5, MI6 and Special Branch agents in Northern Ireland flying into a mountain on the Mull of Kintyre. Every single person on board killed. An entire intelligence cohort utterly wiped out. Kate, Kendrick, all of them.

Pilot error, the inquest will say.

RAF institutional failures that led to pilot error, the inquiry will insist.

You can get the report from Her Majesty's Stationery Office and decide for yourself.

You don't need to see me drop my coffee cup.

You don't need to see my knees bend.

You don't need to see me rush to the telephone and wait all afternoon for confirmation of the bad news.

No, we're done here. The clock poised at 9:05. The clock stopped. We'll take our leave.

Up through the kitchen ceiling, up through the back bedroom, up through the attic and the tiles on the roof ...

Up into the air. Into the world of planes and helicopters.

Into the realm of birds, into the realm of the fey ...

A black crow flaps her oily wings past 113 Coronation Road and turns west toward Knockagh Mountain.

Perhaps it is Morrigan.

Morrigan of the black eye. Morrigan of the sorrows, the great queen, the goddess of battle, fertility, and strife.

The crow flies over hill, high bog, and rain-slicked street.

If it is Morrigan, she is looking down upon a wounded land and she is content, cawing in satisfaction at the patchwork quilt of Ulster, and at the mess on the hillside in the Mull of Kintyre.

Ireland seems to be the exception in a continent that has embraced perpetual and universal peace. But Morrigan the crow knows better. A crow will always be a crow, and to end war you must first change the nature of man.

And as the crow flies over Ulster, giddy with the stench of carrion, she looks east toward Britain and across the North Sea to those great frozen reservoirs of hate behind the Iron Curtain. Ireland is less an anachronism of Europe's bellicose past and more a prophecy of the coming future.

A breeze in the wood.

A ripple on the water.

You'll see, the goddess whispers.

You'll see.

EPILOGUE: A YEAR AND A HALF LATER

No, I never saw Kate again, nor will I, not in this life, but I caught Connolly's jug ears a year and a half later on the BBC news. A lot had happened since. Many cases. More violence. More death. And a girl called Elizabeth . . . but we'll get to that.

I'd almost forgotten about the mysterious Mr. Connolly.

It must have been Marching Season.

God knows what was happening in the outside world, but in Belfast it was all rain and riot.

Riot and rain and the much-delayed christening of John McCrabban's son (a heart ailment/surgery/a secret trip from me to pray for the boy's health at our Lady at Cnoc Mhuire). I put on my dress uniform and drove to the bare windy Presbyterian kirk near Slemish Mountain. They called him Thomas William, and the bairn took his name and the baptismal water without too much protest. As godfather I swore to the dour Raymond Massey—like minister that I would raise the lad in the austere mysteries of the Protestant faith if anything happened to his mum and dad.

Back home to Coronation Road.

Vodka gimlet. The BBC news.

"Holy shit."

I called Lawson.

"Yeah?"

"Put on the news. And call Crabbie. He should be back from church."

"How was the christening?"

"Put on the news, Lawson."

I hung up the phone, unmuted the volume.

Yes, it was Connolly all right. The same sneery face, the pug nose, the meticulously combed hair, the jug ears, the defiantly unintelligent eyes. His real name was Colin Wilson. He was a serving lieutenant colonel in the United States Marine Corps who had been seconded to the National Security Staff of the president of the United States.

"He worked at the White House for the fucking president!" I said out loud.

Wilson was at a Senate Intelligence Committee inquiry investigating a scheme by the Reagan administration to trade anti-tank and anti-aircraft missiles to the Iranians in exchange for the release of US hostages in Lebanon.

The phone rang. "Sean?"

It was Crabbie.

"Are you watching the news?" I asked.

"I can't believe it . . . Or rather, I can believe it."

"I wanna keep watching. I'll call you in a bit."

I watched the story and then I quickly drove down to the newsagents and bought all the broadsheet newspapers to get background. The *Times* had a two-page spread on what, apparently, was a huge and growing scandal for the Reagan White House.

It was called Iran-Contra. It was the biggest scandal in America since Watergate. Sometimes you really had to pay attention to what was in the papers.

I read on. The plan had been to buy missiles that were to be given to "moderate" elements of the Iranian government in exchange for their help in securing the release of American and British hostages in Lebanon. Reagan and Thatcher had been doing deals with terrorists while declaring that they would never ever do deals with terrorists.

Channel Four news was covering the Senate hearing live.

I switched over and there was Lieutenant Colonel Wilson again.

Senator Nields was asking him a question: "Why did you go to Ireland first, Colonel Wilson?"

"A number of reasons. My mother's family is Irish. Her maiden name is Connolly. And there's always been excellent relations between this country and Ireland. We felt that the Irish would be amenable to our interests. Ireland is a place where Americans can do business," Colonel Wilson replied.

The testimony continued. Hours of it.

The *Guardian* said that Wilson had been a naive blunderer right from the start. He had acquired an Irish passport and taken the name John Connolly and, without telling the CIA about his plans, had flown to Ireland to see whether he could buy weapons from the IRA. The IRA hadn't liked the smell of him so he'd gone to the Loyalist paramilitaries instead. The Loyalists hadn't liked the smell of him either, but they'd liked the money.

It was obvious that American spooks had been involved in the Michael Kelly case, but I had never understood why. And never in my wildest dreams would I have cooked up something so completely crazy. And yet there it was. Was this the dumbest administration in history? Or only dumb because they got caught?

I got a can of Bass and called McCrabban back.

"It's definitely him," I said. "He's on Channel Four right now."

"What do you want to do about this, Sean?"

"About what?"

"Now we know everything. The whole story. Do you want to reopen the case files on the Michael Kelly murders?" Crabbie said.

A younger Sean Duffy would have reopened the case files. Would have pulled the temple down about his ears. The me of five years ago. Maybe even the me of two years ago. But this Sean Duffy had learned his lesson.

Sleeping dogs. Whatever you say, say nothing. Choose your cliché.

"I don't think so, Crabbie."

"Me neither," he said.

"We really should have let that one go to Larne RUC," I said.

"Aye. But you weren't to know. I wasn't to know," he murmured.

"No," I agreed.

"No."

"Nice christening today," I said.

"It was."

"I'll let you get back to your family."

"OK, Sean, take care now."

"You too, mate."

He hung up.

I turned the TV off and lay there on the sofa watching the street get dark.

I finished the beer and went to the shed, where I'd put Kate's picture so Beth wouldn't ask any questions about her.

I opened the box.

Kate in Oxford outside the brasserie on Banbury Road. Half tore. Smiling happily in a way she never smiled.

I should have been with her on that helicopter.

If it hadn't been for my injuries I would have been.

If I hadn't been pushed down the stairs . . .

Perhaps she would even have sent me instead of her and maybe that would have been best for all of us.

Maybe.

AFTERWORD

This is a work of fiction and any resemblance to any person living or dead is entirely coincidental. That being said observant readers will have noticed that I have borrowed several elements from several real historical incidents of the time period: the tragic death of Olivia Channon at Oxford; Lt Col. Oliver North's bizarre attempt to obtain anti-aircraft missiles using an Irish passport and the pseudonym John Clancy (borrowing the surname of his favorite spy novelist) during the Iran-Contra affair; the events surrounding the signing of the Anglo-Irish Agreement; the Chinook helicopter crash on the Mull of Kintyre in which an entire cadre of MI5 agents based in Northern Ireland were killed; and the theft of Blowpipe and Javelin missiles from the Short Brothers factory in East Belfast. As this is a novel I have been able to bring together fictional characters who would never have met in real life and I have taken the liberty of compressing events of slow gestation into a tighter time frame.

DI Sean Duffy is a fictional character too, who just happens to live in the house where I was born and grew up: 113 Coronation Road, Victoria Estate, Carrickfergus. Duffy's neighbors are imaginary constructs bearing only a passing resemblance to the actual residents of the estate in that time period, although I did in fact know a guy who kept a lioness in his council house.

ABOUT ... ADRIAN McKINTY

Adrian McKinty was born and grew up in Carrickfergus, Northern Ireland. After studying philosophy at Oxford University, he moved to the United States, living in Harlem for seven years where he worked in bars, bookstores, and building sites. In 2000, he moved to Denver, Colorado, to become a high school English teacher. His debut crime novel, *Dead I Well May Be*, was shortlisted for the 2004 Dagger Award. His first Sean Duffy novel, *The Cold Cold Ground*, won the 2013 Spinetingler Award and was shortlisted for the 2013 Prix du Meilleur Polar and the 2015 Prix SNCF du Polar. The second Sean Duffy novel, *I Hear the Sirens in the Street*, won the 2014 Barry Award for best crime novel (paperback original) and was shortlisted for best crime novel at the 2013 Ned Kelly Awards and for the 2014 Theakston Award for best British crime novel. The third Sean Duffy novel, *In the Morning I'll Be Gone*, won the 2014 Ned Kelly Award and was named one of the top-ten crime novels of 2014 by the American Library Association's *Booklist*.